Murder on False River

To Cassie,
I hope you enjoy
my book! Fondly,
Martha G Manuel

Martha Gabour Manuel

outskirtspress
DENVER, COLORADO

Murder on False River
All Rights Reserved.
Copyright © 2012 Martha Gabour Manuel
v2.0

Cover Photo © 2012 Martha Gabour Manuel and JupiterImages Corporation. All rights reserved - used with permission.

Outskirts Press, Inc.
http://www.outskirtspress.com

ISBN: 978-1-4327-6405-0

Library of Congress Control Number: 2012916848

Outskirts Press and the "OP" logo are trademarks belonging to Outskirts Press, Inc.

PRINTED IN THE UNITED STATES OF AMERICA

Dedication

This book is lovingly dedicated to my family:

To my husband and best friend —
Percy Henry Manuel;

Our children —
Byron and his wife Jeanneca Manuel;
Erica Manuel Kennedy;
Christopher Paul Manuel;
Saundra Anne Manuel;

and

My parents —
Jim and Ruth Gabour.

Thanks for always being there for me ...
through good times and bad.

I love you all!

Special Thanks...

My undying gratitude goes to my mom, Ruth Bryan Gabour, who not only helped edit my book, but also served as my mentor. She has been a constant source of encouragement throughout my life, but never more so than when I was writing my book.

Thanks also to my dad, Jim Gabour, Sr., who put up with our antics and absences while we raced to the library and then to Applebee's on our "mission" to finish this book.

Another special thank you goes out to Amy Catlin, and the wonderful people at Outskirts Press, who provided untold resources and encouragement during this production.

Finally, and most importantly, thank you dear God for all the inspirations during those critical times when I needed them the most! Amen.

FOREWORD

The story born and coddled throughout these pages is exactly that — a story — completely fictional.

Many of the locations prominently featured do exist. A few events referred to bore some similarities to those that, in fact, did take place. Admittedly, many incidents described were enhanced for the reader's entertainment.

At times, the names of individuals of whom I am very fond, were incorporated into fantasy characters. It seemed like a fun way to immortalize them — or their names at any rate. Hopefully they will enjoy the notoriety and ignore my unique and strange sense of humor.

About Pointe Coupee ...

Pointe Coupee (French for "cut-off point") Parish is located some 30 miles northwest of Louisiana's capitol city, Baton Rouge. Its' name (pronounced "Pwent Koo-pay" in French and "Point Koo-pee" in English) refers to the point on the Mississippi River where the river changed course and left a portion of the river cut off from the rest.

Bordered on three sides by inland waterways – Old River, the Atchafalaya River and the Mississippi River – Pointe Coupee is one of the most diversified agricultural parishes in the state. According to parish statistics, approximately 165,000 acres of land are utilized to cultivate cotton, sugarcane, soybeans, corn, milo, wheat, hay, vegetables, rice, pecans, and crawfish.

The parish encompasses four incorporated communities: New Roads, Fordoche, Morganza, and Livonia. New Roads, which is also the parish seat, is situated on the northern end of the picturesque banks of False River, a major tourist attraction.

Until recently a lone ferry was the only way to go from New Roads to St. Francisville without driving long distances in other directions. In 2011 the ferry was shut-down and the new Audubon Bridge opened, albeit a bit prematurely due to excessive floodwaters in Pointe Coupee. How the new Audubon Bridge, bringing with it its added influx of people and businesses, will shape the future of Pointe Coupee parish, only time will tell.

PART I – 2012

CHAPTER 1

Savannah O'Brien Devereaux endeavored to awaken her senses slowly, as through a dense fog, her mind struggling to comprehend what was happening, or had happened, to her body. Her eyes were locked in darkness. She could not speak; and, as hard as she tried to move, she could not feel any part of her body respond in any way.

Working frantically to compose her thoughts, she tried to correlate some reason for the strange phenomenon she was experiencing. The only rational theory at hand was that this had to be a horrendous nightmare.

There was no way Savannah could know that her ailing body was now totally dependent upon I.V.s and other medical equipment surrounding her hospital bed at our Lady of the Lake Medical Center, all while she subconsciously fought for her very life. Doctors and nurses slipped quietly in and out, but no one spoke to her. She was aware of things being done to her body, but none of it made any sense.

Then abruptly, following a long and deafening silence, she heard movement close by and the off/on comments of two women as they drew nearer. One woman with a noticeably Cajun-French accent was asking the other, "What's wrong with her?" pointing toward the bed.

"I forgot you just started working on this floor," the second woman responded in a hushed whisper. "Everyone here knows that's Senator Savannah Devereaux. Her truck crashed into a ditch on New Year's Eve. The talk is that she may have had too much to drink before trying to drive home. She's been like this ever since they brought her in."

"Senator Savannah Devereaux," mused the first woman. "Didn't her husband pass away earlier this year?"

"Yeah, that's the one. In fact, I think that may have had something to do with why she was drinking so much on New Year's Eve."

"What are they talking about? I wasn't drunk ... was I?" thought Savannah.

"I can just imagine how depressed she must have been, her first Christmas and New Year's by herself. I remember that first Christmas after Charlie died ..." Her voice trailed off, as if momentarily slipping back into a different time period. The pause was brief, and just as quickly as she had stopped, she started again.

"Anyway, luckily somebody was driving by and saw her. If they hadn't called 911 when they did, she might not be alive today. It's sad. Everybody says what a wonderful woman she was."

"What do you mean — was! I'm still alive!" Savannah yearned to cry out. Savannah had no way of calculating how long she had been in this condition. She only knew that she was trapped inside a silent, unyielding and uncompromising body.

"You want to get the trash while I get the towels?" the second woman continued.

"Sure. By the way, that bag for her I.V. looks empty. Maybe I should let someone know."

"Nah, don't worry about it. It beeps at the nurses' station when it's finished," replied her counterpart. There was the quiet shuffling of feet, the sound of more movement in the room, then silence.

So this was it! During her brief sojourn in the Louisiana State Legislature, Savannah O'Brien Devereaux had become a legend, noted for her shrewd wit and political power of persuasion. She was regarded as a most influential woman, highly intelligent and self-sufficient.

Now, without warning, this "powerful and beautiful" woman had been reduced visibly to nothing more than a limp and lifeless mass of body parts, trapped inside a world of isolation, and yet, still subjected to the incessant chatter of two hospital housekeepers. Her heart seemed to sink even more deeply into her chest until it ached with fear and self pity.

CHAPTER 2

An eternity of nothingness seemed to have passed before the silence of Savannah's room was abruptly interrupted by a firm heavy-handed knock on the door. Seconds later, she was startled to hear a man's voice at her bedside. His speech was slow and deliberate.

"Savannah, this is Dr. T. You're at Our Lady of the Lake Medical Center in Baton Rouge."

Savannah could feel her hand being gently lifted and held, recording her heartbeat. On recognizing the familiar voice of Dr. Trahan, a close family friend, she submitted to an overwhelming sense of relief, leaving her weak, and desperately fighting off tears.

Dr. Trahan persisted: "Savannah, you were in an automobile accident on New Year's Eve. You've been in a comatose state since that time. Today is Friday, January 27, 2012. If you can hear me, I want you to try to move one of your fingers."

With every ounce of strength in her body, Savannah strove to comply. She wondered if her fingers were moving at all. If they were, she couldn't feel them.

"All right," the doctor continued, "don't you worry – maybe next time."

Out of nowhere a woman's voice intruded. It was Linda Babin, Dr. Trahan's nurse.

"Dr. T., do you think that someone in a coma knows what's going on around them?"

"It's been known to happen, Linda," the calm response came, "but with as much distress as her body has been through with this accident, her mind may have shut down to help her body cope with the situation."

"Then why do you always tell her that she's been in a car accident and how long she's been in a coma?" Linda persisted.

"We never know for sure what someone in such a state can hear and understand. She may not comprehend a thing I say, but just imagine how disconcerting it would be if she could hear us and no one ever spoke to her."

Total frustration and a haunting sense of isolation descended upon Savannah when she heard Dr. Trahan murmur in an exceedingly low voice: "More than likely she can't hear us. We'll just have to wait and see how things go."

As Dr. Trahan turned to walk away from her bed, Savannah could sense a change in the room. There was another knock on the door, then more movement. "Hey Charles, how ya' doing?" Dr. Trahan asked as Sheriff Charles Breaux entered the room.

"I'm doin' okay Dr. T. How's life been treatin' you?"

"Couldn't stand it if it was any better," Dr. Trahan responded with a laugh.

Then, on a more serious note, Sheriff Breaux asked, "How's Savannah doing?"

Dr. Trahan's whole demeanor changed. "She's in pretty bad shape, Charles," he answered in a quiet voice. "I wouldn't give anyone else a chance of pulling through this, but Savannah's not just anyone. She's always been a fighter."

"Is it all right if I visit with her for a while?" asked Sheriff Breaux.

"Sure, just don't expect too much," Doctor Trahan cautioned. "There hasn't been much change in her condition since the accident."

"Yeah, I heard," Sheriff Breaux responded, frowning. "Look, Doc, I'm going to have an officer posted outside her door for the time being. Savannah has now been officially linked to the murder on False River."

"What?" Dr. Trahan exclaimed incredulously. "You gotta be kidding!"

"Wish I was," Sheriff Breaux replied, shaking his head. "I can't discuss it because we're in the middle of an ongoing investigation – but it's serious."

"Have you talked to our hospital administrator yet?" Dr. Trahan continued. "He'll need to let Shawn Dupont know. Wouldn't set well to have the Chief of Hospital Security walk by and see a sheriff's deputy guarding the room of one of the patients without being advised beforehand."

"I was planning on doing that. I just wanted to check on Savannah first," Sheriff Breaux assured him.

Dr. Trahan shook his head sadly. As an afterthought, he said, "Let me know if there is anything I can do to help, Charles."

"Will do," Sheriff Breaux replied.

Turning, Dr. Trahan left the room, Linda following close behind him.

As soon as they were gone, Sheriff Breaux walked over to Savannah's bedside. He leaned over her bedrail and whispered, "Savannah, can you hear me?"

There was no response.

"I wish I could have been there for you when you needed me, Savannah, but I got your call too late. If only I could figure out what you were trying to tell me. You may be the only one who really knows the truth about the murder on False River."

He waited briefly for some recognition from her. Still, there was no response.

"What a shame. A terrible waste," he muttered. He sighed, and heavy of heart, slowly turned and left the room.

Gradually, and fearfully, Savannah began to realize the sobering fact that she had no way to communicate with the outside world. Desperately she prayed that someone, anyone other than herself, knew the shocking secrets locked away in the confines of a waning mind, thus far only accessible to her. She knew that revelation of such evidence would create major changes in her world — and in that of those closest to her.

She had to survive! She had to tell them all!

PART II – 2003

CHAPTER 3

Over the past few years, D.D., Mitch, and Doug, had become inseparable friends. All of them came from what was touted as "upper middle income class families." Other than that, they were as different as night and day.

D.D., now twenty-one years old and the eldest of the group, left home when he was only sixteen. The main source of contention when he lived with his parents was his father. Even though the man was seldom around, on those rare occasions when he was home, he expected D.D. to be perfect.

The animosity between the two grew until the verbal fights no longer satisfied either one of them. Finally, one day in total exasperation over a meaningless issue, his father took his belt off and began beating D.D. When his son grabbed his father's hand to stop the beating, a fist fight ensued.

D.D.'s mother came running in, but when she tried to stop the fight she was accidentally knocked down. Everyone froze for that one moment in time. When D.D. realized what had happened, he ran out of the house, taking with him nothing more than a lifetime of bad memories of mental abuse from his father.

For years he traveled from city to city, sometimes working, sometimes stealing what he needed to survive. It was in Livingston Parish that he met Doug and Mitch. Within a year, D.D. had persuaded Doug to drop out of school and move in with him. Doug hated school and was considered something of a geek by some of the other students. He thought teaming up with D.D. would make him more of a "righteous man."

When Doug moved in with D.D., his relationship with his parents became strained, to say the least. Both D.D. and Doug worked at odd jobs when they could get them to help pay the low rent on the run-down trailer they lived in.

The third member of their group, Mitch, was seventeen years old, and a recent graduate from Live Oak High School. His parents constantly worried about the undue influence D.D. and Doug might have on him. Mitch insisted that they were just good friends and assured his parents that he was going to college in the fall. All of that was forgotten when Mitch heard his cell phone ring.

"Hey, Mitch, Doug and me are treating you to a night at *End of the Line* for your graduation present. How about it?" questioned D.D.

"That sounds great!" replied Mitch. "What time y'all wanna go?"

"Doug's got him a side job over at the Dodge place and won't get off until eight tonight." Before he could continue, Mitch jumped in.

"That's cool. I'll pick up Doug at eight and we'll meet you at *End of the Line* around eight thirty."

"Sounds like a plan," said D.D. "See ya then. Be safe man."

Time passed quickly. By nine-thirty p.m. D.D. was livid. His ride had dropped him off at the bar at eight-fifteen, and Doug and Mitch had yet to arrive. The warm beer he had been nursing for the last half hour was his third. Finally, the front door to the bar opened and in walked Mitch and Doug, still involved in lively conversation.

"What took y'all so long?" growled D.D. as they drew near. "I was beginning to wonder if you were coming."

"I got a new car for graduation and dad had to read me the riot act before I left home," Mitch laughed. "Then I had to go pick up Doug. As usual, he managed to find a sweet little honey on the side of the road where he was waiting for me. If I hadn't promised to go buy him a six pack, he probably would've headed off with her instead of me."

"You gotta admit, she was a heck of a lot cuter than you," moaned Doug.

"Well, maybe marginally," Mitch admitted with a high-spirited laugh.

"What did you do with the six-pack?" asked D.D.

"Oh, that was gone before we got half way here," laughed Mitch.

Both teens ordered shots of Lockness Monster. Their age was conveniently ignored by their friend, Tom, who was bartending. After all, they had to celebrate Mitch's graduation. D.D. ordered another beer. After a few more rounds, Tom finally said, "I think you boys have had enough for tonight. Why don't y'all head on home?"

Mitch was insulted. "Whatta' ya' think you are ... my momma?"

"It's no big deal," D.D. intervened, anxious to avoid a confrontation. "Let's just go somewhere else."

Turning his back on the bartender, Mitch looked pathetically at his two friends. Then abruptly his face broke out into a big grin, and with the slurred speech of a seventeen year old who couldn't hold his liquor, he asked, "Hey you guys wanna see sumpin' really cool?"

"Sure," replied D.D. and Doug in unison, both laughing hysterically at Mitch's antics. At this point, D.D. appeared to be the only one still partially sober.

"Cum' on outside," Mitch continued, barely maintaining his balance as he rose quickly from the bar stool. As his equilibrium continued to fail him, his back pushed up against the bar. When he leaned forward to walk, the force of gravity took hold, and just as he was about to take a nose dive onto the floor, D.D. and Doug raced forward to catch him. With Mitch in tow, the three rowdy friends stumbled out to his car, laughing and joking as they did so.

"Ah, so this is the new ride," said D.D. approvingly as he stood beside Mitch's Camry.

"Yep, this is it. But hey man, check it out," said Mitch. He opened the front door on the passenger side of his car. Then he sat down on the front seat and fumbled with the latch on the glove compartment. When it finally released, the door dropped open in front of him. He reached in and pulled out an old GLOCK G17C 9mm Compensated.

"Man! That is so radical. Where'd you git it frum?" said Doug, in his own inebriated stupor.

Mitch got out of the car before continuing. "My old man had it locked up in his desk drawer at home for years. It belonged to my paw paw. Pop left the key in the desk drawer tonight and," abruptly Mitch tried to bow down in a comical gesture, only to find that he had to sway back and forth to straighten up again, "yours truly decided to set it free." With that, all three boys exploded with boisterous laughter.

"Hey, I got an idea," Doug shouted. "Did you hear that Steve's Curb Market got robbed night before last?"

"Yeah. What about it?" asked D.D.

"Well, since it just got robbed, nobody would be expecting it to get hit again," Doug pointed out. "Why don't we have a little fun and get us some more beer, courtesy of Steve? I got some friends that'll vouch for us if I ask them to. Besides, if we hit the place now, the cops will probably think it's the same losers who robbed it before, just coming back again."

"I don't know," D.D. sighed. "What if we get caught? I can't afford to get into any more trouble right now. I'm still on probation from my last run-in with the law."

"Aw, cum on," said Mitch, staggering towards D.D. He playfully punched D.D. on the chest.

When D.D. realized his friends were serious he began to sober up. "Nah, man. I'm telling you – I can't take a chance on something going wrong."

Before he could protest further, he was shoved into the back seat of Mitch's car and the door shut. Mitch ran around and jumped into the driver's side of the car; Doug rode shotgun as they peeled out of the bar parking lot heading for Steve's Curb Market.

CHAPTER 4

Mitch drove his car to the far end of the parking lot at Steve's Curb Market. Once there, he immediately turned off his head-lights and ignition. It was a quiet night and he didn't want to draw any undue attention to them.

D.D. sat apprehensively, his stomach churning. He watched as Doug pulled the gun out of the glove compartment and handed it to Mitch. Mitch grinned broadly as he stuffed the gun into the pocket of his hoodie.

"Well this is it," Doug said as he pulled the hood on his jacket over his head.

"Yee haw," responded Mitch as he did the same. "You still gonna weasel out, Chief?" he asked D.D.

"You guys are crazy," said D.D. "You'll never get away with this. Count me out."

"Whatsa mattah buddy? You gotta yellow ... strip ... er, uh ... shreek ... uh ... streak down your spine?" Mitch slurred, feeling the effects of his last two drinks.

"Yeah, I guess," answered D.D., now more intense in his demeanor as he contemplated the gravity of what was about to happen.

All three boys got out of the car. Mitch and Doug surveyed the area to make sure there were no customers around. When they decid-ed the coast was clear, they parted company with D.D. He watched in disbelief as they headed for the front door of the store. Then abruptly he turned around, looking in the opposite direction.

His feet began walking as if they had a mind of their own. His steps became longer and longer until finally he was jogging down the road. D.D. felt a sudden urgency to put as much distance between he and his two friends as possible. He had jogged only a short distance when, without warning, a loud noise exploded into the air.

"Oh, God!" thought D.D. *"What was that?"* Heart racing, D.D. immediately came to a standstill on the side of the road. His attention quickly focused in the direction of Steve's Curb Market. For the next few moments he stood in silence, frozen with fear.

Soon afterwards, Mitch and Doug could be seen racing down the gravel road in Mitch's new Camry. The sleek metallic-silver automobile was throwing up rocks and leaving a cloud of dust rising from the rough terrain behind it. On catching up with D.D., Mitch slammed his size thirteen boot down on the brake bringing his car to a skidding stop.

"Jump in," Mitch yelled, as Doug flung open the car door.

"What happened?" D.D. yelled back.

"No time to talk, just get in," screamed Mitch.

D.D. jumped into the back seat as Mitch peeled out, leaving a deep tire rut as rocks scattered. The sound of police sirens in the distance was growing louder.

"What happened?" yelled D.D. again, this time more forceful.

"Mitch got trigger happy and shot a cop," bellowed Doug.

"What!" screamed D.D.

"I couldn't help it," Mitch said. "My hand got all sweaty and the gun was starting to slip. I grabbed for it ..."

From the back seat, D.D. could see that Mitch was shaking.

"... when that crazy cop came up behind me and yelled, 'Drop it!' I spun around and the gun went off. I didn't mean to shoot him. It was an accident." Mitch's shaking was almost spasmodic now.

"Oh, man!" cried out D.D. "Shooting a cop! They don't throw you in jail for shooting a cop. They throw you under it!"

Two police vehicles were in hot pursuit, their blue flashing lights and high-pitched sirens magnifying the intensity of the situation, until at last they caught up with their prey. The first policeman signaled for

Mitch to pull over.

"You better pull over," D.D. groaned. "They'll be ten times tougher on us if we don't."

Mitch reluctantly slowed down and drove his car to the side of the road. Before he had even come to a complete stop, one police cruiser came to a screeching halt directly behind them. The other cruiser raced in front of the Camry and stopped just as quickly.

Leaping out of his car, the first policeman pulled his gun from its holster and crouched behind the door of his vehicle. He ordered Mitch to take the key out of the ignition and put it on the dashboard. The second officer arriving on the scene, barked out orders for the occupants of the car to raise their hands, and keep them in full view.

Both policemen then approached the car, one on either side, and began forcefully dragging all three men out.

"Assume the position!" the first officer snapped. "You punks think you're tough, don't you? Well, let me tell you something! You don't know what 'tough' is 'til you've seen police officers settling the score with some stupid wanna-be big shots that've killed one of our own. You boys are gonna regret the day you were born," he promised.

He held his gun on the three young men while the second officer handcuffed them. Then the officers began painstakingly searching each detainee. Much to their disappointment, although Mitch and Doug were highly inebriated, the additional search failed to produce any drugs or weapons.

The first officer began reciting, "You have the right to remain silent …"

Mitch, again feeling the effects of the alcohol, jumped in, "Hey, bro, I know this one. I seen it on **Law and Order** a zillion times. Is that where you learned it frum?" he heckled.

The officer's face reddened as he continued, "Anything you say can and will be used against you in a court of law…" When he finished he asked, "Do you understand these rights as they have been read to you?"

"I ain't sure," jeered Mitch. "You wanna say 'em over agin?"

The officer looked at the drunken teen in disgust. D.D. and Doug could feel the rage building up inside the man.

Mitch's laugh lost its' vigor as he began to wobble again. Still, he continued, "Hey man, I wuz jest jokin. Can't ya' take a joke? Yeah man, I understand. We all do. Right guys?"

Doug and D.D. were more subdued by this time. Both of them just shook their heads.

The first policeman went back to search their car while the second one entered the names from their drivers licenses into a computer in the front seat of his squad car. During the intensive field investigation, a third policeman appeared. Quickly jumping out of his patrol car, he came running up to the other two officers, yelling out triumphantly, "Look what I found!"

He held up a gun in a plastic evidence bag. "We got you boys now," he sneered. "If you thought throwing your weapon out in a ditch would save you, you guessed wrong."

Mitch looked over at Doug and D.D. and whispered, "Don't say anything until we talk to my dad. He'll know what to do."

"It's a little late for that," mumbled D.D.

"Quiet!" yelled one of the officers.

All three boys immediately stopped talking. It was approaching 4 a.m. by the time the search was completed. The three men were taken to the police station. By seven a.m., Mitch and Doug's parents had shown up, hand-in-hand with their lawyers. Not surprisingly, after a few well-placed calls, both boys were released into the custody of their parents. D.D. remained in jail.

A subsequent search in the computerized criminal records on file at the police station soon revealed that D.D. was on probation for a prior arrest. The police chief assumed that with his record and being the oldest, he had probably been the mastermind behind the robbery attempt and ensuing murder.

Doug and Mitch's parents and lawyers instructed them not to have any more contact with D.D. Their parents convinced the two boys that the only way they could keep from going to jail for an indefinite period of time was to let their lawyers handle the situation. Knowing they had no choice in the matter, they did as they were told.

At the arraignment, Doug, Mitch, and D.D. all pled, "Not Guilty."

CHAPTER 5

D.D. sat in a jail cell surrounded by other prisoners.

"What you in fer?" asked a large tattooed man in the customary prison garb.

"Doesn't matter," replied D.D.

"Hee hee," laughed the man sarcastically. "We got ourselves a real live one here fellas. I think he needs to know what we do with wise crackers like him, don't you?"

Suddenly D.D. was surrounded by five hardened criminals determined to teach the "newcomer" a few lessons. D.D. reeled around after the first excruciating blow to his stomach. Before he could steady himself, he was met head-on by another staggering punch that landed across his jaw. The force of the next hit to his mouth split his lip open and blood began spurting out everywhere. Soon he was in such pain he couldn't keep up with who was hitting him or what direction it was coming from. The relentless punches seemed to continue forever.

When it was all over, he lay unconscious on the jail cell floor. No one seemed to have any idea of how long he had been lying in a pool of his own blood before a prison guard finally found him. He was taken to a hospital in Monroe for treatment and then brought back to prison to recuperate.

By the time his trial came up he knew he was in deep trouble.

Overworked and underpaid doesn't get you much in the line of a defense attorney. To top it off, he was being represented by a public defender that wasn't much older than he was.

The two had met only once before the court date. At that time, D.D. professed his innocence without implicating Mitch or Doug. That didn't go far with his inexperienced attorney. He told D.D. that the investigators had been unable to lift fingerprints from the gun to determine who had been the one to shoot the policeman. Since D.D. was the oldest of the group and already had a criminal record, he was considered the primary suspect, and would be tried for the murder.

Based on the recommendation from the Public Defender's office, his attorney endeavored in every way possible to get D.D. to plea bargain to a charge of involuntary manslaughter. D.D. knew he was innocent and opted for a jury trial.

Before the trial began, D.D.'s charge was changed from involuntary manslaughter to second degree murder and attempted robbery. If his public defender told him that, he didn't remember it. They had also tacked on an assault charge for his altercation in jail.

CHAPTER 6

It was Tuesday, November 5, 2002. A short, stout man in a deputy's uniform walked into the crowded courtroom, commanding in a booming voice: "All rise!"

As the judge entered, the sudden hushed silence was accented only by the shuffling of feet as those present rose to greet him.

"You may be seated," the judge invited as he assumed his post, glancing around to see if his cup of coffee had been properly situated.

Again there was the loud clamor created by the courtroom crowd as they moved around to reposition and become more intimately acclimated to their seats for the final phase of the trial.

Sitting alone with his court appointed attorney, the twenty-one year old D.D. had a haunting, expressionless look on his face. He was a ruggedly handsome man, although barely old enough to actually be deemed a man.

His relatively short life had been filled with heartaches and disappointments, but none as meaningful as today, when he sat alone at the defense table with no family present. He was on trial for murder – a murder he had not committed – but wasn't that what they all said?

Abruptly the door to the jury room opened and the jury filed out and into their seats in the courtroom. None of the jurors looked at the defendant. His attorney knew this was not a good sign.

The judge looked at the jury foreman and asked, "Have you reached a verdict on the case before you?"

"We have your honor," replied the foreman.

The judge then turned his attention to the young man and his lawyer and said, "Will the defendant please rise."

Both men rose in unison: one slightly older; the other slightly taller.

The judge then turned to the jury once again and asked, "…What say you?"

The jury foreman responded, "… we find the defendant … guilty as charged."

At that instant, the young man realized his life was over. Everything else that was said was filtered out; and his troubling thoughts took over. His two best friends had hung him out to dry. In order to save their own necks, they lied about his involvement. His family had deserted him in this, his most desperate time of need. D.D. resigned himself to the fact that there was no one or anything else that mattered.

As if the verdict in itself was not excruciating enough for D.D., the judge decided to proceed with sentencing. Prosecutors convinced the judge that D.D. was a dangerous criminal by revisiting the fight that had taken place with the other inmates in his jail cell. The prosecutor indicated that the fight was further evidence that D.D. should be considered a threat to society.

All things considered, his lawyer assured him that he was getting a good deal by only garnering life in prison instead of receiving the death sentence for killing a policeman.

In no time at all, it became obvious to D.D. that he had been abandoned by everyone. He no longer had a link to the outside world. He was now a "loner" in every sense of the word. The guards came over to usher him out through the side door. He could see the hate in their eyes. Some of the family members of the murdered policeman yelled obscenities at him. His attorney said something to him, but the words never registered.

As the spectators in the courtroom stood and began to file out, an attractive middle aged woman picked up her purse and mingled in with the people leaving. Designer sunglasses covered her red swollen eyes. No one had heard her cry or seen her dab an already soaked Kleenex at the tears that welled up behind the frames of her spectacles, imminently threatening to pour down her cheeks. Her crumpled up Kleenex was well hidden in the confines of her tightly fisted long slender fingers.

She never had a chance to talk with her son before the trial, or maybe that was just an excuse. She knew that her husband would be furious if he found out that she had driven for hours just to sit in a packed courtroom to hear the outcome of her only child's criminal trial.

"It's horrible to be weak," she thought, "especially where your only child is concerned." Unfortunately she had never been a strong person. Maybe if she had been, none of this would have happened.

PART III – 2009

CHAPTER 7

Even at the mature age of fifty-eight, Michael Joseph Devereaux, Jr. was considered an exceptionally handsome man. His smooth tan complexion was enhanced by piercing dark brown eyes, characteristic of his Cajun descent. The thick jet-black locks of his youth had gradually been transformed into a striking salt-and-pepper display of neatly trimmed hair.

Today, he stood alone outside St. Mary's of False River church, his upper body leaning against a large oak tree, the bottom of his right foot pressed up and backwards toward its' protruding roots. His right arm hung by his side as if weighted down by some invisible force. A lit cigarette dangled from the fingers of his hand.

Marriage and this "forever" thing had always bothered him. He was a man of his word, but how could you possibly know what to expect a year from now, let alone a lifetime from now? Besides, he had been down this road once before.

His thoughts drifted back to what seemed like an eternity ago, when he was married to the beautiful socialite, Christine Bennett. Their marriage had been regarded as the perfect merger between two well-to-do families.

He was twenty-nine years of age at the time; Christine was twenty-three. Their marriage might have been different had it not been for Mike's insatiable drive for success and his inherent work habits. After incredibly long hours left alone, Christine sought company in a life of alcohol and pills. Gradually, the two drifted further and further apart.

One night in desperation, after Mike left to attend another out of state business meeting, Christine initiated an all-night drinking binge at a nearby town bar. Had anyone realized her state of inebriation before she left the bar that night, they would never have allowed her to drive home. Obviously intoxicated, she crisscrossed along the winding road heading toward their home.

Unfamiliar with the new, fully-loaded, metallic blue Cadillac Mike had given her for Christmas, and incapable of maneuvering the rain-slicked road, she failed to navigate a sharp turn. The car ran off the pavement, through a low and muddy ditch, and back up into a field. Her car hit a tree, almost simultaneously exploding into flames. The beautiful Christine Bennett Devereaux was burned beyond recognition.

Everyone told Mike there was nothing he could have done to prevent it, but deep down inside he knew that he was not completely blameless for the accident. *"Had I been at home,"* he lamented, *"she wouldn't have been out that night."* Mike's thoughts were suddenly interrupted by the arrival of two of his neighbors dropping by to say hello.

"There's still time to back out!" taunted Larry Ardoin.

"Shame on you!" his wife Alicia reprimanded, slapping his shoulder.

Still on a roll, Larry continued, "I got my truck in the back parking lot. It's filled with gas. Here's the keys – if you want 'em."

Alicia grabbed the keys from Larry as he dangled them in front of Mike, and slid them into her purse. "He just doesn't want anybody to be as happy as he is," she said to Mike with a convoluted smile.

"At least he could have sat in the truck and cooled off," Larry replied as Alicia dragged him into the church, still laughing sympathetically.

Who could blame them for not dallying around outside? It was summertime in Louisiana. Today there was a quiet stillness in the air begging for even the slightest hint of a breeze. Humidity, coupled with the heat, indicated another miserably hot, muggy Louisiana day. To top it off, Mike was dressed in his tuxedo for the ceremony. He could feel the perspiration creeping down his back as he pulled at the collar of his stiffly starched shirt. Unsure as he was of how long he could last outside, going inside scared him more.

Mike had numerous acquaintances, but when it came to close

friends and family he was, to all intents and purposes, a social recluse. His dad had longed for Mike to follow in his footsteps and take over his oil refinery company, but Christine's death changed everything.

He loved his parents, but they worried constantly about him. Their continual urging for him to get out and mingle with other people caused him to realize that the best chance he had for living his own life again, was to leave Shreveport and get a fresh start, free from his past.

While flipping through a trade journal in the waiting room of his dentist's office, Mike chanced across an advertisement that caught his eye. Prominently listed was an established real estate company for sale in New Roads, Louisiana. Somehow it settled in his memory, popping up unexpectedly at odd moments. The more his thoughts turned to the ad, the more interested he became. After making several initial calls he followed up with a trip to New Roads.

Mike made an offer to buy the business, which was accepted with very few changes. Within a matter of months he had sold his home in Shreveport, tied up all the loose ends, and moved to the small quintessential town of New Roads.

It didn't take his parents long to recognize a drastic change in their son. They both agreed the move had been beneficial for him. He seemed more positive and upbeat about everything.

Regretfully, four months after his move to New Roads, he was notified that his parents had been killed in an automobile accident. It was another hard blow to his attempted recovery to normalcy. The large inheritance was of little consolation to him.

Today, standing in front of the church preparing to start life over again, Mike felt mixed emotions. He vowed to make things different this time. Mike couldn't remember ever telling her outright, but he did love Savannah.

At that moment Jim Chandler, Mike's best man, along with Kent Peltiers, his groomsman, walked up to him and said in unison, "Happy Birthday Mike!" "Why didn't you tell any of us that today's your birthday?" asked Jim.

"Don't worry about it," Mike said with a smile. I already got the best birthday present any guy could ever have. She'll be walking out that church door with me as soon as all the formalities are over with."

"Man, he's got it bad," laughed Kent.

"Yeah, I know," said Jim with a big grin. "Mike, I think they're waiting for us to go in."

Mike reluctantly put out his cigarette and together they walked to the side entrance of the church.

There was such a large crowd of people making their way into the church, no one seemed to notice the one lone inconspicuous and uninvited guest in the older model Honda Accord, watching from across the road in the service station parking lot.

The engine of his car was turned off, more than likely to save gas. The windows were rolled up to within two inches from the top, possibly to discourage anyone from coming by and talking with the man inside. This left the stranger behind the steering wheel sitting in the scorching heat, sweating profusely. Any other day someone might have stopped by to see if he needed help. This was not a day for picking up on such minute details.

CHAPTER 8

In stark contrast to the exceedingly proper, and often withdrawn, Michael Devereaux, Savannah Marie O'Brien's personality was reflected as outgoing, fun-loving, and full of surprises. Nevertheless, when she set her goals and identified where she was going, she stayed with the program. Today was no different.

Savannah and her wedding coordinator, Kay Baucuum, had already mapped out all the arrangements for the upcoming nuptials. Kay and Tina Peltiers would pick up Savannah's wedding dress from her home and take it to the Bride's Room at the church, where it could be secured the evening before the wedding. Kay also arranged for Savannah's mother, Grace, who would serve as her matron of honor, and Macy Monroe, her attendant, to arrive at the church an hour early to help the bride get dressed.

Savannah had been so preoccupied preparing for her wedding that she had no time to get jittery. She plunged into a luxurious bubble bath where she lingered slightly longer than usual, and then rose to begin working carefully at her make-up to assure perfection.

Next order of the day was meeting her mother at Kathy's Family Hair Care Center to have her hair styled for the wedding. Kathy Leblanc was a talented hair stylist and a great friend. Her salon in New Roads was one of Savannah's favorite places to go. She could relax, get her hair done, and catch up on the latest gossip, all at the same time.

Kathy had rescheduled today's appointments for her "regulars" to other days so that she would not be rushed when fixing Savannah's hair. Of course she also had an ulterior motive. She was as anxious as everyone else in town to attend the wedding.

Before leaving home, Savannah paused pensively before the floor-length mirror, checking for any small thing amiss. From her flowing shoulder length auburn hair and haunting hazel green eyes to her tall and willowy six foot stature she was, by any standards, a beautiful woman. Not only was she a captivating woman, but also a woman of mystery and intrigue. As far as men's perception of her was concerned, it just didn't get any better.

Staring at her reflection in the mirror, the magnitude of the day's schedule swept over her. Perhaps it had been the loss of sleep, the paucity of food, or merely the realization that she was preparing to make a lifetime commitment; whatever the reason, Savannah began to feel butterflies in her stomach for the first time since she had agreed to marry Mike.

It was not going to be your usual wedding: she was forty-five, Mike was fifty-eight. The thirteen year age difference seemed inconsequential in the overall scheme of things. After all, she had been close in age to her first husband, and that marriage had been a total disaster!

All of a sudden the "Mardi Gras" ringtone from her cell phone jolted her back to reality. It was her mother calling from Kathy's hair salon. "Where are you?" she asked.

"I'm on my way," she sang out.

CHAPTER 9

The marriage of Michael Joseph Devereaux, Jr., and Savannah Marie O'Brien on Saturday, June 13, 2009 was considered the event of the year in the small but up-and-coming town of New Roads. Originally, the wedding had been planned as an intimate family-type gathering. That idea, however, was short-lived.

As word of the impending marriage spread, the realization that many people would be offended if not invited to the wedding stretched the invitation list dangerously near the breaking point. Today, it appeared that the entire population of New Roads and its' surrounding areas were waiting at the church.

It was a beautiful day for a wedding. Actually, it may have been too beautiful a day. Across the road from the church, the sun danced off the sparkling waters of False River, enticing many of the attending fishermen and/or skiers to fantasize being far and away out on the water.

The church approached magnificence as did the flowers adorning the altar. When the music began with the trumpet's dulcet sound accompanied by the organ, Savannah, on cue from Kay, began her solitary walk down the seemingly never-ending aisle. Savannah's father had died in an off-shore drilling accident when she was only twelve years old. She wished he could have been with her today. In a way, she felt he was.

She wondered what other brides thought of as they forced their rubbery legs to conform to go step by step down that endlessly long corridor from single girl to married wife. She could feel her lips shaking as she forced a smile. All eyes were focused on her. It would have been intolerable, had her mind not blocked out everyone around her.

Instead her thoughts focused on Mike.

There had been an instant chemistry between the two of them when they met in New Roads. Not only had Mike sold her a home there, but he also talked her into quitting her job in Baton Rouge and going to work for him as a realtor. First she was getting her realtor's license, then a wedding license. Everything was happening so quickly!

Suddenly pulling out of her daydreams, Savannah realized she was coming nearer to Mike, standing at attention at the foot of the altar. There he stood in full proper severely perfect attire, smiling at Savannah. Mike had already begun to approach her, his hand outstretched to capture hers. Her right hand slipped from beneath her bouquet, revealing an incredibly beautiful diamond-and-emerald engagement ring. It glistened in the light from the stained glass windows of the church.

Mike had commissioned John at "Roy's Jewelry" to create something both beautiful and unique for her, and he had complied in fashion. Both the engagement ring and wedding band drew the attention and compliments of every person that saw them.

The moment their hands touched, Savannah's nervousness disappeared. She knew everything would be all right. Mike's strong hand gently wrapped around her smaller fingers and she was instantly calm.

Everyone said the wedding was beautiful. Savannah didn't really remember. She did recall afterwards her comments on their arrival at the reception arranged at Margaret and Paul McGarity's home.

"Good grief! Look at all the cars. I bet Margaret and Paul had second thoughts about hosting our reception when they saw this crowd start to arrive." The parking areas around their beautiful antebellum home were filled to capacity and the overflow of cars had seeped into the huge empty lot next door. Savannah continued, "Thank goodness it isn't raining. At least they won't have a lot of ruts in their yard from all the cars."

Mike found Savannah's concern for others one of her most loving qualities. "I think Paul can handle it. He has several hired men that keep up his yard. Besides, this is not the first time they have entertained large crowds at their home."

Savannah did not want to even imagine organizing such a large event. The crowd was enormous — once again allowing the stranger from the church to blend in among the invited guests.

CHAPTER 10

D.D., now known as "Loner" because of his inability to form friendships and his desire to be left alone by the other prison inmates, barely made a sound as his long lanky body turned over in the hard unyielding bed. The bunk bed was scarcely long enough to accommodate his entire frame. His eyes slowly opened, and as the light filtered in, he gradually woke up to another abject day.

When he first arrived at East Carroll Detention Center, he muddled through a complex adjustment period. The first night was the worst. Desperation, rage, isolation, humiliation, bone-chilling fear — there just were no words to describe the feelings of a twenty-one year old man sentenced to a lifetime in prison for a crime he did not commit.

Worse yet was the fact that he had been convicted in Livingston Parish, but due to his lengthy sentence, lack of jail space, and the reality that he was now considered a Department of Corrections inmate, he was sent to East Carroll Detention Center (ECDC) in Lake Providence, Louisiana.

At ECDC the majority of the population was black; he was white. Surprisingly enough, it was not the inmates he had the most problems with, but the prison guards and staff. The young man soon realized that in order to survive in prison he had to get tough fast.

At one time he thought he was plenty tough, but that was in his youth and before prison. Tough in prison and tough on the streets were light-years apart. His schooling in prison had been fast and furious and to the point: stand your ground; show no fear; and acknowledge no pain.

He also learned that the worst part of his incarceration at ECDC was, strangely enough, none of the above. It was the sheer boredom that was the central theme of each and every insufferable day.

Certain select inmates were allowed to go out on a work release program. Those were the lucky ones. The remaining prisoners tried to occupy their time by any and all means available. Some played cards or listened to music on their headphones, some stood in line for extended periods of time to work out with the limited weights available, others read their bibles or wrote letters home that would probably never be answered.

A few of the more adventurous ones attempted to make wine with grape juice and anything else they could sneak out of the kitchen without getting caught. The mixtures were hidden in plastic bags until they fermented. This was a dangerous proposition on several counts: it was, of course, against prison rules; guards did not take favorably to inmates that challenged their authority by breaking the rules; and most importantly, if the mixture should leak from the bag and their plot be discovered, they would face severe disciplinary actions.

In the summer months the heat became unbearable in their tin can buildings. Being next to large corn fields was an invitation to the mosquitoes and rats that filled the camp. The chemicals from crop dusting and the excessive dust from the harvesting made it difficult at times to breathe normally.

Visitors were treated almost as badly as the inmates. They met with the prisoners in the cafeteria, with only one large fan blowing the otherwise still, hot stifling air around. At least that's what D.D. was told. He never received visitors, so he didn't know first-hand.

The deteriorating buildings gave way to an occasional prison break by a desperate inmate searching for an escape route to the "real" world. Although independence was usually short-lived, for some, the brief sojourn into freedom was worth it.

In the winter months, inmates used anything they could to stay warm, but there was rarely any relief from the freezing winds and rain that inched its way into their desolate lives. They could complain, but no one cared about what a prisoner said. They had been proven guilty in a court of law. In some parts of society, that equated to being worthless. This was the life to which Loner had been condemned.

As he lay on his bed he watched a rat run lickety-split across the room. Suddenly it stopped, looked around, and darted into a hole etched out in a wooden cabinet in the corner of the room. At one time he might have felt sorry for the old rat looking for food. That time was long gone. Never again would he feel sorry for anything that was free.

CHAPTER 11

People are so naïve to think that hell could be something as simple as burning forever. Loner knew what hell was. He had been subjected to it for years.

Living like a caged animal with other men accused of hideous crimes, fearing for your safety with nothing to protect you but your wits, daily humiliation and abuse at the hands of the guards, lack of proper food and clothing, being susceptible to any disease that was freely allowed to permeate the population, no way to prove your innocence – this was hell.

The tall, thin and wiry, but muscular man bore the tell-tale scars on his arms from having to defend himself on numerous occasions when he first arrived at ECDC. He was thrown into lock-down on a regular basis for fighting, but once he established himself as someone that could hold his own the other prisoners left him alone. Having little contact with anyone else suited him just fine.

The first few years of being continually subjected to time in lock-down had begun to take its' toll on him. He no longer had the gait of a young energetic man. He walked slower and more deliberately now and maintained vigilance in his surroundings.

Since Lake Providence was about as far north as you could go without actually leaving Louisiana, the prison was seldom inspected. On those rare occasions when the facility was evaluated by state inspectors from Baton Rouge, the prison personnel had been notified prior to their coming. Major problems were well hidden by the time of their arrival. At other times, sanitary conditions were appalling.

Loner's body was riddled with the scars from 21 boils that he acquired after only the first few months of imprisonment. One was on his face. Another was under his arm. When the boils first started breaking out, he had to hold his arm out so that it would not touch the rest of his body. Otherwise, if his arm pushed against the boil, the pain became excruciating, and he felt like death would be a welcome relief.

When the boils in the prison population rose to epidemic proportions, two inmates were instructed to wash down the floors. The hot water tank had gone out in the prison, so no one had access to hot water. The same cold, rancid water was used on all the floors. No one took the time to periodically discard the dirty infectious water and replace it with a fresh supply of soapy water. Guards paid no attention to one of the inmates who had developed an oozing boil on his face and was serving food to the other prisoners. The sight drove many of the inmates to forgo their meals in the lunchroom for several days.

Prisoners were forced to undergo strip searches for the amusement of the guards, and if they complained they were severely beaten. This was the life Loner lived.

As Loner lie quietly in his bed, he could hear the supplementary voices of inmates now starting to wake up. He began wondering, as he often did, how long he could endure the raucous noise coming from the never-ending babble of excessive prisoners crammed into such an infinitesimal space.

This was going to be one more of many days where he had too much time on his hands. Although he was in no rush to get up, Loner finally forced himself to get out of bed. He pulled on his pants, and then sat down again to put on his shoes. He looked down into the jar he had hidden under his bed to make sure his pet spider was still there. "Hang in there buddy and I'll bring you something back from the kitchen. If that doesn't kill you, nothing will." Then he headed off to breakfast with the other inmates.

CHAPTER 12

The Devereaux Real Estate Company was housed in a small shotgun type building in downtown New Roads. The stark white framework of the small edifice, enlivened by green shutters, was partially obscured from the road by a large red crape myrtle tree. Mike was more attuned to the total effectiveness of his business dealings rather than the size of his work place when he purchased the small dwelling. In the relatively short time since his move to New Roads, Mike had established and maintained an extremely flourishing business.

As he entered the office, Mike greeted Betty with his usual, "Good morning, Betty. How are you today?"

"I'm fine Mr. Mike. How 'bout you?"

Betty Cormier sat at her small mahogany wood desk in the reception area. Betty was 72 years old, prim and proper, fanatically dependable, and loyal to a fault. For these reasons, Mike had placed a key in her hand shortly after he hired her and made her responsible for opening the office every Monday through Friday morning.

"I'm fine, but I'll be doing even better if you got some coffee going," responded Mike.

Betty laughed out loud and said, "It's ready and waiting."

Each morning, shortly after arriving, and then again right after lunch, Betty made a fresh pot of Community Coffee. Mike wanted it always available for the benefit of their employees and clients. In addition to her coffee-making abilities, Betty served as a receptionist and performed light secretarial duties.

Betty also exuded pride at being the only employee to whom Mike had assigned a permanent parking place. Frankly, no one else cared, but it was of the essence to Betty. Even Savannah knew better than to park in Betty's spot. It did not matter that Betty drove a 1997 Ford Escort, now on its last leg, and Savannah drove a 50th Anniversary Edition Corvette convertible. That wasn't the point. It was all about respecting one's position in life, and Betty's position just happened to include her parking place at work.

A short walk down the narrow hall from the reception area, to the right, was the break room. Jim Chandler, one of the office's two real estate agents, was replenishing his empty coffee cup when Mike passed by.

"Morning, Jim. How'd the fishing go this weekend?"

"I've done better," laughed Jim. "I can't even brag about the one that got away — mainly because there wasn't one."

"I feel your pain," Mike shot back with a chuckle.

Jim was a real hustler. He was a stocky forty-eight year old man with reddish brown hair, a mustache and beard, all kept well trimmed. Jim was always professional and businesslike around clients. Contrary to his mild mannered behavior when clients were present, when left only in the company of staff members, Jim was the office clown. Even Mike, who demanded business-like conduct in the office, could not restrain his laughter at Jim's unexpected antics.

The office adjoining Jim's belonged to Macy Monroe. Already an hour late, Macy finally came bouncing in as if being tardy held no relevance in her world. "Good morning, Ms. Betty. Is Savannah in yet?"

"Not yet. Mr. Mike is here though."

"Okay, thanks. I just wanted to let them know I've got a call to go on in about an hour."

Macy was thirty-four years old, recently divorced for the third time, and enjoying her present-day freedom to the max. Although somewhat sporadic and unpredictable in her day to day activities, Macy was still invaluable to Savannah and Mike. She could read people, an important trait for a real estate agent.

A house showing at ten-thirty this morning had inspired her

present clothing attire: she wore a pair of skin-tight black spandex pants that stopped abruptly just past her knees; and a long, black and red flowered cotton mini-dress that hung loosely down-and-out at the bottom, stopping slightly above her knees.

The dress was enhanced by a scooped neckline, cut low enough to show off parts of her well-endowed figure. Red sandals with wedge heels worked to create the sought-after illusion of a much taller personage. Macy casually sported short black hair because she said it was low-maintenance. Actually, it was quite attractive and accommodated her face very well.

Barely standing 5'5", Macy was addicted to high heels, but avoided them when she was out on a call. She had learned from experience never to wear her Stilettos while showing a home to potential clients. Once while wearing a pair of her favorite Beatrix Ong Naida Peep Toe Pumps (knock-offs of course) to a showing, one of the heels sank in the mud as she stepped from the sidewalk onto the unfinished lawn in the front yard. As she lifted her foot, the entire four inch heel came off the shoe. Since then, she reserved her more elaborate heels for closings, parties, and hot dates.

Macy thoroughly enjoyed eating. This presented an on-going problem due to her short stature. She was constantly on one diet after another. The beginning of the summer months was always the most traumatic for Macy. She postponed donning her bathing suit, with good reason. Extra bulges added during the long, dormant winter months were ever so noticeable when she first forced herself into the skimpy last season two-piece.

This summer, once again, she had vowed to slim down via a rigorous diet/exercise routine. The daily exercise schedule might have done wonders for her, had she avoided the fast food eateries. Her basic theory about her lifestyle was that she enjoyed fast foods because they made her happy, and when she was happy she was so much more likeable.

Once Macy had proclaimed: "you have to be happy yourself to make others happy!" Then she added: "I've never been able to be happy when I'm hungry." If nothing else, Macy was a logical person.

Technically, Macy lived in Lakeland. Judging by the wear and tear on her 2003 Toyota Corolla and her frequent sightings by friends, most thought she lived on the road.

Macy's first daily point of business was stopping in the break room for her morning "jolt" of Betty's strong coffee.

The last office at the foot of the building, encompassing the entire back of the small structure, was shared by Savannah and Mike. Mike was already busy at work in his office.

CHAPTER 13

Savannah had stopped off at Winn Dixie to pick up some donuts for the office crew. Arriving at the Devereaux Real Estate Company she veered her car down the small driveway to the back of the building which had been cordoned off for use as a parking lot for the employees. Getting into the back was always a tight squeeze, but today particularly so.

Savannah found herself inching her Vette back and forth so as to be able to park between Betty's Ford Escort and Mike's Hummer. She knew she could get into the space, but with her wide doors, she wasn't sure she would be able to get out without damaging somebody's car.

As she squeezed out into the small area between her car door and Betty's car, she started mumbling to herself. "Good grief, Betty! Why can't you pull that car over a little more, so every once in a while I might have a little extra room to get out?!" Looking up she saw Harold Stout, their attorney, waving to her from the porch of his law office next door. With an embarrassing grin on her face she waved back. "*I hope he didn't hear me,*" she thought.

Harold had been on contract with the Devereaux Real Estate Company since Mike first opened his doors almost five years ago. His office was a large gray house, accented by tall red shutters, practically dwarfing Mike's small office. The sign out front boldly proclaimed: "Stout and Stout Law Firm." Harold's son had moved away shortly after passing the bar exam, and it wasn't until two years ago that Harold had been able to convince him to move back to New Roads and join him in his practice.

Across the street from the Devereaux Real Estate Company was "Raymond's Pharmacy." Raymond and his wife Carol had opened the pharmacy back in the days when the doctors gave suckers to children after their exams or routine shots. Most practitioners had stopped giving the delicacies years ago, but Raymond's Pharmacy still puts a couple of pieces of candy in the bag with your prescription. Mike would always laugh and say that if the medicine didn't help, at least you could get a little "rush" from the chocolate tootsie rolls and peppermints.

New Roads was a small town, but it was in a great location: it was close enough to the big cities where some of the local residents worked; yet, remained far enough away to maintain its' small town appeal. Best of all, it was a mere five miles from Savannah and Mike's home in Ventress.

CHAPTER 14

"Mike, someone named Tony Prejean called this morning about the ad you have in the paper for a groundskeeper," Savannah said as they sat down to dinner. I told him he needed to call back this afternoon and talk with you."

Almost on cue, the phone began to ring. Savannah answered the phone and handed it to Mike.

"Mr. Devereaux, this is Tony Prejean. I'm calling about the position you advertised for in the paper."

"Yes, my wife told me you called," replied Mike. "Tell you what, Tony, why don't you come on over around seven-thirty and we'll talk."

"Yes sir, Mr. Devereaux. I'll see you then."

At seven-thirty the sound of a vehicle could be heard coming up the driveway. Mike met Tony at the back door.

"Come on in Tony," he said, as they shook hands. Turning towards Savannah, Mike continued, "This is my wife, Savannah."

"I'm pleased to meet you ma'am," smiled Tony.

Tony was twenty-eight years old, with a strong masculine physique, sun-bleached blonde hair, blue eyes, and a healthy tan. Although he could have his pick of the young girls that continually flung themselves at him, Tony had yet to find the girl of his dreams. Had it not been that Mike and Savannah were so much in love, Mike might have felt a twinge of jealousy. Instead, the two men seemed to form an instant camaraderie.

Sitting at the kitchen table they began discussing the job, salary and benefits, and finally, the living accommodations in the cottage at the back of the property. Almost an hour later, Mike realized that he had gone from talking in the abstract, to giving Tony the particulars of his job duties. "Well, Tony, what do you think? You interested?"

"Absolutely!" Tony responded enthusiastically.

Unexpectedly, Mike let out a hearty laugh. "Okay, then, let's go take a look at your new residence. We can talk some more on the way," Mike replied, still grinning.

Savannah watched as the two men left the house, got into Mike's truck, and drove down the road to the cottage.

CHAPTER 15

"I was talking to Erica last week. I told her that since you hired Tony as our groundskeeper, you've been after me to hire a housekeeper," Savannah said to Mike with a mischievous grin. "Do you remember Erica Kennedy?"

"Sure. She was that tall, good-looking friend of yours with the dark brown hair and beautiful tan complexion," teased Mike.

"I see you remember her well," Savannah replied with a sarcastic laugh.

Mike grabbed Savannah and pulled her close to him. "Savannah, there will never, ever be anyone else for me but you," he whispered. "I love you more than I ever thought possible."

Savannah could feel herself melting in his strong, comforting arms. "Good grief, Mike. You almost made me forget what I was going to say," she scolded as she looked lovingly into his sensuous dark brown eyes.

"Anyway," she continued, as she pulled herself away from his embrace, "Erica called me back yesterday and told me she mentioned what I said to her housekeeper, Maria Conswella.

Maria works on Mondays and Wednesdays for Erica, and for the Davids on Thursdays. She told Erica that she would love to work for us Tuesdays and Fridays, preferably from ten a.m. until two p.m."

"What did you tell Erica?" asked Mike.

"I told her I wanted to mention it to you first."

"Why don't you hire her on a trial basis? That'll give you a chance to see for yourself how she works."

"That's a good idea," Savannah answered. "I'll call Erica back and let her know."

CHAPTER 16

It was seven-thirty a.m.

Mike had barely pulled out of the driveway when his cell phone began ringing.

"Mike Devereaux," he answered.

"Did you know that FOX news has started working with some of our 'acquaintances' on what is panning out to be a major documentary – probably one of the biggest exposes in the history of journalistic reporting?" the voice on the other end jumped in.

"Yeah, I heard," said Mike, a little less than enthusiastic.

"They're gonna blow some people out the water if they use all the names they got. Man, this could create a scandal, the likes of which have never been seen around here before. I don't need to tell you, it could come back to haunt us. What 'cha wanna do?"

"Nothing," said Mike emphatically.

"You talked this over with your wife yet?"

"No," said Mike, "and you better not either."

"Hey, man, not me. I ain't talkin' to nobody. I don't know nuthing!"

"Good. Let's keep it that way."

With that, both cell phones went silent at the same time. Everything that needed to be said, had been said.

CHAPTER 17

Five months had passed since Maria had begun working for the Devereauxs. She was just as Erica had described her, a very humble and respectful middle aged woman who talked little but smiled a lot, and Savannah could not have been more pleased. Although the Devereauxs seldom saw Maria, since she came and cleaned while they were at work, there was never any doubt that she had been there on her scheduled work days. The house was always immaculate and dinner was cooked and waiting for them on the stove.

Their lack of communication may have been one reason why, when Savannah answered the phone at her office Thursday morning, the last person she was expecting to hear from was Maria.

"Good morning, Ms. Savannah," said a very subdued Maria. "I know I not come to work today, but I much need to talk to you."

"Of course, Maria. You can call me whenever you want. Is something wrong?" asked a puzzled Savannah.

"I so sorry Ms. Savannah, but I no can work for you now. I get call from doctor's office today. They tell me they get back tests." Suddenly, Maria stopped talking. Savannah could hear her crying quietly in the background.

"Is something wrong Maria?" asked Savannah, more concerned than ever.

"Ms. Savannah, they tell me … I got … the cancer." She could hardly get the words out.

"The doctor, he say for me to come and they do the chemotearipy, but I no sure how long it take. I talk to my Mary. She say if okay with you, she do my job for me now."

Savannah was stunned. "Maria, don't worry about your job. The most important thing is for you to take care of yourself and get better," replied Savannah. "If your daughter would like to come to work for me that would be fine, but I don't have to have a housekeeper right now. I could just wait until you finish your chemotherapy to see how you feel."

"Oh, no," said Maria. "Mary already tell me she like to work for you. She been housekeeper for old man who pass away in December. She been going to look for new job soon anyway. She good girl, Ms. Savannah. She work hard for you. You like her. Is okay with you?"

"That's fine, Maria. Is there anything that I can do for you?"

"No ma'am. I gonna be all right, but I thank you and Mr. Mike for all you do for me. My Mary, she say she start tomorrow, if okay with you. I come with her and show her what to do."

"That would be fine, Maria. But I want you to remember that you're like part of our family now. If you need anything at all, please call me."

Tremendously disheartened, Savannah hung up the phone. It would be difficult to have Maria's daughter in the house. It was as if they were being disloyal to Maria. Still, if that's what Maria wanted, Savannah was determined to honor her wishes.

CHAPTER 18

On Friday, December 4, Savannah and Mike were busily working on separate projects in their office. Without warning, Savannah blurted out, "Mike, I'm going home. Maria's daughter, Mary, is going to be working with her at the house today, and I haven't even had a chance to meet her yet."

"Sure, go ahead," Mike said with a smile.

Savannah grabbed her purse from the bottom drawer of her desk. As she was leaving, she looked back and threw a kiss to Mike. "See you later alligator," she chuckled.

"After while crocodile," came Mike's response.

When Savannah pulled into the driveway of her home, she saw Maria's car parked in the usual spot. "*Good*," she thought. "*They're still here.*" Without delay, she walked into the kitchen where Mary Conswella, Maria's daughter, was working.

"Good afternoon, Ms. Savannah," sang out Mary's soft melodious voice. "I'm Mary."

"Good afternoon, Mary," replied Savannah.

Mary was a petite 5'5" 27 year old Hispanic girl. She had long black hair and glowing brown eyes. She looked radiant in her unpretentious soft grey uniform with her hair twisted up in a big clip on the back of her head.

"Momma's in the back bedroom. Would you like for me to go get her for you?"

"No, that's all right," answered Savannah. "I was hoping we'd get a chance to talk by ourselves for a few minutes anyway. Come sit down."

Savannah and Mary made themselves comfortable in two of the plush swivel chairs at the table in the breakfast nook. "Your mother said the man you had been working for just recently passed away," Savannah continued.

"Yes, ma'am," replied Mary. "I was very fond of him. I had been in his employment for over six years. He began having problems with dementia, but it never changed his attitude towards me. He was always very kind and generous, and I loved him like a father. I miss him a lot."

As they talked, Savannah was surprised to learn that Mary was a college graduate. She had been conscientiously saving her money, in hopes of one day opening her own floral shop. Her determination and goals were impressive, but it was the love Mary had for her mother, that instantly drew Savannah to her.

Fifteen minutes had passed before Mary looked up and saw Maria come into the kitchen. "Oh momma, I'm so sorry. I didn't mean to leave you to clean up the bedroom by yourself. I started talking with Ms. Savannah and I forgot about the time."

Maria was grinning when she mockingly scolded her daughter, "You not forget your work!" Then she turned to Savannah and said, "You tell her — no talk — work!"

"Don't worry Maria," said Savannah, as she broke into laughter over Maria's antics. "It's my fault. I asked Mary to sit down and talk with me." The die had been cast. While Savannah had thought it impossible, she now realized that she was going to love having Mary around as much as her mother Maria.

PART IV – 2010

CHAPTER 19

Savannah and Mike were enjoying a leisure breakfast Wednesday morning, when they were startled by the loud ring tone on their home phone. They both cast worried looks at each other. It was seven a.m. No one ever called this early in the morning unless there was trouble. Savannah rushed to the phone and with a quick jerk plucked the slender object from its' solitary stand. "Hello," she answered laboriously, as if winded from her short sprint to the phone.

"Savannah, this is Heath Johnson. I'm sorry to be calling so early in the morning, but I need to talk with Mike."

"Sure Heath," Savannah replied, startled by the tone of his voice. She promptly handed the phone to Mike, with a questioning look in her eyes.

"Hi Heath, what's up?

"It's a mess over here at the Capitol," blurted out Heath. "There was a news release this morning from Ed Norton, one of the federal agents from Washington, D.C., in charge of approving housing grants for the victims of Hurricanes Katrina and Rita. He said that all the funds set aside to help the victims in Louisiana are about to be cut off.

Everyone knew eventually the steady stream of government money would end; it's just that we had no warning the announcement would come today. With all the red tape people have had to go through, some of them still haven't gotten their loans approved. Now they're worried the money won't be there when they finally do get approved.

To add insult to injury, some of those who finally got their loans approved, are now having problems buying a home. In their haste to help residents rebuild after the hurricanes, the state legislature passed bills relaxing rules on new home construction. The legislation made it easier for places like New Orleans to begin rebuilding, but it's also resulted in numerous inferior and shoddy housing structures. That, coupled with the kickbacks being received from housing contracts, has made efforts to rebuild or buy homes just one nightmare after another for people."

"Sounds bad," Mike replied.

Heath continued. "I just talked with Jeanneca Neff, a friend of mine who's a real estate agent. Last week she went to sell a new home. When the building inspector came out, he found so many problems created by the construction crew bypassing the building codes, he told her there was no way he could put his stamp of approval on the house. So now, the family has an approved loan, the money to buy a home, but no home to buy.

Anyway, this morning's news sent a shockwave throughout the state. Everyone's scrambling trying to find out what it will mean to them. I don't need to tell you, the housing industry is going to be hit hard if something is not done immediately to help diffuse the problems with the sub-standard homes now being built.

"What do you suggest?" questioned Mike.

"During the last legislative session, we drafted some proposed legislation to try to reinstate the prior building codes, but it fell on deaf ears. A group of us are getting together Friday night to discuss other viable options. We could use your input."

"Sure, where and what time?"

"Six p.m. at Parrains in Baton Rouge. Please invite Savannah too."

"Okay, see you Friday," Mike replied. As he ended the call, Savannah prepared for a lengthy conversation.

CHAPTER 20

It was crowded when Savannah and Mike walked into Parrains on Friday evening. Mike mentioned Heath's name to the hostess, and they were immediately ushered into a separate dining room. Several lively conversations were going on simultaneously.

Heath, President of the Louisiana Realtors Association, waived them in and began introducing them to the group: Cary Bani, President of the New Orleans Real Estate Association; Keith Gallagher, President of the Louisiana Homebuilders Association; Christopher Paul, President of the Electrical Contractors Association; and Lloyd Thomas, President of Howell Property Management, and the Federal Political Coordinator for Senator Frank Joseph.

Lloyd introduced his wife, Maxine. Maxine's father had been in politics since she was a child, and although he had recently retired, he was still no less a man to be reckoned with. Because of her father, Maxine was very influential with the legislators. That is, until this time. The hurricanes had put a strain on everyone. Legislators were gun-shy about introducing legislation that might possibly backfire on them. As Maxine so aptly put it, "Where the hurricanes are concerned, you're derned if you do, and derned if you don't."

After greetings and salutations, including the usual barbs back and forth, the waitress came in, took their orders, and left the room. Her departure indicated the start of their meeting.

"Y'all know the reason why we're here," Heath began. "Because of the housing loan failures, banks and other financial institutions have started tightening their lending practices. It's getting harder and harder to get a loan. And then when people do get a loan approved, they can't find suitable housing.

Homebuilders that are still abiding by the codes enacted prior to Katrina and Rita are being slammed. They can't compete with the cheaper homes being built with defective building materials and illegal laborers. Legislators were quick to pass legislation that has too many loopholes in it, and now the housing standard rules are not being uniformly adhered to in the construction business. We've got to face the fact that we may get stuck with a lot of substandard homes to sell.

Some retired legislators helped us draft legislation to get the housing industry back on track. But none of our current legislators want to consider it. We're worried about getting caught in the crosswinds of some real battles if nothing is done. If we're reduced to selling substandard homes, knowing their deficiencies, I'm not sure what our liabilities may be. I think it's time we take our grievances to our congressmen in Washington, and ask them point blank for their support. It may be the only chance we have to be heard." Everyone agreed.

"When are you planning on doing this?" asked Mike.

"The sooner the better," responded Heath. "I suggest we choose representatives from our group to fly to Washington next Tuesday, and stay through Thursday if necessary."

With no objections, the group was formed and plans for leaving were finalized.

CHAPTER 21

When Savannah and Mike returned home following the meeting at Parrains, their conversation inevitably turned to Mike's upcoming trip.

"Savannah, instead of going to Washington with the group on Tuesday, I've been thinking about going up on Monday instead. Do you remember me telling you about my friend, Tracy, who lives in Shreveport?"

Before Savannah could answer, Mike continued. "Tracy told me about a business entrepreneur he knows named James Maxwell. James bought some large parcels of land in Shreveport for development purposes. From what I understand, he's extremely good at what he does.

When he heard about the new Audubon Bridge being built in Pointe Coupee parish, he told Tracy he was very interested in looking at property here. If I go up on Monday, Tracy may be able to set up an informal meeting for me with James. This would be the perfect opportunity for us to get to meet, and maybe even talk a little business."

"That sounds like a great idea," responded Savannah with a smile. Secretly she wished she were going with him, but knew someone had to take care of their business at home.

CHAPTER 22

All the necessary arrangements were made for Mike to meet Tracy in Shreveport on Monday. Savannah drove Mike to the airport in Baton Rouge early Monday morning. He was wearing a business suit for his meeting with Tracy and James.

"You're so good-looking, I'm not sure it's a smart move for me to let you make this trip alone," Savannah said, smiling broadly.

Mike looked into Savannah's sparkling hazel green eyes and smiled back. "Take good care of yourself while I'm gone," he whispered. "I love you, baby."

"I love you too, Mike," she said softly.

Impulsively, Mike dropped the briefcase he held in his left hand. It fell by his foot with a heavy thud. With his hand now free, Mike pulled Savannah gently to himself and kissed her as if no one else existed. Then, just as quickly, he picked up his briefcase once more. He turned to leave, pulling his carry-on luggage behind him.

Before entering the enclosed walkway that led to his plane, Mike stopped and looked back at Savannah. Her eyes lit up when she saw her strapping, handsome, and ever so distinguished husband wave to her. Strands of silver and jet black hair intermingled to accent his strong tan facial features, and his masculine physique put the much younger men boarding the plane to shame.

After Mike disappeared from sight, Savannah gazed out of the large plate glass window in the waiting area of the airport for what seemed like an eternity. Finally, her eyes caught sight of his plane as it began its taxi to the runway.

Savannah gently touched the large window pane and murmured in an almost inaudible voice, "Please hurry home. You just left and I already miss you!"

CHAPTER 23

Arriving in Shreveport, Mike walked down the long corridor from the plane into the concourse. He looked around the terminal and immediately spotted Tracy moving hurriedly towards him.

"How was your flight?"

"Not bad," said Mike. "I appreciate all the trouble you went through to set up this meeting with James. I know I didn't give you much advance warning."

"It was no trouble at all, Mike. James was booked up all day, so I told him we would meet him for dinner at *2 Johns* in Bossier City this evening. Is that all right with you?"

"Fine," said Mike.

"In the meantime, I thought we could go to *Ralph and Kacoos* for lunch."

After lunch, Tracy drove Mike to his home where their lively conversation finally honed in on the serious dialogue that they both knew was imminent.

"Mike, things are starting to get rough. Somehow or another, word has gotten out that you've been one of the ringleaders in the investigation. With your cover blown, it's not safe for you to keep going on this anymore. I know you don't want to involve Savannah, but there's no way she can be left out if you continue the work you're doing."

"I know," said Mike. "Believe me, I've been thinking about it. It's just that we're so close to wrapping this up. A little longer and we may be able to bring everything to light."

"You realize that some people aren't going to be happy when they find out about your involvement. You know way too much about too many individuals, and that's going to scare some people. Maybe you better back off until things settle down a little."

"I wish I could Tracy, but like you said, I'm in too deep. If I stop now they win, and I'm not ready to concede defeat."

Once Tracy realized that Mike was resolute in his determination, he took him into his study. "If you plan on sticking with this, I have some information that you'll need to know," he said. Tracy moved the deer head he had hanging on his wall, revealing a combination safe. Turning the knob back and forth, he opened the safe and pulled out a stack of papers that he handed to Mike.

"This information comes from some extremely reliable sources. I think you will probably want to examine it carefully before going any further." The two men studied and discussed the vast array of papers before them for the rest of the afternoon.

Evening found Mike and Tracy being greeted by a hostess at the entrance to *2 Johns* restaurant. They were quickly ushered to the table where, only minutes earlier, James Maxwell had settled in to wait for them. As they approached the table, the older aristocratic looking gentleman rose from his seat to shake hands with them. In record time, all three men seemed to find bonds that connected them.

That night, as Mike's plane departed Shreveport en route to Washington, he recounted his friend's warning. Maybe Tracy was right, but it was too late. He couldn't back down now.

CHAPTER 24

It was in the early morning hours when Mike's plane finally reached Washington. He knew Savannah would be waiting to hear from him, so as soon as he told the cab driver the name of his hotel, he pushed the speed dial number for Savannah on his cell phone.

She answered on the first ring. "How was your flight?"

"Miserable," said Mike.

"Why?" asked Savannah, with a worried tone of voice.

"…because you weren't with me."

She laughed, relieved. "I miss you too," she conceded in her sweetest southern drawl. "Did you get to meet Tracy's friend?"

"Actually our meeting went extremely well. James is planning on visiting New Roads after he gets along further on his current building project in Shreveport. I want to show him the property that Gil's been talking about selling."

Mike was so involved in his conversation with Savannah that he ignored the erratic maneuvers of his taxi cab driver. He was surprised a short time later when they pulled up to the entrance of the hotel. "I gotta go, sweetheart," he said, as he paid the driver and rushed to remove his baggage from the taxi.

Mike checked into the hotel, and was soon riding the elevator to the 14th floor. When the doors opened he stepped out into the silence of the carpeted foyer and followed the numbers towards his room.

A door to his right unexpectedly opened and out stepped a man dressed in a black business suit. He was obviously in a hurry to leave, probably hoping that he wouldn't be seen by anyone. The man was followed by a woman, clad only in a flimsy black negligee, still holding on to his hand. Unfortunately for him, it was too late to escape unnoticed. Not only had Mike seen him, but he also recognized the illustrious Senator, Jacob Adams, from Louisiana.

Senator Adams hurriedly pushed the woman back inside the room, closing the door behind her. Then he walked to the elevator as if nothing out of the ordinary had just taken place. It was an awkward moment for both men. Mike walked straight to his door and was busying himself opening it as Senator Adams passed by. Neither man acknowledged the other.

"*This is just great,*"thought Mike. "*I wonder what affect this will have on our negotiations when, or even if, we are allowed to meet with him this week.*"

Mike had a few flings in his younger years, but never while he was married. He considered himself open minded, but not when it came to cheating on a spouse. His philosophy was, "*If a man can't be faithful to his wife, how can we expect him to be faithful to the voters who elected him?*"

Mike was well aware of the wheeling and dealing that went on behind the scenes in politics. He arrived in Washington anticipating problems – but none like this one. His first night in Washington and already he was on Senator Adams "hit list."

CHAPTER 25

Tuesday morning came way too soon. Mike had arrived in Washington at an ungodly hour and was hoping to get in a few extra hours of sleep this morning. With the curtains drawn, he was surrounded by total darkness. The heat flowing throughout the room engulfed him, leaving him to feel as if he were in his own private cocoon.

The bed was so comfortable he fairly floated in and out of dreams that he wished would never end. But abruptly they did. The loud ringing of the hotel phone, on the nearby nightstand, jolted him into consciousness. It took a minute for him to get oriented and locate the phone.

"Hi, Mike!" came Maxine's way too cheery voice. "We all got checked into our rooms and thought we'd meet in the restaurant downstairs for breakfast. You want to join us?"

"Sure," said Mike. Give me a few minutes to get cleaned up and I'll be down."

As Mike approached his band of cohorts in the restaurant downstairs, he was quickly drawn into their festive mood and high-spirited discussions.

"You barely made it in time," goaded Cary. "We were just getting ready to order without you."

"What time did you get in last night?" asked Heath.

"Last night?" questioned Mike. "Try two-thirty this morning. With jet lag, I figure I should be fully awake in time to go to bed again tonight."

Heath laughed heartily, "Yeah, I'm with you on that one."

Maxine jumped in, continuing the discussion she started before

Mike arrived. "I'm still amazed we found all the pieces of luggage that we checked in." Then she sighed. "You know, I had a friend who said her luggage got lost on a trip she took and they never found it. They had to pay her for everything that was missing. I knew I couldn't be that lucky. My luggage was some of the first to come off of the plane. It sure would have been nice to go on a shopping trip courtesy of Delta," she whined.

Everyone started laughing at Maxine's crazy antics. She could always be counted on to liven up just about any gathering.

Lloyd broke in next. "This is a woman whose father was a great judge and legislator, and you know what fascinates her on a trip to our nation's capitol?"

"Lloyd, you don't need to tell everything," blurted out Maxine.

By this time he had aroused the curiosity of all the other men.

"Come on, Lloyd, tell us. The suspense is gonna kill us," said Chris.

"She was fascinated with the way they folded the first sheet on the roll of toilet paper in our bathroom. I mean, aren't we just the height of sophistication?" quipped Lloyd.

But Maxine was on a roll and wasn't fazed by her husband's "tell all" documentation. "You think I'm bad. You should have heard the commotion in the bathroom at the airport in Dallas. I went into one bathroom stall, and then an elderly woman and her daughter came in. One went into the stall on my right, the other on my left. When the old woman finished and stood up the toilet flushed. I thought I would lose it when all of a sudden the old woman said, 'Well if that don't beat all! The dang thing flushed all by itself!'

When I started laughing, her daughter said, 'We don't let her out much. Besides, we're pretty much 'country come to town.' By that time everybody in the restroom was laughing, including the old lady. One of the airport attendants came in and said, 'I thought I'd come in and see if I could get some of whatever you guys are on.'"

"Need I say more?" questioned Lloyd. "I tell you, there is never a dull minute with Maxine around." The other men in the group laughed heartily as Lloyd shrugged his shoulders in playful despair.

Suddenly, Tina, a tall, thin, high-spirited waitress appeared to take their orders. "Boy, this sounds like a lively group," she said. Her wide smile revealed a mouth full of recently whitened teeth. "What can I get for you fine folks that you don't already have?"

Maxine jumped in, "How about a winning lottery ticket?"

"Honey, if I could do that, I wouldn't be working here."

"I know what you mean," Maxine conceded with a snicker.

After everyone had finished eating and Tina was serving the final round of coffee, Heath began their informal meeting. "We have two Senators and seven representatives. In order to see them all, I suggest we divide up into groups."

After their assignments were given out, Heath continued. "Let's get out there and see what we can do today. If you're not able to get in to see everyone today, try to set up appointments for tomorrow or Thursday. Remember, be pushy if you have to. We need to see every single one of these people if we can. If everyone is in agreement, we can meet back here this evening for dinner at six-thirty." Soon the enthusiastic party set out on their mission.

CHAPTER 26

Their first day of trying to visit congressmen had been somewhat uneventful for most of the group. "It's too bad we only got to see Lesurge today," complained Heath. The only good thing about going to see him was getting to talk with that knock-out secretary of his."

"Be careful," recounted Mike. "You don't want to end up another statistic in Washington's scandal tabloids."

"Oh, it's okay. I'm playing it by the book. Beverly told me I could look as long as I don't touch. It's tempting, though."

When they arrived back at the hotel, Mike asked Heath, "You want to join me for a drink in my room? Maybe we could come up with a way to bring Hastings and Albritton around to our way of thinking tomorrow."

"Sure," responded Heath.

When the elevator opened on Mike's floor, Mike led the way to his room. He slipped his card into the slot above the handle on the door, quickly pulling it out and pushing the door open at the same time. The maid service had cleaned his room while he was out, leaving the thick plush dark blue curtains wide open. Only the sheers were partially pulled together. This gave ample opportunity for what was left of the sun's brilliant rays to come streaming in through the long, clear, plate glass window.

The bed was made, towels and toiletries had been replaced, and the mini-bar in his room had been replenished, although he had only taken out bottled water the night before. Mike pulled a few drinks out of the mini-bar and raised them up. "Want one?" he asked.

"Sure," said Heath.

Mike poured the cold drinks into glasses and handed the first one to Heath. Both men seated themselves in chairs situated next to a small round table near the window.

"I saw Senator Adams when I came in this morning," said Mike spontaneously. "He was coming out of one of the hotel rooms followed by a very young, good-looking, scantily-clad blonde. I assume they had more on their minds than legislative issues."

"What did he say?" blurted out Health with an astonished look on his face.

"Nothing," said Mike. "When he saw me he pushed her back into the room and closed the door behind her. Then he passed by me like I wasn't even there."

"Did he recognize you?"

"Undoubtedly. He was probably wishing a big hole would open up, and I'd be pulled in, never to be seen again."

"Wow, another one bites the dust!" exclaimed Heath. "What are you going to do?"

"Nothing right now," commented Mike. "I have to admit, though, I'm totally disgusted by his behavior. I know his wife, and she's not only an exceptionally nice woman, but very good-looking as well. She doesn't deserve to be treated like this. On top of that he has two kids. Adam's been re-elected so many times, no one even runs against him anymore. He's got it made, and what does he do? He cheats on his wife."

Heath replied, "I don't understand why a man like Adams would risk everything he has on a fling with another woman. Why do you think people like Adams keep getting elected?"

"Who knows? Maybe the people back home don't know, or don't care what's going on here. But, if you really want the inside scoop on anything at the capitol, all you have to do is get in good with the secretaries. They know everything: who's sleeping with whom; whose marriage is in the crapper; who's a workaholic; and who's an alcoholic — you name it, they know it."

"You're probably right," laughed Heath.

CHAPTER 27

It was six-fifteen p.m. when Mike and Heath made their way downstairs to the crowded hotel restaurant on the first floor. The rest of the group had just been seated. Maxine was asking their waitress, "Is Tina still here?"

"No, she's on the morning shift. My name is Rosa and I'll be your server tonight." After Rosa brought their drinks, and then went to place their orders with the cook, Heath asked, "How'd everybody do today?"

Lloyd immediately jumped in. "Maxine and I struck out completely. Everybody we wanted to see was either out of their office or in scheduled meetings for the rest of the day. But we do have appointments set up for tomorrow and Thursday.

Cary said, "Chris and I saw Representatives Billings and Hayworth. They both gave some nice talks, but I'll be totally amazed if we get any help from either one of them. We're going back in the morning to see Representative Lofton."

"Don't feel bad," said Heath. "Mike and I got basically the same results. We saw Lesurge, which was a total waste of time. We see Albritton and Hastings tomorrow."

After dinner a slightly less enthusiastic group split up: some going out to see the local sights; some going to their rooms to relax and watch television; and Heath and Mike who strolled over to the lounge where they ordered drinks.

"Mike, don't look now, but I think those two girls that were sitting in the corner over there are coming this way." Before Heath could finish, two very attractive women approached them.

"Hello, there," said one of the women in a low, sexy voice. My name's Sonya and this is my friend Wendy. We were wondering if you two good-looking fellas would like to join us at our table for a drink."

"That's very kind of you ladies," replied Mike quickly, "but we have some business we need to finish discussing, and then I have to call my wife."

"We can wait," said Wendy.

Mike looked at Heath in disbelief. Heath laughed heartily and said, "Afraid not tonight, ladies. Thanks anyway."

Sonya grinned and replied, "Suit yourself." The two women turned and left in search of other prey.

"Mike, my wife will fall in love with you when I tell her about this," sputtered Heath. He was laughing so hard he could barely talk.

After they finished their drinks, Mike and Heath went their separate ways. "See you in the morning," Mike said as he left the lounge.

Mike trudged into the empty elevator and punched the button for the 14th floor. He mumbled to himself, "*Sure hope there's no fire while I'm here.*" Then he smiled to himself. "*It's kind of a shame, though. I hate being on the 14th floor, and Savannah would have loved it. She would have opened the curtains the minute she got in so she could see off in the distance. She gets so excited about even the simplest things. Man, I miss her.*"

CHAPTER 28

As soon as Mike entered his room, he pulled off his coat and tie and tossed them across a chair. He snatched a drink from the mini-bar, pulled out his cell phone and said, "Savannah."

"Which location?" came the reply. "Mobile," he instructed. At the sound of the first ring, he started taking off his shoes.

Savannah answered her cell phone immediately when she saw Mike's name on her phone's display. "Hey good looking, what 'cha got cooking?" she asked jokingly.

"I guess I'm the one cooking," he said with a chuckle. "I've been throwing everything I could in the pot, but at the end of the day it seems like all that's stewing is me."

It was good to be able to laugh and joke with Savannah. It made him feel a swift upsurge in his energy level, even though only seconds earlier he felt a bout of depression setting in. As long as he stayed busy he didn't have time to think about how much he missed her. But when things settled down at the end of the day he knew he needed to hear her voice.

"We didn't get much accomplished today," he said, as if apologizing. "Hopefully we'll do better tomorrow. We have appointments to see Hastings and Albritton. We saw Lesurge today, but he wasn't any help at all." All of a sudden Mike stopped talking. There was a moment of silence.

"Mike, are you O.K.?" asked Savannah nervously.

"I miss you Savannah. You don't know how much."

With a sigh of relief she responded in a whisper, "I know. I miss you too. I don't think I'll ever let you go off alone again. The bed looks so big and empty without you. I've been sitting in the recliner watching television, wishing I could fall asleep. At least then I wouldn't have to go to bed alone."

Thinking about Senator Adams, Mike added, "I'll be home soon darling. Don't let anybody take my place."

With a lightning fast response, Savannah promptly answered, "There's no chance of that happening. No one could ever take your place."

Mike knew her reply was heartfelt. "I don't know how I was so lucky to find you. You could have had anyone you wanted. I still don't know why you picked me."

"If only you knew," thought Savannah. *"You make my heart sing all day long just thinking about you."* In the end all she could say was, "I'm the lucky one."

CHAPTER 29

Heath and Mike met for breakfast Wednesday morning. By nine-thirty a.m. both men were sitting in the waiting room of Representative Albritton's office. It was not until nine-fifty-five that they were ushered into his private office.

Representative Francis Albritton was a tall, slender man. Thinning brown hair, a receding hairline, and wire-rimmed glasses gave him a distinguished and intellectual look.

Once seated, Mike began, "Thank you for taking the time to meet with us this morning, Representative Albritton. I know you're busy so I'll try to be brief. We have, unfortunately, found ourselves in somewhat of a dilemma in trying to work with our local legislators. A stalemate has occurred regarding some important issues, and we were hoping we could solicit your help in bringing them around to our way of thinking."

As Mike went on to explain the problems they were encountering, Representative Albritton knowingly shook his head.

"I understand what you're saying, Mike. I've talked to a number of my colleagues in Louisiana about similar issues. They tell me that the problem is they've got such a backlog of issues to deal with they don't have time to consider anything else right now. I wish I could help you, but if you can't get the legislators in Baton Rouge to listen to you after what you've told me, I doubt I could do any better pleading your case."

Mike and Keith then walked over to Representative Hastings office. Again they were offered little encouragement.

Representative Hastings said, "Off the record, there's been a lot of talk here in Washington about lawmakers back home getting kickbacks from dealing with programs associated with the hurricanes. The word is that no one wants to support any new legislation that might end up eventually cutting off some of the legislators' extracurricular funding sources. No one wants to 'rock the boat,' if you know what I mean."

Mike and Heath did indeed know what he meant. There would be no endorsements coming from Washington.

It was getting colder, and both men pulled their coats tighter around them as they ventured outside. "Let's go get some lunch," said Heath. "Maybe it'll make us feel better. Or, we could go look up Sonya and Wendy," he said flippantly.

Mike tried to look stern as he replied, "Don't we have enough problems already?"

They stopped at a restaurant on the way back to the hotel where they continued their discussion. "Look Heath, why don't you and the others go ahead and plan on taking off? I know y'all need to get back home. Lloyd and Maxine still need to meet with Representative O'Neal tomorrow. I'll stay over and go with them. Other than that, I think we've all done everything we could here in Washington."

"Yeah, I guess you're right," said Heath. "As soon as we get back to the hotel, I'll call everybody and let them know our plans. I'll leave Lloyd and Maxine up to you. By the way, Mike, I'm not sure any of us told you how much we appreciate all you've done. You've really been a big help."

"No problem," responded Mike.

Upon entering the hotel lobby, Mike and Heath saw Lloyd and Maxine coming in the side door. Mike told Heath, "You go on ahead. I'll tell Lloyd and Maxine what we discussed."

"Good deal. Thanks," replied Heath.

Mike walked over to Lloyd and Maxine and asked, "How'd things go for y'all?"

"Same as yesterday," said Lloyd. "We hit bottom."

"Yeah, us too," said Mike. Heath and I thought it would be best if we just turned the others lose so they could head on home. I know you two still have to see Representative O'Neal tomorrow. If you want, I'll be glad to go see him with you, or if you need to get back, I can see him by myself tomorrow."

"We don't mind going to see him, but man, if you want to go with us that would be great," said Lloyd. "We meet with O'Neal tomorrow at eleven-thirty. You want to meet us for a late breakfast or early lunch before going over there?"

"Sure, that sounds good. Why don't we meet at the hotel restaurant around nine a.m.? Maybe that'll give Maxine time enough to get into another discussion with Tina."

Maxine started grinning and said, "You read my mind."

Mike went back up to his room and called Savannah to let her know what his plans were. As they began to talk, Mike pulled several of the pillows out from under his bed covers and shoved them against the headboard. When he propped himself up on the pillows, he instinctively pulled his feet up on the bed, shoes and all. *"Good thing Savannah can't see me,"* he thought, with a tired expression on his face.

After talking with Savannah, Mike picked up the control for the television and flipped through the channels. The sun began to go down and suddenly Mike realized, *"I'm going home tomorrow and I haven't gotten anything for Savannah. If I'm going to do it, I better go now."*

Once outside, he wandered the streets of Washington for what seemed like an eternity before finally finding the treasure he had been looking for. It was a pair of long, dangling diamond earrings. *"She'll love these,"* he thought. When the clerk finished wrapping the small package he stuffed it into his coat pocket and started walking back toward the hotel.

CHAPTER 30

It was freezing cold. The sun had gone down long ago. The lights from all the surrounding shops illuminated the streets just enough to keep them navigable.

To top it off, there was a light drizzling rain mixed with a biting wind. It seemed to penetrate every piece of clothing Mike had on. Lowering his head into the collar of his coat, he stuffed his hands down deeper into the fleece lined pockets of his coat trying to keep them warm.

When Mike looked up again, the lights of his hotel in the distance were a welcome sight. He walked at a faster pace until finally reaching the hotel lobby. The warm air that greeted him upon entering was an instant reprieve from the outside weather. As he began to relax he trudged wearily over to the elevator.

The only noticeable person in view was the hotel clerk. The clicking noises made by her long painted nails on the keyboard of her computer so preoccupied her, she never even noticed the late arrival of another hotel guest. Mike stepped quietly into the elevator. Begrudgingly, he took his hand from the warmth of his coat pocket and pushed the 14th floor button. Immediately afterwards, he shoved his hand back into the pocket. The door closed in front of him. A slight second later there was movement as the elevator began its upward assent. Mike watched as the numbers on the side panel began to light up as they passed each floor.

Suddenly, the elevator abruptly stopped on the 7th floor. Two heavyset men dressed in coveralls stood waiting in the hallway. They had erected an "Out of Order" sign by the door. As soon as the door to the elevator opened, they pulled hoods over their heads and rushed into the elevator. Caught off guard, Mike was easily shoved back.

Inside, the man closest to the door locked the elevator. The other man grabbed Mike from behind, forcing a foul smelling rag into his mouth. The first man turned around quickly. Without a moment's hesitation, he began strategically thrusting several powerful blows to Mike's face. The first punch landed right above his eye, causing blood to gush out and blur his vision. Then the unidentified man sent several well positioned blows to Mike's rib cage.

The man's hands were wrapped like a boxer's. They were covered with thick material-like gauze. It seemed like forever to Mike as the heavy-set man continued to use him as a punching bag. Never so much as a word was spoken. The rag in his mouth not only kept him from yelling out, but also began to suffocate Mike as he tried to gasp for air. He was getting light-headed and was on the verge of passing out.

The man standing behind Mike tightened his grip, preventing him from falling. "That's enough," he said to the combatant in front of him. With the same menacing tone he whispered into Mike's ear, "It's time you quit your investigation. If you think this was bad, just tell anybody about it, and see what happens to that pretty little wife of yours. This is our first and last warning. Don't get involved in things that don't concern you. You may be a big man with your friends, but you're nothing to us."

With that, the first man turned the elevator back on, and the door opened. The one that had been behind Mike turned him loose. He dropped to the floor like the dead weight that he was. The two men stepped out, picked up their 'Out of order sign,' and walked hurriedly towards the exit door for the stairs. Before Mike could do anything, the doors of the elevator slowly closed and continued upwards towards the 14th floor.

Fighting against insufferable pain, Mike struggled to get to his feet. He inched himself up against the wall of the elevator as it continued to rise. When the door finally opened on the 14th floor, he was again in an upright position.

Mike stood still for a moment to steady himself. The pause was brief; anything longer and he knew he would be unable to continue. Awkwardly, he began forcing his feet to carry him out of the elevator, and then step by step to his room. His hand shook as he slid the card key into the door slot and then pushed the door open. As soon as he stumbled across the doorway to his room, he let the heavy coat he was wearing slide off his arms. It dropped with a thud to the floor. The door to his room automatically closed behind him.

With great effort Mike managed to walk into the bathroom and lean against the marble counter top, looking into the ornate mirror that covered the wall above it. The image revealed horrified him. Blood was still seeping out of a deep gash over his eye. Suddenly he coughed, and blood poured forth from his mouth. The pain became more intense than anything he had ever experienced. His ribs were throbbing, and the skin covering them was red and bruised. From the acute pain he was experiencing, he assumed he might have a broken rib.

Mike snatched a washcloth from the counter and soaked it in warm water. Leaning against the sink, he tried to wash the blood off. It was no use. He knew he had to lie down before he passed out. He staggered back to his bed. Every bone in his body was aching as he tried in vain to find a way to lie down without causing more pain.

When his eyes finally opened again, Mike knew he must have passed out for a while. There was only a glimmer of moonlight streaming in from the outside.

"Savannah," Mike cried out, before passing out again — this time for the night.

CHAPTER 31

The sun was shining brightly through the sheer curtains covering the window of Mike's hotel room. The privacy drapes had never been drawn. "It's morning?" he said drearily as he felt the sun on his eyelids. "It can't be!"

Even before exposing his eyes to the light, Mike could feel sharp stabbing pains in his chest. As his eyelids slowly began to open and focus on the existing surroundings, the large accumulation of blood matted to his shirt instantly grabbed his attention. The wet washcloth he had wiped his mouth with the night before had dried and fallen to the floor, but still he didn't have the energy to pick it up.

A half an hour passed before Mike decided the situation wasn't going to get any better. With great difficulty, he managed to go from a sitting to a standing position. Inch by inch he worked his way into the bathroom. The grotesque face in the mirror affirmed what he already knew. This had been no nightmare. He had been the principal victim of a brutal assault.

"Savannah's earrings!" he cried out. Mike hobbled back over to the coat still lying on the floor. Unable to lift the heavy jacket, he fell to his knees and began searching the pockets until his hand felt the small wrapped package. He grabbed it immediately. "At least they didn't get that!" he said aloud.

Mike looked at the time on the clock by the bed. It was 8 a.m. He had to call Lloyd and Maxine and cancel his meeting with them. If he was lucky, he could get out of the hotel and to the airport while they were meeting with Representative O'Neal. There was no way he wanted them to see him in his current state of affairs. After a few rings, Maxine answered the phone.

"Maxine, this is Mike. I hate to do this to you, but I think I'm going to have to cancel out on you this morning. I'm not feeling very well. I'm really sorry."

"Oh, Mike, don't worry about that," said Maxine with great concern. "Is there anything we can get for you?"

"No thanks. I'm just going to rest for a while, and then I'm going to go ahead and try to make it on home. I'll talk to y'all when you get back, if that's all right."

"Sure, Mike. You take care of yourself."

Mike hung up the phone and laid down again. He was too weak to do much of anything else. Finally, with great difficulty, he forced himself to get back up, knowing he would have to clean up and finish packing if he were to catch an early flight out. An hour later, with his luggage in hand, Mike went downstairs. The hotel porter hailed a cab for him.

"Had a rough trip?" asked the cabbie with a concerned look as he entered the cab.

"You'll never know how rough," said Mike with a grimace.

The short answer and the look on his face set the stage for the rest of the trip to the airport. There was absolute quiet as Mike began thinking, *"What am I going to tell Savannah?"*

CHAPTER 32

Mike had only been gone four days, but to Savannah it seemed like an eternity. Her eyes continued to fixate on the large wall clock at the Baton Rouge Metropolitan Airport as she waited impatiently for Mike's arrival.

Finally the announcement was made. A flurry of people began excitedly moving about in anticipation of the incoming flight. The loud roar of the plane's engine could be heard inside the building. Savannah stood close by the window and watched as the approaching aircraft dropped its landing gear and slid gracefully onto the long paved runway. Soon afterwards, the travelers were making their exit from the walkway into the airport terminal.

Just when Savannah thought she could take it no longer, Mike entered the terminal. Her excitement quickly turned to horror when she saw his bruised and swollen face. She ran up to him and cried out, "Mike, what happened!"

"It's all right," he said quietly, trying to calm her down. "I had a little accident, but I'm all right."

As she reached up to hug him he cringed in pain. "Oh my gosh, Mike! We need to get you to a doctor."

"Savannah, really, I'm okay. Let's just get out of here."

"Not until you tell me what happened," she insisted.

"I got mugged, Savannah. It's embarrassing that I let myself get into a situation like that. I really don't want to talk about it right now."

"I'm sorry Mike," Savannah said as tears welled up in her eyes.

Mike pulled her close to him and whispered softly in her ear, "Please don't get upset. I'm just a little shaky on my feet, but I'll be fine once I can get home and relax." Then he leaned over and kissed her so tenderly that her whole body trembled. It was like the first time: soft, gentle, strong and passionate; all rolled into one.

"I'm so glad you're home," she said affectionately. "You'll never know how much I missed you."

The purpose of the trip and Mike's battered body escaped them momentarily. Their only thought was that they were finally together again. Savannah took Mike's luggage from him and he quickly put his freed arm around her waist as they walked towards the parking garage.

At home, Mike tried to eat, but the pain consumed him. Weak and unable to argue, he finally acquiesced to Savannah's continued pleas to let her take him to the hospital emergency room.

Dr. Ryan Leonards walked into Mike's room after reviewing the x-rays and lab work. "Mr. Devereaux, you have two cracked ribs and multiple lacerations and contusions. You have suffered a mild concussion as well. Frankly, I'm amazed that you were able to make it back from Washington in the condition that you're in. You had to be in terrible pain. Did you report this altercation to the police while you were in Washington?"

"No. It was my last night there and I was anxious to get home. I didn't want to be stuck at some police station for hours filling out paperwork," Mike said truthfully.

"I understand. Well, we've cleaned up your injuries as much as we can. I'm not going to wrap your ribs tonight. We need to let some of the swelling go down first. You'll be in a lot of pain for several days, so I'm prescribing some pain medication for you. The injection we gave you should help until you get your prescription filled. Do you want me to call the prescription in to your pharmacy so that it'll be ready to pick up on your way home?"

"I'd appreciate that," responded Mike. "I'd like to get back home as soon as possible."

"That's a good idea," said Dr. Leonards. "In fact, the sooner you get home the better. At this point there's not much more we can do anyway. I want you to check in with your regular physician in a day or two. That way you can be checked to make sure there are no other complications and that everything is starting to heal properly. In the meantime, if you have any other problems at all, don't hesitate to call me."

After picking up his prescription, Savannah drove Mike home. She helped him get changed and into bed and then returned with his medicine. All night long, Savannah kept a vigil in the recliner in their bedroom. She had never seen Mike so frail. She was afraid that if she lay down beside him she might accidently bump up against him and cause him more pain.

It was not the homecoming Savannah had hoped for, but he was home, and he would get better.

CHAPTER 33

Mike had been taking pain pills and sleeping most of the time since his return from Washington. Early Sunday morning, Mike slowly turned over in bed, only to discover that Savannah was gone. It was not unusual. Since Thursday evening when she drove him home from the hospital, she had done everything in her power not to disturb him while he was resting. On his first night back Mike woke up around two a.m., and glanced over to see Savannah sleeping in the recliner in their bedroom.

He wanted to tell her to come to bed, but the medicine he was taking left him in a fog. All he could do was look at her long slender body curled up in the recliner, her auburn hair cascading around her neck. Her skin looked as soft as the clouds, and her lips were parted ever so slightly, almost on the verge of a smile. Finally he drifted off into dreams that could never compete with his 'real life' love.

As morning dawned, Mike could smell coffee brewing. It was a sure sign that Savannah was making breakfast. Savannah's face lit up as Mike managed to walk into the kitchen. "Good morning," she said with a huge smile. "How are you feeling?"

"I think I'm gonna live," said Mike. "You know what they say – only the good die young."

Another big grin lit up Savannah's face. She rushed over to Mike, gently wrapping her arms around his neck, and said, "Oh, then let's be bad." With that she placed a kiss on his lips, trying not to brush against the cuts and bruises still prominent on his face.

"I love you so much, Savannah. I don't think I ever tell you that enough," whispered Mike.

Savannah pressed closer to Mike and gently stroked the side of his face. Then, with a flirtatious laugh, she turned and walked back to the stove. "I thought I would try to entice you into eating breakfast this morning. Want some coffee first?"

"Yeah," said Mike, as he moved slowly towards the kitchen table. Then, in a defeatist tone, he spontaneously blurted out, "The trip to Washington was a total bust. We accomplished nothing."

"I wouldn't say that," Savannah grinned mischievously. "Seems to me I ended up with some absolutely gorgeous diamond earrings!"

"Yeah," said Mike absentmindedly. Then, with a one track mind, he continued. "The trip just confirmed for me what I guess I already knew. Legislators, for the most part, are just a different breed of people. They say what they think you want to hear, and then go ahead and do whatever they want. We couldn't get any of them to actually commit to anything."

"Oh, I'm sorry Mike," responded Savannah.

"The whole trip was just one frustration after another. I don't know why I should have expected anything different."

"I think you're just worn out from everything that happened to you," Savannah said in a soothing voice. "After you've rested and start to feel better, I wouldn't be at all surprised if you begin to look at your trip in a totally different light."

"Maybe," Mike continued. "I just don't know. There's talk in Washington that some of the officials in Louisiana have made out like bandits on a number of programs set up after the hurricanes. They've helped promote companies they either own, or have major stock interest in. Legislators have been seeing to it that their friends continue to get contracts with the state to help rebuild Louisiana.

It appears that the corruption associated with the hurricanes is more rampant than we originally thought. At this point I'm not sure who we can trust in the legislature. There are people in some very powerful positions that are going to be implicated in charges now being investigated. It doesn't look good, Savannah."

"What do you mean?" Savannah asked with a startled look on her face. The governor's not involved, is he?"

"I don't think so. At least it doesn't look like it."

"Who else, then?" questioned Savannah.

"I'll reserve my comments until the investigation is finished, except for Senator Adams. I'm completely disgusted with him, now that I know firsthand what a sleazebag he is."

Savannah appeared shocked. "Why? What did he do?"

"When I got to Washington I checked in at the hotel. My room was on the 14th floor. When I got off the elevator and started down the hallway, I saw Senator Adams coming out of one of the rooms. It was very late and I was tired, but I can assure you it was not his wife standing in the doorway behind him. And, she was definitely not dressed for a business meeting. Come to think of it, you would have looked downright incredible in that flimsy little black negligee she had on."

"Oh, Mike, that's horrible."

"I don't think so. You're a good looking woman," laughed Mike.

"No," Savannah blurted out. "That's not what I mean." Suddenly, after a slight hesitation, and the realization of what they had both said, Savannah and Mike broke out laughing. Then, refocusing, Savannah began again. "Seriously, Mike, I know Senator Adams' wife, and she is such a sweet person. They also have two children."

"I know. That's what makes it even worse. I may be old fashioned, but I don't have much use for a man that's unfaithful to his wife."

"I'm glad to hear that," teased Savannah.

"One good thing that did come out of this whole fiasco, was my trip to Shreveport. In fact, when I got to Washington I called Tracy back to thank him for hooking me up with James Maxwell. James turned out to be quite an astute businessman. I have to admit, he really impressed me, which doesn't happen often. I'm going to put together a proposal for him after I talk to a few people here. I know of several large tracts of land that he may be interested in buying."

"That's great," exclaimed Savannah. "You see, there's always a silver lining."

Mike laughed at the ever optimistic Savannah and replied, "Yeah, come to think of it, I'm pretty happy about that meeting. While I had Tracy on the phone, I told him about the word we had been getting in Washington regarding all the illegal contracts and corruption going on back home in Louisiana. I was surprised when he told me that they had been hearing the same things in Shreveport.

Tracy said he was already checking out a few things for some friends of his and that he's going to let me know what he comes across. With his contacts, he's in a better position than I am to find out if there's any truth to what we're hearing. By the way," Mike continued, "Heath called yesterday and wants us all to get together on Wednesday."

"Are you sure you're up to it?" questioned Savannah.

"As long as, 'I got you babe,'" he laughed.

CHAPTER 34

There were shocked expressions on the faces of Heath and the rest of their group when Mike and Savannah walked into Parrains on Wednesday evening. Mike was still brandishing the scars of his altercation in Washington.

"Mike, what happened?" cried out Maxine. "You look terrible!"

"Always the flatterer," grinned Mike.

"Seriously, what happened to you?" she persisted.

"I got mugged in Washington. I must have had a magnet on my back that said, "This is the one. At least I have an original souvenir from our nation's capitol."

"That's so terrible," continued Maxine. "Why didn't you tell us?"

"There was nothing you could do. Besides, I was hoping you and Lloyd could convince O'Neal to help us out so our trip wouldn't be a total disaster."

"I'm afraid we let you down, Mike," Maxine said regretfully.

After Mike and Savannah sat down, Heath asked Mike if he would like to start their meeting. Mike's comments began unemotional and straightforward: "We've talked to our state legislators. We've visited our U.S. Senators and congressmen. We've gotten nowhere."

As he continued to speak, his words became more heated and his actions more fired up. "It's time we change our strategy. If we can't get the people we elected to work with us on an issue as important as this, then we need to replace them!"

Applause broke out. Several members of the group all started talking at once. After a lively discussion back and forth, Heath spoke up. "What are you suggesting Mike? You know it would be impossible to replace the whole bunch."

"I realize that," said Mike. "But just think about this. All we need is one person in the legislature that would really go to bat for us: someone that would not be afraid to speak out on important issues; someone that would champion our cause at the state capitol; someone that would actually listen to our concerns.

If we had someone like that, I think we'd have a chance at getting back to where we need to be. Regardless of how it's done, we need to find one person that we can count on. Then we all need to pull together, and get that person elected. Meanwhile, as individuals and as a group, we need to police our legislators and scrutinize their actions. If we find that they are doing something illegal or morally reprehensible, we need to make sure the public is made aware of their actions. It's time we quit looking the other way. I'm tired of being ashamed of who we have elected to office."

"Great speech," said Heath enthusiastically. "Why don't you run, Mike?" At once everyone started clapping their hands and urging Mike to throw his hat in the ring.

"Oh no," he chortled. "I've got no desire whatsoever to run for office. I've got enough to keep me busy as it is." Mike grinned as he looked over at Savannah. "Besides," he said on a more somber note, "we need someone with a real fire in their belly that can get out there and fight for us with no reservations. We need to start thinking seriously of what qualities we want to see in the person we would be willing to back."

"I think it would be to our advantage not to have another lawyer in office," said Maxine. Almost half of the Senate is already filled with lawyers. If you ever read one of their briefs you would know why we have so many problems. You can't understand a word they're saying. They complicate everything with their legal jargon."

The room filled with laughter.

"You may be right," consoled Mike. "Fortunately we don't have to decide everything tonight. Let's think it over and meet back in about a week. Whatever we do, we need to be in agreement so we can concentrate our efforts on getting the right person elected."

Their group had now grown to 23. Each one pledged their support and efforts to actively seek out a candidate that they thought would exemplify the goals of their assembly.

In the meantime, Mike began receiving strange phone calls, both at home and at the office. The calls were untraceable. No message was ever left on the answering machine. When they answered the phone, the message was always the same, "Tell Mike Devereaux to leave things alone."

CHAPTER 35

"We're getting nowhere fast," grumbled Mike. "The primaries are coming up in October, and we still haven't found anyone to run for State Senator. Nobody wants to run against L. J. Brasseaux. All the judges and lawyers always stick together, and they contribute heavily towards his campaign.

Add to that, the fact that his family is very wealthy and politically powerful. Those are some pretty insurmountable hurdles for almost any opposing candidate. A campaign is tough enough to begin with, but who wants to get into one that they don't think they have a chance of winning?"

Savannah sat quietly for a moment. Then, unpredictable as usual, she stared at Mike and said emphatically, "I could do it!"

"Do what?" replied Mike questioningly.

"Run for State Senator," she shot back.

Mike turned pale. "Savannah, do you know what you're saying? Even if the campaign didn't kill you, just being a senator probably would. It's a mean, tough job. People expect miracles from you. When you don't do everything they want, they gang up on you and try to get rid of you."

Savannah let Mike get it all out of his system. When he finally stopped talking, she smiled sweetly at him and asked, "Are you through?"

"I guess it doesn't much matter," he replied. "You're going to do whatever you want to do anyway."

"That's not true, Mike," Savannah said dejectedly. "If you say you definitely don't want me to run, I won't run. But Mike, this would be such a great opportunity. I've always wanted to be in a position where I could make a difference. Just think of all the changes we could help instigate. Think of the good we could do if I were in the senate. People are tired of being ignored. They're looking for someone to elect that they can trust. They want someone who will actually represent them in the legislature."

"What would you run as?" asked Mike. "You're an Independent. You know you don't have much of a chance if you're not registered as a Democrat out here."

"Yes. But I don't think that's going to make a big difference. Neither the Democrat nor Republican parties are the same as they used to be. I know some people still vote strictly along party lines, but I think they would be shocked if they ever asked to see a copy of their party's current platform. I know I was. Besides, if elected as an Independent, I don't owe anybody anything. I am my own person. I can truly be for all the people in my District and not just looking out for the interest of one particular party. At least think about it. Okay?"

Mike knew it was all over when he saw that beautiful smile slowly spread across Savannah's face. Being a man, though, he considered it his duty not to give in right away. "Okay, we'll both sleep on it. I just can't believe you want to run for office. Then again, I can't imagine anybody wanting to run for office."

That night Mike tossed and turned as his thoughts tried to conjure up what he would say to Savannah in the morning. Mike had serious misgivings about Savannah running for office. He knew she could do the job — that wasn't the problem. It was more a concern of how brutal people could be. He still had the scars from Washington to prove it. *"What if they come after Savannah as ruthlessly as they came after me?"* he thought.

Mike also thought of the call he received from Tracy, informing him that he was able to acquire notebooks full of documentation proving corruption charges within the Louisiana state capitol itself. The information had been given to him in strictest confidence, informa-tion that could be dangerous in the wrong hands. There was genuine concern that if anything leaked out prematurely about the "deals" that were being made, many of the major players would instigate cover-ups and avoid prison time. They were intent on this not happening. The al-legations of wrong-doing went all the way up to Governor Claiborne's Office, but there was nothing to indicate that he had been personally involved. There was, on the flip side, serious implications that others in his office were.

Although Mike was worried about Savannah running for office, he could never deny her anything. The next morning as they sat down to drink coffee, Mike told Savannah, "If you want to run for office, I won't stand in your way. Just be sure this is what you really want."

Savannah jumped up and ran over to Mike and threw her arms around him. "I love you," she shouted in excitement as she repeatedly kissed him all over his face.

"Yeah, I know," he replied sarcastically. "Just prepare yourself. It's going to get rough before it's all over."

CHAPTER 36

A s soon as he got to work, Mike put in a call to Heath. "You're not going to believe this," he began as soon as he heard Heath's voice. "Savannah has decided to run for State Senator."

"All right!" shouted Heath. "That's great! I'm going to call everybody I know, right now. I can't think of anybody I'd rather campaign for. What made her decide to run?"

"You know Savannah, Heath. What makes her decide to do anything?"

Heath laughed heartily. "Yeah, I know. Who can figure out women?" And once again he laughed. "Honestly, Mike, this is great. Let me know what I can do to help."

Thanks Heath, I'll do that," said Mike, before hanging up. *"Well, it's started,"* he thought.

Shortly after Mike left for work, Savannah was on the phone calling her mother. "Mom, guess what?" Without waiting for a response Savannah continued, "I'm going to run for State Senator."

"What!?" exclaimed Grace. "Are you serious?"

"Yes, ma'am, and I want you to be my campaign manager."

"I can't believe this! What made you decide to run?"

"Somebody had to," said Savannah with glee.

"Is Mike okay with this?" Grace asked.

"I think he's still trying to get used to the idea."

"I can understand that," Grace moaned. "I think what you need to do is to get someone who knows what they are doing to be your campaign manager. I'll be glad to help, but I don't know anything about running a campaign."

"Okay, as long as you promise to help."

"You couldn't drag me away," said Grace with a high spirited cackle.

When Savannah arrived at work an hour later, the entire office was buzzing with excitement about the prospect of her running for office.

"I'm sorry Savannah. I should have let you be the one to break the news to everybody," said Mike.

"I don't mind one bit. I'm glad to see you're getting involved," smiled Savannah.

"Savannah," said Macy. "When Mr. Mike told us you were going to run for senator I just had to call my friend, Kay Begue. She has never been fond of L.J. and always said if anyone ran against him she would be more than happy to help in their campaign.

In fact, Kay told me, 'I would love to see someone run against L.J. Brasseaux and beat the pants off that son-of-a-gun. The man is incorrigible!' I gave her a call and told her that you were going to run. She's thrilled. Kay has served as a campaign manager in several political campaigns before, and wanted to know if you could use her help. She's willing to volunteer her services. I told her I would ask you."

"You're kidding!" yelled out Savannah. "That's fantastic!" Give me her number and I'll call her right now." Within minutes Savannah was on the phone with Kay. "Kay, this is Savannah Devereaux. I understand you might be interested in working on my campaign for State Senator."

"I sure am," replied Kay. "I've worked on several campaigns before, and was the campaign manager for two of them. So, if you need me …."

"Seriously?" Savannah jumped in. "You are a godsend. I wasn't sure what I was going to do. This is pretty new for me. I have people already volunteering to help, but none of them have any experience working on a campaign.

"That's no problem. We just need to get them organized," said Kay.

"How soon can you start?" prompted Savannah.

"I'm getting dressed now. Where do you want to meet?" shot

back Kay.

"Why don't we meet over at the Top Spot on the corner of False River Drive and Hospital Road? I'm sure Mr. Ali won't mind us taking up one of his tables for a while."

"That sounds good. I'll meet you there in thirty minutes," said Kay, as she dropped her cell phone in her purse and reached for her shoes on the floor next to her.

CHAPTER 37

Savannah rented an office building less than two blocks from the Devereaux Real Estate Company to use as her campaign headquarters. For the next several months, she and Kay worked non-stop in their efforts to get her operations into high gear. Grace, Savannah's mother, took over as receptionist, and Kay worked non-stop on just about everything else.

The first day of qualifying for office, Savannah was eagerly waiting in line at the Clerk of Court's Office in New Roads for the doors to open. She and the other candidates were met by Lanell Landry, the Clerk of Court, who explained how to fill out the necessary paperwork and pay the required fees to run for office. For many it was business as usual. For others, like Savannah, who had never been a candidate for any office before, it was the ultimate rush.

After three painfully slow days, the qualifying period officially ended. It was then that she realized she was the only one in the race against Senator Brasseaux. "Great news!" she told her staff with an air of excitement. "I'm the only one running against Brasseaux for Senator."

All at once the group began cheering and clapping.

"Dathene and Patsy asked, "Why is everybody so excited?"

"Because if you have more than two people running, and no one gets over 50% of the vote, there has to be a run-off in November," answered Kay. "With only two people running, the October primary will decide the winner. We won't have to go through another election."

"Oh, that is great," said Dathene with a smile.

"You're going to be a shoo-in," echoed Patsy.

"This is a major plus for the campaign," continued Savannah. We can concentrate all our funding on this one election, without having to worry about saving some of the money for a run-off." After work Savannah rushed home, greeting Mike with an affectionate hug. She was still exuberant when she announced, "Just the two of us. Can you believe it?"

"Two of us as in you and me, or two of us as in you and L.J.?" asked Mike with a faked sense of despair.

Savannah's excitement could not be contained. Her eyes lit up and her face seemed to glow.

Mike could only smile and say, "You really did get a lucky break." Then he continued, "Remember Savannah, this is just the beginning. It's going to be a rough race."

"I know, Mike. Please don't worry so much. I'm a big girl and, believe it or not, I can take care of myself."

"You think you can take care of yourself, my love," thought Mike, *"but you have no idea of what people will do in order to win an election."*

CHAPTER 38

As election time drew near, the overly-confident L. J. Brasseaux began to realize that he had some serious competition on his hands. Campaign attacks became more vicious as Savannah's numbers rose in the polls.

Tuesday, September 1, was the deadline for registering to vote in the upcoming election. Savannah was reviewing the layout of her district when she noted some curious information. She called Mike from her campaign headquarters. "Hey good looking, what 'cha got cooking?" she asked Mike when he answered.

"Nothing much," he answered with a chuckle. "What's going on with you?"

"I thought I'd see if you were free for lunch."

"I may not be free, but for you, I'm always available," Mike jumped in with a high-spirited laugh.

Savannah ignored his remark and quickly resumed her conversation. If you want, I could grab us a couple of lunches from Tex Mex and meet you at your office in about an hour."

"That sounds like a winner," said Mike. "I don't get to see you enough like it is."

Savannah assembled all the information she had printed from the Internet, made some phone calls, then left to pick up lunch. Once she got to the Devereaux Real Estate Office, she and Mike cleared off the desks in their office and sat down to eat lunch.

"Did you know that Sam is getting ready to sell Tex Mex?" asked Savannah.

"Really?" said Mike.

"Yes. He's opening a restaurant in Baton Rouge called Sadaf Café. He's going to serve Greek and Lebanese food."

"Good for him," responded Mike.

Before he could comment further, Savannah continued, "Mike, I want you to see something." She began pulling out stacks of papers from her brief case. "It's really strange. The parishes in our district are not all grouped together. In Pointe Coupee Parish you actually have to skip over West Feliciana Parish, which is not part of our district, in order to get to East Feliciana Parish, which is part of our district.

It appears to me that district lines were changed to coincide with areas that L.J. does particularly well in. I think there's a lot of gerrymandering going on here.

"Hmm," said Mike. "That may be true, Savannah, but I don't think L.J. was responsible for that. The legislature is mandated every ten years, after the new census comes out, to review and make adjustments to district boundaries where necessary. There are a lot of variables involved. And then, after the legislators have redefined the boundaries, the maps have to not only be approved by the Senate and House of Representatives, but also have to be approved by the courts."

Savannah realized, try as she might, she was not going to win her argument with Mike. Just out of stubbornness she added, "I still think it's quite a coincidence."

"Yeah, I agree," said Mike trying to appease her.

CHAPTER 39

Nighttime was approaching and, as usual, Grace was the last of the volunteers to leave. She walked to the open doorway of Savannah's office and stated in a subtle, concerned voice, "Savannah, I'm getting ready to leave. It's getting dark outside. You better come lock the door behind me if you're going to stay a while longer."

Grace had tried to discourage Savannah from staying so late at the office by herself, but it had all been to no avail. When Savannah made up her mind to do something, there was no way to convince her to do otherwise.

"Okay. Thanks mom. I'll be right there."

After watching Grace get safely into her car and drive off, Savannah locked the door, turned the "Open" sign over to "Closed," turned off the lights in the reception area, and went back into her office. She paid little attention as the hours flew by, the parking lot became deserted, and darkness settled in.

After a while, she became so mesmerized by the words on the computer in front of her, that she didn't notice when the strange scratching noises on her window screen began. As they got louder, she suddenly froze at her computer, holding her breath, waiting to see if the sounds would be repeated. Silence filled the room.

The absence of any trees or bushes close to her window, and the fact that it was an exceptionally still night outside, made Savannah shudder. There had to be someone outside making the noises. She waited for a few minutes, but heard nothing else.

"Just my imagination," she thought to herself. Feeling rather foolish, she started back to work on her computer. A few minutes passed

and suddenly, even louder than the first time, she heard indisputable scratching on the window screen. In a near panic, she again held her breath, as if that one action would prevent anyone from knowing of her presence.

She reached over and gently lifted one of the thin wood slats in the closed mini blinds behind her. She peeked out, but it was hard to focus. The frightening darkness of the night permeated the outside area of her office. The light from inside prevented her from seeing anything in the black void exterior.

With great difficulty, she settled back into working on her computer and tried to ignore the nagging thought of what might have caused the noises she heard. *"Probably just kids playing,"* she rationalized to herself. *"Although it's dark outside, some parents let their kids stay out late at night."*

As the evening wore on, Savannah became so immersed in her work that the outside world ceased to exist. She was oblivious to the barely audible tunes coming from her radio on the desk next to her printer. Even the constant clicking noises from her nails typing on the computer keyboard didn't register with Savannah. She was in exceptional form and totally absorbed in her work.

Suddenly, without warning, there was a loud knock on the door! Savannah jumped in her chair. Silently, she slipped into the front office. She made her way to the door and carefully pulled back one of the blinds to see who had been knocking. She could see someone running off in the distance.

"Enough is enough!" she yelled out loud. Grabbing her phone, she dialed 911 as fast as her fingers could push the buttons. Savannah hated to admit that she was scared, but she was. Whatever weird game someone was playing with her was really starting to wreak havoc with her nerves. Luckily the police were on patrol in an area close by and responded within minutes.

"I feel a little foolish. having to call the police over something so trivial, but I just wasn't sure if I should be worried or not. Thank y'all for coming so quickly."

"It's no problem at all," said Officer Donald Ashley. "We didn't have anything to do anyway," he said with a mischievous grin. "It's been a quiet night. Besides, that's what we're here for."

His partner, Officer Victor Vead, agreed. "Actually, Captain James Rivers was in the office when we came on duty. He insists we stay busy, so we were sent out on patrol as soon as we checked in."

Both deputies laughed in unison and then excused themselves so they could complete their investigation. They checked around the outside of her office but, as suspected, were unable to find anyone.

"We didn't see anyone, but if you're planning on spending more time here tonight, we'll run by again in about 15 minutes to check on you. You can't be too careful at night," Officer Vead cautioned.

"I can't thank you enough," said Savannah. "I'll probably be leaving pretty soon. I think I've just about finished everything I was going to work on tonight anyway."

After they left, she quickly stacked up paperwork that could be handled in the morning. Her focus was on getting out to her car and leaving before anything else could happen. Driving home she continued to look in her rear view mirror to make sure no one was following her.

A sense of relief flooded Savannah as she pulled into the driveway of their home. When Mike came out to meet her, she blurted out nervously, "I had to call the police tonight."

"Why? What happened?!" asked Mike who was shocked by her blunt statement.

"I thought I heard something scratching on my window," said Savannah trying to regain her composure. "Then someone knocked on the front door and ran off. It was probably nothing more than kids playing around."

"Not at this time of night," said Mike. "Savannah, I don't want you working late over there at night by yourself anymore," he insisted.

"But Mike ..."

"No. I'm completely serious about this. I don't think it's safe. I don't want you working over there late anymore. Understand?"

It was rare that Mike got so insistent on anything, so Savannah thought it best to agree. "You're probably right. I'll try to get home earlier from now on," said Savannah. Secretly, she was relieved. Maybe Mike was right. Maybe there was more to this than just kids playing around at night. But who would have it in for her like this? Surely it wouldn't be Senator Brasseaux. This would be too low, even for him. But then ... who?

CHAPTER 40

It was a beautiful Saturday morning. All the campaign workers were scattered throughout the district, putting up signs and handing out push cards. Cindy, at the New Roads Printing Company, had explained to Savannah that they were called push cards, "Because when a politician meets someone new they 'push' one of their cards into the person's hand."

Savannah was busily preparing a campaign speech, when Grace walked into her office at noon. "You want me to pick us up some lunch?"

"Thanks mom. I'd appreciate it," replied Savannah.

Soon after Grace left, the silence of the office was broken by a loud thump against Savannah's window. *"What was that?"* she thought.

A quick glance outside revealed the culprits. Two young boys were playing ball. Impulsively she rushed outside and around to the side of the building. Both boys looked startled to see her. The youngest boy immediately hid the ball behind his back.

"Hi," she said. "I don't think I know you boys."

"I'm sorry if we hit your window," the older boy said defensively. "It was an accident."

"That's all right," said Savannah. "Accidents will happen, and there was no damage done. By the way, y'all weren't out here the other night were you?"

"No ma'am," answered the older boy. "We only got here this morning. We're just visiting our aunt. My name is Ronnie, and this here is my brother, Kyle."

"Well I'm pleased to meet you both," said Savannah cheerily. "You know what? I may have some candy in my office if y'all would like to come in and get some."

Their eyes lit up and both boys answered, "Yes, ma'am," in agreement. When they entered the office, Savannah walked over to a small round table, removed the top from the glass candy dish sitting on it, and let both boys take some candy out. The boys' comical antics as they were trying to decide which pieces they wanted tickled Savannah. After they got their candy Ronnie asked, "You want to come see us do some tricks on our bikes? We're real good. Aunt Trenetta said she never saw anybody do tricks better than us."

"I'd love to fellows, but I got a lot of work to do," replied Savannah. When she noticed the crestfallen looks on their faces she quickly changed her mind. "You know what?" she asked. "I think all work and no play makes somebody pretty dull. Let's go see what you can do."

Both boys yelled with excitement. Each one grabbed one of her hands as they pulled her outside with them. They took her back to the large concrete parking lot on the side of her office where few cars ever parked. Savannah laughed and clapped as they showed off for her. They held her attention for much longer than she had planned. Finally Ronnie glanced over as if looking for someone. Then, rather abruptly he stated, "We gotta go. Our momma will be looking for us." With that, the two boys raced off on their bicycles.

"Momma?" thought Savannah. *"I thought they said they were staying with their aunt. Oh well, that's kids for you."*

As they disappeared from sight, Savannah turned and walked around the corner and back into her office. What she viewed when she walked in the front door sent her into a state of shock. Her bottom jaw dropped down, and her eyes opened wide in disbelief. Everything was in shambles. Her desk had been opened and files pulled out. Papers were thrown everywhere. It was obvious that someone had been in a hurry to find whatever they were looking for, and to get out before she returned.

"How could this have happened!" she exclaimed in horror. "I wasn't gone that long. How would anybody know there was no one in here for that short a period of time? How would they know — unless this was a set-up. Good grief, I'm getting paranoid," she sputtered. She ran outside to see if she could determine which way Ronnie and Kyle had gone, but they had mysteriously disappeared. Grace drove up at the same time Savannah was turning to go back into her office.

"Hey, what 'cha doing out here?" asked Grace.

"You wouldn't believe me if I told you. Come on in. I want you to see something."

When Grace walked into the office she threw her hand over her mouth and screamed, "Oh my gosh, Savannah! What happened?"

When Savannah finished relating the events that had taken place, Grace said, "I can't believe this! Don't touch anything. We have to get the police over here." With lightening speed, Grace picked up the phone to call the police as Savannah called Mike on her cell phone. Within minutes of each other, both the police and Mike arrived at Savannah's campaign headquarters.

Officers Atwood and Templeton, both seasoned police officers, at once began an intensive search of the premises. Atwood went through the entire office to ensure there was no one still hiding inside, while Templeton patrolled the outside area again for the two boys. In spite of their extensive search, neither Ronnie, Kyle, nor their intruder was found.

"What do you think they were looking for?" asked Officer Atwood.

"I have no idea," Savannah replied, still quite disturbed, "but they sure didn't give themselves much time to look. I couldn't have been outside more than fifteen minutes."

"You would be surprised what someone can do in fifteen minutes," replied Officer Templeton.

"Savannah, you need to start keeping your office door locked during the day. People can knock if they need to come in," said Mike.

"Mike," Savannah laughed, "you can't be serious. What kind of an office locks its doors during the day?"

"The kind that is worried about strange people breaking in," replied Mike.

Feeling the tension in the room starting to mount, Grace quickly jumped in. "Don't worry, Mike. From now on we'll just be more careful. We usually have more than one person in here during the daytime anyway. What gets me is the fact that whoever did this had the audacity to come in during broad daylight, knowing that someone had to be close by."

Savannah knew what Grace was doing. Her mom was good at calming people down and right now no one needed that more than Mike.

"You know what I think?" asked Savannah. "I think this was someone's feeble attempt to try to scare me so I would drop out of the race for Senator. Well I can tell you now – that's not going to happen. I'm too mean and stubborn," she said with a smile as she grabbed Mike's arm and playfully pushed him.

As the elections approached, Savannah's phones in her campaign headquarters began to ring non-stop. People were coming in and out and conversations were loud and festive. For the most part, Savannah now took comfort in the unrelenting noise around her. She would never acknowledge it, but after everything that had happened, she felt a little safer in the company of others.

CHAPTER 41

Early voting for the primaries ran from September 18 through September 25, and from unofficial polls taken it appeared that L.J. was in the lead. Still, spirits were high in Savannah's cramped headquarters. At the conclusion of early voting, Savannah met with Kay to update her on final plans and campaign strategies. "Kay, how are we doing on our lists of people that still have not voted?"

"We've got a few problems," responded Kay. "When we were going through our lists of registered voters, marking off the people who had already voted, Janith saw her Aunt Leona's name among the absentee voters."

"What's the matter with that?" asked Savannah.

"Her Aunt Leona died two years ago."

"Really?" Savannah replied. "And who says you can't take it with you? Obviously Aunt Leona took her absentee ballot with her," laughed Savannah trying to keep upbeat.

"She's not the only one that found something wrong," Kay continued. "Juanita said her cousins Ralph and Alsee are on the registered voters list. According to the polls, they cast their ballots during the early voting. But Juanita said they moved to Washington five years ago, and haven't been back since then." JoAnn and Janith pointed out several more instances of voter fraud to Savannah. She began to get a sinking feeling in her stomach.

"We may not be able to do anything about it during this election," she said, "but after the election we need to make sure we report all these problems so they won't occur again."

As word of the voter discrepancies got out, no one seemed to be surprised. Some even went so far as to say, "Looks like business as usual."

CHAPTER 42

Saturday morning, October 2, 2010 – at long last it was Election Day! The polls opened at six a.m. Savannah met her mom and Kay at the office at five-thirty a.m. to get everything organized for their volunteers. As workers filed in, their mood was jovial and upbeat. Everyone seemed to be running on nervous energy and lack of sleep. By mid-morning, volunteers were everywhere handing out push cards and carrying signs.

Back at the office, the phone bank was in high gear and going strong. Everyone seemed to be talking at the same time. Normally, voting for Senator and local elected officials would draw a decent voter turnout in their district. Today, however, some very controversial amendments had been added to the ballot which was sure to generate a heightened level of interest in the elections.

At three-fifteen p.m. Clara and June rushed into Savannah's campaign headquarters completely out of breath, but still ranting furiously. "Savannah, you won't believe what Brasseaux's campaign workers are doing!" yelled June. "They're actually out on the streets paying people not to go vote! Have you ever heard of anything so devious and underhanded? What do you want us to do?"

"What do you mean they're paying people not to vote?" asked Savannah.

"Everyone knows L.J. gives his workers money to pay people to go vote for him. Most people they only pay about five dollars. But this time they got worried that some of the people they paid may still not vote for him once inside the voting booth, so they started paying people not to go vote. That way they don't have to worry about how they will vote when they go in," said June.

Savannah looked puzzled. "But how would they know if the people didn't go back and vote after all?"

"L.J.'s got volunteers at every voting precinct," said Clara. "Some of the volunteers look like they probably work as bouncers at local bars or night clubs in Baton Rouge."

"These guys are big and scary looking," added June. "The word is out that they are monitoring the voting precincts. Some people have become so intimidated by what they've heard that they're actually afraid to go vote."

Savannah turned to Kay and asked, "Do we have enough volunteers to send out to every precinct to make sure our voters feel safe?"

"We're spread pretty thin, but I'll do the best I can," said Kay.

"Peggy told me that L.J.'s volunteers are picking up bus loads of people. When they arrive at the polling precincts, they're given a piece of paper that has the numbers they're supposed to vote for on it. Half the time, these people don't even know who they're voting for. When they get back on the bus to go home, they get paid off," reported Clara. "She also told me that some of his more seasoned volunteers have even been able to talk some people into signing papers stating that they needed assistance in voting. In those cases L.J.'s volunteers go into the voting booth with them and vote for them."

"Look at it this way, Savannah," Kay said with a smile. "L.J. must be getting pretty desperate if he is resorting to intimidating people trying to vote. I think he was incensed in the beginning, that a political unknown would have the nerve to run against him. And then when people started rallying around you like they did, it had to scare him. Even the news coverage has started picking up your race. Some reporters are actually saying that there may be a real upset in this election."

"Really?" said Savannah with suppressed excitement. "I've been out campaigning and haven't been able to keep up with the news."

Kay continued, "People are really worked up about this race.

Nobody expected you to be a bona fide contender. That may be why L.J. is sending out more volunteers to make one final last ditch effort to do damage control, and prevent too much of a landslide."

Savannah broke out in laughter. It felt so good. She had been stressed out for so long that she had almost forgotten how great it felt to laugh. It was fantastic to have friends like Kay.

CHAPTER 43

The polls closed at eight o'clock. By seven o'clock everything was beginning to wind down at the campaign office and Savannah encouraged Kay, Grace, and several volunteers to go over to the Scott Civic Center to get everything ready for the crowd that was to follow.

They had decided to set up camp at the Civic Center so there would be plenty of room for everyone to watch the election returns, have something to eat, and enjoy themselves. Mike had picked up chicken and ribs for barbecuing. He and several of his buddies had a full-fledged barbeque going on in the parking lot. Next to them was Paul Colomb and Stan Mead who were cooking jambalaya. In the midst of all the laughter and good-natured barbs back and forth was a large sound system cranking out familiar tunes.

Inside a huge pot of gumbo was sitting on a large burner. Rice cookers sat ready to be turned on. The refrigerator was stocked with side dishes and drinks. Savannah told Mike, "Even if we don't win the election, I want to make sure that all of our volunteers have a good time tonight."

Three large televisions had been placed strategically on separate tables in the main gathering area so spectators could take full advantage of being able to watch the election returns on three different channels, all at the same time. There was also a longer table on one side that had a computer hooked up to the Internet. Once the Secretary of State's office began receiving election returns, the numbers would be tabulated and entered on their website where they could be viewed immediately.

By seven-thirty everyone had left the campaign office except

Savannah. She ran to her computer and typed up a short acceptance speech – just in case. Then she typed a conciliatory speech – just in case. She printed both speeches, folded them and put them in her pocket. On the outside she labeled the first one with #1 and the second one with #2. If she won, she would pull out #1. If she lost – she didn't want to think of that right now. She was feeling exceptionally confident at this stage of the game. She moved the second envelope over into her other pocket. With a huge grin on her face, she grabbed her purse and rushed out of the office.

As soon as she got to her car, she remembered she needed to put a note on the door to let anyone coming by after they left, know they were at the Civic Center. She turned around to go back in when, in a flash, someone rushed up from behind her. Before she could react, a gloved hand grabbed her waist, while the other hand forced a cloth in her mouth. She was viciously pushed back into her office. She heard the door slam as she struggled to keep from falling. A spine-chilling voice whispered in her ear, "Tell Mike Devereaux to back off, or the next time his beautiful wife may not be handled so gently."

She fought as hard as she could, but her oppressor was much stronger and towered over her. Savannah felt his hand clamp mercilessly across her mouth. Within seconds the room started swirling around her. The last thing she remembered before losing consciousness was reaching backwards in an attempt to scratch her attacker.

Her head was pounding and the phone was ringing unmercifully as she began to regain consciousness. Savannah looked straight up from her vantage point on the floor and tried to focus on the wall clock. It was eight-thirty. She hurriedly looked around. The office seemed deserted, but she wasn't taking any chances. She grabbed the ringing phone so she could summon help, if need be.

The voice on the other end was Mike's. She could hear the panic in his voice. "Savannah, where are you? I've been worried sick about you. I've been trying to call you on your cell phone, the home phone, and the office phone for the last half hour. Are you all right?"

She only had a split moment to decide her course of action. If she told Mike what had happened, the whole night would be ruined. "I'm so sorry Mike," she said. "I got involved in writing up a silly little acceptance speech and the time just got away from me.

I must have gone out to my car when you called, because I didn't hear the phone ring." She knew she had just lied to her husband. She had never done that before. It made her feel sicker than she already was. "I'll be there in twenty minutes or you can send out a search party for me," she laughed tensely. Unknown to Mike, while she was talking with him on the phone, she was also checking the office to make sure no one else was still in there. Once she was convinced that she was alone, she locked the front door.

After they finished their conversation, Savannah went into the restroom to put on some fresh make-up. She moaned out loud when she saw the big bruise on her cheek. She couldn't remember what would have caused it. Even the best make-up artist would have difficulty trying to conceal the gruesome bluish-black discoloration. Still, Savannah knew she had to make do with her make-up and powder. Nighttime might help her get away without an explanation tonight, but what would she tell Mike in the morning? She wondered if saying she ran into a door would suffice for Mike.

Savannah grabbed a diet cola from the refrigerator and took some Advil to try to help relieve her pain and steady her nerves. On the way to the Civic Center she kept thinking about what had happened. *"Why would someone go after Mike for helping me look into corruption charges at the state capitol?"* she questioned. *"I'm the one running for senator. I'm the one that can do the most damage with whatever Mike uncovers.*

Maybe they think if I'm scared and I tell Mike what happened, Mike will quit his investigation. Well, that's not going to happen. Their scare tactics are too little, too late. Mike will never find out about tonight — at least not from me," she thought with her usual self-determination.

CHAPTER 44

When Savannah got to the Scott Civic Center, even before entering the building, a round of applause broke out. People were cheering and calling her "Senator." Mike rushed over to her, hugged her affectionately, and whispered in her ear, "Even with all their dirty dealings, it looks like you may have a winning number tonight."

"Do you really think so?" she asked jubilantly. She was thankful it was dark outside and hoped no one would be able to see her hidden bruises.

"You must be one of God's angels. He always seems to be watching out for you," said Mike affectionately.

"If only you knew," thought Savannah. *"If only you knew."*

"The newscasters are having a ball with this story. They're saying that according to the exit polls, a political unknown may actually unseat Senator L.J. Brasseaux. I think you're even taking the attention away from some of the amendments on the ballot."

Savannah was thrilled to see Mike getting so involved in her campaign. She knew it had been hard on him, but he never complained. It made her all the more determined not to ruin the night for him by discussing her earlier run-in.

By nine p.m. the vote tallies had begun arriving at the Secretary of State's office. At first they were painfully slow. By nine-thirty p.m. they were coming in at a steady pace. With each new count posted on the state's website, a new tally was posted on the billboard erected on the stage in the Civic Center. Each time the count favored Savannah, cheers resonated throughout the assembly and out into the crowded parking lot.

Savannah had been closely monitoring the returns as they came in precinct by precinct. When she finally had the time to analyze what was going on, it dawned on her that she had taken an early lead and had been staying on top throughout the night. She nervously thought, *"I might just win this election after all!"*

Returns came in quicker than anticipated and by ten p.m. it was unofficially over. There was no need to wait for the last votes to be posted. It became evident that Savannah had walked away with the election. Print and broadcast reporters raced in to get interviews with the woman who had pulled off the shocking "surprise victory," and declared her election the biggest upset of the night.

Still woozy from her earlier encounter, Savannah was amazed that she had the presence of mind to remember to pull out her paper labeled #1, and begin thanking everyone. Her win would not be official until all the votes had been tallied and the winners declared by the Secretary of State's office. Still, at this point, there was no question as to the outcome.

Savannah earnestly told her supporters, "They said it was impossible. They said that a virtual unknown running against a powerful incumbent didn't have a chance. They said I couldn't win. And you know what? They were right. I couldn't win – not without all of you. Tonight we have all won a victory, and I thank you from the bottom of my heart."

It was the perfect rhetoric to get the crowd cheering wildly. Flashes on cameras lit up the room and video equipment appeared from thin air. There was no way to contain the euphoria among her supporters tonight. She watched as they gave each other high-fives and pats on the back. Tonight was their night as much as it was hers.

The celebration lasted well into the wee hours of the morning.

It had been a long day and Savannah and Mike were both tired, but it was a good tired. Savannah leaned over and softly kissed Mike on the cheek, her own cheek still throbbing. "I love you more than you will ever know," she said.

"I know. I love you too," he replied.

PART V - 2011

CHAPTER 45

Excluding Mike, Savannah's greatest supporter was unquestionably her mother, Grace. They had always been close, but during the brutal and exhausting election campaign they grew even closer.

On January 11, 2011, when State Senator Savannah Devereaux officially took her oath of office, she looked over at her mother and realized how pale she appeared. Grace had never been one to complain or discuss her ailments, but today Savannah sensed something was wrong.

After the activities at the capitol, a large group of newly elected officials and their supporters went out to lunch together. Mike drove Savannah and Grace to meet them. It was the perfect opportunity for Savannah to question her mother.

"Mom, are you feeling okay?"

"I'm fine honey," Grace replied. "Why do you ask?"

"You look a little pale today. Maybe now that the elections are over you should go and see Dr. Vincent," Savannah persisted.

"You know, Savannah, I'm the mother and you're the daughter. I'm supposed to be the one telling you what to do, not the other way around."

"I know," Savannah said with a grin. "...and you do tell me what to do so well." Then they both broke into laughter. "It would make me feel better, though, if you would go and get a check-up. We've both been under so much stress lately; it can't be good for either one of us," Savannah continued.

"Okay. As soon as I can get an appointment I'll go. Happy?"

"Yes ma'am. Thank you," said Savannah half mockingly.

At lunch, Savannah went into high gear with her plans for the immediate future. They had already transformed Savannah's campaign headquarters into her new legislative district office, and Savannah quickly changed Kay's title from Campaign Manager to Executive Assistant. Kay was thrilled. "I'm going over to the office this afternoon to see if we have any calls and check the mail," Kay reported.

"Great," responded Savannah. Then she looked over at Karen Ryder. "Karen, I just got my office assignment at the capitol. I really need someone that's good at researching and digesting important documents to keep me on track and to help me run the office. I was hoping you'd take the job. Are you interested?"

"Absolutely!" responded Karen with her usual enthusiasm.

"I have to be at the capitol on Wednesday. That's when they give out committee assignments. It might get a little hectic then. Why don't we meet at the Capitol on Thursday? Just give me a call Thursday morning and we'll decide what time we want to get together."

"Okay, great! I'll call you Thursday," said Karen.

"Don't worry about the real estate business," Mike replied with a smile. "I'll handle that until you get a chance to visit us again."

Savannah gave Mike a playful push and said, "Thanks." Then, almost as an afterthought, she looked lovingly at him and said, "Thanks for everything, Mike. I couldn't have done it without you."

CHAPTER 46

Immediately following the swearing in of the new legislators, and the committee assignments, Governor Percy Claiborne called an extraordinary session on February 14, 2011. During the special session there were only two issues on the agenda to be discussed and the Extraordinary Session lasted less than two weeks.

Mike and Savannah planned a dinner party on Sunday following the completion of the extraordinary session. As the festivities began to die down and the guests began to leave, Savannah noticed that Grace had disappeared. When she walked into the bedroom, she saw Grace taking some medicine. "What's the matter, mom?" she asked.

"It's nothing honey. I've just got another one of my headaches. They do seem like they're getting worse, though."

"Mom, having headaches like this isn't normal. Something's wrong. Didn't you tell me that Dr. Vincent said you had a sinus infection? The medicine he gave you should have cleared up a sinus infection by now. It's been well over a month since you first went to him. Why didn't you tell me you still weren't feeling good? I could have taken you to Baton Rouge to one of the doctors there."

"Don't worry sweetheart. I'm sure Dr. Vincent knows what he is doing. I probably should have gone back, but I just hate to be a bother to people."

"Look mom, you shouldn't worry about that. Let me call Dr. Vincent's office tomorrow morning and find out if they can work you in."

"Well, if you really think I need to go."

"I do. I'll call you tomorrow to let you know what time Dr. Vincent can see you. Are you sure you don't need me to stay with you tonight, though?"

"Oh, I'll be fine tonight," Grace said with a smile, as she tried to make light of the situation. I just took some medicine, and when I get home I'm going to put a cool washrag on my head. I'm sure it'll help."

Savannah asked her mom, "Do you promise you'll call me if you need me?"

"Sure I will honey," said Grace. "Don't you worry about me. I'll be fine."

Savannah wasn't sure her mother would be fine, or would even call her if she started feeling worse, but she could only do so much.

CHAPTER 47

The following morning Savannah called Dr. Vincent's office and spoke with his nurse, Becky Bergeron. They had been friends for a long time, and more than once Becky had squeezed her into Dr. Vincent's packed schedule so that she could be seen quickly.

"Becky, I'm worried about mom. She had a really bad headache yesterday and I've never seen her look so pale. Could Dr. Vincent see her this morning?"

"Sure," Becky replied. "How about 9:30?"

Dr. Vincent was appalled when he walked into the examination room and saw Grace's pale face and feeble condition. "Grace, didn't I tell you to come back if your headaches didn't get any better. Why did you wait so long to come back?"

"Well every time I started to call, I began to feel better," she said with a giggle.

Dr. Vincent examined Grace and then told her he was going to refer her to Dr. Babin in Baton Rouge. He explained that Dr. Babin was a specialist in internal medicine. Grace never questioned the doctor.

The following morning she and Savannah were in Baton Rouge for Grace's appointment at the clinic. Dr. Babin had so many tests run that they spent the better part of the day there. When they finally got through it was already four-fifteen and both Savannah and her mother were exhausted. Savannah decided to take Grace to Applebee's. She wanted to make sure her mother would have something good to eat after going so long with only cookies and crackers.

At dinner, Grace felt compelled to describe to Savannah every good looking doctor she saw at the clinic. They laughed and joked about everything and everybody. Savannah blamed her giddiness on her lack of sleep. Grace blamed hers on just being in a silly mood.

By the time Savannah got Grace home, they were still laughing. Savannah was happy to see her mother in such a good mood. Her earlier state of depression had seemed to vanish.

CHAPTER 48

On Wednesday, Savannah found herself trying to play catch up after being off Monday and Tuesday. Around eight-fifteen a.m. she received a call from Grace. Her voice was trembling.

"Savannah, Dr. Babin just called me. He said that as soon as he read my x-rays, he consulted with Dr. Reuben, a neurosurgeon at the clinic, to verify his findings. They both agreed that I have a brain tumor that needs to be removed immediately.

There was an accident on the Interstate, so Dr. Babin called Acadian Air Med Services. They're going to send a helicopter to Pointe Coupee General Hospital to pick me up, and then take me to Our Lady of the Lake Medical Center in Baton Rouge. Lord, Savannah, I've never been in a helicopter before. I'm scared to death. Why do you think they're in such a rush to get me over there?"

"I'm sure it's just a precaution, mom," Savannah said, trying to sound optimistic. "Don't worry, I'll be right over." Savannah grabbed her purse and informed Mike of the situation as she bolted from the room.

Savannah was scared, but she didn't want her mother to know how much. She was at her mother's house before Grace even had time prepare for the trip. "Don't worry about putting an overnight bag together right now," she told her mother. "I can come back later and get that. Let's just get you to the hospital. The helicopter will be waiting for you."

As soon as they arrived at Pointe Coupee General, they were ushered out to the helicopter pad where the pilots and paramedics assured Savannah that her mother would be well taken care of. Of course Grace balked when they told her she would need to lie on the stretcher for the trip.

"Is that absolutely necessary?" asked Savannah.

"We were told to start getting Ms. Grace ready for surgery on the trip to Baton Rouge," replied Peter, one of the paramedics. "It won't be so bad," he said as he smiled at Grace. "I may not have great bedside manners, but I'm a lot of fun in a helicopter."

Grace laughed out loud and at once seemed to relax. The young man certainly knew just how to handle her. Savannah felt better too.

Peter suggested that Savannah go ahead and drive her car to the hospital so she would have it later if she needed it.

Savannah's heart ached when she saw the look on her mother's face. Grace looked like a frightened little girl. Savannah had never seen her mother look like that before. She had always been so strong. "Don't worry mom. Everything's going to be all right. I'll meet you at the hospital. Heck, I'll probably beat you to the hospital. You know how I drive. Besides, once you get to the hospital it will still take some time for them to get you checked in. Okay?"

"Don't you worry about me. I'll be fine. And don't you get in too big a hurry to get to the hospital either. I don't want anything happening to you," said her mother.

CHAPTER 49

As soon as the helicopter took off with Grace on board, Savannah drove like a woman possessed trying to get to Baton Rouge. The radio had evidently alerted motorist to avoid the Interstate because of the overturned truck on I10. Savannah decided to take Airline Highway to try to avoid the inevitable traffic jam. Unfortunately everyone else seemed to have the same idea. The large volume of traffic threw her into a panic.

By the time she arrived at the hospital and found a parking place, her nerves had gotten the best of her. She ran into the lobby and dashed over to the reception desk. Winded, she ignored the usual formalities, and quickly demanded: "I need to find out where they took my mother. Her name is Grace O'Brien. They were bringing her here by helicopter from New Roads."

The receptionist was a petite elderly woman who wore a Volunteer badge. She smiled sweetly, and with a slow southern drawl replied, "I'm sorry ma'am, but we're not allowed to give out any information on patients without a written consent."

"You've got to be kidding," wheezed Savannah in a near panic. "Did you hear me? It's my mother I'm asking about."

"I don't know," the white haired grandmother responded nervously.

"You don't know! Let me tell you something lady," began Savannah, her voice rising and a frown on her face, "if you don't tell me where my mother is right now, I'm going to make your life, and the life of everyone in this hospital, miserable. Do you understand?"

The woman turned pale. She immediately picked up the receiver on her phone and called someone. She turned her back to Savannah as she whispered into the phone. When she completed her call, she turned back to Savannah and said, "Someone will be with you in just a minute. Please have a seat."

Defiantly Savannah stood at the desk to wait. She looked at her watch so as to note the time.

Once she heard of the situation, Dr. Renee Harris came rushing from the back hallway to meet Savannah.

"Renee," Savannah cried out. "I'm so glad to see you. They brought mom in and I can't find out where she is, or what's going on with her."

"I know," responded Dr. Harris. "I just spoke with Dr. Ruben. Let's go back to my office so we can talk." Dr. Harris led Savannah out of the reception area and into a small office in the back. Savannah sensed that something was terribly wrong.

"What's the matter Renee?" she said. "Is something wrong with mom?"

Dr. Harris slowly closed the door and turned back around to face Savannah.

"Savannah, I'm sorry to have to tell you this, but your mother didn't make it. She passed away before they could get her into the operating room. Dr. Ruben had hoped they could perform the operation in time, but it just wasn't possible."

Savannah felt her body go limp. She struggled to maintain her composure. Her head felt like it was spinning in circles, going out of control.

"What?" she asked weakly. "Mother is … dead? Are you sure?"

When she could hold it in no longer, she began to sob uncontrollably. She felt Dr. Harris' arm around her as she helped guide Savannah towards an arm chair. Dr. Harris reached over and handed Savannah a box of Kleenex.

"I'm so sorry Savannah. Is there someone you would like for me to call for you? What about Mike?"

"No," she said. "If I could just sit here for a few minutes, I'll be all right."

"Of course," said Dr. Harris. "Why don't you let me order something to help settle your nerves?"

Savannah could only shake her head no.

"All right then. I'm going to get you something to drink. I'll be right back. You can stay in here as long as you want."

When Dr. Harris left the room, Savannah's thoughts quickly turned back to her mother. How would she ever be able to forgive herself for letting her mother get into the helicopter without her? She should have been there with her to comfort her before she died.

Savannah's sorrow was compounded by the fact that she had just completed her first legislative session and now had three weeks until the first day of the regular Legislative Session. *"Why couldn't I have had those three weeks to spend with mom?"* she lamented. Night after night Mike watched helplessly as Savannah cried herself to sleep. Savannah had counted on Grace for so many things. They were soul mates, best friends, and true confidants. Grace's death would have been an insurmountable loss had it not been for Mike.

CHAPTER 50

The week of March 28, 2011 had been exceptionally busy for Savannah. It was the start of the first regular legislative session at the state capitol in Baton Rouge. Even following her mother's tragic death, Savannah appeared calm and composed as she entered the Senate chambers. She had style and grace, and Mike felt a tremendous sense of pride when she took her place among the other senators.

By Friday afternoon, she was beginning to settle into the routine. Savannah walked into her capitol office she quipped, "Hi, Karen. How are things going here on the old home front?"

"Your desk is full of names and numbers of people you need to call back. I was able to help a few people out, but most of them just want to talk with you. By the way," Karen continued, "you got one really strange call. When I answered, the man said, 'Tell Senator Devereaux to remember the message we gave her on election night.' Before I could say anything, he hung up. I tried to get the number he was calling from, but it just showed up as unknown name and unknown number on the caller I.D. list."

Savannah turned pale. It was starting again.

"Are you okay Savannah? Is anything wrong?" asked Karen with a concerned look."

"Oh, I'm fine. I imagine everyone encounters at least one loose cannon during an election campaign. This one just doesn't seem to know when to quit."

"If he's still contacting you after the election, don't you think you ought to report him to the police?"

Savannah answered, "Karen, do you know how many weird calls

I get? I mean, in addition to my friends?" Then she laughed out loud. "This is just one more to add to the stack."

The response seemed to appease Karen, but Savannah wasn't so sure she had been completely honest. She didn't want Karen to worry, but she remembered the incident that occurred the night of her victory celebration, and the man that had accosted her. She had been lulled into a false sense of security when everything seemed to settle down after that confrontation. Now it was starting all over again.

Savannah stayed long enough to take care of pressing matters and then told Karen, "I'm going to head on out to New Roads. I'll probably spend a few hours at our district office before I go home. If you need me, call me on my cell phone. Have a good weekend."

"You too," replied Karen.

CHAPTER 51

Savannah had arrived at her New Roads office just as Kay was getting ready to close up. Actually she was relieved. She could get so much more done when the office was closed and no one else was there.

After several hours of peaceful bliss, Savannah was startled when the loud ring of the telephone brought her out of the self-induced trance she had been in while working on her legislative paperwork. It was Mike.

"Hey, I was just wondering if you planned on coming home tonight?" he asked.

Savannah looked at the clock on the wall. It was nine-fifteen. "Good grief. I didn't realize how late it was. I'm on my way home now. See you in a minute."

Savannah picked up her purse and some papers and locked the door on her way outside. It was pitch-dark, but her car was parked in front, so there was no need to put on the outside lights of her building. As soon as the unlock button on her key chain was pressed, Savannah slid into the driver's seat of her beloved Vette, quickly pulled the door closed behind her, and immediately pressed the door lock. Once again she felt safe.

The ignition key slid into place, and as she turned it, she heard the deep roar of an engine ready for action. Before she could put the car in reverse, a warning popped up on the information bar of her car: "Right front tire flat; then a second message popped up – Left front tire flat; then a third message – Right rear tire flat; and finally – Left rear tire flat."

"That's impossible, she thought. *How could all four tires be flat? Something's not right!"*Savannah grabbed the cell phone from her purse

and called Mike. "You won't believe this," she stuttered. The information bar on my car keeps flashing a warning that all four of my tires are flat. Is that possible?"

"Anything's possible," he said, "but I don't see how that could be. You might just have a faulty sensor. Did you check your tires?"

"No. It's so dark and I don't see anyone around. I'm a little nervous about getting out of my car to inspect the tires."

"Okay, just come on home and I'll check them when you get here." Mike replied.

"You think it'll be all right to drive home if they're flat?" asked Savannah.

"It'll be fine. Even if your tires were flat you can still drive another 50 miles. That's those special tires they put on the Vettes. Just take it easy coming home."

Mike had the lights on and was waiting outside when Savannah drove up. Her heart began to race as she saw the startled look on Mike's face. Immediately she jumped out of the car to look for herself. The tires were not just flat. They had been slashed to shreds.

"You got that number for the police still stored in your cell phone?" Mike asked tersely.

"Yes," she replied.

"Call them," he said.

His abruptness was frightening to Savannah. With trembling hands, she grabbed the phone from her purse and called the police.

"Police Headquarters, Captain James Rivers speaking."

"Captain Rivers, this is Senator Devereaux. Someone slashed all four of my car tires while I was at the office tonight. I got the car home, but the tires look really bad."

"All four of them were slashed?" asked the surprised captain. "I'll get one of my officers out to your house right away," said Captain Rivers. "Do you have any idea of who might have done this?"

"No," said Savannah. "I did get a strange call at the office today, but it didn't make much sense. It was something about being careful about what we do. I'm not sure what they were talking about." The color drained from Mike's face.

"Senator, I don't want to alarm you, but I think it would be wise for you to take added security precautions for a while, especially when you go out by yourself. You're free to call my men here at the station when you're working late, and we'll be glad to have our officers keep an eye on your office while they're on patrol.

An officer should be there in about 10 minutes. I'm also going to have your house on our watch list tonight, so don't be alarmed if you see patrol cars passing by your house throughout the night."

As they waited for the police to come, Mike became increasingly agitated about even the slightest small annoyance. Savannah had never seen him like this before. She knew something was bothering him, but couldn't get him to discuss it with her. Although the tires for her car would be expensive, she knew it was more than just that.

Finally she said, "Mike, I know my tires are going to be a big expense, but you seem overly edgy. Is there something besides the tires that is bothering you? Have I done something to upset you?"

His tense facial features loosened up and his voice softened as he replied, "No, Savannah, it's not you. I'm just worried about how vulnerable you are as a state senator. Some people are just crazy. Slashing your tires was not the work of a rational person. What if this person comes back again and tries to do you bodily harm? I may not always be around for you."

"I love you so much," Savannah said as she softly stroked his hair, "but I'm a lot stronger than you give me credit for. I can't just quit the minute something doesn't go my way. Frankly, I think you worry way too much about me." Then she kissed him and smiled.

That was it. Mike knew the discussion was over. He would never be able to convince her that she was in a dangerous situation, even more dangerous than she actually knew.

CHAPTER 52

The long winding rural highway, scarred with its potholes and rutted surface, stretched endlessly onward. The only visible scenery for miles were the fields of sugar cane on either side of the road, waiting to be harvested.

It had been threatening rain all morning. Even though the downpour predicted by the weatherman had yet to materialize, the skies remained overcast, adding an even gloomier outlook to Marcus Traylor's current situation.

Marcus had been driving for almost five hours. The trip from Denham Springs to Lake Providence normally did not take this long. Unfortunately, there was construction going on and somewhere along the line he took a wrong turn, resulting in the unbearably slow procedure of trying to get re-routed. With all that now behind him, if his new calculations were right, he would soon be arriving at his destination.

Marcus had been a practicing attorney with the Public Defender's Office in Livingston Parish since 2001. This was his first trip to Lake Providence, Louisiana, and in particular, East Carroll Detention Center.

The silence in the car had become deafening hours ago, but Marcus could not bring himself to turn on his music and enjoy the great Bose sound system in his car. It was just another way of punishing himself. He had done wrong and he knew it. All morning long, he had been trying to convince himself that everything would be all right. The problem was that he knew he was only kidding himself.

Try as he might, he had still not found the right words to tell his client how downright pathetic he had been as his defense attorney. The poor guy was only 21 years old at the time. He counted on Marcus, and Marcus failed him miserably.

When Marcus was hired in the Public Defender's Office, he was not much older than D.D., his first client. Marcus was a new attorney and anxious to please his boss. His supervisor, Leon Biddle, had instructed him in no uncertain terms, that his primary objective was to get his clients to agree to plea bargains.

He could still hear Leon telling him, "None of us want to go to trial. It takes too long and our budget can't handle it. We have too many cases and too little time." In all these years he had done exactly what he was told to do, except for his first client.

D.D. had insisted on going to trial and there was no way Marcus could convince him otherwise. Leon had been so angry with Marcus for not being able to arrange a plea bargain that he gave him little help in the way of guidance during the trial. When the verdict came down, D.D. was sentenced to life in prison.

After that trial, all of Marcus' cases ended up as plea bargains. One total failure was enough for him. In fact, it appeared that his entire career was going to end up as a string of plea bargains. That is until recently, when a glitch in one of his cases made him take a second look at his life, and that of those he defended.

His trip today to ECDC was to try and right one of the wrongs he had done. If he had been stronger, or a more experienced attorney, maybe he would have fought harder in his first case involving D.D. Marcus remembered him as a quiet man. In fact, his demeanor was more that of a downtrodden boy. Through the entire trial he barely uttered a word. It was only after he was taken back to his prison cell that D.D. had finally resorted to verbal obscenities, after realizing he had been railroaded into an unjust and unwarranted prison term.

Today, almost nine years later, Marcus had proof handed to him on a silver platter that his client never committed the murder for which he had been accused. Marcus was carrying a letter addressed to him from Mitch, one of the other two boys that had been involved in the attempted robbery and murder of a policeman.

Mitch had finally decided he could no longer live with the guilt he bore for shooting the policeman during the attempted robbery at Steve's Curb Market. He and Doug had botched up miserably, and it was their fault D.D. had been wrongly accused.

Mitch decided there was only one way he could ever achieve peace again. He drove out to a quiet, lonely stretch of woods and parked his car. Then he reached under the seat of his car and pulled out a small box. Inside the box was the handgun that had been used in the robbery so many years ago – the same gun that had cut short the life of a dedicated police officer, left his wife and children without a father and husband, put two young men on probation for years, and sent a 21 year old man to prison for the rest of his life.

"This is so screwed up," Mitch thought as he took the gun out of the box and laid it on the seat next to him. He stared long and hard at the metal piece, just as he had done countless times before. He detested the object that had ruined his life and that of so many others.

Mitch pushed the front seat of the car back as far as it would go. In an excruciatingly painful moment, he reached over into the glove compartment of the car, removed some paper and an envelope, and began to write the letter he had gone over in his head at least a hundred times before.

His handwriting was shaky, but the intent of the letter was obvious. Mitch took full responsibility for shooting the policeman. He admitted it was an accident, and admonished himself for being a coward and not coming forward with the truth before now. The letter went on to say that D.D. had not even been with them during the robbery.

Mitch begged D.D. to forgive him, although he admitted that if it were him, he doubted he could be that generous. He had kept his silence far too long. After he finished with the letter, he addressed the envelope, placed the papers inside, and sealed it. He picked up the gun and replaced it with the envelope. Without a moment's hesitation, he put the gun to his head, and pulled the trigger.

The letter had been written to D.D., but the envelope was addressed to Marcus, D.D.'s attorney. When Marcus received the letter, he instantly related to Mitch's feelings of guilt. They had all let D.D. down in one way or another. Marcus had never even assumed that anyone other than D.D. could have been responsible for the shooting. Now it was up to him to make things right. Marcus was on his way to tell an innocent client that he had been deprived of eight years of his freedom and the alienation of his family and friends, all because his court-appointed attorney had been too incompetent to do his job.

All at once he become conscious that his meandering thoughts, coupled with the tall stalks of corn on the side of the highway, had obscured his vision for the last few miles. He had passed up the road that led to the prison. It may have been his subconscious mind trying to avoid the inevitable, but again he found himself making a quick detour in the opposite direction. As he finally reached the side road that led to the prison, he followed the lonely path to the end. On the right was the parking lot for visitors. On the left was the prison. Tall barbed wire fences surrounded the encampment.

Marcus had not called ahead, but he was an attorney and knew he should be able to see his client. In order to enter the facility he had to show his driver's license and his state bar membership card. Then he was searched and patted down like a common criminal. His brief case was inspected and then re-inspected. He felt sure they were just flexing their muscles since they were obviously not trying to read anything.

When the guards had finally satisfied themselves that he was suitable to enter, they ushered him to the kitchen complex that doubled as a visiting room. It reminded Marcus of an old-styled school cafeteria. He was told to wait there until they called back to D.D.'s cell block and had his client brought in.

The place was hot and muggy, and the dust in the air almost choked him. Marcus had come from his office in Denham Springs and still had on his suit, but was thankful that he had left his coat and tie in the car. Before long he was sweating so much that his shirt was sticking to his body.

He looked around the old building and spotted roaches scurrying back and forth. The mosquitoes were so big that when he made the mistake of hitting one that had landed on him, it left a large spot of blood on his shirt. *"Great,"* he thought. *"I'll probably never get the blood out of my shirt. Whatever possessed me to wear a white shirt over here?"*

The tables in the cafeteria were scratched and weather beaten, more likely than not, a reflection of the prisoners housed there. A guard entered from the side door and walked slowly over to Marcus.

"There's been a mistake made. The prisoner you came to see is in lock-down. Prisoners are not allowed visitors while they are in lock-down."

"But I'm his lawyer," protested Marcus. "A prisoner cannot be denied his right to speak with his attorney."

"You may be a lawyer, but you ain't my boss," responded the irritated guard. "He's in lock-down and that's where he's staying."

"Where's the warden?" asked Marcus.

"He's outta town and won't be back in 'til tomorrow."

"Then whose the next person in charge?" questioned Marcus.

"That would be the deputy warden, but he's out sick today. Like I said, you're gonna have to come back another time. The prisoner's in lock-down and that's where he's gonna stay until I'm told differently by the boss man."

Marcus was furious. He had driven for hours on end, the whole time searching for the right words to explain what had happened, and to beg for his client's forgiveness. Now he couldn't even talk with him.

He left the prison and walked across the road to his car. He climbed in, turned on the ignition, and turned the air conditioner up full blast. Then he reached down and picked up his cell phone. He tried to call his office ... but there was no signal.

CHAPTER 53

For a new State Senator, Savannah Devereaux took on challenges few in her position would have undertaken. Standing at the podium before her fellow colleagues in the Louisiana State Legislature, she began explaining a Senate Bill she had authored.

"Louisiana was plagued with two major hurricanes in 2005, and still to this day, we have not resolved all of the problems encountered by those catastrophic events. Many of Louisiana's eligible applicants are still waiting to collect housing grants awarded to them.

At the same time that many building codes and regulations were waived in order to expeditiously provide housing for those in need, bids were also awarded to contractors with little, if any, monitoring being done, and now we're all suffering the consequences.

The hurricanes are over. It's time for us to reinstate the codes and regulations previously put on hold. I believe the passage of this legislation is critical. We have reached a time when we must demand more accountability within the housing industry.

This legislation will ensure clear guidelines on how any future money is to be doled out and to whom. It dictates the accountability and transparency that we all expect. Your passage of this bill will bring a welcome relief to countless individuals."

Her posture at the rostrum gave no indication of the turmoil she felt inside. The vote was announced and it was recorded, "The bill has passed."

Savannah's bill, which was intent on closing loopholes that were encouraging profiteering, was sent to the house floor where it passed just hours before the session ended. It was quite a feat to have such substantial legislation passed not only in her first year in office, but even more impressive, in her very first regular session in the state legislature.

Savannah wondered if this would finally stop the calls she and Mike had received about staying out of things that didn't concern them. *"Maybe they'll realize now that everything concerns us,"* thought Savannah.

When the gavel went down ending the session, Savannah suddenly became conscious that it was the first breather she had had in a long time.

Her next thought was, *"We need to celebrate."*

CHAPTER 54

The end of the regular legislative session did not bring with it the lull in her senatorial duties that Savannah had anticipated. She had always considered herself the queen of multi-tasking, but the past year, with all its ups and downs, had finally began to take its toll on her.

"Good morning, Savannah," Kay said as she walked in. "I left some messages for you on your desk."

"Thanks," responded Savannah. As she approached her desk, she exclaimed, "Good grief! It looks like my part-time job as Senator has turned into a full-fledged job, and it doesn't look like things are going to slow down any time soon." She and Kay enjoyed joking about the piles of work, but by lunch time both women had organized their tasks into doable objectives.

"I'm going to pick up some lunch and then afterwards I'll get on those letters for you. Do you want me to pick up something for you while I'm out?" Kay asked.

"No, thanks. I think I'll call Mike to see if he wants to join me for a bite to eat later on." Soon after Kay left, the phone rang. Savannah was pleasantly surprised when she heard Mike's voice.

"Is this that gorgeous Senator Devereaux?"

"Hi, Mike," she laughed. "What are you up to?"

"I promise you my vote in the next election if you'll go out to lunch with me," he replied.

"Why, Michael Devereaux, if I didn't know better, I'd say you are trying to offer me a bribe."

"And...?"

"And normally I would never accept such an offer, but in your case, I'm afraid I can be bought. The only problem is that Kay has already left for lunch and I can't leave until she gets back."

"How long you think she's going to be gone?" asked Mike.

"She just went to pick up her lunch, but I need to give her some time to eat when she gets back."

"Okay. It's 11:45 now. Why don't I come over around 12:45? If you want, we could just walk over to *Ma Mamas* for lunch."

"That sounds wonderful," said Savannah. She hung up the phone and began frantically trying to finish as much work as she could before Mike got there. When he arrived, Savannah was waiting for him. "I'm starved," she said. "I hope you brought a fat wallet."

When Kay heard Savannah's remarks to Mike she fell out laughing hysterically. "I feel your pain," she said to Mike, as they walked out the door.

The lunch crowd had begun to thin out at *Ma Mamma's* by the time Mike and Savannah arrived. Once they placed their order Mike began talking quietly to Savannah. "I have a surprise for you," he said. "I've made reservations at the Paragon Casino hotel in Marksville for Friday night. I thought we could have dinner and take in a show. Then instead of having to drive home we could spend the night there."

"Oh, Mike, said Savannah with a worried look. I'd love to go, but I've just got too much work piled up right now."

"Come on, Savannah," Mike said in total frustration. "I'm not talking about taking off for a week — just a night. You can't continue to work 24/7 for the rest of your life."

Savannah looked deeply into Mike's eyes. They twinkled when he smiled, but he wasn't smiling now. *"What a jerk I am,"* she thought. *"This handsome and thoughtful man worships the ground I walk on, and I'm ignoring him. I'm going to lose the best thing I ever had if I'm not careful."*

Out loud she replied, "You know what? You're absolutely right, Mike. I have been pushing myself a lot lately. On top of that, we never seem to have much time together anymore. I think, Mr. Michael Devereaux, you're just what the doctor ordered. Taking some time off with you really does sound great. Let's do it!"

CHAPTER 55

Friday, at noon, Mike and Savannah closed their offices, loaded the Hummer, and drove to the Paragon Casino in Marksville. "I've got reservations for dinner and tickets for a show afterwards," Mike beamed.

"Oh, this is so exciting," said Savannah, as she reached over and lovingly patted his arm.

"Do you realize this is the first time that we've had just for ourselves since I can remember?" questioned Mike.

"I know, Mike, and I'm sorry. Sometimes I get so wrapped up in what I'm doing that I forget about everything else. Please forgive me."

Mike grinned as he pulled a package out from under his seat. "Here," he said.

"What's this?" asked Savannah with a surprised look on her face.

"Open it and see," he said as he tried to watch her and the road at the same time.

Savannah carefully opened the package and then burst into laughter. It was a small wall plaque that had brightly painted roses on it and words that read, "Take Time to Smell the Roses."

"This will go on my wall at work as soon as we get back." Savannah unbuckled her seat belt and slid over to Mike. She flung her arms around his neck and kissed him on the cheek. Then she quickly slid back to her seat where she buckled up again. "Isn't love grand?" she sang in a melodious voice, smiling from ear to ear.

The first order of business once they checked in at the Paragon hotel was to take their bags up to their room. Savannah looked out of the glass back of the elevator onto the people scurrying below. There was even an area fenced off where baby alligators were lazily treading in and out of the water. A bridge crossing over their habitat allowed visitors to watch them from a safe distance.

When the elevator stopped on the top floor, Savannah and Mike got out and walked down the long hallway to their room. At the door, Mike abruptly took Savannah's small bag and purse from her and put them on the floor next to his bag. Without the slightest pause, he lifted Savannah up into his arms, pushed open the door, and carried her over the threshold.

"Mike, I'm going to break your back," laughed Savannah hysterically. With Savannah laughing and squirming around, Mike had to struggle to carry her into the next room without dropping her.

"This romantic junk is highly overrated," he said straight-faced as he let her fall onto the bed. Then he rushed back outside to pick up their luggage. Mike had reserved a suite for them; obviously sparing no expense. A beautifully simple bouquet of red roses adorned the small but decorative table in the foyer. Inside on the counter was an ornate edible fruit sculpture, and a bottle of pink champagne.

With so much to take in at first, Savannah almost overlooked the small neatly wrapped box next to the champagne. Mike grinned when she asked, "What's this? More reminders of the woman I should be?"

"Actually it's more to celebrate the woman you are," he smiled.

She carefully opened the package, trying not to tear the paper. Inside she found a heart shaped locket with a tiny cluster of diamonds in the middle. On the inside of the locket was a miniature picture of Mike and Savannah.

"Oh Mike," she cried, "it's beautiful."

"Just like you," he replied. "You know, Savannah," he continued, "the heart may be what keeps us alive, but I never started living until I met you. Don't ever forget that."

Savannah flung herself into Mike's arms and softly exclaimed, "I love you so much, Mike. You're everything I ever dreamed of. I never knew how good life could be until I met you."

"I feel the same way about you," he replied.

CHAPTER 56

It was Labor Day. Their offices were closed, so Mike and Savannah decided to barbeque. Once the fire was going good and the meat seasoned and placed strategically on the grill, Mike inevitably began to talk shop.

"I got a call from Tracy yesterday. He said James Maxwell is getting ready to start expanding his business again. After our meeting in Shreveport in January, James told Tracy he was definitely interested in talking to me more about the possibility of acquiring land in Pointe Coupee Parish. I think I need to make another trip to Shreveport soon.

In fact, if he's available, I thought I'd take the Cessna and fly up there sometime this week. I could bring him back and show him the land that Gilbert Mouton has been talking about selling. It would be perfect for his land development project. If you don't mind, I'll invite him to spend the night with us. We could take him out to dinner and let him see the sights. Then I could fly him back the next day."

"See the sights?" laughed Savannah. "That shouldn't take too long. During the week the sidewalks close up by eight p.m. Of course on the weekends the nightlife continues well past eight until probably nine or nine-thirty." Savannah was on a roll. "No, Mike. I don't mind you inviting him to spend the night. As a matter of fact, I'd gladly serve as your stewardess on the plane, but I have to prepare for a possible sale this week."

Mike laughed out loud at the thought of Savannah serving as a stewardess on their four-seated Cessna Corvalis TT airplane. Normally when he flew longer distances and planned on being somewhere more than a day or two he flew commercial. But for short trips or even overnight trips he preferred to take his own plane.

Tuesday morning, Mike called James Maxwell. "James, this is Mike Devereaux. I was talking to Tracy and he tells me you may be in the market to purchase some property here in Pointe Coupee Parish. I know of some land that I think you would be very interested in.

If you have time this week, I would be glad to fly up to Shreveport and pick you up. Then on our flight back I could point out some particularly nice areas of land that I think might fit your criteria. Savannah wanted me to invite you to stay over with us as our house guest. That way you would have time to see more of New Roads before having to go back to Shreveport."

"That sounds like a great idea, Mike," said James. "Let me check what I've got going on this week and I'll call you back to see when we can set something up."

By that afternoon James had called back and the two men made arrangements to meet at the airport in Shreveport on Saturday.

CHAPTER 57

Saturday morning Savannah drove Mike to False River Regional Airport so he wouldn't have to leave the Hummer there while he was gone. Mike went through his customary check of the airplane before preparing to leave. He had always been overly cautious with his Corvalis TT. Savannah used to laugh and say that they had two children; one was her 'Vette, the other was his Corvalis.

After one last check and assuring himself all was in order Mike strolled over to Savannah, looked lovingly into her eyes, and then without warning kissed her with such passion she was left breathless.

"Are you trying to make me beg you to stay?" she asked. "If you are, you're doing an outstanding job."

Mike looked longingly at Savannah and replied, "You know what I love the most about you?" Without giving her a chance to reply he said, "It's the way your eyes sparkle when I look at you. You're so beautiful."

"Mike, if you keep this up I'm not going to let you go. I'm going to take you back home instead."

"Why go home? We have a perfectly fine hanger here. We can pull the hanger door down and have all the privacy we want."

"Mike!" said Savannah, feigning shock.

Mike laughed heartily as he climbed into the cockpit. "I'll give you a call this evening when I get back with James so you can come pick us up."

Mike was gone all morning and well into the afternoon. She knew that if Mike and James got back before it started getting dark they would be flying over New Roads and the land Mike wanted to show to James. There was no doubt in Savannah's mind, that if there was any possibility at all, by the time Mike finished talking with James there would be a sale in the making.

When Savannah finally got the call from Mike, she was dressed and waiting. She jumped into the Hummer and drove to the airport. Mike smiled when he saw Savannah walk up, and proudly made the introductions.

"I'm pleased to meet you Savannah," said James as he extended his hand to Savannah. "Mike tells me that you're the number one senator in Louisiana."

"Mike likes to brag a little too much," laughed Savannah, shaking the outstretched hand. Savannah could tell that Mike and James's trip to New Roads had gone exceedingly well. He seemed relaxed and self-assured as he talked with James at dinner, and later that night at their house.

Savannah got up early the next morning to start breakfast. Soon afterwards both Mike and James came into the kitchen. "Good morning," she said. "Coffee's ready if y'all want some."

After a leisure breakfast, Mike took James to the Devereaux Real Estate office to show him charts and descriptions of the various tracts of land they had been looking at. Then they had lunch and drove around New Roads and out to surrounding areas. By the time they returned it was already late afternoon, and time to take James back to Shreveport.

"Mike, since we're getting off to such a late start, if Savannah doesn't mind, why don't you just plan on staying over at my house tonight?" suggested James. "There's plenty of room. I really hate to see you have to fly all the way to Shreveport, then have to turn around and fly right back."

"That sounds like a wonderful idea, Mike," said Savannah. "That way I don't have to worry about you flying back so late at night."

"I'll see how things go," said Mike. He threw some extra clothes and other essentials in an overnight bag, just in case he decided to stay over as James had suggested. At the airport, Savannah walked with

Mike and James out to the hangar. James put his bag in the back seat of the plane and began talking with Savannah while Mike began his walk around the plane, examining everything on his mental check-off list as usual.

When Mike finished, James climbed into the aircraft, while Savannah silently followed Mike to the other side. She kissed him goodbye before he entered the plane. "Be careful," she whispered.

"I'll see you soon," he replied with his usual smile.

CHAPTER 58

"Hey Loner, I hear you're getting out. How'd you rate that, bro?" asked Cruiser.

"Don't have a clue," answered Loner.

"You must know somebody, man. Nobody gets out of a life sentence around here without having some kind of super connections."

"I told you, I don't know!" shot back Loner aggravated that he had to repeat himself.

"I bet it was your old man," Cruiser persisted.

"Not likely. I haven't heard from him since I've been here. I doubt after all these years he has suddenly had a change of heart and wants to reclaim me. Anyway, what difference does it make? As soon as they open those doors for me, I'm outta here."

"Where you gonna go?"

"Don't know and don't care," replied Loner. "Just wanna get as far away from here as I can."

"I hear that," replied Cruiser, "but one thing I wanna know. You plannin' on gettin' even with certain people when you git out? You know, make em pay for what happened to ya?"

There was a brief silence. Loner looked at Cruiser but did not reply.

Look Loner, I hate good-byes so I ain't gonna say that. And I ain't gonna say I hope I see ya again, cuz that would mean you'd be back in here, and I don't wish that on nobody. So I'll just say, be safe man."

Cruiser continued, "I gotta git goin' if I'm gonna make the chain gang today," he said with a chuckle. "Some of us without early paroles, or who ain't got no miracles goin' for 'em, still gotta work. Good luck to ya on the outside."

"Thanks," mumbled Loner.

The two men shook hands, and for the slightest moment, their weary eyes met. "I'll miss you bro," Cruiser said as he turned and made a hasty retreat from the small cell.

Eight years and Loner had never opened up to another inmate. Cruiser was the closest he had ever come to having a friend. Eight years and all Loner could say at the end of their co-existence was, "Thanks."

He watched, without so much as an utterance, as Cruiser hurried to catch up with the other inmates heading out into the fields. Everything he had that belonged to him was packed and rolled up in his shirt sleeve – which was to say, all he had to his name was a pack of Camel cigarettes that Cruiser had stolen for him as a good-bye gift.

"Ready to go?" asked Haney, one of the prison guards.

"Been ready since the day I got here," shot back Loner.

"Okay then, let's put on these handcuffs so I can take you up front to get your final paperwork processed."

Haney was short but stocky. Loner was tall and lanky, but muscular. Both guard and prisoner walked briskly down the recently deserted halls, the only noise coming from the heels of Haney's shoes as they stomped heavily against the plain cement floors.

"Here he is Captain."

"Good. You can go ahead and take off the handcuffs."

Deputy Haney did as he was told.

"Thank you, Deputy Haney. That will be all. Please close the door on your way out."

"Yes sir," said the deputy as he walked out of the room.

"Come in and sit down," the warden said to Loner as he motioned to the chair across the desk from his.

Loner obediently sat in the chair as he had been instructed.

"You're getting an opportunity most men in your situation never get. Your sentence has been overturned and you're being set free. Do you know what that means?"

"It's been a long time, but I can still vaguely remember what the word 'free' means," said Loner, attitude coloring his voice.

"Look boy, you may be getting your walking papers today, but if you cause any trouble out there, you can be back in here in a heartbeat. You hear?"

Loner wanted desperately to tell the warden exactly what he thought of him, but he had no intention of jeopardizing his chances of getting out. Instead he answered, "Yeah, I hear."

A short conversation ensued, with the warden warning Loner to stay clean. Moments later, without any fanfare, Loner was walking out the gates of East Carroll Detention Center and into a prison van that would take him to the bus station. He was given barely enough money for food and a bus ticket to Somewhere, USA.

CHAPTER 59

Monday morning Savannah woke up early and went to check the caller ID on both her cell phone and the home phone. There were no messages. *"Mike's probably out of reach of a cell tower,"* she reasoned. *"I'm sure he'll call soon to let me know when he's getting in."*

After drinking a cup of coffee and reading the morning paper, Savannah decided to pamper herself with a hot bath in their oversized whirlpool bathtub. She poured bath salts into the water, turned on the whirlpool action and stepped in, then gently slid deep into the circulating soft ripples of water. Mike had only been gone overnight, but she could hardly wait for him to get back. She wanted to look her best when he got in.

Savannah arrived at the Devereaux Real Estate office at ten-thirty. Betty was talking on the phone, extolling the benefits of becoming a Devereaux Real Estate client; Macy and Jim were working in their offices. Savannah waved at Betty as she passed by her desk.

As usual, the first task of the day for Savannah was to check messages left on her voice mail. After listening to the last entry, she became acutely conscious of the fact that she had still not heard from Mike. Opening her bottom desk drawer, Savannah pulled the cell phone out of her purse and pressed the speed dial number for Mike's cell phone. The phone continued to ring without going into voice mail.

"That's strange," she thought as she dropped the cell phone back into her purse and shut the bottom drawer. She picked up her coffee cup and headed for the break room. As Savannah was getting ready to pour her coffee, Macy walked in.

"Savannah, remember when I told you I was going to get a dog?

Well, I got one! He is so adorable! I named him Moxie. You want to see his pictures?" asked Macy as she pulled out an album and plopped it down on the table.

"Pictures?" laughed Savannah. You just got him and you already have an album full of pictures?"

"Yeah, pretty cool, huh?" said Macy as she opened the album.

"What kind of dog is this?" asked Savannah.

"A Bichon Frise. Isn't he gorgeous?" Macy gushed.

"He is cute," said Savannah. "But he's so little. Why didn't you get a big dog that could protect you and look after your house when you're gone?"

"Well you see, it's this way," she began earnestly, "I wanted someone to share my life and my bed with: someone that would keep me company; that wouldn't take up the whole bed; that wouldn't expect anything more than food out of a bag; and an occasional pat on the head."

Savannah burst out laughing. "Only you, Macy – only you!"

After looking at Macy's pictures, Savannah glanced down at her watch and said, "Good grief. I've got to get busy. I have a dozen things to do before Mike gets back."

"Where is Mr. Mike?" asked Macy.

"He took the Cessna up to Shreveport this weekend to pick up James Maxwell. Mike wanted to show him some property that he thought James might be interested in. James spent Saturday night with us and Mike flew him back to Shreveport late yesterday afternoon.

Mike was going to stay overnight with James and fly back this morning. I'm really surprised that I haven't heard from him yet," Savannah said quietly.

"I wouldn't worry," replied Macy. "He probably just got tied up and hasn't had the chance to call yet."

Lunchtime came and went, and still there was no word from Mike. Savannah became increasingly worried with each passing hour. It was uncharacteristic of Mike not to call her if his plans changed. Finally, since she could not reach Mike, she decided it was time to call James. He picked up on his private phone after the first ring.

"James Maxwell speaking."

"Hello James. This is Savannah Devereaux."

"Savannah, how are you?" Before she could answer, he continued, "I want to thank you again for your most gracious hospitality this past weekend. I can't remember when I've had such a nice time."

"Thank you James. We certainly enjoyed your visit as well. I'm not going to keep you long because I know you're a busy man, but I wanted to check with you to find out what time Mike left Shreveport this morning."

There was a moment of quiet hesitation before James, obviously concerned, responded. His voice softened. "Savannah, Mike told me he couldn't stand to be away from you overnight, and decided to return home last night. I tried to talk him into staying, but he had made up his mind. As soon as he dropped me off, he turned around and headed home. He should have arrived in New Roads last night."

"James," began Savannah with a slow and unsteady voice, "Mike hasn't even called me. Normally we talk several times during the day, and when he's away from home he always calls me at night."

"Let me see what I can find out over here. I'll call the airport to see if there have been any calls from pilots that have reported problems with their planes."

Savannah knew exactly what James was telling her. He was going to call air traffic control to see if any planes had crashed. He was probably also going to call hospitals and the police to see if Mike's name turned up anywhere.

"Don't worry, Savannah, we'll find him."

"Thanks James," said Savannah as her voice began to quiver. She tried her best not to cry. She hung up and immediately called Yvonne Chenevert, the manager at the False River Regional Airport. "Yvonne, this is Savannah Devereaux."

"Savannah, how are you doing?" came back Yvonne's cheery voice."

"I'm not sure," Savannah shot back. "Mike left to go to Shreveport yesterday afternoon and he never returned. Could you tell me if you've heard of any pilots reporting problems with their planes – or ..." her voice cracked slightly, "if you know of any plane crashes between Shreveport and New Roads?"

"I've been here all morning," Yvonne answered quickly, "and the only thing I've heard about is a plane crashing into the Potomac River outside of Washington. Maybe Mike stopped over in Natchitoches or Alexandria. If you want, I'll get on the phone and start calling around. He may have just had engine trouble and made a stop on the way here. How long overdue is he?"

"He was supposed to be in last night. I thought he had stayed over in Shreveport, but I just found out he didn't. I'm really worried."

"Let me call around and see what I can find out," replied Yvonne.

"Thanks Yvonne," said Savannah as she ended the call.

CHAPTER 60

At 3:45 p.m. Savannah received the call she had been dreading all day. "Savannah, this is James." Without waiting for a reply he continued, "I'm afraid I have some bad news for you. They found Mike's plane."

Savannah's muscles began to tighten and her breathing became erratic.

"It crashed into the Potomac River after a mid-air explosion. They told me that it appeared Mike was trying to make a landing at the Washington National Airport right before his plane caught fire and exploded. I wish I didn't have to be the one to tell you, Savannah, but it looks like Mike died in the explosion."

Savannah fell back in her chair in utter shock. There were no words she could say, no thoughts she could think, and not even any tears that she could cry. Her body went limp.

She had no idea how long it was before she was brought back to consciousness by James's voice on the other end of the line calling her name over and over again.

"Savannah, are you all right?" James kept repeating.

"…are you sure?" Savannah eventually replied in a hushed whisper. "That can't be right. Why would Mike go to Washington? He would've called me if his plans changed. Even you told me he was on his way home."

"I don't know, but the coroner in Washington asked if you could send a copy of Mike's dental records to him as soon as possible so they can make a positive identification. I have the address if you want it, or if you prefer I can contact his dentist and request the information for you."

"If they want his dental records, then that means they're not positive it's Mike," said Savannah with the slightest glimmer of hope. "Where do we send his dental records? I'll call Dr. Mitchell and get him to send them off right now."

James knew the dental records were just a formality, but he gave Savannah the information and said nothing more about the possibility of Mike's still being alive. As soon as they hung up, Savannah called Dr. Mitchell and explained the situation to him.

"I'll take care of it for you Savannah," Dr. Mitchell assured her. "If you need anything else, please let me know."

"Thank you so much," said Savannah in a robotic voice. *"It can't be true. This has to be a mistake,"* she thought.

Then the second call came through. It was Yvonne at the New Roads airport.

"Savannah, I wanted to make sure they got hold of you to let you know that they retrieved a piece of the plane that crashed in Washington. It was registered to Mike. I'm so sorry. Is there anything I can do for you?"

"I don't think so. I can't really think straight right now," answered Savannah.

"I'm so sorry, Savannah," Yvonne repeated again.

"I know," whispered Savannah. "Thanks for calling me back, Yvonne. I appreciate all your help."

"Sure," said Yvonne. Before hanging up she added, "You know our thoughts and prayers are with you."

Savannah walked into the front office and called the staff together so that she could relay the news to them all at the same time. Although she clung to the fact that it had not been confirmed yet, she said there was a definite possibility that Mike had died in a plane crash. After her announcement, a morbid silence fell over the office, and it remained that way until closing time.

When Betty turned the 'Open' sign over to 'Closed' at the end of the day, nobody rushed to leave. Savannah seemed to be in a daze and no one wanted to leave her alone. After much protesting and insisting that she would be all right, Savannah finally left the office. She went straight home where she remained secluded for the rest of the evening.

"Why, Lord, why?" lamented Savannah. She sat in the recliner in their bedroom holding Mike's keys in her hands. With her bare feet curled up underneath her, her body began to sway back and forth. She sobbed quietly at first. Affectionately she watched as Mike's keys flipped over again and again in quick rotation in her hands.

As she began to grasp the concept that Mike may never be coming home again, her quiet weeping became louder and more forceful until finally she could hardly catch her breath. "Mike, please don't leave me. I need you so much. I never needed anybody like I need you. I can't live without you," she wailed out loud.

"Dear God," she cried, "First you took my mom, now you take Mike. What more can you ask of me? I'm not that strong. I know you have your reasons, but please God, if you're going to take everything in my life that means anything to me, please take me too."

She leaned back in her recliner, and as she did so the foot rest raised upwards. Her body begrudgingly began to stretch out until finally, out of desperation, her tense body began to relax ever so slightly. She drifted off to sleep from sheer exhaustion, and was pulled into a strange world of nightmares.

First she saw Mike trying to reach out to her, but demons surrounded her and would not let her get close to him. Then they pulled her further away and into a dark wooded forest overgrown with brush and thickets. She saw her mother, and called out to her, but her mother was frozen in time and could not move to help her.

Abruptly, the demons left her and started chasing a man she had never seen before. When they caught up with him they grabbed him and unmercifully began stabbing him repeatedly with a knife. Savannah watched in horror as they took him to a river and forced his head underwater. He began thrashing about gasping for air until, in the final moments, he gave up the ghost.

A sudden jerk of her body roused Savannah from the deranged psychotic state of mind she had been trapped in only seconds earlier. The cool morning air only served to send a chill down her spine as she awoke in a cold sweat. There was nothing, or no one, that could alleviate the devastating fear and apprehension that wracked her trembling body.

It was only three a.m., but Savannah feared more nightmares if she went back to sleep. Instead, she wandered around aimlessly from one room to the next. At the first sign of dawn she made a pot of strong coffee and sat down in her cushioned chair in the study. She knew it was true. Mike was dead.

CHAPTER 61

The phone rang at seven forty-five a.m. Savannah considered not answering it, but knew that would only delay the inevitable. "Hello," she answered softly.

"Is this Senator Devereaux?" replied the stranger's voice.

"Yes, it is."

"Senator, this is Warren Riley with the Washington Coroner's Office. I know Mr. Maxwell called you yesterday to tell you that your husband's plane had crashed in the Potomac River. We wanted to confirm our suspicions before we contacted you. I am sorry to have to tell you, but unfortunately after receiving the dental records from Dr. Mitchell, we have now been able to verify that the person found in the plane crash was your husband, Michael Devereaux."

Savannah could no longer hold it all in, and began to weep quietly.

"I know this is a terribly difficult time for you, but we will need to know what you would like for us to do with Mr. Devereaux's remains. They were badly burned because of the fire. If you would like to have his body cremated, we can do that here. Or, if you prefer, we can have the body sent back to you in a simple pine box and you can select a casket from a funeral home there in New Roads to use for his burial. I'll give you my phone number so that you can call me back after you've had time to think about it."

Savannah wrote down the phone number Warren Riley gave her and somehow managed to thank him for his call. After their conversation the words, *"What do I do now,"* continued to play over and over again in her head as if on some sheet of continuous music on a player piano.

"I can't keep doing this," she thought. *"I have to pull myself together. First I need to decide what to do about getting Mike home. Then I need to make the arrangements for his funeral."*

At eight a.m., Savannah called the office and was relieved to hear Betty's voice. Betty had heard on the morning news about the plane crash in Washington. Although the name of the pilot was not given, she assumed it must have been Mike. She answered the phone in a somewhat subdued voice, "Good morning, Devereaux Real Estate Company, Betty Cormier speaking."

"Betty, this is Savannah. The plane that crashed on Sunday night was Mike's, and now they have confirmed that it was him in the plane." Savannah stopped talking to keep from crying.

"I'm so sorry Savannah," Betty said as she began to cry.

"Has Jim made it in yet?" Savannah continued, still trying to stay in control.

"Yes, honey, he's here. Just a minute and I'll get him on the line for you." Before transferring the call, Betty hesitated, "Savannah, please let me know if there's anything I can do for you, or if there's anything you need."

"Thanks, Betty. I just can't seem to get a handle on this yet. Nothing seems real."

"I know," said Betty, trying to sound reassuring. "Just be sure to call me if you need anything at all. I'll ring Jim now."

Seconds later Jim was answering his phone. "Savannah, Betty just told me about Mike. I can't tell you how sorry I am. We're all in a state of shock. What can we do to be of help?"

"Jim, I'm going to need you to take over the office for a while," Savannah said. "Until I can get everything settled, I need someone in charge, and I know you can do it."

"Sure, Savannah, don't worry about the office," said Jim. "If there's anything else you need, all you have to do is ask."

"There is one more thing," she continued. "Would you or Macy get a wreath to put on the office door? We can include a note with the date and time of Mike's rosary and funeral when we get that set up."

"Good idea, Savannah. We'll take care of that. Anything else?"

"I'm going to try to arrange to have the funeral on Friday if I can, but first I need to make sure they can get Mike's body back here by that time. I'll let you know as soon as I find out something. Also, I think we should close the office tomorrow through the rest of the week. Make sure Betty and Macy know what we're planning so they can make arrangements to reschedule appointments if necessary."

"Do you want me to make the arrangements for Mike's funeral?" asked Jim.

"No, I'll take care of that. I really need to stay busy so I won't go crazy thinking about Mike. That's probably the only way I'll survive. I don't even know why I want to do that."

"Savannah, please don't talk that way. You know that we all love you, and we're all here for you. I promise you that together we'll get through this."

"Thanks, Jim. I love you too."

CHAPTER 62

Jim did just as he said he would. Before the end of the day, there was a beautiful wreath hanging at the front entrance of the Devereaux Real Estate Company, with long black ribbons flowing down from its underside. A day later a small announcement was added, giving the time for the rosary and the funeral service.

For the rest of the week, every time Savannah passed their office she saw the wreath Jim had placed on the front door for Mike. Occasionally the black ribbons would flutter in the breeze, catching the attention of those passing by, and serving as a reminder of the impending services.

The rosary, which had been set for Thursday evening, had an overflow crowd in attendance. Mike had included in his will that at his death he wanted his casket to remain closed. Under the circumstances, that was a foregone conclusion. Savannah longed desperately to see him one last time, but his untimely death robbed her in a cruel and sadistic way of ever realizing that dream.

Standing beside Mike's casket at Niland's Funeral Home on the night of the rosary, Savannah lovingly stroked the shiny bronze metallic casket. Huge tears rolled down her ashen cheeks and fell like rain onto the coffer. She could think of no reason to want to live any more. Everything important had been taken from her.

Macy quietly walked over and put her arm around her friend. Ever so gently she guided Savannah back to the front pew so the rosary could begin.

After the rosary had been said, and the endless line of people wanting to pay their last respects had left the funeral home, Macy asked

Savannah if she would like to have some company for the night. Macy was surprised but delighted when Savannah replied, "I would love for you to come over. I really don't feel like being alone right now."

"Do you want to drive your car home, or would you prefer to ride in my car, and we can pick up your car tomorrow?" asked Macy.

"I'll take my car home. I don't want to leave it here overnight. Just give me a chance to say goodnight to Mike first."

"Sure," said Macy sadly. "I'll meet you outside."

Savannah moved over to the casket. Placing her hand gently on the front, she let her fingers glide across the glossy polished finish below the large spray of flowers that adorned the top of his casket.

"I love you, Mike. I'll always love you," she said in a faint whisper. Then she slowly bent down and kissed his casket. Rising, she wiped the falling tears from her eyes and then turned and walked briskly outside to catch up with Macy.

"Let's go," she said,

CHAPTER 63

Savannah gave Macy a pair of her silk pajamas with a matching housecoat to wear.

"I haven't been to a pajama party in a million years," laughed Macy trying to lift Savannah's spirits. Suddenly, realizing she may have crossed the line, she said, "I'm sorry Savannah. I guess that sounded kind of heartless."

"It's all right Macy. I've cried so much it feels good to get my fingers out of the Kleenex box for a change. I need to get my mind on other things." Both women pushed back into their adjoining recliners in the den, accompanied by mugs of hot chocolate with marshmallows floating on top.

"I guess I really bombed out on y'all this week," Savannah sighed.

"You've been under a lot of strain," said Macy. "Give yourself a break." As an afterthought, Macy scrunched up her face and continued, "Something did happen on Tuesday though that I thought was a little strange ..." Immediately Macy stopped talking, as though she had said something she shouldn't have.

"What?" Savannah prompted, her curiosity aroused.

"Oh, it's probably nothing. I shouldn't have even brought it up. Let's just wait until you get back to the office to talk about it."

"Look, we've got nothing but time right now. I'm not in the least bit tired, are you?"

"No, I guess not."

"Okay then, out with it," demanded Savannah playfully.

"You were so upset when you left on Monday, and we were all so stressed out on Tuesday morning, that nobody was doing any work.

Betty and Jim went into the kitchen to sit down and have a cup of coffee. I was sitting at Betty's desk when this man came in. I've never seen him before.

He handed me an envelope and said that he was told if anything ever happened to Mike he was to give this envelope to Savannah Devereaux. It was a sealed long white envelope with just your name on it. I told him you were not in at the time but that I would see to it that you got it. He thanked me and left.

I put the envelope in my purse because I knew I would see you at the rosary tonight. Actually, I forgot about it until just now. I don't know if it's good news or bad. You may want to wait to read it until later."

"Do you have it with you now?" asked Savannah.

"Yeah, it's still in my purse." Macy picked up her purse, pulled the envelope out, and handed it to Savannah.

Savannah took a moment to look at her name typed on the envelope. Mrs. Michael J. Devereaux. She had not seen it written that way in some time. Usually she was addressed as Senator. She opened the envelope and immediately began to read the familiar handwriting.

Savannah —

Please don't discuss the contents of this letter with anyone. If anything happens to me, place a notice in the obituary column of the paper. After that you will be contacted by a man with the initials B. H. I don't want to put his name in here, but after you think about it, I'm sure you'll figure out who I'm talking about. Tell him they finally got me and that he needs to be careful.

And you, my darling, must also be careful. B.H. will explain.

Remember that things are not always what they seem. The only thing you can be sure of is my love for you — even in the hereafter.

Always yours,

Mike

"Bad news?" asked Macy.

"I have no idea," said Savannah. "You didn't tell anybody else about this, did you?"

"No. It was addressed to you. I figured it was nobody's business but yours."

"Good. I'll have to think about this later. I've just got too much going on right now to try and make any sense out of it."

Talk turned to small talk. Small talk lasted well into the early morning hours until finally both women dozed off to sleep in their respective recliners.

CHAPTER 64

Savannah and Macy topped off the few hours of sleep they managed to get with early morning cups of coffee. "Savannah, I need to drive over to my house and get dressed for the services. Will you be okay while I'm gone?"

"Of course," said Savannah attempting a feeble smile. Don't you want something to eat before you go?"

"No thanks. I'll pick up something at the house. Do you want me to meet you back here or at the funeral home?"

"Let's just meet at Niland's," Savannah replied. "I want to get there a little early anyway. Mary and Maria are coming in this morning to clean the house and prepare some food for anyone that comes over here after the funeral. They said they would stay and keep the house open for visitors so I don't have to rush to get home."

"That's a good idea," said Macy, her voice trailing off as she realized how difficult this day had to be for Savannah.

As soon as Macy left the house, Savannah got dressed and rushed over to the funeral home. *"I don't want Mike to be alone when people start arriving,"* she thought.

Gradually, friends started showing up, some bringing trays of food they took back to the kitchen. She remembered some people had brought food the evening of the rosary. She wasn't sure who had brought it, but most of it was gone by this morning.

An hour before the body was to be taken to the church for the funeral, Jim Chandler and his wife Shelia showed up. "How you holding up, Savannah?" asked Jim as he walked over and kissed her on the cheek.

"I don't know," she replied honestly. "I feel like I'm in another world. Nothing seems real. I want it all to be over with, but then again, I don't. I know Mike's not here, but his body still is. Once that's gone, I feel like I won't have anything left of him."

"Knowing you, Savannah, Mike will always be a part of your life," said Jim.

Savannah knew he was trying to comfort her, but the words sounded trite and lame.

Before she could respond, Mr. LaFleur, the funeral home director, appeared at her side. With all the self-assurance and dignity associated with a man in his position he whispered, "Senator Devereaux, it's time we take your husband to the church. Would you like for me to go ahead and make the announcement?"

The words pierced her heart. She felt weak and dizzy all at the same time. Somehow she managed to nod her head in agreement.

In proper form, Mr. LaFleur stood in front of the casket and announced to the crowd, "The time of visitation has now ended. Please return to your vehicles as the family pays their last respects, and we prepare for the procession to the church."

Savannah watched as the crowd of people filed out. At long last she stood as a solitary figure before Mike's casket, unable to fathom how she had come to this point. Her hand lovingly passed over the casket as she whispered, "I wish I could be with you Mike. There's nothing left here for me now." Slowly she turned and walked out to the waiting group of friends.

Savannah stood beside Macy and watched as the pall bearers carried the casket out and loaded it into the hearse. "You know what the worst part is?" she whispered to Macy. "I never got a chance to see him one last time. It doesn't seem fair. I said goodbye when he left for Shreveport. I never thought it would be our last goodbye." Macy gently put her arm around Savannah and led her to the waiting limousine.

The mass was beautiful. Savannah had picked out the readings and the music. "Mike would have been proud to see how many people showed up," she whispered awkwardly to Macy.

Once the mass was over and the graveside services concluded, people once again paid their respects and left the grave site. It was a beautiful day. The sun was shining brightly and there was a slight breeze that thwarted what might have been another scorching Louisiana day. Birds were singing nearby, but Savannah didn't hear them.

She never even heard what was supposed to be words of comfort from Father Young's eulogy, or from all the many friends that approached her at the graveside. Her heart was beating too loudly in her ears.

Macy walked over to Savannah, who was still standing beside Mike's casket. The sun created sparkles that bounced off its glossy exterior surface. Savannah thought they looked like angel's wings. "If you want to stay a little while longer, I'll go over to your house with Betty, and you can drive my car back when you're ready," said Macy as she slipped her keys into Savannah's hand.

"Thanks, Macy," Savannah whispered wearily.

"Take your time," Macy replied as she rushed off to catch up with Betty and to tell the limousine driver he could leave.

Savannah knew the cemetery workers were waiting for her to go to her car so they could begin their job of burying Mike. She wondered if they even knew Mike and what a great man he was, or if this was just another day to them, just another body to be buried. She broke down and cried at the thought.

When she could cry no longer, she slowly dried her eyes, and turned to leave the cemetery. There in the distance, she saw a man standing by a tree watching her. He wore dress slacks and a dress shirt, but no jacket or tie. She wondered if he had been a friend of Mike's.

A loud noise startled her and she turned around to see the men lowering Mike's casket into the ground. She watched for a brief moment and then quickly turned her head back. The man standing by the tree had disappeared. Silently relieved by the fact that she had just skirted another forced conversation intent on making more small talk, she walked to Macy's car.

Savannah tried to put the key into the door of the car, but her hands began shaking uncontrollably. Finally, with one hand supporting the other, she was able to place the key into the lock, open the door, and slip inside.

Once inside, she took a quick look around at the interior of Macy's car. A pair of light blue stockings with intermingling silver threads were thrown on the floorboard of the passenger side of the car, among a slew of non-discriminately tossed candy wrappers. Oversized yellow and red flowered sunglasses hung from the rearview mirror.

A stuffed dog sat on the back seat amidst a clutter of real estate books and this month's copy of Cosmopolitan. Savannah started to cry, but then it turned into laughter. *"Good ole Macy,"* she thought. *"She is what she is. Even her car is a reflection of her personality."*

CHAPTER 65

Slightly more than a week following the funeral, Savannah was back at work. The wreath had been removed from the door and, except for an occasional bout with depression for Savannah, life went on as usual inside.

Thursday morning Macy came bouncing in; a pair of long, thin, red and black sparklers hanging from her earlobes. Her matching necklace made up of strings of thin red and black beads, with long natural white simulated pearls intertwined in between, accented her ensemble.

Her watch had a wide black velvet band. To offset the watch on her left wrist, she wore a thick red and black hand-carved bracelet with silver backing on her right wrist. She had a wide array of rings on three of her fingers on her left hand, and two on the right hand. Her fingernails were manicured and touted Romancing Red nail polish. Her short sandaled heels revealed the same Romancing Red nail polish on her toenails. Macy was definitely in top form today and ready for business – be it work or after hours.

Savannah could hear Jim let out a wolf whistle in the reception area and Betty collapse with laughter. She walked into the front office to see what was going on.

"Wow, Macy, where are you going today?" she said with a teasing smirk.

"I think I may have a sale in the making," Macy grinned broadly. "And if I don't end up selling a condo to this absolutely gorgeous man I'm meeting at eleven this morning, I'm going to see if he's available to go out this evening."

"Well please try to remember to keep business and pleasure separate. Otherwise, it could end up being a problem," lectured Savannah good-naturedly.

Savannah had only been back at her desk for a short time when she began to get a nagging sensation, as if someone were watching her. Gazing upwards she saw Betty standing in the doorway, all the color drained from her face, and looking as if she had seen a ghost.

"What's the matter Betty?" she quickly inquired with an element of alarm in her voice.

"There's a phone call for you. It's a man."

"All right," said Savannah with a questioning look on her face.

"He says he's Mike's son," she stammered.

Savannah felt herself go limp. It was as if the rug had been pulled out from under her, and she was now free falling into a deep, bottomless pit.

"What?" she said incredulously. "Mike didn't have a son. Are you sure that's what he said?"

Betty looked offended that Savannah would question her. "That's what he said. Do you want to take the call or shall I tell him you're busy?"

Savannah hesitantly replied, "I'll take the call. What line is he on?"

As she looked down at the phone on her desk she realized there was only one line blinking. She looked back at Betty, somewhat embarrassed, and said, "Thanks, I got it."

Picking up the phone, Savannah tried to answer as usual. "This is Savannah Devereaux. May I help you?"

"Yes," came back the reply. "This is Dylan Devereaux, Mike's son.

I'm sorry that my first conversation with you had to be just after dad died. I didn't know he had passed away until I got into town today. In fact, I didn't know my mother had died and dad had remarried. We haven't been in contact with each other in quite some time."

"Mike never told me he had a son," whispered Savannah, as much to herself as to the caller. "Why have I never seen or heard from you before?"

"I guess I can understand why dad kept me a secret," replied Dylan. "We had a falling out a long time ago and were never able to resolve it. I don't know why I came to see him now. Maybe I was just hoping we could come to terms with some of the issues that pulled us apart.

I know my timing stinks, but I was wondering if we could get together and talk. You are the only link I have to the father I never really knew."

"Where are you calling from?" Savannah asked.

"I'm in Livonia. I came by bus as far as Baton Rouge and then just hitched a ride the rest of the way over here."

"Are you anywhere near 'Not Your Mama's Café'?" continued Savannah. The walls at the office seemed to have ears, and she wanted to find out what this was all about before everyone else did.

"Yes. It's just down the road from where I am right now."

"Okay. If it's not too difficult for you to get to, why don't we meet there around eleven-thirty?" asked Savannah.

"Sure. That would be great. I'll see you at eleven-thirty."

Savannah's hands began to tremble as she placed the receiver back on its base. *"Mike's son,"* she thought. *"Could this be possible? Mike never told me he had a son. Why would he keep that a secret from me? I can't believe he wouldn't tell me something that important."*

Regaining her composure, she picked up the receiver again and called Harold Stout. Harold was not only her attorney, but also a good friend.

"Harold, this is Savannah," she said, talking softly so as not to be overheard. "Something very strange has come up and I need your opinion on what I should do."

"Sure, Savannah" Harold said. "What's the problem?"

"Have you got a few minutes so that I could come over and talk with you?"

In less than five minutes Savannah found herself sitting in one of the deep maroon leather chairs in front of Harold's ornate mahogany desk with the door closed behind them.

CHAPTER 66

Harold Stout's office was attractive in a masculine sort of way. The beautiful heavy furniture accented by the long salient drapes cascading down from the heavy duty Fleur-de-lis curtain rods were obviously chosen by his wife. His contribution to the decor consisted of the piles of papers and folders that cluttered his desk, chairs, and even the floor around him.

Harold was a tall, slender man, in his early 70s. His silvery white hair was beginning to thin on the top. His dark blue eyes had bags under them this morning, probably the result of a late night reading some of his legal briefs. Although he usually wore a business suit to work each day, the coat and tie usually came off as soon as he entered the office. This morning they were hanging in their usual place on the coat rack behind his desk.

"So, what's up, Savannah?" asked Harold in a questioning manner.

"I got the strangest phone call just a little while ago. The man on the phone said his name was Dylan." Savannah paused for a moment and then continued hesitantly. "He said that he's Mike's son. He wants to meet with me at eleven-thirty this morning."

"Mike's son?" questioned Harold with surprise. "I didn't know Mike had a son."

"Neither did I," answered Savannah. "I'm not sure what to do."

"Well, I certainly hope you're not going to meet with him until I have a chance to check him out."

"Actually, I did agree to meet with him at 'Not Your Mama's' in Livonia this morning."

"Savannah, what were you thinking? You don't know who this man is. Do you want me to go with you? Tisha can fill in for me while I'm gone."

"No, Harold. Don't do that. I know how busy you are. Besides, what's he going to do in a crowded restaurant in Livonia? I know how close you and Mike were, and I guess I just wanted to find out if he had ever mentioned having a son to you."

"Savannah, I don't want to sound cruel," Harold said, "but sometimes people crawl out of the woodwork when someone like Mike dies. They want to see what they can get out of the family members. It's very important that you don't let this man get the upper hand on you. I've seen way too many cases where deceptive and outright cruel individuals try to take advantage of a person who has just lost someone they loved. If this is the first time you've heard of Mike having a son, how do you know that it's true? Don't you think Mike would've told you if he had a son?"

"I just don't know," said Savannah, "I want to think he would've."

Harold asked, "How old is this fella?"

Savannah realized that she had no idea how old he was. She was so flustered by his call, she had not been able to think rationally again until after hanging up.

"I don't know" she admitted.

"Well, it doesn't matter," Harold continued. "Mike had a legal will leaving everything to you. If this guy is trying to get some of Mike's estate, son or no son, he is flat out of luck."

"Gosh, Harold, I hadn't even thought about Mike's will. Do you think that might be what he's after — some of Mike's money?"

"There's no telling Savannah. That's why I'm saying you need to be careful." When Savannah stood up to leave, Harold rose from his chair and came from behind his desk to walk her to the door.

"Thanks for your time, Harold. I feel better already. I guess that's why Mike and I always depended on you so much. You always think of everything."

"Well, keep me informed," he said as she walked out.

Back at her office, Savannah peeped in the front door and waved at Betty. "Betty, I'll be out for a while. Hold down the fort for me, okay?"

Betty smiled and said, "Will do."

The trip to Livonia gave Savannah ample time to try to digest the strange series of events that were unfolding. Mindless thoughts struggled to understand the incomprehensible: why Mike wouldn't have told her that he had a son. Strange thoughts filled her head, with nothing to fill in the voids except countless, "Whys?"

CHAPTER 67

Savannah pulled into the parking lot of 'Not Your Mama's Café' at eleven-twenty. Sarah, the head hostess, greeted Savannah as soon as she walked into the restaurant.

"Good morning, Senator Devereaux," she said sweetly. "There is a gentleman sitting at a table in the lounge who said you would be joining him. Please follow me."

"Thank you," replied Savannah.

"Ms. Savannah," Sarah continued on a more informal basis, "mom and dad didn't get a chance to talk with you at the funeral because there were so many people there. They said they were going to wait for a while, and then call to see how you were doing."

"That's so sweet of them," Savannah replied. "Please be sure to tell them I said hi."

Larry and Cecile had lived on the island side of False River for years. The entire family had been supportive of Savannah during her campaign, but it was Sarah that worked in her campaign office on a regular basis.

Sarah took Savannah over to a small booth in the bar area which was more secluded than the regular tables and booths in the main section of the restaurant. As they approached, a ruggedly handsome young man stood up and extended his hand for Savannah to shake.

A chill went down her spine and she froze in place for the slightest moment. She was so taken aback that she actually felt her heart skip a beat. She could see Mike in the stranger in front of her. Maybe the connection was not so much in his outward appearance: he was tall and thin; his coal black hair was long and shaggy; and he had a rough looking beard and mustache.

Muscles bulged out from under his short sleeve black t-shirt, and slightly hidden under the right sleeve of his t-shirt was a very intricate tattoo. Savannah figured he must be around 30 years old.

Notwithstanding some of the above characteristics, he had Mike's eyes and his smile. Looking into those beautiful dark brown eyes, she could see the same insecurities and longing to be loved that she had seen in Mike's eyes when she first met him. *"How's this possible?"* she thought. *"He's Mike all over again."*

"Good morning, Mrs. Devereaux," he smiled.

"Good morning," was all Savannah could utter as she tried desperately to keep her voice from trembling."

As they both sat down she continued, "I'm not sure what to say, Dylan. I have to admit that I didn't even know Mike had a son. He never told me about you, and I don't know why. I thought we shared everything."

Dylan seemed to relax as Savannah started talking. He had known that his call would be a shock to her, and wasn't sure what her reaction towards him would be.

The waitress appeared to take their order. Savannah asked for a glass of tea, while Dylan ordered a beer. She returned with their drinks and then was off to take another order.

"I guess this is kind of awkward for both of us," he said. "First off, I want you to know that my only reason for being here is to meet you and talk about my dad." Dylan looked at Savannah and knew immediately why his dad had fallen in love with her. She was a beautiful woman.

"Why now?" questioned Savannah. "I don't understand. Why didn't you come to see Mike before he died?"

"I've been in prison for the past eight years." Dylan answered reluctantly.

Savannah could hardly contain the shock she felt, and shuddered in disbelief.

"I got left holding the bag in a murder case."

"Murder," cried out Savannah, who was quickly rendered speechless.

"Yeah," repeated Dylan in a low voice that reflected the hurt he had endured for so many years. "Just recently my conviction was overturned. The one who was actually responsible confessed. It's kind of ironic, but the first thing I wanted to do was tell mom and dad.

I know I was a thorn in dad's side for a long time. I guess the murder conviction was just the straw that broke the camel's back. I wanted to explain everything to him, but now I guess that's impossible.

No one told me about my mom. It wasn't until after I got to Shreveport that I found out she had died and that dad had moved to New Roads. In fact, I'd barely found out that dad had gotten married again before I heard that his funeral was last week. It's been just one blow after another for me. That's why I just wanted to talk with someone that would be a connection to everything I've lost. I hope you don't mind me calling you like I did."

Savannah could see the hurt look in his eyes, but knew there was nothing she could do or say to relieve his pain. *"Be careful,"* she warned herself. *"Remember, like Harold said, you don't really know who he is or if what he's telling you is true."*

"Tell me about your mother," she asked inquiringly.

"I loved my mom, but she was never a strong person. She started drinking when I was very young. By the time I got older, I didn't realize she had become an alcoholic. I thought that was just the way she was." His head gradually slumped downwards as he said in an almost inaudible whisper, "She loved me the best she knew how."

Regaining his composure, Dylan continued. Dad tried to make the best out of a bad situation, but mom with all her problems, and me with mine – well let's face it – we were sometimes just more than he could handle; the perfect example of a dysfunctional family.

When I first landed in prison, mom sent me a few letters. She told me not to write back. She said dad would get mad if the postman saw letters coming from a prison to our house. After a while, mom stopped writing. I thought she gave up on me too. I didn't know that she had died. It makes me sick to think I couldn't even attend her funeral. They tell me she died in a car accident. I don't know much more than that about her death. I wish I could have been there for her.

One thing's for sure, prison gives you a lot of time to re-evaluate your life. My youth was not a time I'm particularly proud of. I decided that if I ever got the chance, I would visit mom and dad and try to tell them how sorry I was for everything. To be honest, I just figured that would never happen and that I would end up dying in prison all alone."

Both Dylan and Savannah got very quiet. It was almost noon and Savannah knew that if Dylan was just getting out of prison, more than likely he had little or no money.

"Why don't we get something to eat?" she suggested. "It's my treat."

Dylan appeared a little embarrassed. "I am a little hungry," he said. "Once I get my feet back on the ground, maybe I can repay the favor."

"Don't worry about it," smiled Savannah. "I'm enjoying the company." With that, Savannah called the waitress over and they ordered lunch. During the course of their meal, Savannah asked Dylan, "Do you have any plans on what you're going to do now that you're out on your own?"

"I guess the first two things I need to do are to find a place to live, and try to find a job," Dylan replied.

"Do you think you might be interested in settling down in the New Roads area? I know a lot of people and I could put in a good word for you if you'd like."

"That would be great," replied Dylan, his voice reflecting relief. Since he learned of his father's death he was beginning to realize how limited his resources were.

"What type of work are you interested in?" asked Savannah.

"Any I can get," answered Dylan earnestly. "I'm sure when people find out I've been in prison, even if it wasn't my fault, it's not going to be easy to find employment."

"You might be surprised," answered Savannah. "I would think people would be more sympathetic towards you knowing that you had to serve time for something you didn't even do. Is there anything in particular that you like to do?"

"Well, I'm pretty good with electronics and computers. While I was in prison the guards used to bring me video games and other electronic gadgets to work on. After I fixed them they would give me a pack or two of cigarettes, which was as good as money in prison."

"Electronics," mumbled Savannah, as she methodically went through a list of places in her mind where she thought Dylan might be able to find employment. "Tell you what," she began. "Why don't you come and stay a while with me until you can get your own place? I have a large home with plenty of spare bedrooms."

"Are you sure you don't mind?" Dylan asked in disbelief.

"Not at all," she responded, surprising even herself.

CHAPTER 68

Dylan grabbed his meager belongings, now stuffed in a Winn Dixie bag, from under the table as he and Savannah got up to leave the restaurant. Once outside, his eyes got as big as saucers when he saw Savannah walk towards her Corvette.

"This is yours?" he asked in total awe.

"Yes," she replied. "Do you like Vettes?"

"Is the pope Catholic!" he exclaimed. "Jeeze, I'm sorry," he said. "I just mean this is a dynamite car!"

"That's all right," she replied while laughing out loud. "I love it too." Savannah remembered when Mike first saw her Corvette on the showroom floor at Brockhoeft's Chevrolet in Grosse Tete. Mike asked John, "How do you get into this thing? It's so low to the ground." Then he asked, "Savannah, why in the world would you want a car like this?"

She had wanted to say, *"If you have to ask a question like that, you could never understand the answer."* It pleased Savannah that Dylan appreciated her car. "You know your dad had a tendency to lean towards the more extravagant conventional cars. Even though he wasn't extremely tall, he still had to practice learning how to get his legs into my car."

Dylan laughed at the thought of his ultra conservative dad riding in a Vette.

Once they were on the road, Savannah lifted her cell phone from her purse and called Betty. "Betty, this is Savannah. I decided to take the rest of the day off. Would you mind closing up for me this afternoon?"

"Sure," Betty replied, sounding a little apprehensive. "Is everything all right?"

"Yes, everything's fine. I'll see you tomorrow. Okay?"

"Okay, she said, with some reservation. You take care."

Savannah dropped her cell phone back into her purse. "Have you been through downtown New Roads?" Savannah asked Dylan.

"No. I've never been in New Roads before."

"My office is on the right up ahead. I'll point it out to you as we pass," Savannah continued. "Tomorrow I have to go into the office for a few minutes. When I get through, I'll give you a tour of the town if you like, and while we're out, I'll introduce you to some of my friends."

"Another thing you may need to know," said Dylan sheepishly, "I don't have a high school diploma. I did get my G.E.D. though. My buddy said that stands for 'Good Enough Diploma.'"

Savannah broke out laughing uncontrollably. When she finally regained her composure she said, "No Dylan, I think that stands for General Equivalency Diploma."

"Good," he replied. "I thought it was a joke, but I wasn't really sure."

"It was a joke," Savannah assured him as she wiped tears from her eyes.

"I'm not sure anybody is going to want to hire me with as little experience and education as I have," Dylan added more seriously.

"Well, let's not worry about that tonight."

Savannah's head was spinning. What had she gotten herself into?

CHAPTER 69

From downtown New Roads, it was only a matter of minutes before Savannah was turning into the driveway of her home. The white stone rock driveway glistened as the sun bounced off its multi-faceted sides. Manicured grass fed into the liriope that lined both sides of the driveway.

Hidden among the trees and beautifully landscaped yard, there stood a huge two-story Louisiana Plantation home. Thick white columns rose from the bottom of the first floor to the top of the second floor. A wide outside balcony the length of the front of the house led into bedroom doorways on the second floor.

The massive back yard included an oversized, intricately designed, swimming pool. A large pond could be seen in the distance where the back yard trailed off into a wooded area.

"This is beautiful," Dylan said approvingly.

After Savannah parked the car, she saw Tony in the back yard and called out to him. As he approached them Savannah said, "Tony, I want you to meet ..." There was a slight moment of hesitation before she continued. "... Mike's son, Dylan." For the first time, Savannah realized she had to come to grips with who Dylan was, or said he was. "Dylan's going to be staying with us for a while," said Savannah.

"Nice to meet you Dylan," Tony said as he reached his hand out to shake Dylan's.

"Same here," Dylan came back.

"I hope you enjoy your stay," replied Tony in his usual friendly manner. "If there's anything I can do for you while you're here, just let me know."

Savannah could just imagine how shocked Tony must have been, but to his credit he never let on. "Tony's our groundskeeper," Savannah told Dylan. "He lives in the cabin at the back end of our property."

Dylan envied Tony's strong looking physique and incredible tan. He wondered how close Savannah and Tony really were. After all, he thought, she was probably closer in age to Tony than to Mike. Savannah was obviously a very attractive and wealthy woman, and Tony definitely was a good-looking man on all counts.

Interrupting Dylan's thoughts, Savannah asked, "Tony, I'm getting ready to throw something together for dinner tonight. "Would you like to join us?"

"Thanks for the offer Ms. Savannah, but I've still got a lot of work to do before I call it a day," smiled Tony. He turned and went back to picking up branches in the yard. Tony stayed to himself most of the time, but on those rare occasions when he did invite friends over, he usually brought them by to meet Mike and Savannah. Savannah had always thought that Mike looked on Tony as if he were his own son. It seemed impossible to her that this was the same man that denied Dylan's very existence.

Once they were settled inside, Savannah invited Dylan to go through Mike's closet to see if there was anything in it that he might be able to wear. He selected a few items and then went upstairs to one of the guest rooms to get cleaned up and changed.

Savannah changed into some comfortable jeans and a pull over top and made her way back into the kitchen to prepare dinner.

By the time Dylan came back downstairs, Savannah had put on a pot of spaghetti and taken out the spaghetti sauce Mary had made and frozen for just such occasions. The spicy aroma from the spaghetti sauce began to drift through the house, but it wasn't until Dylan walked into the kitchen that he got his first good whiff.

"Boy, that smells good," he said grinning from ear to ear.

When Savannah looked up she was overwhelmed by how incredibly handsome he was. She had thought that before — even with his scruffy beard, long hair, and grungy clothes. But now, after getting cleaned up and shaved, with his wet hair hanging down almost to his shoulders, he was downright gorgeous. That was probably not the right word to use for a man, but handsome just didn't seem to get it.

"I'm fixing some spaghetti and a salad. How does that sound to you?" Savannah asked.

"Sounds great!" Dylan said with wholehearted approval.

Savannah was relieved that he was not a finicky eater. *"I guess he couldn't be in prison,"* she thought. She wondered if there would ever be a time when she would be able to forget about Dylan's stint in prison.

"Why don't you put the spaghetti and salad on the table while I get the French bread out of the oven?" As she opened the oven, the smell of garlic mixed with butter atop the warm toasted bread filled the room. Savannah had loved to cook for Mike when they first got married, but that seemed so long ago. With their busy schedules she had to eventually turn the cooking over to Mary.

At the dinner table, Savannah and Dylan laughed and talked until long after the last of the spaghetti had been eaten and they had gone through several glasses of red wine. When the leftovers were finally put away, both Dylan and Savannah decided they would make it an early night.

Upstairs, Dylan turned on the television set in his room and pulled off his jogging suit. He pulled back the quilted covers on the king size bed and sunk into the plush feather mattress. He was a grown man, but he had never known the feeling of happiness that he was experiencing this first night in his departed father's home. There was a sense of belonging that was completely foreign to him. If everything fell apart tomorrow, and he was tossed out into the streets once again, it would have all been worth it to live like this for one night.

For the first time in years, Dylan prayed, "Thanks God. Maybe you are up there after all." With that, he fell into a deep slumber.

Savannah took a long hot bath. She had dimmed the bathroom lights and had put her leftover glass of wine on the inset of the Jacuzzi. With the jets spewing out warm bubbles of water all over her already smooth and silky skin she felt her body relax. Whether it was the wine, or the pleasant conversation, she wasn't sure.

Having Dylan show up in her life at this time could be a good omen of things to come, she thought. She didn't know how long she would be comfortable with him living here, but she didn't have to decide everything tonight.

CHAPTER 70

"I can't believe it's already seven-thirty," Savannah said, more to herself than out loud. "I can't remember the last time I slept this late. I wonder if Dylan's up yet."

She jumped out of bed, quickly dressed, and quietly slipped into the kitchen. The coffee had just finished brewing when Dylan walked in. "Good morning," said Savannah with a smile.

"Good morning," Dylan replied. "Were you up early, or did I sleep late?"

Savannah began to laugh. "Don't worry, I just got up too. I think we probably both needed the sleep. I thought today, if you're up to it, I'd take the day off and see if we can't find you some new clothes. If you're going to be looking for a job, you'll need to look the part," said Savannah lightheartedly.

"I really appreciate everything you're doing for me, Savannah. As soon as I can find a job, I'm going to figure out a way to start paying you back."

"Well, let's not worry about that right now. Let's just take things one step at a time. First on the agenda, we need to run by my office so I can take care of some business. Then I want to take you around town so you can get a chance to meet some of the local townspeople.

If you like, we could stop by the barber shop and see if Clipper has time to give you a haircut. Most of the business people here are pretty conservative. You might have better luck looking for a job if your hair were just a little shorter."

Dylan started laughing. "Ahh, the perfect politician – trying to get me to do something without hurting my feelings. It's all right

Savannah. I already knew I needed a haircut."

They both broke into laughter. Then Savannah continued, "Okay smart guy. After that we can go shopping for clothes and shoes. Does that sound better?"

"Sounds to me like you're going to waste your whole day on me," said Dylan with a flirtatious grin.

"It'll be my pleasure," responded Savannah.

As promised, their first stop was a quick visit to the office. When Savannah walked in with Dylan around eight-thirty, a deafening silence filled the room. Savannah realized that Betty must have told Jim and Macy about Dylan's call the day before, and she assumed they must have been talking about it when she walked in with Dylan this morning. "Good morning," said Savannah, obviously in an upbeat mood. "I'd like for y'all to meet my stepson, Dylan."

Betty's jaw dropped open, and for the first time since Savannah had known her, she appeared speechless. Savannah continued, "Dylan, this is Mrs. Cormier, she's our sweetheart of a receptionist."

Trying to recover from the initial shock of learning that this was Mike's son, Betty replied, "Just call me Ms. Betty. Mrs. Cormier sounds too formal."

"Yes m'am, Ms. Betty," Dylan replied.

"And this is Macy and Jim, two of the best real estate agents in the country. The only one that can top them is me," Savannah laughed.

"Pleased to meet you both," responded Dylan as he shook their hands.

Savannah was delighted to see Macy's eyes light up when she met Dylan.

Macy smiled broadly and extended her hand. "Gollee Savannah, I never knew you had such a good looking stepson. You've been holding out on us," she said in a flirtatious manner.

Dylan smiled sheepishly, obviously more than just a little embarrassed.

Savannah laughed out loud and thought jokingly, "*you shameless little hussy.*"

Jim shook hands and gave the customary, "Nice to meet you Dylan," greeting.

Savannah took Dylan on a tour of the small office, and once inside her private office she realized there were several messages on her desk that she needed to take care of. "Dylan, you might want to go get a cup of coffee in the break room while I return some of these calls. It shouldn't take me too long," she said apologetically.

"Sure," he responded as he turned and left the room.

In less than a minute, Savannah could hear Dylan, Jim, Macy, and Betty laughing hysterically in the outside office. She expected Betty and Macy to get along with Dylan, but was a little surprised when Jim joined in. He was usually all business around strangers, but today he seemed to be enjoying another man's company in the office. It never dawned on Savannah, that since Mike died, Jim was now the only man in their small office.

Today was like old times – "good" old times with all the laughter and chatter.

Savannah's first returned call was to Gilbert Mouton, a wealthy cattle farmer. Gilbert was getting up in age, and with no sons to help him out, his wife had finally talked him into selling a large portion of his land. This was the property Mike had showed to James Maxwell.

"Hi, Gilbert," Savannah began. "I'm sorry it's taken me so long to get back with you. I wanted to let you know that Mike showed your property to a man from Shreveport and he is definitely interested in it. "

"Sha, I wasn't trying to rush you, no," said Gilbert. "I just thought I'd check in with you to see what was going on. You know I'm not crazy about the idea of selling my property anyway, but Mary Louise's been after me to either retire or at least cut back on how much I do. I don't like to admit it, but she's probably right. The old grey mare, he ain't what he used to be," mocked Gilbert. "Besides, even if I sell off what we talked about, I'll still have more than enough to keep me busy."

Savannah remembered Mike's excitement at the prospect of show-ing Gilbert's property to James. She also recalled how pleased Mike was that James had taken an instant liking to the beautiful and vastly wooded area. Now Savannah would be responsible for closing the deal that Mike had worked so hard to bring to fruition. It left her in a tre-mendously melancholy mood.

"Mr. Maxwell is looking for land to develop and Mike thought he would really be impressed with your property. That was the weekend Mike's plane crashed, and I haven't talked with Mr. Maxwell about it since then. However, I'm sure he is still interested. I'll give him a call back and see if he's ready to sign a purchase agreement. I'll let you know as soon as I hear anything.

By the way, how's Mary Louise doing? I heard she has a new cook-book coming out."

Gilbert said, "Yeah. I wish she'd quit trying out all those new recipes on me. I bet I've gained 60 pounds since she's been writing cookbooks. I'm gonna have to start working out again."

Savannah giggled. The thought of the heavy set 68 year old Gilbert working out was more than her mind could fathom.

"Well, tell her I said hi," Savannah responded.

"Will do," replied Gilbert, and then like so many others added, "We're really going to miss Mike. If you need anything at all, you give us a call, you hear?"

Even though he couldn't see her, Savannah gently nodded her head and answered, "Thanks Gilbert. I will."

Savannah knew she should call James Maxwell, but just didn't have her heart in it. *"I'll call back later,"* she thought. *"Gilbert didn't really sound like he was in a hurry and James is aware of the circumstances here."* The re-mainder of the messages she gave to Jim on her way out of the office. "I'm taking off the rest of the day," she reported. "If you need me, just give me a call."

CHAPTER 71

Savannah knew that finding a job in New Roads would be difficult for Dylan. With as little experience as he had in any one particular line of work, and as few available jobs as there were in the surrounding area, she felt certain he would have to go to Baton Rouge to find employment. And even then, it would not be easy. Still, he had been out every day since he arrived, putting in applications. When she left for work the following Wednesday, Dylan left for another day of job hunting.

Savannah had been working on her computer at the office all morning when she noticed the light on her phone start to blink. Betty's cheery voice on the phone's intercom system broke the silence. "Line 1 is for you."

"Thanks, Betty," responded Savannah.

Pressing the crimson blinking light she answered, "Devereaux Real Estate, Savannah Devereaux speaking."

"Senator Devereaux, this is Joe Granger over at the power plant. Your stepson, Dylan, has filled out an application with us and I'm just checking his references. Would you like to say anything on his behalf?"

Savannah was thrilled. "It's good to hear from you Joe. I appreciate your call. I'm sure that Dylan has probably told you that we are really just now getting acquainted. He's Mike's son, but I never had the opportunity to meet him before. From the short time we've spent together though, I believe that Dylan would be a real asset wherever he goes to work. He tries hard to please people and is anxious to do whatever he can to help out. I have no trouble at all recommending him for any position that you may have open."

"That's all I wanted to know, Senator. I think we may have a position for him as soon as we get the drug test and background check completed."

"That would be terrific, Joe. Thanks so much." Savannah wondered if Dylan had said anything to Joe about being in jail. She decided it was not her place to mention it.

In less than five minutes, Savannah received a call from Dylan. "Savannah, guess what?" he sputtered. "I got a job. Mr. Granger just called me and asked me to come in to fill out some paperwork and get set up for a drug test. I'm on my way over there now."

"That's great, Dylan," she said. "Good luck."

When Savannah arrived at home that evening the lights in the house were on. Dylan was sitting in the living room watching television. When he heard Savannah come in the back door, he immediately jumped up and rushed into the kitchen to meet her.

"Well, how'd it go?" she asked, smiling at Dylan.

"It looks like I may have a job. I told Mr. Granger about my past, but his call to you helped me secure the job. Thanks, Savannah."

"I'm glad I could help, Dylan. What are you going to be doing, and when do you start?"

"I'll be a lineman in training. He wants me to go in tomorrow to finish filling out paperwork and if everything works out all right I may be able to start as early as next Monday.

I know it's asking a lot, Savannah," he continued, "but if it's not too big a problem for you, I was wondering if it would be all right if I could stay here and use dad's truck to get back and forth to work, just until I can get my own place and my own vehicle. Once I start getting a paycheck, I'll begin paying you back for everything. Just tell me how much I owe you, and I'll give you money every payday until I pay you back. It may take me a while, but I'll do it."

"Of course you can stay here as long as you need to, Dylan," Savannah said. "I'm so happy for you. And don't worry about using

Mike's truck. I'm not using it right now anyway. Just be careful."

Secretly she was happy to have Dylan at home with her. He reminded her so much of Mike. It was lonely since Mike died, and the house had seemed cold and empty. Dylan made Savannah feel like she had a family again.

CHAPTER 72

Friday afternoon, Savannah called Mary and asked her what she was fixing for dinner. When Mary told her, Savannah surprised her by asking if she would like to join Dylan and her for dinner. The dinner was delicious and the conversation was lively and upbeat. Dylan and Mary seemed to thoroughly enjoy each other's company.

Savannah, Dylan, and Mary had no sooner finished dinner and Dylan gone outside to walk Mary to her car, than the phone rang. Savannah didn't recognize the number on the caller I.D., but answered anyway.

"Is this Savannah Devereaux?" the caller asked.

"Yes it is," replied Savannah in a questioning tone.

"This is Brian. I was a good friend of Mike's. Unfortunately I was out of the country when he passed away, and I just recently found out about his death. I wanted to express my sincerest condolences to you."

"Thank you so much. I still have a hard time believing he's gone," Savannah said while trying to hold back the tears.

"Mrs. Devereaux, I have been working on a very important and highly confidential project with Mike for quite some time now. I think that in light of his death, it is equally important for you to be aware of this information. I'll only be in town for the weekend, so I wanted to know if it would it be possible for us to meet this evening?"

"A project … ?" questioned Savannah. "What kind of a project?"

"I'd rather not discuss it on the phone, if you don't mind. Mike had asked me to research some issues you were concerned about in the legislature. I was supposed to meet with him and go over everything I found out. It may take a little while for us to discuss."

"Well, you're more than welcome to come by my house if you'd like."

"Are you alone?" asked Brian.

"What a strange question," thought Savannah. "My stepson is here," she replied. "Why do you ask?"

"Stepson?" questioned Brian in a surprised tone.

"Yes, he just recently moved to Ventress and is staying with me for a while."

"Mrs. Devereaux ..."

"Please call me Savannah," she quickly jumped in.

"Thank you, Savannah. As I was saying I'd be glad to stop by your home, but the information I have is highly confidential and I can't discuss it with anyone else around. Would it be possible for you to meet with me at Jim's Place instead? Do you know where that is?"

"Yes, I remember going there when I was campaigning."

"I'm over here now and I won't keep you long tonight, but I do think it's imperative that we talk. Also, it would probably be best if you don't mention my name to your stepson. I know this must all sound like the old cloak and dagger routine, but I'll be able to explain everything to you when we meet. "

Savannah hesitated for a moment and then replied, "It'll take me about fifteen minutes to get there."

"Thank you. I'll see you then."

Savannah could hear Mary driving her car down the driveway when Dylan came back in. "Dylan, I need to run out for a little while. I shouldn't be too long. Why don't you see if you can find a good show on television or a video in the cabinet to watch? There's ice cream in the freezer if you'd like some. If I'm not back when you get ready for bed, don't worry about waiting up for me. You know where everything is, so just make yourself at home."

"Nothing's wrong, is it?" asked Dylan.

"No, everything's fine," Savannah replied. "I just have some business I need to take care of." Savannah went into her bedroom and picked up her purse and car keys. On the way back she passed through the living room where Dylan was sitting. When he looked up, she playfully called out, "See you later, alligator."

Dylan grinned broadly and replied, "After while, crocodile."

"*Ahh*," she thought, "*he knows the lingo.*"

CHAPTER 73

"What am I doing?" Savannah asked herself. "I'm on my way to meet a complete stranger in a bar – by myself – at night. I'm just not like this. This is insane. Whatever made me agree to this?" As she drove up to Jim's Place, her nervousness intensified. What would people think if someone saw her in a bar with another man this soon after Mike's death? Bad idea or not, it was too late to back out now.

It was Friday night, and the small parking lot was packed. Savannah noticed that the majority of vehicles were pick-up trucks. The tail-lights of someone leaving caught her attention. Moving quickly, she was able to maneuver her car into the spot they had just vacated close to the front door of the building.

After parking her car she reached into her purse for some paper and a pen. Then she began to feverishly write: "I am on my way to meet a man named Brian at Jim's Place. He has some information to give me that he said he put together for Mike." Then she took the note and stuffed it under the seat of her car. *"At least if anything happens to me, maybe the police will search my car and find the note,"* she thought. Whether it would do any good or not was another matter. She couldn't even be positive that the man's name was really Brian.

When she walked into the jam-packed bar it took a moment for her eyes to adjust. The grappling darkness that surrounded her was intensified by the thick blending haze of cigarette smoke. Several people congregated around the only pool table in the room, while a few others played on one of the three video poker machines at the far end of the bar.

The card table close to the front door sat empty.

To the right of the door was the long wooden counter top of the bar; set off by the eleven tall weather beaten bar stools pushed up against it. Making an abrupt turn to the right, three additional stools were firmly planted against the far short end of the bar. Almost every bar stool was filled tonight.

There were large colored light bulbs that lined the top of the bar from one end to the other. Against the wall was a menu board surrounded by small white lights. Below the menu, on the back counter, was an assortment of liquor bottles filled to varying degrees and waiting to be poured into the next set of glasses.

Ceiling fans hung over the long narrow area where the two bartenders, one an exceptionally striking woman with red hair, the other a short, thin, middle aged man, hustled back and forth trying to keep the regulars supplied with their favorite drinks.

Two television sets were positioned high on the wall on each end of the bar with captions being displayed as the programs played. Playing on the set that caught Savannah's attention was the television show, "Cops." The words to the song being played ran across the bottom of the screen ... "*Bad boys, bad boys, what you gonna do when they come for you?*" Against the wall opposite the bar, the juke box was playing some country music.

There was a large hand printed sign standing against the bar that read: Crawfish for sale $25 a sack. Once Savannah's eyes began to focus more clearly, she realized that except for the attractive red headed bartender, there were very few women in the bar.

As she glanced around the room, she saw a single table in the far left corner. There was a man sitting alone who appeared to be watching her. Hesitantly she walked towards him. He stood up as she approached the table. Trying to raise his voice above the sound of the music without actually yelling, he said, "Good evening, Savannah." As he held out his hand to shake hers, he went on to say, "I'm Brian."

Savannah shook his hand and smiled, "Hi Brian."

Brian was not what Savannah had expected. But then again, she didn't really know what she had expected. He was much taller than Mike, probably around 6'1". He looked as if he might have played football in his earlier years. While he wasn't an exceptionally handsome man, he had a kind face and blue eyes that seemed to sparkle even in the dark.

They shook hands and Brian continued, "Perhaps you would be more comfortable sitting at one of the tables on the back porch where it's not quite as noisy."

Savannah was relieved to be distancing herself from the staring eyes. "That would be fine," she said."

Brian picked up his drink and they both walked outside.

CHAPTER 74

The night air had just a hint of a breeze and it was much easier to talk without the music blaring in their ears. The waitress came out and after the normal pleasantries asked, "What can I get for y'all?"

Brian turned to Savannah and asked, "Would you like something to eat?"

"No, thank you. We had just finished dinner when you called."

"How about a drink?" he suggested.

"Sure, that would be nice." Savannah wasn't much of a drinker so she added, "I'll just have whatever you're having."

Brian smiled awkwardly and said, "I was just going to have another beer."

Savannah laughed and said, "That's fine with me. Just make mine light."

Looking up at the waitress Brian said, "We'll have two more (and he held up his beer); a light for the lady and high octane for me."

The waitress smiled and said "Coming up," and then headed back inside. As soon as their waitress was out of earshot, Savannah turned to Brian and asked, "Brian, please forgive me, but I don't remember Mike every mentioning your name before. Where are you from?"

"Oh, I'm sorry Savannah. I go by Brian in business dealings, but Mike and all my friends back in Shreveport always called me Tracy. Sometimes I forget who I'm talking with."

"Tracy," said Savannah with a relieved look on her face. "Of course I know who you are. Mike spoke about you often. You're the one he went to see in Shreveport that introduced him to James Maxwell."

"That's right," said Brian who was now smiling broadly. "I'm sorry about the confusion. I should have said Tracy to begin with. When I was young I wanted to be a detective like Dick Tracy, so all my friends started calling me Tracy. For some reason, it just stuck. You can call me whatever you like," Tracy grinned."

"Thanks," said Savannah, eager to continue. "But now, would you tell me what's so secretive that we couldn't meet at my house to discuss it?"

"Savannah, Mike and I have been good friends for a long time. We went to school together and even enlisted in the service at the same time. He ended up as a pilot. I ended up as a foot soldier. But that was many years ago. When we eventually both returned from the service we met up again. We confided in each other on some very important matters. Do you remember during the campaign when you got that strange call telling you and Mike to stay out of things that didn't concern you?"

"Yes," said Savannah a little startled. "Mike told you about that?"

"You thought the phone call was connected to the shady dealings regarding the hurricanes and the Louisiana legislature," continued Tracy.

"Wasn't it?" asked Savannah with a puzzled look on her face.

"Actually … no. Savannah, for the time being, none of what I tell you can be revealed to anyone else. If it is, you and I both may suffer some grave consequences."

"What do you mean?" asked Savannah, suddenly disturbed by Tracy's choice of words.

"I'm not sure where to start. Mike and I discussed your running for Senator. He was worried that if you became a political figure, your life might be in danger because of what he knew. He wanted to tell you what was going on, but he was afraid if he did it might endanger your life. During our last conversation, Mike made me promise that if anything ever happened to him, I would tell you everything. He also asked me to beg your forgiveness for keeping a secret from you. He had hoped he could take care of it and move on without ever getting you involved.

When I heard about Mike I came as soon as I could. I know how much he loved you, Savannah. No one can ever deny that. I also knew that I had to carry out his last wish and tell you everything. I'm sorry it's come to this."

CHAPTER 75

Tracy grew increasingly uncomfortable in his chair. His fingers traced over the label on his beer that was beginning to warm in the bottle in his hand. "This will come as a shock to you Savannah," he started, "but Mike has been working as an undercover agent for the CIA since before you were married. He began during the Al Collins drug smuggling investigation."

"No way," laughed Savannah out loud. "You've got to be kidding. Mike?"

"I'm afraid so Savannah," said Tracy with a disturbed look on his face.

"You're talking about the Central Intelligence Agency – that CIA?" responded Savannah sarcastically. "I doubt anyone who lives in Ventress, Louisiana would be involved in something as multifaceted as the CIA."

"Where do you think they get all their undercover agents?" asked Tracy adamantly. "They want people that no one would suspect, and Mike was perfect. When they first enlisted him he was married, had a child, was very wealthy, did a tremendous amount of traveling, and for all practical purposes, was his own boss. He could come and go as he pleased and no one would be the wiser, not even his own family."

"I can't believe this," said Savannah, suddenly disturbed over the strange turn of events. "Why would Mike be involved with the CIA – and why with Al Collins? Wasn't Al Collins the one from Baton Rouge who was involved with a major drug operation?"

"Yes. Mike met Al in Baton Rouge at a Civil Air Patrol meeting shortly after graduating from LSU. They seemed to take an instant liking to each other and soon became close friends. Al was a little older than Mike, and for Mike I think it started out as a form of hero worship. After Mike went back to Shreveport they kept in touch with each other. Every time Mike went to Baton Rouge he made a point of getting together with Al. Al did the same when he went to Shreveport.

Then in the early 1980s, the CIA contacted Mike. They told him that it was imperative that they meet with him on a matter of national security. Of course Mike had no idea what they were talking about.

During a CIA investigation it was discovered that Mike and Al were good friends. When the special agent in charge met with Mike, he told Mike that they suspected Al Collins of being involved in smuggling drugs for the Contras. The CIA wanted Mike to infiltrate Al's business enterprise and find out if he was using it as a front for his drug smuggling operation. If his findings proved them right, they wanted Mike to collect evidence for them.

Of course Mike didn't believe them. He was outraged that they would think he would even consider getting involved in such a diabolical plot aimed at discrediting his friend. But when the feds decide they need your help, they don't give up.

Their first endeavor to get Mike to work with them was subtle enough. They asked for his help. When he refused, their persuasive tactics became more forceful, until finally they turned up the heat on Mike. They told him that if he didn't do what they asked, they would turn their focus on his business and personal life. They would leave no stone unturned. Anything and everything he had ever done wrong, no matter how inconsequential, would be brought to light.

Mike wasn't concerned about himself, but he was worried about Christine and Dylan. Christine was beginning to have problems with alcohol and Mike secretly worried that she might be getting involved with drugs as well. He knew he had to protect her. With that in mind, he finally agreed to help them as long as they promised that his family would never be the target of any investigation. In fact, he was so sure they were wrong about Al that he agreed to take the lead as an undercover agent in what was fast becoming their top covert operation. He was determined to prove Al's innocence."

Tracy stopped talking as the waitress returned with their drinks. He paid her and she left. Then he continued.

"As it turned out, Al was in deep. The information Mike gathered was going to be used to help issue an arrest warrant for him. That was hard on Mike. He wanted nothing more to do with the CIA. He worried that if it ever leaked out he had been involved, something might happen to Christine or Dylan. It's a well known fact that when you get involved with drug lords, anything and everything is fair game."

"Why didn't he get out after their investigation was over?" asked Savannah nervously.

"It's not that easy. Their investigation never seemed to be over. The CIA kept insisting on additional information in their attempt to build cases against everyone involved. Dylan was still young at the time, but he was beginning to have his own set of problems. Mike wasn't sure he could count on the CIA to leave Dylan alone.

I know it may sound paranoid, but you have no idea of what the government can do to you. They can turn your life upside down if you fail to cooperate, and believe me, once they do you will never be able to get it straightened out again. Your life is no longer your own once you enter their system. Mike kept receiving untraceable calls from the CIA demanding more and more data on Al's operations. They knew he was invaluable. No one knew all the background on the case like Mike did, and if they were going to be able to rein in Al, it was imperative that they have Mike onboard.

All the while this was going on, Mike continued to tell Christine he was going on business trips. He hated lying to her, but he couldn't afford to take a chance on any slip-ups."

"Did Christine ever find out?" asked Savannah hastily.

"No. I think Christine went to her death thinking that Mike had been cheating on her, and that his trips out of state were to see another woman. The sad part is that I've never known anyone more totally devoted than Mike. When he makes a promise to someone, his word is as good as gold. He loved Christine, he loved Dylan, and he loved you. I always thought it would have been easier on Mike if Christine had known. But that's another story."

"What about you, Tracy? How did you get mixed up in all of this?" asked Savannah.

"I found out what was going on strictly by accident. Mike would have never drawn me into all of this if it had been up to him. He didn't want to get anyone else involved, but when I confronted Mike with what I knew, he decided to confide in me. He had no doubt that he could trust me. We've been around the block a few times together, if you know what I mean."

"Yes, I think I do." replied Savannah thoughtfully.

Suddenly a cool breeze drifted through the air and Savannah and Tracy sat in silence.

CHAPTER 76

Savannah could see the pensive look on Tracy's face and knew he was trying to decide on how to continue. "I see you wear a wedding ring. Didn't your wife ever get suspicious or wonder what was going on?" asked Savannah.

"My wife and I are separated. We just never could seem to get it together. We've gone back and forth so many times, but I think this time it's for good. She wants a divorce."

"I'm so sorry," said Savannah.

"Yeah, well sometimes that's just the way it goes. I guess I wasn't that great a prize anyway. Who knows?" he said as he shrugged his shoulders. Quickly changing back to the subject at hand, Tracy continued, "At any rate, Mike was considered one of the CIA's best agents until about ten years ago."

"What happened then?" asked Savannah, now spellbound by Tracy's revelations.

"That's when Al was indicted in Florida for smuggling Quaaludes and laundering money. When Al realized he was about to be sentenced to an extended prison term, he entered into a plea bargain with the CIA in which he agreed to organize an undercover sting operation. It was a tremendous success. Because of Al, during the next few years the Feds were able to get some very serious criminal convictions. Some major drug lords were among those arrested.

After the arrests, the judge reduced Al's lengthy prison sentence to six months probation. A lot of people got upset about that. To make matters worse, the judge commended Al for his work against the Sandinistas and ignored the fact that he had been a drug smuggler himself. Just like the judge, we all thought Al was on his way to turning his life around. Mike was so relieved that everything was starting to work out for him, and even more thankful that his friend never knew of his involvement in the case brought against him.

Unfortunately, shortly after Al's probation was up, he got arrested here in Louisiana for flying in a cargo of marijuana. He was released on a half a million dollar bond. At first we thought Al might have reverted to his old ways and was back into dealing drugs. Then we heard from other sources that he was still working as an informant for the feds. At that point, even Mike and I were baffled. It got hard to tell who the good guys were. When Al had to appear before a federal judge in Baton Rouge for his current charges, he was found guilty of two felony drug convictions.

The rumor is that Judge Barlow was told by the CIA that Al was not to be given jail time because of his cooperation as an informant for the government. Judge Barlow was furious. He had fought for years trying to get rid of the drug traffickers, and all of the sudden he was being told that he had to let Al go with probation.

Judge Barlow did as they told him and sentenced Al to six months of supervised probation. But he also tacked on an added condition to Al's probation. He had to report in at the Salvation Army halfway house on Airline Highway every night at six p.m. He was required to spend the night there, and could not leave before six a.m. the next morning.

A Baton Rouge newspaper ran a feature story about Al, giving the conditions of his probation. When Mike saw the article he immediately called Al. Al was adamant that he was being set-up. After the story ran in the paper, he said he was like a sitting duck. Every person that wanted to get even with him now knew where he would be, and when he would be there. He told Mike that as a convicted felon he was not allowed to carry a gun or be around people with a gun. He argued that he had no way to protect himself.

Mike told Al that he would talk to people he knew and ask them to try to reason with Judge Barlow. When that didn't work, Mike called in every favor he could think of to try to help Al. The people he contacted at the CIA assured him they would take care of things.

But it was too late. The drug dealers knew Al had turned informant, and after the story broke in the news, they knew where he would be every evening. Two weeks after he had begun serving his probation, Al pulled into the Salvation Army parking lot, as usual, and parked his car. He had just started to get out when two men, one with a machine gun, drove by and started shooting at him. By the time the car drove out of sight, Al's body was torn to pieces by the force of the bullets.

When Mike found out what had happened, I thought he was going to fall apart. He blamed himself for Al's capture and eventual death. Many a time after that, he told me he wished he had never gotten involved with the investigation. He said he had betrayed a good friend, and he would never forgive himself for that."

"Oh, that's horrible," whispered Savannah, obviously distressed.

"Mike was determined to find out who killed Al," Tracy continued. "The word on the street was that it was a hit job. Mike knew it had to be, and wanted to find out who was responsible. I think he was on to something big, Savannah. I just don't know what.

Mike and I were working on a number of investigations together. We kept all our sensitive material in a strong box in my safe deposit box at the bank. Mike thought it would be safer there. He didn't think anyone would associate the two of us when it came to what we were actually working on. If they discovered he was investigating something, it would be highly unlikely they would connect it with me, and vice versa. We had two keys to my safe deposit box. Mike kept one and I had the other.

When Mike came to Shreveport, he told me that if anything happened to him he wanted me to do two things for him. First, I was to give you access to the strong box with all the information we gathered. Mike said it not only contains documentation needed for convictions relative to corruption we uncovered in the state legislature, but also gives details about ongoing drug smuggling operations here in Louisiana. Two weeks before Mike died, he sent me his key in the mail. The note with it said, that if anything happened to him, I was to give it to you. I don't have a clue why he sent me his key," continued Tracy. "I was out of the country, and didn't get it until I returned. By then it was too late for me to call him. I brought the strong box with me. It's at the camp where I'm staying.

Whatever you decide though, Sanannah, it might be wise for me to take the box back with me after you've had time to look through its' contents. I can return it to my safe deposit box until you decide what you want to do with it."

"What was the second thing he asked for you to do?" asked Savannah as she solemnly placed the key in the change compartment of her wallet, and closed it.

"He was worried that if something happened to him, you may not be safe either. He wanted me to watch over you and protect you the best that I could. Savannah, no one knows all the things that I'm telling you now. If anyone finds out, I'm not sure how safe any of us will be," said Tracy, who was obviously agonizing over his doomsday prediction.

"I won't tell anyone until I know for sure what's going on," promised Savannah. "But if I uncover corruption in Louisiana, regardless of who is involved, or where it is discovered, as a legislator I will be morally bound to inform the authorities."

"I understand. One last thing ..." cautioned Tracy. "Mike and I found out that there is going to be a documentary on the FOX news channel next year that will include an in-depth look at drug smuggling cartels, and in particular, the life and death of Al Collins. We don't know how it happened, but Mike's name was leaked to an investigative reporter working on the documentary. He was listed as an undercover agent involved in the discoveries that led to Al's arrest. Mike had hoped after he talked to the reporter that his name would not be used, but just recently I found out that Mike had been under surveillance himself.

I'm not sure if it was the CIA or one of the drug cartels he infiltrated that was keeping tabs on him. That why, when I heard of Mike's death, I had to come and find out what happened and make sure you were all right."

"Mike died in a plane crash," responded Savannah, still in disbelief from everything she had just heard.

Tracy looked down at his beer as Savannah continued to watch him. He took a long swig, placed his beer bottle gently down on the table in front of him, and then stared at it for a moment. Finally, in somewhat of a whisper, he continued.

"I don't want to upset you any more than you already are, Savannah, but don't you find it strange that a man as knowledgeable and with as many hours in the air as Mike should suddenly have a plane crash in beautiful weather over the Potomac? We've flown together into that airport more times than I can remember. Mike never had a problem landing. And I know Mike is a fanatic about checking out his plane before he flies."

"What are you trying to say?" gasped Savannah.

"There are too many unexplained circumstances surrounding Mike's death. Why did he go to Washington instead of coming home as planned? Why did an experienced pilot with as many hours in the air as Mike had, crash going into an airport he was very familiar with on a beautiful day – no storms, no wind shears, nothing to hamper his flying?

Savannah, I think Mike's plane may have been tampered with," said Tracy cautiously.

CHAPTER 77

Savannah was still reeling from Tracy's statement that Mike's plane may have been tampered with, when he made another startling announcement. "Savannah, I hope I'm wrong about this, but it looks like you may have another issue that warrants checking into."

"What do you mean?" questioned Savannah, now feeling the effects of being completely drained from worry and confusion.

"As I mentioned before, I've known Mike for a long time and we've shared a lot together. I've never know him not to be truthful with me," began Tracy. "After Christine died, Mike indicated to me that Dylan had been in the car with Christine when she died. I've been wracking my brain for clues ever since you told me Dylan was at your house. I can't be positive that Mike told me outright that he was dead, or if I just assumed it from our conversation. I know it was talked about in hushed whispers among all his friends.

Christine was cremated, and her ashes buried. No one ever talked about Dylan after that, but some people said they thought Dylan's body may have been cremated too and buried with Christine's. Mike never had any other children that I know of."

"Oh, dear God!" cried Savannah. "This is just too much. I can't believe it. Tracy, the man at my house just has to be Mike's son, Dylan. He looks exactly like him. He has his eyes and his smile and even sounds like him."

"You don't think that maybe this young man might just be trying to take advantage of an obviously kind hearted woman at a time when she's most vulnerable?" asked Tracy.

Savannah hesitated for a split second. She had harbored some of the same thoughts when Dylan first contacted her. "I wondered at first, too," she said, "but once I saw him, I knew I couldn't deny him. He just **is** Mike. I mean, I do have to admit that I was surprised when he showed up," Savannah continued. "I never thought Mike and I held any secrets from each other. Then, all of the sudden, there's Dylan … and there's you … and there's Mike's hidden life…"

"Where does Dylan say he has been living all this time?" asked Tracy.

"He told me he had been in jail."

"Really? That surprises me. I'd think an imposter would say anything rather than admit that he had been in jail. I guess it's possible I'm wrong about Dylan, I just don't know. I'll do some more investigating if you'd like. In the meantime, please be careful about who you trust."

"Be careful about who you trust?" thought Savannah. *"What about you? I'm not even sure if you're who you say you are."*

"Tracy, please forgive me for asking, but if you were as close to Mike as you say, why haven't I met you at least once during the time we were married, and even more so, why didn't you come to our wedding."

"It's complicated Savannah. Mike and I had to be extremely cautious about everything we did. For a while we thought it best to only openly communicate with each other when absolutely necessary. I know this is a lot for you to take in all at once, and I don't blame you for doubting me. But if you will meet with me again tomorrow I will bring documents to prove everything I've been saying.

One of my friends is letting me use his camp on False River for the weekend and I left everything there. I have documents relating to the investigation conducted on Al as well as a myriad of other papers, tapes, and videos of sworn testimony outlining possible corruption charges and scandals associated with high officials in Louisiana and Washington. The discoveries we made are mind boggling."

Savannah sat speechless. It was too much information to internalize all at one time.

Tracy suspected that he had told Savannah enough for the night. "Savannah, I'm afraid I haven't been fair to you. Why don't we wait until tomorrow when we can meet again and I can go over everything with you in the light of day? It'll give you a chance to think about what I have told you and put together any questions you may have for me."

He reached into his pocket, pulled out his business card, and handed it to her. As Savannah took the card she read the logo at the top of the card: Handy Building Contractors – Brian Handy, Owner. The card also had a Shreveport address and phone number.

Savannah thought to herself, *"That probably gave Mike and Tracy the perfect excuse to get back in touch with each other. A contractor would definitely be interested in the state's housing problems."*

Tracy said, "My cell number is on the card. Please feel free to call me at any time."

"Thanks Tracy," Savannah said as she slipped his business card into her purse. Then, out of habit, she reached back into her purse and pulled out one of her business cards. "Here's one of my cards. If you need to get in touch with me, my cell number's on my card too."

"Thanks," he said, and quickly stuck the card in his wallet.

Savannah thought, as she began to divide her attention once more between Tracy and her warming drink, that Tracy had carried himself with an air of distinction throughout this whole ordeal. It must have been hard for him to tell her all of this. He had a kind face and small wrinkle lines at the edge of his eyes as if he smiled a lot during happier times. His face had taken on a much more serious look tonight.

After a few more moments and several more sips of her beer, Savannah and Tracy's talk turned less solemn and their discussions took on a lighter air. As they slid into mediocre chit-chat, Savannah replayed all the discussions they had just had back over in her head. *"Was there anything else she needed to ask Tracy?"*

"Oh yes. When did you say you were leaving to go back home, and where did you say you were staying?" Savannah asked.

"A friend of mine has a camp on False River. I'm going to take his boat out in the morning and do a little fishing. Do you like fish?"

"I love fish," Savannah said. "Mike and I used to go fishing together a lot …" she said as her voice began to betray her attempt to appear more positive and in control."

"I love fishing too," said Tracy. "If I do any good I'll give you a call. If you're free, you're welcome to come over for a fish fry. You can even bring the new stepson if you want," he said hesitantly.

"Thank you, Tracy," replied Savannah. "I guess I better get back home now." She didn't want Tracy to know that she had suddenly become a little leery of her new stepson. Even if he was who he said he was, it might be wise to be cautious about what she did and said in front of him until she was certain of his identity.

"It was good to finally get to meet you, Savannah. I'm sorry it was under these circumstances. I'll give you a call tomorrow, but please don't hesitate to call me at any time if you need me," he said.

As Savannah got up to leave, Tracy stood up as well. "Would you like for me to walk you to your car?"

"I appreciate the offer, but it's really not necessary. I'm parked right next to the front door." As an afterthought she added, "By the way, if you don't catch any fish tomorrow, give me a call anyway, and I'll see what I can throw together for us to eat at my house."

"I'll do that," he replied. "Thanks."

Savannah walked though the bar area and out into the hot muggy air. The humidity was terrible, and almost immediately she could feel beads of sweat starting to run down her body. She climbed into her Vette, fastened her seat belt, and turned on the ignition. The sudden blast of cool air was an instant reprieve from the stifling heat.

Immediately with the turn of her key, she heard the low rumble and the vibrations of her muscle car, reminding her of the power she held within her hands. Not much calmed Savannah like a ride in her

Corvette. The gentle continuous purr of the powerful engine hidden under the long sleek hood of her car, the radio belting out her favorite music, and always the stares from men, women, and children alike, gave her the feeling of being in total control. She loved it all.

She drove home slowly, enjoying the stillness and darkness of the outside combined with her favorite music on the inside. Even though her nervousness had subsided, her troubling thoughts jumped from one problem to another. *"Should I question Dylan about the issues Tracy brought up, or just keep quiet for the time being?"* She finally decided, *"I'm not going to mention anything until I do some research on my own."*

Upon arriving at her house, Savannah pulled into the large garage in the back. There was Mike's black Hummer and his grey Silverado pickup truck still waiting for him. *"I guess eventually I'll have to sell at least one of these vehicles,* thought Savannah. *There's no sense in paying insurance for three vehicles when I can only drive one at a time."*

Still, the Hummer was so convenient when she needed to drive real estate clients around, and the truck was great when they had to pick up branches after a storm or drive in the fields. And her Vette – well there was no way she was parting with that.

CHAPTER 78

Dylan walked in the direction of the stairway leading to his bedroom. But before he reached the first step, his eyes caught sight of the open door to Savannah and Mike's bedroom. Curiosity aroused, he decided to take one more look through their bedroom.

The door to their enormous walk-in closet was wide open. The closet was divided in half, although clearly more than two-thirds of the space was filled with Savannah's belongings. The scant remaining room was left for Mike.

He had just begun rummaging through Mike's wardrobe when he heard the low rumble of Savannah's car.

"Oh great!" he thought. *"That's all I need: to have Savannah come in and find me going through her closet."* He immediately dashed out of her bedroom and bolted upstairs.

Savannah entered through the back door of the house, automatically turning and locking the door behind her. In the kitchen, she dropped her purse on the counter just long enough to fill her favorite wine glass.

With glass in hand, she picked up her purse and retreated to the sitting room in her bedroom. As soon as she was comfortable in her recliner, she began flipping through channels looking for a good show to watch. Nothing was on but *Law and Order*.

"Well that's about right," she thought. *"That seems to be the story of my life – always looking for some semblance of law and order."* She scooted back onto the soft oversized cushions in the large chair facing the television. Her legs curled up next to her body.

Mike's recliner sat empty next to hers. She leaned back against the padded pillows in her chair, as if once again she was waiting for him to join her. For a brief moment, it was as if he were still there with her. Before she knew it, she had drifted off to sleep with happier times on her mind.

CHAPTER 79

Savannah waited for Tracy's call all day Saturday. By late afternoon she decided it was time to give him a call. Immediately upon dialing the number, her call was directed to his voice mail. "Hi Tracy, this is Savannah. I'm surprised I haven't heard from you by now. I guess things didn't work out like you planned. I was thinking about taking Dylan to Satterfield's this evening for dinner, and was wondering if you'd like to join us.

If you come, please don't mention anything to Dylan about what we discussed last night. I need to find out what he knows before I say anything to him. Obviously I'm still upset about our discussion. I really need to talk with you. I just don't want to talk in front of Dylan. You have my number, so please give me a call as soon as you can. I can't stress how important it is to me that we talk again soon."

Savannah waited another hour before finally deciding that Tracy was not going to call back any time soon. Instead of inviting Dylan to go out to eat, she located some of Mary's frozen entrees in the freezer and fixed dinner for them at home.

All weekend long Savannah kept her cell phone with her, waiting for a call from Tracy. By Sunday evening, she was certain that something must be wrong. Even if he had decided to leave early, she felt sure he would have called to let her know. His business card indicated the office hours were from eight a.m. until five p.m. Monday through Friday.

By eight a.m. Monday morning, Savannah was calling Tracy's office.

"Handy Building Contractors," the cheery voice on the other end of the line answered. "This is Bonnie Brown. May I help you?

"Yes," replied Savannah rather curtly. "I'd like to speak with Mr. Handy please."

"Mr. Handy is not in. May I take a message for him?"

"This is Senator Devereaux. Mr. Handy was supposed to call me back on Saturday regarding some business we were discussing. I never heard from him, so I just wanted to make sure he was all right," Savannah replied.

"I'm not sure why he didn't get back with you Senator. He's usually very good about calling people back. Unfortunately, Mr. Handy is not expected back in the office for the next two weeks. He had airline tickets for Madrid, where he is about to bid on a major contracting deal. If you would like to leave your name and number, I'll be happy to give it to him the next time he checks in with the office."

"That's all right," said Savannah. "He has my number. He probably just got busy like you said. Thanks anyway." As they hung up, Savannah began to wonder about Tracy. At first she was worried about him, but after talking with his secretary she began to get irritated.

"If he can't call me back like he said he would before taking off for a two week stay in Madrid, then to heck with him. Now I'm beginning to wonder how much of what he said was really true. All of this is so strange. But he really seemed sincere. Why would he tell me all of the things he did, and then suddenly leave? What's happening to me? I don't even know who to believe any more. How could I have been so gullible? I feel so ridiculous for believing him.

Still . . . what about the key he gave me?"

CHAPTER 80

O ut of sight, out of mind. By the time Saturday rolled around again, Savannah had conveniently pushed thoughts of Tracy out of her mind. She had other more pressing matters at hand.

When she opened her closet door and saw Mike's clothes staring at her as they had done every day since his death, she knew it was time to do something. Savannah got some boxes from the garage and headed back to the bedroom. She had already given everything to Dylan that he could use. The rest she began lovingly folding and putting into the boxes. Without the constant reminders, she hoped she might eventually be able to start her life over again.

Though her vision was clouded by tears, she continued to check each pocket in Mike's clothing to make sure nothing was still in them before giving them away. It seemed like a waste of time. Mike had never been one to store things in his pockets. Lifting his black pin striped suit off the hanger Savannah reached into the coat pocket. To her surprise, she pulled out a piece of paper folded in half.

Hurriedly she opened it. There, in front of her, was a handwritten note that read, "*You can meet me the last Friday of this month at the address listed below anytime between 4:30 and 5:30 p.m. Don't worry if you end up running a little late. I'll wait for you until you get here. I think you will be pleased with what I have arranged. I look forward to seeing you again – Saundra.*"There was a Dallas address with a phone number scribbled under it. Savannah felt her heart start to race faster. "*I think you will be pleased with what I have arranged.*" "What do you mean?" demanded Savannah out loud, as if Saundra were in the room with her.

In her wildest dreams she could not imagine Mike being unfaithful to her. Even Tracy had said how Mike could be counted on to be true to his word. But then what did she really know about Tracy. Soon the words *"I look forward to seeing you again,"* began to burn a hole in her heart. She had to know who Saundra was.

Unexpectedly, Dylan knocked on her open bedroom door and then walked in. Savannah quickly slipped the paper into her pocket. "So here you are. I've been looking for you. What are you doing?" he inquired.

"Just packing away some things," she said. "I didn't know you were awake yet. Are you hungry?"

"Yeah, why don't I fix some breakfast while you finish up in here?" Dylan found himself growing increasingly fond of Savannah. He knew that this morning was probably a very trying time for her when he saw her packing away Mike's clothes in the boxes surrounding her on the floor. He wished he could help ease her pain, but he had never been good at small talk.

"Thanks Dylan," she said. As he walked out of the room she reached back into her pocket and pulled the paper out once more. She picked herself up off the floor and walked over to the small bedroom table that held her purse. Reaching into her bag, she quickly felt for the familiar shape of her cell phone, pulled it out, and immediately began dialing. It was answered on the second ring by a woman with a captivating voice.

"I'm sorry to bother you," Savannah said. "I must have the wrong number. To whom am I speaking?"

"Who are you trying to reach?" the quick reply came back.

"Rats!" thought Savannah. Trying desperately to think of another approach she said, "I have a paper with this phone number on it." She quickly read off the phone number.

"That's the number you got," came back the voice. "Who are you trying to reach?"

Finally, in desperation she said, "I'm calling regarding my husband,

Mike Devereaux."There was a long silence. Then the phone went dead.

"Well, I guess that was just about as dumb as it gets," thought Savannah. *"Of course no woman is going to talk to a man's wife when she calls her out of the clear blue like I just did."* Savannah called back again. This time the phone continued to ring. No one answered it.

"Don't worry Saundra," Savannah thought. *"You haven't heard the last of me. I am going to find out who you are — one way or another."* With that being said, she put the note back in her pocket, slipped into her flip flops and went to meet Dylan in the kitchen.

Dylan seemed to be having a great time preparing their breakfast. He had always loved cooking, and while in jail he used to imagine what it would be like to be a famous chef.

"I'm going to get as big as a house if I eat all this food," Savannah laughed.

"Yeah, like that's gonna happen," Dylan said with a teasing smirk on his face.

When breakfast was finished Savannah said, "Dylan, I have some things I need to give to Goodwill. Would you mind loading them up in the truck and taking them for me?"

After he carried the last of the boxes to the truck, and Savannah saw him pass by the window on the way down the driveway, Savannah's thoughts once again turned to Saundra. *"Why would she hang up on me?"* Savannah wasn't sure she really wanted to know the answer.

CHAPTER 81

Savannah pulled the note from Saundra out of her pocket and quickly tapped the last number she had called on her cell phone. To her surprise, Saundra answered on the first ring.

Without giving her a chance to hang up, Savannah blurted out, "Please don't hang up. My husband recently passed away and as I was packing away some of his things I found your note. I was wondering if you were a good friend of his." The ensuing silence was deafening. Finally Savannah asked, "Is this Saundra?"

"Yes ma'am," came back the reply. "You said that Mr. Mike is dead?"

"Mr. Mike!" That certainly wasn't the response that Savannah was expecting to hear.

"Yes," said Savannah solemnly. "I just assumed you knew."

"No ma'am, I didn't. I've only talked with Mr. Mike a few times and I just saw him in person one time. He was a good friend of my father's, John Miguel. He found out about my business through my dad."

"Your business?" asked Savannah.

"Yes ma'am. I'm in the jewelry business. I've been fortunate enough to be able to design and make exclusive jewelry for some most influential people in this country as well as abroad. Mr. Mike had looked at some of my pieces and seemed impressed with my work. He commissioned me to make a special necklace with matching earrings for you for Christmas.

He was very definite in what he wanted and how he wanted it made. He was so excited about having this done for you. In fact, his enthusiasm spilled over to me. I don't think I have ever been so excited about making jewelry for someone.

We set up a time to meet at my shop in Dallas, so that he could look at a drawing of the necklace I designed for you. Mr. Mike seemed very pleased with my drawings and went ahead and paid me for the jewelry based on the pictures I showed him. He was such a nice man, and all I could think of was how amazing it must be to have a husband who loved his wife so much.

I told him I would call him when everything was finished and he could either come back to Dallas for a final inspection, or I could insure the items and send them to him by UPS or FedEx. I had no idea that he died. I am so sorry Mrs. Devereaux. I know his loss must be heartbreaking for you."

Savannah was at a loss for words. Finally she said, "Do you think you can go ahead and make the jewelry like he wanted?"

"Oh yes ma'am," she said. "I've been working on the pieces he ordered, and like I said, they will be ready by Christmas. If for any reason you are not completely satisfied with what I have done, I will either fix the piece you are not satisfied with, or I will refund your money. I am proud to say that after 15 years in the business, I have never had an unsatisfied customer. Would you like for me to describe the necklace and earrings that I'm making for you?"

"No," said Savannah. "If Mike told you he wanted to surprise me with it, let's keep it that way. I'll see it when you're through."

"You two must have been an awesome couple," said Saundra wistfully. "I can't wait to finish your jewelry for you. You'll definitely receive your package shortly before Christmas."

The design on both the necklace and the earrings was the fleur-de-lis, a favorite of Savannah's. Mike had wanted small diamonds and amethyst stones, which were her birth stones, on both the necklace and the earrings.

Saundra had gotten very good with this design because many of the ladies in the south were partial to it, and she had designed many variations of the popular style. This gift of love would be one that both Saundra and Savannah would cherish, each in their own way.

CHAPTER 82

Sunday evening Savannah and Dylan decided to go to Satterfield's for dinner.

"Boy, it looks like even the sidewalks close up by eight p.m. in New Roads," laughed Dylan as he viewed the deserted streets.

"You're just about right," joined in Savannah. "We don't have a lot of the big city nightlife here in downtown New Roads. In the evening, Satterfield's, a few of the restaurants, and the bars, are going to be about the only choices you have for entertainment."

Although there was a downstairs stairway on the side of the restaurant that led up to what was actually considered the main entrance, Savannah and Dylan, like most patrons, parked on Main Street and used the entryway there.

Immediately upon entering, on the right side, was an old antique car – a reminder that the building once housed a car dealership many years ago. On the left was "Nelda's Place," now closed for the evening. Dylan and Savannah followed the long hallway which served as a focal point leading to Satterfield's; its walls plastered with old pictures and memorabilia of times past.

As Dylan and Savannah reached the hostess station, they were greeted by Pam, a friend of Savannah's and a waitress at the restaurant.

"Good evening Senator Devereaux," Pam responded as she smiled at Savannah. "Our hostess is seating someone else right now. Would you like me to show you to a table?"

"Thanks Pam," Savannah replied. "I'd appreciate it."

"Would you like to be seated inside or outside tonight?"

"It's such a beautiful evening; I think maybe we'll try outside,"

Savannah said. She then quickly turned to Dylan and asked, "Is that all right with you?"

"Perfect," he responded.

They passed through the large dining area. The walls were blue with exposed wood beams slanting upwards. The huge glass picture windows were accented with a thin black metal, giving way to a magnificent picturesque view of False River. From inside you could vaguely see the wrap-around porch, and the diners on all three sides of the restaurant.

"Look, Dylan," Savannah said as she pointed to a display set up to resemble a small pier. Lying on the deck was a long stuffed alligator looking quite foreboding.

"Cool," responded Dylan.

Piped in 50s and 60s music filled the room and flowed out into the seating area on the wrap-around porch outside. Once outside, Pam asked, "Will this be all right?" as she pointed to one of the many decorative black wrought iron table sets.

"This will be fine," said Savannah. "Thank you."

"Can I get you something to drink while you look at the menu?" asked Pam in true southern dialect.

"I'll just have some tea," said Savannah. "What would you like to drink, Dylan?" Savannah asked.

"I'd like a beer. Whatever's on tap is fine."

"All right then, I'll be right back with your drinks," said Pam, turning to go back inside.

"Oh Dylan, look," said Savannah as she gazed out onto False River. They both watched as a boat slid gracefully by on the glistening water below. The lights reflecting from the restaurant above bounced off the tranquil water, giving the illusion of glittering sparkles on a gently floating path, its only disturbance being tiny frothing waves feigned by the boat that had just passed.

Tonight was incredible. It was the perfect night – if there ever could be such a thing. There was a quiet breeze that lifted off the calming water lapping against the pier. The sky was filled with a million twinkling stars that mirrored onto the dark part of the water where the lights from the restaurant failed to reach. "Isn't it a beautiful night!" exclaimed Savannah.

Soon Pam returned with their drinks, and took their orders. As she hurried off, Savannah began to comment on how peaceful it was.

But before she could continue, and without warning, the serenity of the evening was shattered by a sudden blast from a loud siren in the distance. A police car, fire truck, ambulance, and a boat used by the Sheriff's department, all appeared, seemingly out of nowhere, on the island side of False River. Flashing lights lit up the night.

Some of the patrons and waitresses rushed outside to see if anyone knew what was going on. Cell phones materialized from thin air as diners called friends who lived across the river, trying to get some information, but all to no avail.

The excitement across the river continued to hold the attention of diners for the rest of the evening. By the time Savannah and Dylan were finishing their meal, they had learned that a dead body had been found floating face down in the water. How the person died, when they died, or who it was, no one seemed to know.

Savannah whispered to Dylan, "I wouldn't be surprised if, in a small town like this, everyone knows all the details by tomorrow morning."

Dylan paled as the talk around them continued. Savannah began to worry about him. She asked, "Are you all right? You don't look like you feel well."

"Oh yeah," he said. "I'm fine. I guess I'm just tired."

"It has been a busy day," said Savannah. After eating dessert they decided to call it a night and drove home.

CHAPTER 83

Simultaneously, two scenarios were being played out. While the excitement at Satterfield's over the activity on False River continued to escalate during Savannah and Dylan's dinner, happenings on the island side of False River were far different.

Beth and Bert Roubique were sitting outside their campsite in a swing on the pier. It was Saturday evening and they were enjoying another beautiful sunset over False River. From where they sat, they could see across the river into the softly lit dining room of Satterfield's.

"Looks like they got a full house tonight," said Bert.

"It sure does," said Beth. "We haven't been to Satterfield's in a while. Why don't we go tomorrow?"

"If you want to," replied Bert.

Beth and Bert had both retired several years ago. At first they divided their time between their home in Baton Rouge and their camp on False River. Gradually, the time spent at their home became almost non-existent. Finally, last year they decided to sell their house and make their camp on False River their permanent residence. While their camp was smaller than their house, it was every bit as beautiful. Tonight as the water lapped against the poles in the ground supporting their pier, Bert suddenly got very quiet. "What's the matter?" asked Beth.

"Do you see something bobbing up and down in the water by that tree trunk?" Bert replied.

"Where?"

"Look over there by that clump of bushes," said Bert.

Beth turned pale in the moonlight. "It ... it looks like a body!"

"That's what I thought. I'm going out to get a better look."

"No," Beth cried out. "Let's just call the police."

"You call Sheriff Breaux while I go out and make sure it's not just some old clothes or trash. I don't want to feel stupid if the cops come out here and find nothing but junk in the water."

While Beth called the sheriff, Bert got in his bateau and cautiously trolled towards the object. As soon as he neared it, he knew they had been right. "It's a body!" Bert called out to Beth. Bert rushed back over to the pier where Beth now had Sheriff Breaux on the phone. Let me have the phone," he said as he grabbed the phone out of Beth's hand.

"Hey Sheriff, this is Bert. Beth and I were sitting out on our pier tonight when we saw something floating in the water. I went out to see what it was and, man I hate to tell you this, but I found a body in False River. There's no telling how long it's been in the water. It's all bloated up and looks like something's been eating on it. It really looks bad. Can you get over here quick?"

"I'm on my way," the sheriff responded. "Don't let anybody get around it." In less than ten minutes Sheriff Breaux and his deputy pulled up in Beth and Bert's driveway with lights flashing. Behind them a myriad of neighbors began to show up.

"Keep those people back," shouted Sheriff Breaux to his deputy. "Can you take me over to where you saw the body, Bert?"

"Sure," said Bert. With that, he and Sheriff Breaux got into his bateau and trolled over once again to the spot where the lifeless body lay face down in the water.

"Look over there," the sheriff shouted out. "It looks like ropes in the water. Can you get us closer?" he asked.

"I can, but we're going to have to be careful," said Bert. "There's no telling what else might be around there. For all I know there might be another body. It's hard to see in the water this late at night."

"Okay. Just get us as close as you can," responded Sheriff Breaux.

"Look, there!" the Sheriff exclaimed. "See those ropes?"

When Bert pulled up closer to the ropes in the water, Sheriff Breaux remarked, "They're all tattered on the ends. It's like they were attached to something, but finally tore away."

"I bet I know what caused that," called out Bert. "Late this afternoon a man and his wife were out on the water close to where we are now. They were having trouble with their boat, so I asked them if they needed help. The man called back and said that they had been at the far end of the lake where he thought he might have gotten too close to some underbrush. It was after that when his boat got very sluggish.

After he started examining his boat, he told me he figured out what the problem was. His propeller had gotten tangled up in some rope. He cut the rope off his propeller and his boat started right up. He and his wife waved bye and went on their way. I didn't pay any more attention to them after that."

By the time Bert and Sheriff Breaux returned to the landing, the Wildlife and Fisheries officers had arrived. A special team of divers accompanying them were dispatched into the water. Immediately they went to work securing the body in a mesh body bag so that no possible clues would be washed away as they lifted the body from the water.

Once the body had been retrieved, they used their night equipment to scour the area looking for clues or even possibly another body.

"Got it!" one of the men exclaimed, as the hoist on their boat worked under great pressure to pull up a large cement cylinder block from the bottom of the river. "It still has parts of the ropes attached."

When the body was brought to shore, the Coroner, Dr. Harry Kellerman, and the Deputy Coroner and Chief Investigator, Ty Chaney, were waiting. Both men quickly examined the body for any obvious clues as to identity or the special circumstances surrounding the unusual death before ordering the body to be loaded inside the coroner's van and taken away.

A small crowd of people had begun to appear from nowhere. On top of that, as if by magic, the news media showed up. "Let's get this area roped off with Crime Scene tape right away," said Sheriff Breaux. "The more people we have underfoot, the harder it's going to be for us to do our job."

Left in the still of the night was Sheriff Breaux and his deputy, the police, members of Wildlife and Fisheries, the news media, and an assemblage of horrified people. There had never been a murder on False River before.

CHAPTER 84

Sunday morning Savannah sat in her living room watching the local news on television as she drank her coffee. "Shocking news of
a body found in False River leads our news this morning!" exclaimed
the excited reporter. "Saturday evening a couple sitting on the dock
outside their False River campsite were horrified to discover a body
floating in the water nearby."

Pictures of the body being pulled out of the river and later
loaded into the coroner's van followed the reporter's initial report.
Immediately afterwards, the news clip with Beth and Bert being interviewed was played.

"It was horrible," said Beth. "I've never seen anything like it before."

"We called the sheriff's office as soon as we realized that it was
someone's body," continued Bert.

After the interview the reporter concluded his story with the customary, "We'll have updated information on this startling discovery as
soon as it becomes available."

With a Legislative office and a Real Estate office to keep up with,
Savannah had no time to dwell on the tragic news. She was getting up
to go into the study to finish some paperwork when Dylan walked in.
The news of the murder was just going off. "Did you hear about the
murder on False River?" she asked Dylan.

"Yeah, I heard the last of it when I was coming in. Did they say who
they thought it was?"

"No. They haven't even said if it was a man or a woman yet," responded Savannah. "It's all so unbelievable."

"Boy, that's something," responded Dylan. Looking down at his watch he continued. "I hate to run out on you, Savannah, but I gotta get to work."

"Oh, that's right. I forgot you had to work today."

"Yeah, when they offered me the job I told them I would work whenever they wanted me to. I guess I'll get all the hours and days nobody else wants until I put in more time over there. It doesn't really matter, though," he continued, "I really need the money."

"I understand," said Savannah. "Sometimes you just have to tough it out until things start to come around for you. I think if you work hard and do a good job, you may have an opportunity to advance and build a career at the plant. A lot of people have done just that."

After Dylan left, Savannah got another cup of coffee and walked into the study. She decided to try to get a few hours of work in before it would be time to get ready for church. She and Mike had never totally agreed on the church issue. While Mike, without a doubt believed in God, he never felt the need to sit in a church pew every Sunday and listen to sermons that generally were wasted on him. Savannah, on the other hand, seemed to get her strength from the very things Mike dismissed.

Savannah began to review the state budget. Then she pulled together work from the real estate office. *"Without Mike, it's going to be hard trying to keep up with both jobs at the same time," she thought.* Savannah longed to have Mike around again as a sounding board. She loved being able to bounce ideas back and forth with him. Those days were gone. She was definitely on her own now.

CHAPTER 85

Wednesday morning Savannah arrived at the office just as Betty was turning over the "Open" sign in the window pane of the front door. "Good morning, Betty. How are you today?"

"Fine, Ms. Savannah. How about you?"

"I'm hanging in there," said Savannah with a lackadaisical smile.

Betty began making coffee while Savannah went into her office toting the paperwork she had worked on at home. Soon Savannah heard Jim and Macy come in. In no time at all, the phones started ringing and it became obvious that another busy day at the Devereaux Real Estate Company had begun. It was close to ten a.m. when Betty buzzed Savannah on her telephone intercom.

"Ms. Savannah, Sheriff Breaux is here to see you."

"Fine, Betty. Please tell him to come on back."

When Sheriff Charles Breaux walked into her office, Savannah was a little surprised to see him. Even though Charles was a good friend of hers, and Savannah had been instrumental in helping with his campaign for sheriff last year, he seldom if ever visited her office. "Good morning Charles," Savannah began. "I hardly ever see you anymore. What are you doing in my neck of the woods today?" she asked cheerfully.

Charles was tall and muscular. His well fitted uniform made him look as if he came right off an officer's training academy poster. "Savannah, I'm afraid I've got some bad news. I have to bring you in for questioning," Charles said.

"Questioning for what?" asked a startled Savannah.

"A body was found floating in False River on Saturday. It had been weighted down by thick ropes and an anchor. Somehow the ropes came loose and the body floated upwards towards the surface. From the initial investigation it appears that the body had been in False River for about a week. Dr. Kellerman and Ty Chaney both came out on the call. They've already had the body transported to the pathology lab in Lafayette. Ty said he would be running some extra tests at the coroner's office in New Roads while he is waiting to get back a more detailed lab report from Lafayette, but there is no doubt that we're investigating a homicide.

"How horrible!" Savannah exclaimed. "Dylan and I went to Satterfield's Saturday evening and heard the sirens and all the commotion on the other side of the river, but we didn't know the details of what had happened until I heard about it on the news Sunday morning. Do you know who it was, and ... by the way, what has this got to do with me?" asked Savannah, suddenly realizing what Sheriff Breaux had said.

"We received a Missing Person's report from the Shreveport Police Department on Saturday morning. The man's wife had waited to report him missing. He was leaving on a trip out of the country, and she couldn't be sure that he hadn't already left without calling her. She said he had come to spend the weekend at their friend's camp in New Roads and she hadn't heard from him since then. He was supposed to have called her before he left on his trip."

Savannah felt a sinking sensation in the pit of her stomach. *"Shreveport ... trip out of the country ... friend's camp on False River. No, it couldn't possibly be — could it?"*

Sheriff Breaux continued, "His wife, Kris, called their friend Bob Gabour, who lives in Lafayette, to get the address of his camp for us. When we went to investigate, we found Mr. Handy's car in the driveway, but there was no answer when we knocked on the door."

"It's true," Savannah thought to herself. *"Tracy's dead!"*

"We contacted Mr. Gabour and got permission to search the premises. He told us that one of his neighbors has a spare key to his camp that he keeps in case of an emergency, and that we could get the key from him. When we entered the house, everything looked normal; nothing seemed out of place.

As it turns out, one of my deputies knows Mr. Gabour. He said that he has a really nice boat that he keeps in the boat shed on the side of the house. When he went to check on Mr. Gabour's boat, he discovered that it was missing.

Originally we thought that we might have a boating accident on our hands. After searching the lake, we found the boat tied up to a dock at the far end of False River. Foul play wasn't apparent at first so we checked with neighbors and businesses in the area and decided we would canvass the area thoroughly before we determined a search of False River was warranted.

Before we ever got to the point of dragging False River for a body, we were called out to investigate a body found in False River on Saturday evening. From that moment on everything started having a domino effect.

We went back to the camp to do a more thorough investigation and in the course of that investigation we found a note with your name and phone number on it. We also recovered a cell phone hidden in the microwave with calls to and from you."

"In the microwave," blurted out Savannah. "Why would anyone put a cell phone in a microwave?"

"People can be tracked down using the signals from their cell phone. If a cell phone is placed inside a microwave oven it can't be traced because the same protective covering of the microwave that keeps the potentially harmful electromagnetic waves inside, will also keep in the electromagnetic waves from a cell phone, rendering tracking devices inoperable. Someone obviously did not want to take any chances on us finding our murder victim through his cell phone." The sheriff continued, "From everything we have gathered so far, it appears you may be one of the last ones to have seen our John Doe, who we now believe to be Brian Handy, alive."

Savannah felt her bottom jaw drop and her heart rate increase dramatically. She suddenly felt very dizzy. Her mind was racing in a million different directions. "You said Brian Handy?" she stammered.

"Yes," replied Charles. "I assume you know him from the messages left on his phone."

"I only met him about a week ago. He was a friend of Mike's," Savannah sighed.

"I knew this had to be a mistake. Why don't you come with me to the station so we can get this all cleared up right now?" asked Charles.

"All right. Just let me tell Betty I'll be out for a while." Savannah grabbed her purse and, trying to act nonchalant as she passed by her, told Betty that she would be back later.

"Shall I take my car and follow you, or am I under arrest?" quipped Savannah once they were outside the office.

"You're not under arrest," answered a red faced sheriff. "Savannah, please don't make me feel any worse than I already do."

CHAPTER 86

Sheriff Breaux and Savannah did not have far to go before reaching his vehicle. "Savannah, this is a major investigation and we're bringing in anyone that may have any knowledge of any kind regarding this case. We don't have many clues to go on right now. The story of the murder is being run on all the major television networks. This is the worst possible news coverage of Pointe Coupee Parish that we could get. Even the weekend visitors who like to fish in False River are going to be more hesitant to come now.

What's even sadder," Sheriff Breaux continued, "is that we're not positive where the murder occurred just yet. We're still in the early stages of our investigation and we don't want to rule out any possibilities regarding how, why, or even where the murder may have taken place. It's obvious we're dealing with a homicide. Other than that, we're not certain of anything. For all we know, the murder may have occurred elsewhere and the body just disposed of in False River. We're working closely with Captain James Rivers of the New Roads Police Department, Detective Van Calhoun with the U.S. District Attorney's office, the Secret Service, and numerous other law enforcement agencies. Anyone that can be of help has been called in."

"I understand all of that," replied Savannah. I'm just confused on why you want me to go to the station with you."

"Actually, I'm worried about a few comments you made to Mr. Handy on his voice mail. Some of your remarks could be construed as incriminating," said Charles.

"In addition to that, the body pulled out of the river looks as if it had been in the water about a week. It appears that the last contact

Mr. Handy had with anyone was with you about a week ago. It doesn't look good Savannah. Between us, you are going to be asked to account for your time last Friday and Saturday a week ago. Do you have a good alibi?"

"Alibi? I need an alibi?" stammered Savannah.

"I'm afraid so," said Charles.

"Friday a week ago was the first time I met Brian Handy. By the way, his friends call him Tracy. He asked me to meet him at Jim's Place."

"Good grief, Savannah. Tell me you didn't go there to meet him by yourself?"

"Yes, I know Charles. It was a stupid idea. He caught me off guard when he called, and I agreed to meet him before I had time to think it through."

"I wish I had thought to tell you to call Harold while you were at your office," said Charles. "He's still your attorney, right? I don't want to see you get implicated in a murder."

Savannah began to panic. "Call Harold?

"Yes, why don't you go ahead and call him now?" suggested Sheriff Breaux.

Savannah reached into her purse, pulled out her cell phone, and called Harold. On the second ring his assistant answered.

"Hi, Tisha," Savannah began. "Is Harold in?"

"He sure is, Senator. Just one minute and I'll connect you."

"Hey Savannah, What's up?" came Harold's booming voice over the phone.

"Harold, I think I have a serious problem and I need your help."

"What kind of problem?" bellowed back the affable Harold. "What'd you do, forget to put something on your tax return?" he joked.

"Did you hear about the man they found dead in False River on Saturday?" Savannah asked quickly.

"Shucks, that's all anybody is talking about," said Harold. "I ran down to Winn Dixie Sunday morning and everybody over there was upset. An out and out murder is what they're calling it. Heck, we're getting to be like the big cities now. A visitor comes to New Roads and gets murdered. Who'd have ever thought it? Brenda said when the word gets out; nobody's gonna wanna come to visit New Roads anymore."

When he took a breath Savannah jumped in before he could continue.

"Well, they want to question me regarding the murder. Charles said I should give you a call. He said this is very serious."

"You gotta be kidding! What do they wanna to talk to you for? Where are you right now?"

"I'm in the car with Charles on our way to the Sheriff's office."

"Let me talk with Charles."

Savannah handed the phone to Charles. "He wants to talk with you," she said.

"Harold, Charles here. I told Savannah it might not be a bad idea if you were to meet us at my office. We need to question her regarding the body we found on False River, and I would feel better if she had you there to advise her on what she should or should not say. I'm the sheriff and I have to stay neutral."

After a back and forth conversation in which Savannah was only privy to one side, Charles handed Savannah's phone back to her.

"He'll meet us at the office," said Charles.

There was silence for the rest of the ride to the station.

CHAPTER 87

Once inside the sheriff's office, Charles asked one of his deputies to bring coffee for both he and Savannah into the interrogation room. Another officer came in to take notes and record the proceedings. By the time they settled in, Harold had arrived and was being ushered into the room. Soon afterwards the questioning began.

After an hour of probing questions regarding a man they had now come to believe was Brian Handy, and Savannah's involvement with him, Harold spoke up. "I think Savannah has told you everything that she knows. Obviously this is not a person she knew a lot about. Why are you questioning her in such detail?"

Sheriff Breaux paused as if trying to find the right words. "It appears that Savannah may have been one of the last persons to see Brian Handy alive. The message she left on his phone implies he knew something that she didn't want to get out. We just need to know why Savannah was meeting with him Friday night at Jim's Place."

Horrified, Savannah looked at Charles and whispered, "Charles, surely you don't think I could have had anything to do with something so terrible, do you?"

Charles saw the stunned look on Savannah's face. He knew she was innocent of any wrongdoing, but he had to do his job. "Savannah, if you could just tell me about your meeting with Brian Handy, I'm sure it would clear up everything."

"My meeting with Mr. Handy was confidential in nature and I am not at liberty to discuss it," replied Savannah, a little more forceful.

Savannah didn't know what to think anymore. How would she ever find out the truth? *Was Tracy being honest with her all along? Was*

Dylan really Mike's son? What was the big secret Mike and Tracy had been in-volved in? Was it genuinely possible that Mike had not died from an accidental plane crash?

"We have contacted Mr. Handy's wife in Shreveport. We suggested she send his dental work to the lab in Lafayette to help identify the body. Having been in the river so long, I doubt she could have recognized him anyway," added Sheriff Breaux.

Savannah was glad Harold was with her. She wanted to tell him everything she knew, but her loyalty to Mike prevented her from doing so. She had to find out a few things for herself first.

Sheriff Breaux looked apologetically at Savannah and said, "I'd appreciate it if you didn't take any long extended trips without checking with me first; at least not until after the investigation has been completed."

"Surely you don't think I had anything to do with this man's death, do you Charles?"

Sheriff Breaux motioned for his deputy to turn off the recorder and replied, "Of course not, Savannah. I'm just trying to do my job."

Harold asked, "Savannah, do you need a ride home?"

"I'd appreciate a ride back to my office, Harold." Then turning back to Sheriff Breaux she asked, "Am I free to go Charles?" She was anxious to distance herself from the interrogation she had just been through.

"Of course," said Charles. "I'm sorry I had to bring you in, Savannah, but I appreciate you coming."

Charles may have just been doing his job, but Savannah had never been interrogated before and she didn't like it at all. She felt it was humiliating and degrading.

On the way back to the office Harold said, "Savannah, I want you to take what I'm saying very seriously. For the time being you need to be careful who you talk with, and what you discuss. Since you are the only person they know of that was in touch with Brian Handy before his death, whether they want to or not, they will be watching you closely until they can find a better suspect."

"Do you think they really consider me a suspect?" blurted out Savannah, obviously upset.

"I don't think so, but let's not give them any reason to want to question you further."

"Don't worry about that," she said as they neared their respective offices. Inwardly she knew her investigation had just begun.

CHAPTER 88

"Would you like to come in and have a cup of coffee before you go back to your office?" Savanna asked Harold.

"I appreciate the offer, but I got a bunch of work I have to finish before I go home this afternoon. Today's Brenda's birthday, so I promised her I would take her out to eat tonight."

"Oh, how sweet," said Savannah. Then, hesitantly, she continued. "Harold, I know you're very discreet about your clients," Savannah began, "and I know you'll understand when I ask that you not discuss what went on today with anyone else, right?"

"Savannah, you know me better than that. There's no way I'd betray a confidence, especially when it involves you."

"Thanks, Harold."

"You bet. Call me if you need me."

As Savannah walked into her office she looked up at the clock on the wall. It was already one-thirty. *"Good grief,"* she thought, *"I've been gone all morning. I didn't even eat lunch. That's probably why my stomach is in knots."*

Even though she hadn't eaten, food didn't appeal to her. She fixed a glass of iced tea, got some cheese crackers from the vending machine, and went back to her office. Usually Savannah was one of the last people to leave the office, but not tonight. She felt completely worn out, both physically and mentally.

At home she changed into her sweat suit and immediately went to sit in the recliner in her bedroom. Dylan was still at work, and the house was exceptionally quiet. She looked over at the picture of Mike on her bed stand.

"Mike," she cried, *"I miss you so much."* She reached over and picked up her purse from the end table next to her chair and began rummaging through it to see if she could find a Kleenex. As she did so, her hand brushed against the envelope Macy had given her when she spent the night. She pulled it out and looked at it in disbelief. Her eyes focused on one part. She read it over again. "... *After that you should eventually be contacted by a man with the initials B. H. – tell him they finally got me and that he needs to be careful."*

"Oh, no!" she cried out. "B. H. – could that have stood for Brian Handy? Was I supposed to have told Brian to be careful?" "... *they finally got me."* "Who finally got him? What was he trying to say?" She felt a rush of tears fill her eyes. Unable to hold them back, they flowed like a driving rain down her pallid cheeks, and would have soaked the precious note in her hand, had she not moved it a split second earlier.

"Tracy was right. Mike may have been murdered," thought Savannah. *"After all, Tracy was murdered. Maybe someone found out that he had been talking with me and were worried about what all he would tell me."*

Savannah had a sinking feeling in her stomach as she thought, *"Tracy was murdered and I did nothing to warn him. I failed both Mike and Tracy. What do I do now?"*

CHAPTER 89

Savannah admonished herself. *"I have to pull myself together. It's time to start thinking with my head, and not my heart. If Mike was murdered as Tracy suggested, what could that mean? Was Tracy right about Mike's cover with the CIA being blown? Could the drug dealers have caused his death? Surely the CIA was not involved ... or were they? How can I find out for sure without asking a lot of questions? People are going to think I've gone crazy if I start questioning Mike's death based on what a man that I barely knew, and who is now himself dead, told me. But I need answers,"* she said to herself as she rushed into the study and turned on the computer.

After pulling up the Internet, she entered the name Brian Handy. Instantly she was linked to numerous web addresses for him. Then she spotted a web address that took her to a site for Handy Building Contractors, Inc., Brian Handy, owner. Now, more than ever, she questioned what he and Mike had discovered that may have cost them their lives. She wondered who else may have been involved. When she thought she had pulled up all the information she could on Brian Handy she turned to another search.

Savannah remembered Mike's first wife's name was Christine. She looked up Christine Devereaux on the Internet and found a link to the Pineville News, a weekly newspaper in Pineville, Louisiana. There was a lengthy article and a sizeable picture of the late "Christine Devereaux, wife of Michael Joseph Devereaux, CEO and co-owner of Devereaux Oil Refineries, Inc., Shreveport, Louisiana."

Savannah read through the article with great interest. It was just like Mike had told her. Christine was driving when her car went out of control, flipping over several times. As it flipped one last time, the

car exploded. By the time the fire trucks and emergency personnel got there, the car was engulfed in flames. Christine was burned
beyond recognition. The accident had taken place at 3 a.m. on a deserted stretch of road. Savannah could just imagine what people must
have thought. Although Mike had told her it was also reported that
Christine had been seen drinking quite heavily in one of the local bars
before the accident, probably out of respect for the family, that was
not mentioned.

The article about the memorial service held for her included an
extensive list of all the "who's who" in attendance. "Very impressive,"
Savannah said to herself. Evidently there was a large insurance policy
on Christine which she and Mike had taken out, leaving him as the sole
beneficiary. After the article in the paper, the trail ran cold. There was
no more mention of Christine Devereaux. There was also no mention
of their son, Dylan Devereaux.

CHAPTER 90

"Hi Tommy. This is Savannah. How are things at the Banner?"

"It's really heated up today. The news is all about the murder on False River. As a matter of fact, I was just getting ready to call you. How did you get involved in all this mess?"

"What do you mean, Tommy?" asked Savannah.

"Don't play coy with me," he said with feigned indignation.

"Who told you I was involved?" Savannah persisted.

"Sammy Rodriguez," replied Tommy.

"I thought I knew everybody in New Roads, but I never heard of Sammy Rodriguez. Who is he?" questioned Savannah.

"He told me he's a private investigator who was hired to secretly follow Brian Handy, the guy they say was murdered. I think they're still trying to get positive identification on the body. Rodriguez wouldn't tell me why he'd been following Handy, but he did say that he was going to talk with the sheriff and offer his help in trying to solve the case. He was really interested in trying to find out where Handy had been staying before he was killed."

"Did you tell him?" asked Savannah.

"No. I didn't know," replied Tommy. "Funny thing, though," he continued, "When I talked to Charles to get his comments for the story I'm writing, I asked him if he and Rodriguez had found out anything else about the murder on False River. Charles said, 'What makes you ask an odd question like that?' I told him straight out, 'Rodriguez said he was going to be working with you on the investigation.' Boy, Charles was as hot as blue blazes. He said, 'I don't know who this Rodriguez character thinks he is, but I sure don't need the likes of him getting involved with my investigation.'

He told me, 'I want you to call me if you hear from him again. He's probably just trying to make a name for himself – probably trying to get an exclusive report for some tabloid or out of town paper.' Charles asked me to be sure to call him if I heard any more strange comments like that from anybody."

"What did he tell you about me?" asked Savannah.

"Who?" asked Tommy.

"Sammy Rodriguez," sputtered Savannah impatiently.

"Only that he heard you had met with Handy before he died. In fact, Rodriguez said Handy was reported to have had a clandestine meeting with a certain state senator before he died. You want to tell me about that?"

"I hope you told him that I don't have clandestine meetings," Savannah said sarcastically.

"Sure did," said Tommy beaming. "Makes my blood boil when somebody comes in and tries to tear down good people that live here!"

"Thanks, Tommy," replied Savannah. "I'm lucky to have a good friend like you." Then she continued. "Do you have any idea where Sammy Rodriguez is now?"

"Not a clue. Sure wish I did, though. I have a feeling that guy could be a story by himself. I think he knows a lot more than he was telling."

"Tommy, I'm really nervous about this whole thing. I barely knew Brian Handy and all of the sudden it seems that I am being dragged into his murder. I sure would appreciate it if you let me know if you find out anything else."

"Sure will, Savannah."

When she finished talking with Tommy, Savannah began to wonder about Brian Handy, alias Tracy. Had he really been working with Mike, or was he just trying to find out if she knew anything about the bizarre conspiracy Mike was supposedly being implicated in?

But he said he had information – and the note from Mike ... no, she had a gut feeling about Tracy. She believed he was sincere. At this point she had to believe in someone.

And now — who was this mysterious Sammy Rodriguez that had suddenly appeared and just as suddenly disappeared? Was he really a private detective or was he from "the other side." The more Savannah tried to sort things out, the more confused she became.

Not realizing how long she had been working on her own private investigation, Savannah was startled when she heard a noise at the door. She looked up to see Dylan. "I'm sorry Dylan. I didn't realize you were there. How was work?"

"Well, I haven't been fired yet," he laughed.

"That's a good sign," she laughed back.

"Am I interrupting you?"

"Yes you are, but I'm glad. I need a break. Why don't I throw a pizza in the oven for dinner tonight?" asked Savannah. "I'm just going to put away these papers and I'll be right out."

"You look tired, why don't you let me fix it?" Dylan came back.

"No, I really don't mind," said Savannah. "I need to get my mind on something else."

Dylan left the room and Savannah put everything away that she had been working on. The phone rang and when Savannah answered, she immediately recognized Macy's voice on the other end.

CHAPTER 91

"Savannah, guess what! Remember that home you pulled up for me to show the Bertrands? They loved it!

Mr. Bertrand just called and asked me to come over. They want to discuss the possibility of making an offer on it tonight. I think they're going to want to go back inside the house before signing a purchase agreement, so we'll probably end up going back over there again tonight."

"That's fantastic Macy. Do you need me to come along?"

"I was hoping you'd ask!" gasped Macy. "We make such a great team."

"Okay," laughed Savannah. "Why don't you come on over here, so we can take the Hummer. That way we'll have more room if the Bertrands want to go look at the house again."

"Right," said Macy. "I'm on my way over."

As soon as Savannah got off the phone she called out to Dylan, "I'm afraid I am going to have to cancel out on you tonight. Macy has a house she's trying to close on, and asked me to go with her. I'm not sure how long we'll be. I haven't started the pizzas yet, so you can either fix something yourself, or if you want to go to town to get something, you're welcome to use Mike's truck."

"Thanks Savannah. I think I may take you up on that."

Savannah rushed to her room to change before Macy got there. She slipped on rust colored pants and a nickel colored silk boat neck blouse with a wide belt. Her hair was brushed and pulled back and up with an oversized decorative hair clip. She finished putting on her make-up and jewelry and slipped into a pair of Sergio Rossi patent leather pumps. Grabbing the matching bag, Savannah hurried into the kitchen just as Macy was driving up.

"I'm off," she called out to Dylan.

"Have a good time," he shot back, "and good luck."

Savannah told Macy to pull her car into one of the spaces in the garage while she pulled the Hummer out of the space on the far end. With the motor of the Hummer running, Macy jumped into the passenger side and shouted, "Let's go get 'em. Yee haw!"

Savannah started laughing. This was so typical of Macy. She could be so much fun, and she did love going in for the kill, especially when Savannah was with her.

"I made another copy of all the stats you gave me," said Macy. "I knew Mrs. Bertrand was interested, but to be honest, I thought Mr. Bertrand would talk her out of it. I didn't need to pre-qualify them because their credit rating is out the roof. They got more money than God."

"Macy!" laughed Savannah. "Shame on you," she said with a feigned sense of shock.

It didn't take long to get to the Bertrand's house. It didn't take long to get anywhere in New Roads.

"This house always reminded me of a castle," Savannah whispered. The intricately designed black wrought iron fence surrounding the entire circumference of the property was set off by a heavy gate with an intercom system. Tonight the gate had been left open.

"I'm surprised the Bertrands left the gate open," said Macy. "It's usually locked. I hear that very few people ever get invited inside."

The decorative brick sidewalk created a charming access to the wide cement stairs going up to the sizeable wrap-around front porch. On one side of the sculptured glass doorway was a quaint white swing hanging by chains from the lofty roof. On the other side were two large old-fashioned woven white rocking chairs.

Mrs. Bertrand greeted them cordially at the doorway. "Mr.

Bertrand is waiting in the kitchen. I just brewed us a fresh pot of coffee if you'd like some."

"That sounds great," replied Savannah and Macy, as they followed Mrs. Bertrand down the hallway and back into the kitchen where Mr. Bertrand was sitting. "Good evening, ladies," he commented. "Sorry to get you out so late."

It was only seven-thirty, but there was much to discuss.

"It's no problem at all." Before long Savannah and Macy were discussing the Bertrand's extremely large kitchen, complete with a bar and bar stools, a massive wood table large enough to seat eight people comfortably, and a long hanging wooden chandelier over the table. "It's just amazing how you can have such a big spacious room that still feels so cozy."

Macy could see Mr. Bertrand warming up to Savannah almost instantly.

"We added this room on to the house about eight years ago," bragged Mr. Bertrand.

"It's going to be hard for us to move," said Mrs. Bertrand. "We have so many good memories here. But I'm looking forward to a change. A lot of our friends have died and some have moved into retirement villas. The neighborhood's just not the same any more.

"I can certainly understand how you feel," agreed Savannah. "This is a magnificent home, and I know you've both done a lot to make it that way. But I have no doubt your new residence will reflect the same warmth and personality that you instilled in this house."

Mrs. Bertrand smiled as she poured coffee for all of them.

The house and property that the Bertrands were looking at was listed at over two million dollars. If the Bertrands bought it, they would then, in turn, sell their house, which Savannah estimated at well over a million dollars. Savannah could not imagine the Bertrands wanting to sell their stately old home, but then again, as Mrs. Bertrand pointed out, times were changing and so was their neighborhood.

Soon Mr. Bertrand began discussing the house they were considering buying. He said in his opinion the house was highly overpriced. To her credit, Savannah never even flinched. "Well, you know Mr. Bertrand, that's why we have purchase agreements. It's the old barter system. You tell me what you are willing to pay and the owners will come back with either an agreement or a counter offer on what they are willing to take. If you both don't agree, the deal is off and you're free to look for something else."

Mrs. Bertrand looked a little pale thinking that Mr. Bertrand might back out after she had worked so hard to get him to this point. But Savannah knew men. Most men loved the thrill of the hunt, and the challenge of negotiating a good deal. Mr. Bertrand was no different.

After coffee, Savannah suggested, "Why don't we take a ride back out to the house so you can go through it one more time? It might help you to make up your mind on what you think a fair purchase price would be."

Mrs. Bertrand was quick to answer. "I'd love to go back over there again, if it's not too late for you girls. What do you think honey?" she asked as she smiled at Mr. Bertrand. At this point, although he tried to convince himself otherwise, Mr. Bertrand knew it was all over but signing the papers.

CHAPTER 92

The drive to Maringouin was an enjoyable one. Savannah and Macy answered numerous questions for Mr. and Mrs. Bertrand while en route.

By the time the Bertrands went through the house one final time they were ready to sign the purchase agreement. Savannah saw the color drain from Macy's face as Mr. Bertrand decided to offer considerably less than the stated purchase price. After much discussion, both Mr. and Mrs. Bertrand signed the document and Macy put it in her briefcase.

"Once Macy submits this, the owners will have 24 hours to respond to your offer. As soon as we hear from them we will be back in touch with you," smiled Savannah.

Savannah drove the Bertrands back to their home in New Roads. As soon as they had gone inside, Macy turned to Savannah and asked, "What do you think? Is there a chance that the Robillards will take their offer?"

"Oh, I think there's a very good chance," smiled Savannah.

"Really?!" shouted Macy in amazement. "I was worried about the purchase price."

"Well, it's not sold yet," Savannah reminded Macy. "But we're definitely on the right track. Have you figured out your commission yet?" Savannah teased.

"I don't think I can count that high," replied the overly giddy Macy.

"And remember, if you sell this house, the Bertrand's are going to want to sell their house, which will result in another commission for you."

"For us," encouraged Macy. "We split this commission. I couldn't have done it without you."

"Well, we'll talk about that later," laughed Savannah. Both women felt like they were on the ultimate high with the possibility of earning such large commissions.

"Macy, look on the paperwork and see who the listing agent is."

Macy grabbed the paperwork from her briefcase and scrolled down to the name of the listing agent. "Byron Daigle," she said.

"Okay, pull out your cell phone and give him a call. Let's not wait until tomorrow if we can help it."

Macy pulled out her phone directory of real estate companies and their agents and quickly found the number she was looking for. Within seconds she was dialing Byron's cell number.

The discussion seemed to move very smoothly and soon Savannah heard Macy saying, "That sounds great. We'll probably grab a bite to eat while we're waiting for you. We're driving a black Hummer. My name is Macy Monroe and I'm with Savannah Devereaux."

After a few more comments, Macy replied, "Okay, we'll meet you at the Burger King on Hospital Road in about thirty minutes." As she hung up, Macy looked over at Savannah. You got that?"

"Burger King – Hospital Road – thirty minutes – right?"

"You got it," beamed Macy.

When Savannah and Macy got to Burger King, Savannah wasn't hungry, so she just got something to drink. Macy, on the other hand, was always hungry, and ordered a full meal. A little thing like nerves wasn't going to slow down her appetite.

After she got her order, the two women found a seat close to the window so they could keep an eye out for Byron. It was then that they realized they had no idea what he looked like. They found themselves smiling broadly at every man that came in alone. They received more than a few smiles back in return.

This is ridiculous," said Savannah. "I'm not acting like a crazed woman anymore. He's going to have to figure out who we are."

"Oh, he already knows," said Macy. "When I told him your name he asked if you were Senator Savannah Devereaux. He sounded all excited about getting to meet you."

"Great," said Savannah. "You've had me practically throwing myself at men all this time when you knew all along that he would be able to identify us?"

"It was immensely entertaining," Macy replied with a big grin on her face.

At long last, both women were pleasantly surprised when an extremely handsome young man walked in and headed straight for their table. Savannah and Macy knew this had to be Byron. "Good Lord, he's a hunk if there ever was one," whispered Macy. "He must work out on a regular basis."

"Hush," Savannah whispered back in a playful mood.

Always stylish and impeccably dressed, Byron had been the heart throb of many a young girl wherever he went. Macy wondered why they had never met.

"Good evening," he began. "My name is Byron Daigle."

"Good evening," responded Savannah. "I'm Savannah Devereaux and this is Macy Monroe. Won't you have a seat?"

Just when Macy was thinking her life couldn't get any better, it did. First, she was on the verge of making the biggest sale she had ever made, and now, in walks Byron Daigle.

"I've already called the Robillards and told them that I was about to pick up a purchase agreement on their house," said Byron. "They told me to go ahead and bring it over as soon as I got it, so I think we're in business."

This is a good sign. They're anxious to sell, thought Savannah.

"How does the purchase agreement look compared to their original selling price?" asked Byron.

"The Bertrands are making a counter offer. It's less than what the

Robillards were asking, so I guess we'll just have to wait and see," Savannah replied.

After some lively discussion, Byron said, "It was great meeting you both. I'm going to go ahead and take this purchase agreement over to the Robillards, and I'll let you know what they decide by tomorrow morning. I'm sure they're going to want to think it over tonight."

"Where are the Robillards staying right now?" asked Savannah. "I know they already moved out of their house."

"They bought a house in Baton Rouge and moved in about a month ago. It's over in Country Club Estates."

"That's a nice area," replied Savannah.

"Strange, though," mused Byron. "Most people I talk with want to move out of the city. The Robillards wanted to move in. I guess different strokes for different folks."

"You're right," laughed Macy, trying to keep from drooling.

CHAPTER 93

After Byron left, Savannah and Macy were both so keyed up they decided they would stop by Satterfield's to celebrate. It was getting late and there weren't many people inside. The relaxed atmosphere inside was perfect for some wind down time. Macy and Savannah ordered drinks and settled in for some high-spirited conversation.

"What do you think the Robillards will do?" asked Macy.

"I'm pretty sure they'll come back with a counter offer. Mr. Bertrand wasn't even close to the selling price. Still, the Robillards have already moved out and are anxious to sell, so there's always the possibility they may accept the offer. It's really a toss-up."

After a while, talk gradually changed to other topics. "By the way Savannah, how are things going with you and Dylan?" Macy inquired.

Dylan. Savannah had all but forgotten about him. "Fine, why do you ask?"

"I know it's none of my business Savannah, but he's a grown man, and you really don't know that much about him. Are you sure it's a good idea to take him in like you did?"

"Look Macy, he's Mike's son. I have this huge house, and I just wouldn't feel right sending him off to fend for himself, when I have so many empty rooms. Besides, once he gets established and has a steady income, I'm sure he'll want to start looking for his own place."

Suddenly Savannah got a little more serious than usual. Half talking to herself, half talking to Macy she said, "The only thing that bothers me about Dylan is why Mike never told me about him. I just don't understand that. I never thought Mike and I kept secrets from each other."

"What do you mean?" asked Macy.

Savannah wasn't sure if it was the drink, the excitement from the day, or finally just having a trusted friend to talk with, but suddenly she began vocalizing some of her worst fears. "It just seems like everything is happening to me at once. Do you realize how complicated my life has become during this past year? First I'm elected to the Senate. Then mom dies. Then Mike dies. Then Dylan shows up and tells me he's Mike son when I didn't even know Mike had a son. Next Brian Handy comes to town, is murdered, and I am pulled into the investigation just because I met and talked with him."

"Whoa!" exclaimed Macy. You're being investigated for the murder on False River? I didn't know that. Why didn't you tell me?"

"That's why Sheriff Breaux came over this morning. He took me to his office to question me about how I knew Tracy."

"Tracy?" asked Macy questioningly. "I thought you said his name was Brian."

"His name is Brian, but they call him Tracy. Sheriff Breaux thinks I might have been one of the last persons to see him alive. Obviously, someone saw him after me since he was murdered, and I didn't do it. Right now there are more questions than answers concerning Tracy's death."

"Macy, if I tell you something, will you promise to keep it to yourself? I haven't told anyone else yet and I'm still not sure what I'm going to do."

Savannah looked so serious that Macy knew this was going to be something dramatic. "Savannah, you know if you tell me something in confidence it goes no farther than us."

In her heart Savannah knew this was true. Macy was a loyal friend. Savannah had trusted Macy with other secrets, granted, none as big as this one. Still, she had never been betrayed. Tonight Savannah desperately needed someone to talk to.

"Friday before last," Savannah began, "I got a call from a man named

Brian Handy. I didn't realize who he was at first. He told me he was a friend of Mike's and that he needed to talk with me. He suggested we meet at Jim's Place."

"At Jim's Place ..." began Macy with a surprised look on her face.

"I know. I know. Anyway, he told me to be careful about trusting Dylan and he also told me..." Savannah took a deep breath, "... he also told me that there is a chance that Dylan may not be Mike's son."

"What!" exclaimed Macy. "That is so not right! How could he say that? You don't believe him, do you?"

"I don't know what to believe anymore," Savannah said with a deep sigh. "I was so upset at the time I couldn't even think. Tracy said he was staying at a friend's cabin and was going fishing the next day. We even talked about getting together for a fish fry on Saturday. When I called him the next day he didn't answer so I left a message on his voice mail. On Sunday I tried to call him again on his cell phone. I left a message for him, but I never heard back from him.

This past Saturday, Dylan and I went to Satterfield's for dinner. There was a big commotion, and some talk about finding a body in False River. It never dawned on me that it could be Tracy until this morning, when Sheriff Breaux showed up at the office and wanted me to go in with him for questioning."

"Wow!" said Macy completely taken aback.

"That's not even the worst part," Savannah continued. "From what I've been hearing, Tracy was being stalked by a man named Sammy Rodriguez. Sammy was trying to find out where Tracy had been staying while he was here." Savannah stopped herself from telling Macy too much more. She wanted to tell her everything, but it was just too much, and some of it was hard even for her to believe.

"Do you think this Sammy guy could have been the one to do in Tracy?" asked Macy.

"I don't know," responded Savannah. "I mean, if he was the one, he would have had to know where Tracy was staying, don't you think?

Sheriff Breaux seems to think that Tracy may have been killed near the camp."

"Oh yeah, that's right," sighed Macy.

"I don't know who to trust or what to think, Macy. I can't afford to tell anybody about what I know or don't know until I have a chance to find out the facts for myself. I don't want people thinking Dylan is not Mike's son if he really is, but at the same time, I don't want people thinking Mike was keeping secrets from me."

"You're probably right. Look Savannah, Mike was a good guy and he loved you. If something looks suspicious, I guarantee you Mike had a reason for doing what he did. What about Dylan? Have you told him about any of this?"

"No. We've just started getting to know each other and he seems so sincere and is so sweet. I just can't bear to tell him what Tracy said. He's had enough bad times for an army of people."

"Well then, what are you going to do?" Macy asked.

"I'm not sure yet. But please don't tell anybody about this, Macy. I need to keep it quiet until I can find out what's going on."

"Your secret is safe with me," replied Macy.

CHAPTER 94

Macy leaned over toward Savannah and whispered, "Do you know the guy sitting at the table next to the window over there?"

Savannah glanced over and then back again. "No, why?"

"He's been watching us ever since he came in. I think he walked in right behind us. I'm beginning to wonder if he's been following us."

"What makes you think that?" asked Savannah nervously.

"I just get this creepy feeling, that's all."

"Well, we've got work tomorrow, so it's probably a good time to leave anyway. We'll see what he does when we get up," whispered Savannah. After paying their bill, both Savannah and Macy walked outside. As they made a feeble attempt to stroll nonchalantly over to their car, Savannah glanced back over her shoulder. "I think he's still inside," she told Macy, beginning to feel a little foolish.

They were putting on their seat belts in the Hummer when Macy spotted the same man coming out of Satterfield's. "There he is again," she said. "He's getting into a Honda Accord that's parked two cars behind us."

"Macy, I'm starting to think you may have been right."

"Rats! What are we going to do?"

"First I want to make sure it's not just our imagination. I'd be so embarrassed if we accused a guy of stalking us, when all the time he was just out to have a nice quiet evening. Let's sit here for a few minutes. If he doesn't leave, we'll take off slowly, and then I'm going to wind down some different roads to see if he keeps following us."

Both Savannah and Macy sat nervously in the Hummer until finally Savannah said, "Well, I guess we can't wait here all night. Let's go." As she slowly pulled out of their parking space, the man in the Honda Accord started up his engine.

The speed limit downtown was twenty-five mph. Savannah was up to thirty-five mph when suddenly, she made a sharp turn to the left without giving any signal. Mr. Honda Accord kept going straight. Both women breathed a sigh of relief. Savannah went down to the end of the road and made a right turn. As she did, she spotted Mr. Honda Accord on the other side of the road coming towards them. "Good lord, he's at it again," she gasped. "Okay, so now I'm starting to get nervous."

"What are we going to do?" cried Macy.

"Do you have Sheriff Breaux's number?"

"I sure do," replied Macy. "You want me to call him?"

"Yes. Tell him we think we're being followed, and we're going to drive by his office. Ask him if he could have someone outside to check on the car following us."

Before Savannah could get the last words out of her mouth she could hear Macy talking to Sheriff Breaux on her cell phone.

"Sheriff Breaux, this is Macy Monroe. Savannah and I were out showing a house tonight, and now we think we may have someone following us. We're going to drive by your office. Could you please have someone check out the car behind us when we do? It's an older model Honda Accord."

Sheriff Breaux asked Macy a few more questions. By the time she finished they were turning down the street that led to the sheriff's office. They could see Sheriff Breaux standing outside with another deputy. When the driver of the car behind them saw the sheriff, he quickly pulled into a driveway, turned around, and headed off in the opposite direction.

Savannah pulled up next to Sheriff Breaux.

"Yeah we saw him," the sheriff said before either woman could comment. "I have one of my men posted on both ends of the street. They'll stop him and find out what this is all about. You want me to have someone follow you home?"

"No thanks, Charles," responded Savannah. "I hated to bother you, but I've been a little squeamish about everything lately. As long as you give us some lead time to get out of here, we're fine."

"I'll do that," the Sheriff promised. "We'll keep him here long enough for you to get home."

"Thanks, Charles."

Soon Savannah was pulling into her driveway. "You want to come in for a while?" she asked Macy.

"No, I better get on home. I want to be long gone by the time Sheriff Breaux's men let our stalker go."

Savannah laughed at first, but then said, "Macy, why don't you call me when you get home so I'll know you made it back safely?"

"Now Savannah," said Macy. "You know it's going to be a while before I get home. I'll be fine. You go ahead and get to bed."

"You sure?" asked Savannah.

"Absolutely," answered Macy.

"All right then. But please be careful. I'd hate to have to keep that big old commission check for myself." Savannah went inside as Macy drove off. She was shocked when she saw the time. It was already well past midnight and Savannah, at long last, realized just how tired she was.

The house was dark and quiet inside. It appeared that Dylan had already gone to bed. She slipped quietly into her bedroom. As usual, her thoughts turned to Mike, and it was hours before her mind could turn loose and let her drift mercifully into an overdue slumber.

CHAPTER 95

Normally Savannah woke up long before her alarm clock went off. This morning was different. As the buzz began its irritating noise, she pushed the snooze button. Slowly she tried to focus her eyes on the numbers before her. Five a.m. She was just about to doze off again when the alarm sounded once more. This time she reached up and turned it off.

Savannah did not realize that she had gained an extra hour of sleep until she was awakened by the loud clanging sound of a pan Dylan dropped in the kitchen. *"He must be trying to fix himself some breakfast,"* she laughed out loud. *"I guess I could get up and help him out before he tears the whole house apart."*

As usual, Savannah's mind began making a mental list of everything she had to do, as she reluctantly crawled out of bed and headed for the shower. *"I hope Macy hears something from Byron this morning,"* Savannah thought. *"She was so excited last night about the possibility of making a big sale."*

Dylan looked relieved when Savannah finally walked into the kitchen. "I'm sorry for making so much noise," he apologized. "It seems like I'm all thumbs this morning. I did manage to make coffee though. Would you like a cup?"

"Thanks," replied Savannah. "Why don't you let me take over now?"

Dylan was more than happy to turn over his kitchen duties to Savannah. After breakfast Dylan and Savannah left for work, each going in a different direction.

When Savannah pulled into the parking lot of the Devereaux Real Estate Company, she saw Betty's Ford Escort already at home in its' assigned parking place. The aroma of fresh coffee greeted Savannah as soon as she walked in the office. Betty was sitting at her desk, reading the newspaper, and drinking a cup of coffee.

"Good morning, Ms. Savannah," she cheerfully exclaimed.

"Good morning, Betty" Savannah replied. "How are you this morning?"

"I guess I'm as good as could be expected for someone my age," she chortled. Without hesitation she continued, "I got stuck going with Cal to his sister's house for dinner last night." The dinner was good, but her husband wasn't. He is so weird.

After dinner we played cards and listened to Huey's warped views on politics, past elections, and how the youth of today are all going to hell in a hand basket. Cal and Huey ended up drinking too much, as usual. I thought Sally and I were going to have to pull them off of each other when they got to talking about freeloaders on society and who should get Medicaid and who shouldn't. Yes ma'am, that was one fun evening!" said Betty sarcastically.

"The only good thing that came out of it was that Cal agreed with me when I told him that I thought I had fulfilled my obligation as a good wife, and that I didn't think I should have to go back to his sister's house for at least another 10 years. Cal is 79 years old now. He will probably be dead in 10 years if he keeps smoking and drinking the way he does.

It's kind of a shame though. I really like Sally, and we could be such good friends if it weren't for the old geezers we are married to."

Savannah started laughing out loud. "Betty, you are something else!"

She was still laughing as she walked into her office, put her purse in the bottom drawer, and checked the messages Betty left on her desk. Then she went to the break room where she filled her coffee cup and quickly took a sip from it. "Betty, your coffee sure hits the spot this morning," she called out.

As soon as Savannah walked out of the break room and into the hall, she saw Macy coming in. "Good Lord, Macy, it's not even eight-thirty yet. I figured since you got home so late last night, you'd be coming in late this morning. You must've been up all night figuring out how much you're going to make in commission on your big sale today."

"What big sale?" asked Betty.

"It looks like the Bertrands are going to buy the ole Robillard place," Macy proudly responded.

"Way to go," smiled Betty. "And when do you plan on taking us all out to lunch to celebrate?"

"You sound just like Savannah. A girl tries to make a living around here, and the next thing you know, everybody thinks she's adopted them," she joked. Then she added, "I'm just kidding, Ms. Betty. Don't worry, if this sale goes through, I'll treat everybody to an ice cream cone," Macy laughed enthusiastically.

"That's our Macy. Generous to a fault," chuckled Betty.

When Jim walked in and saw everybody, including Macy, joking and having a good time he quickly looked down at his watch. "Am I late?" he stuttered.

"No, you're on time," laughed Savannah.

"But it's only eight-thirty and Macy's already here. What's going on?" he asked. "Did y'all call a meeting and forget to tell me about it? Was I fired and no one let me know?"

By this time Savannah, Betty, and Macy were laughing uncontrollably. "No, we just got a case of the sillies," said Betty.

"Actually we're just celebrating early. It looks like Macy may have a buyer for the old Robillard place," said Savannah.

"Congratulations, Macy! That's great news." said Jim.

"Y'all better not jinx me," said Macy. "The deal hasn't gone through yet. We're still negotiating."

"You can do it, Macy. We have faith in you," said Jim.

"Well, we all better get to work so that Macy doesn't turn out to be the only one who can pay her bills this month," said Savannah. With that, she took her coffee and went into her office.

The morning passed quickly: checking e-mails, answering phone calls, monitoring the Internet for new pieces of real estate on the market, and people stopping by to talk. Savannah had hoped that Byron Daigle would be by before she had to leave. She had a meeting with Gilbert Mouton at two p.m., and needed to leave the office by one-forty p.m. to make it in time. Of course, even when Byron brought the purchase agreement, Macy would still have to take it to the Bertrands to get their reaction to any changes made.

She wasn't sure how long her meeting with Gilbert would take. Mike had already gone over everything with him before, so this was more of an opportunity for Savannah to make sure that she had all the facts straight before talking with James Maxwell again.

With the current market situation like it was, several banks having to be bailed out, and people defaulting on loans, everyone in the money lending business was extremely nervous. However, if a client had a steady credit record and no major problems, they were probably going to be all right. She felt confident that would be the case with both Gilbert and James.

Jim knocked on her door and looked in. "I'm getting ready to walk over to Espresso Etc. to pick up sandwiches for lunch for Betty, Macy, and myself. Would you like one too?"

"Thanks, Jim. That sounds great. Would you get me one of their Mediterranean wraps?" Savannah reached into her Gucci bag which was tucked away in her bottom desk drawer and pulled out a fifty dollar bill. "You've all been working so hard, that I'm treating today."

"Thanks," Jim grinned. As he was passing Betty's desk she said, "Jim, if you give me the orders I'll call them in so they'll be ready when you get there."

Jim waited a few minutes after Betty called, and then walked down the block to the cafe. On his return, Jim called Betty, Macy, and Savannah into the break room for lunch. "Lunch today is courtesy of our generous boss," he quipped.

The break room was not much bigger than their small offices. It was just large enough to include a wrap around counter with a kitchen sink, a built-in stove, a small refrigerator, and a microwave. Centered in the middle of the room was a round wooden table barely large enough for the five chairs that circled it.

"Betty where are you going?" asked Savannah as Betty headed for the door.

"To my desk, so I can answer the phone."

"Not today. Just put the answering machine on and come join us."

Soon they were all sitting around the table in a most festive mood. Jim said, "You know Savannah, I think this is the first time, in a very long time, that we've all had the chance to sit down and eat together. This is really nice. Thanks."

CHAPTER 96

By the time the office staff had finished lunch it was one o'clock. "I guess it's time to get back to work," said Savannah. "I have some last minute business I need to finish before my call this afternoon. You haven't heard anything from Byron yet, have you Macy?"

"No," Macy replied nervously.

"Don't worry. They have until this evening to get back to you," Savannah reminded her. "I imagine Byron is pushing as hard as he can to get everything completed. After all, he's going to make quite a bit on this transaction too."

Before she knew it, time had flown by and Savannah found herself rushing to her car to make sure she would not be late for her meeting with Gilbert and his wife, Mary Louise.

The Moutons were the perfect hosts. After going over all the paperwork with them, and eating several different samples of cookies that Mary Louise was planning on including in her cook book, Savannah left for the office. She was anxious to learn the outcome of the purchase agreement Macy had drawn up for the Bertrands.

As she pulled into the office parking lot, Savannah immediately spotted Byron's vehicle. It was a beautiful steel gray pickup truck with the extended cab. She quickly parked and rushed into the front office. The thrill of negotiations never seemed to grow old with Savannah.

Betty smiled broadly when Savannah walked in and pointed to Macy's office. "The agent with the purchase agreement is here. Lord, he's good looking!"

Before she could catch herself, Savannah laughed out loud. Hoping Byron had not heard her, she regained her professional demeanor and replied, "Thanks." She was on her way back to her office when Macy called out to her.

"Savannah, come on in. Byron just brought back the purchase agreement from the Robillards."

"What did they say?" asked Savannah in excited anticipation.

"Actually I was very surprised," Byron reported. "They agreed to everything. I thought they would balk at the price offered, but I guess they were getting tired of having it on the market for so long."

"That's great," said Savannah. Macy, have you called the Bertrands yet?"

"No, Byron just got here and we were going over the paperwork when you came in."

"Why don't you go ahead and call them now? Let's make hay while the sun shines."

Byron started to laugh. "I can see you two have everything under control. Macy, you have my cell number. If you would, just give me a call when you finish talking with the Bertrands so I can call the Robillards. I think everyone is on edge waiting for the outcome of this deal."

CHAPTER 97

After Byron left the office, Savannah couldn't tell if the flushed look on Macy's face was from the excitement about the prospect of such a big sale, or from coming in contact with Byron again. She grinned broadly at her.

Macy ignored the look and asked Savannah, "Are you going with me again?"

"Sure, if you want me to. Just find out when they want you to come over and let me know."

Macy picked up the phone and called the Bertrands. "Mrs. Bertrand, this is Macy Monroe. I just got the purchase agreement back from the Robillards. If you and Mr. Bertrand are free, I'll be happy to bring it over for you to look at."

Mrs. Bertrand started laughing. "Macy, honey, Mr. Bertrand and I may not be free, but we're reasonable. You just come on over." She was still laughing as she hung up the phone.

"Let's go," Macy yelled out to Savannah. "Mrs. Bertrand is in rare form, and like you always say, we need to strike while the iron is hot." Once inside the car, Macy could hardly contain her excitement. "Do you realize, Savannah, this is the biggest sale I've ever made."

Mrs. Bertrand was waiting at the door when Savannah and Macy arrived. After the customary greetings she ushered them back to the kitchen. Mr. Bertrand was sitting at the table drinking coffee.

"Would you girls like something to drink?" asked Mrs. Bertrand.

"No, thank you," both girls replied. They didn't want to appear rude, but they were anxious to give the Bertrands the good news.

"The Robillards have agreed to your offer," Macy beamed.

"Really!" exclaimed Mrs. Bertrand. "I can't believe it!"

"I'm surprised too," said Mr. Bertrand, obviously pleased.

"There are only two stipulations: The first is that we go to closing by the date they've indicated, which should not be problem; and the second is that since they're coming down drastically on the purchase price, they will not be putting anything towards the closing costs."

The Bertrands were satisfied with the changes and quickly initialed and dated the stipulations. Macy carefully placed all the paperwork in her briefcase. After congratulating the Bertrands on their successful negotiations, Savannah and Macy excused themselves so they could return to the office and ready the paperwork for Byron. As they left the Bertrands, everyone had a smile on their face, even Mr. Bertrand.

Inside the car, Macy let out a whoop. "I can't believe it!" she exclaimed. "This is absolutely my best day yet as a real estate agent!"

"Wait until you get your commission," Savannah reminded her. "You better call Byron right now and let him know the Bertrand's approved the contract. Tell him he can come by and pick up a copy of the signed purchase agreement."

Macy pulled out her cell phone and pushed the number she had already pre-programmed for Byron.

"Byron Daigle speaking."

"Hi, Byron, this is Macy. I just wanted to let you know that the Bertrands have agreed to the closing date and will pay all the closing costs, so it looks like we're good to go."

"Great!" said Byron. I'll let the Robillards know and then I'll be by your office to pick up the paperwork."

Savannah and Macy returned to the office just as Betty was getting ready to close up. "Don't worry about shutting everything down today, Betty. Macy has to wait for Byron to pick up the Bertrand's purchase agreement, so we'll be here for a little while longer."

"How'd it go?" asked Betty.

"Fantastic!" Macy gushed.

"Good for you Macy. Now you be careful around that cute little Byron Daigle. That boy's too good-looking for his own good. You know, the good-looking ones are the ones you have to watch out for."

"I'll be careful, Ms. Betty," Macy replied with a giggle.

Savannah told Macy, "While you're waiting for Byron, I'm going to try to get in touch with James Maxwell about Gilbert Mouton's property."

"Sure, no problem," said Macy.

Before calling James, Savannah remembered seeing a sold sign on the house across the street from the Bertrands. *"It might be a good idea,"* she thought *"to see just how much that house sold for. It would give us a good indication of the price Mr. and Mrs. Bertrand might reasonably expect to get for their home."*

Savannah connected to the Internet and was soon pulling up the stats on the sale price and the purchaser. "No!" she yelled out loud.

Macy came running in. "What's the matter?" she asked nervously.

"You're not going to believe this," Savannah answered, completely stunned. "Guess who bought the house across from the Bertrands."

"I don't have a clue," Macy replied.

"It was none other than Sammy Rodriguez, the guy that told Tommy he was a private investigator. And, get this – he paid the asking price for the house, which wasn't cheap! Why do you figure a private investigator would spend that kind of money on a house in New Roads?"

"Beats me," said Macy. "Is he married, or is it just in his name?"

"Good question. I only saw his name, but let me double check." After going through a few more sites, Savannah said, "It appears that only his name is on the deed. What do you make of that?"

"It seems kind of strange to me," replied Macy. "I mean, he appears out of nowhere and just as suddenly establishes residence here. There's been no talk about him setting up a business. Usually somebody new that moves into town ends up being the latest gossip. It's really weird that we haven't heard anything about him."

"There is one good thing about him paying top dollar for that house, though," continued Savannah. "It means the Bertrands should be able to ask more for their home. You are going to be selling their home, aren't you?"

"That's the plan," smiled Macy as she turned to go back to her office.

About twenty minutes later Byron pulled up to the Devereaux Real Estate Company office. Savannah heard him come in, but before she could stand up she heard Macy rushing out to the front office.

Macy and Byron quickly engaged in a lively conversation so Savannah decided not to butt in. After all, if Macy needed her, she would come and get her. Savannah snickered at the thought, *"Yeah, like that's gonna happen."*

About fifteen minutes later Savannah heard the front door shut, and soon Macy was at her door. "How'd it go?" she asked.

"As soon as the deal goes through, Byron is taking me out to celebrate."

"Wow, a double whammy," Savannah marveled, "closing on two deals at the same time."

"Yeah, I got to admit, it's been a good day," proclaimed Macy as she danced out of the room.

It was getting late. Savannah had called James and arranged to meet with him on his next trip to New Roads. She neatly stacked her paperwork in the top drawer of her desk, locked up the office, and went out to her car. It was past time to go home.

CHAPTER 98

When Savannah woke up Saturday morning her mind quickly turned to thoughts of Tracy, or as everyone kept referring to him, Brian Handy.

Tracy said he had important information for her at the camp where he was staying. Sheriff Breaux had never mentioned finding a strong box, and at the time of her interrogation, Savannah hardly had the presence of mind to ask about it. Maybe that was good. If she had asked, it might have implicated her further in his murder. Savannah wondered if it was possible that they found the box but left it behind, thinking it belonged to Mr. Gabour.

If a strong box really existed, it could prove to be invaluable in discovering who might have a motive for killing Tracy. She began to feel a knot in her stomach as she realized that it may also include a link to Mike's death. Ultimately, she was held captive by the thought that it would indeed contain information that Tracy and Mike had gathered regarding sinister activities at the capitol.

Savannah still had lingering thoughts about Tracy. What was it about him that continued to keep her on edge? Tommy said that Sammy Rodriguez had been hired to follow Tracy. Could he have been following Mike too?

Clearly Mike and Tracy were working on something of vital importance that certain individuals did not want to become public knowledge.

Savannah decided it was time to start her own investigation. The police were not working fast enough and did not know everything she knew. It was time to drive out to the Gabour campsite.

Arriving at the campsite, she quickly noted the entire area had been cardoned off by the police. Yellow and black caution tape was everywhere. Savannah viewed the empty house from a distance.

The campsite, camp, or cabin that everyone had been referring to, was in reality, a beautiful brick home. It included a pier off the back of the lot, leading directly onto False River. Well-kept landscaping surrounded the home. As she neared the cabin, the fuller branches of trees and bushes made it difficult to see inside.

The boat shed to the back side of the house now sat empty. She heard that blood stains were found in the boat and it had been impounded for DNA testing. Tracy's car, which was also missing, had been taken as well.

There was a place on the ground close to the river that had chalk markings on it. The arrows were pointing towards the other side of False River. *"These markings look as if they're pointing to the spot down the river where Tracy's body was pulled out,"* thought Savannah.

There were noticeable signs indicating a full-fledged investigation had taken place. Grass and contiguous flower beds had been trampled by investigators looking for additional clues.

As she walked around the house, Savannah was surprised to find a window with the blinds open. Brightly colored shrubs filled the yard in front of it. Trying not to disturb the landscaping, she reached forward to grab hold of the window sill in order to see inside. As she leaned in, she lost her footing and slipped, falling into the thick shrubbery below.

Her hand hit on something sharp beneath some overgrown foliage and started to bleed. As she tried to regain her balance, several of the plants were pushed aside. There, beneath the mass of plant growth, she spotted a shiny metal box that was still partially buried in the ground. Savannah quickly looked around to see if anyone may have seen her. Confident that she was still alone, she began digging out the remainder of the buried box.

"This is it!" she thought with great excitement. *"This is the strong*

box Tracy told me about. He must have known someone was after him. Why else would he have tried to bury the box in the flower bed?"

The box was locked. Savannah remembered the key she had in her purse back in the car. Suddenly a noise on the other side of the house made her freeze in her tracks. The agonizingly long minute that followed convinced her that it must have been the wind. Still, whoever was after Tracy would surely be back looking for the information she now possessed. There was no sense in dallying around.

Rushing to her car she unlocked the door from the button on her key chain and jumped in. Immediately afterwards she closed and locked the door again. She drove off at a steady pace, trying not to attract attention. As an afterthought, Savannah reached into the glove compartment of her car and found some napkins to press against her injured hand.

When she pulled into her driveway at home she was relieved to see that Dylan was still at work. She covered the box with a plastic bag she found in her car, and then got out. As she was putting the house key in the back door a man's voice resounded, "Hello."

Savannah's hand jerked wildly. Her key fell to the ground as she yelled out in fear. When she whirled around she was embarrassed to see Tony smiling at her.

"I'm sorry. I didn't mean to scare you," he said.

"Oh Tony," Savannah moaned in relief. "You caught me off guard," she laughed.

"I just wanted to let you know, I'm going to town to pick up some supplies. Is there anything I can get for you while I'm out?"

"No, but thanks for asking," replied Savannah.

Once inside, Savannah secured the back door behind her and went straight to her bedroom. She locked the bedroom door and walked into the bathroom, gently placing the strongbox on the counter. Then she took out a washcloth and peroxide and began to clean her bleeding hand.

When Savannah was through washing and putting a Band-Aid on her hand, she wiped the dirt off the box and took it back into the bedroom. She opened her purse and took out the key Tracy had given her. Then she dropped her purse on the floor beside her. She kicked off her shoes and sat in the recliner, the box in her hand. Gently she placed the key in the lock. It opened easily. One by one she began taking the papers out.

The first set of papers was preceded by a note that stated, "Things to tell Savannah:

    1.   I've been trying to find out more about Dylan. Still a blank page on that one. I did find a picture recently that had Dylan's name on the back of it along with the name Hank Myers. I don't know where it came from. Could they be one and the same? Is Dylan really who he says he is?

    2.   Mike's cover with the CIA has been blown. I don't know who is responsible for his death. It could be drug cartel figures or the CIA themselves. I'd hate to think the latter. We may all be treading on thin ice at this point.

Savannah wasn't sure she wanted to continue, but she had gone this far and couldn't stop now. The next stack of papers included information about scams and improprieties going on at the state capitol in Baton Rouge. As Savannah's eyes skimmed over the details she became distraught at the revelations before her.

The cumulative contents of the metal box were mind boggling.

CHAPTER 99

Some time passed before Savannah returned all the documents to the metal box. Her fingers grabbed hold of the frame on the large picture hanging on the bedroom wall. With little effort, it swung out to reveal the safe behind it. Soon, with the smooth gliding action of the combination lock, the safe was opened. The box was placed inside, the safe closed and locked, and the picture returned to its stationary place on the wall.

Savannah changed clothes and rushed into her home office. On the internet she typed in the name, Dylan Devereaux. He was listed as the son of Michael Joseph Devereaux, nothing more. Then she typed the name, Hank Myers. There were several sites, but none that appeared to be related to Dylan.

It was time to call Tommy, at the Banner, to see if he had found out anything else about the murder investigation.

"I was told the police have some leads, but if they do they sure are keeping a tight lid on it," he reported. "They interviewed people up and down both sides of the river. Nobody saw anything."

"Are they sure the body they found was Brian Handy?" Savannah questioned.

"No doubt about that. His wife sent in dental records and they matched up."

"Is there any more information on who may have killed him?"

"No, but it was a pretty brutal attack. They said he had been unmercifully stabbed repeatedly with a knife, and then held underwater until he drowned. Brian Handy was definitely done in by someone who had a real grudge against him."

"If you find out anything else, would you let me know?" asked Savannah. "I feel so strange having been pulled into all of this. I'd really like to know why."

"Sure Savannah," said Tommy. But I'll be honest with you. We just keep getting bits and pieces. Nothing seems to be fitting together yet."

"I understand. Thanks, Tommy."

CHAPTER 100

After talking with Tommy, Savannah became increasingly troubled. If Tracy was killed the way Tommy said, it was in your face and personal. Someone had intentionally gone after him in a very brutal and terrifying way. If they found out that he had been in touch with her, would they come after her too? In addition to that, she worried about Dylan, and the possibility that he might not be Mike's son.

On Monday morning, Savannah decided it was time to have a serious discussion with Sheriff Breaux. As soon as she got to the office, she placed a call to his office.

"I'm sorry Savannah," said Jean. "The sheriff's out until after lunch. Do you want me to have him call you back then?"

"Yes. Thanks," replied Savannah.

Savannah worked until eleven-thirty and then decided to take an early lunch.

"Betty, I'm going out for a little while. If Sheriff Breaux calls would you ask him to call me on my cell phone?"

"Sure," said Betty.

Less than an hour later Savannah was back at her desk. It wasn't until one-thirty that she received a call back from Sheriff Breaux.

"Charles," she began, "I have some information that I think you need to know about concerning Brian Handy. Do you have some time when we could talk today?"

"Sure Savannah. Any time you want to come by will be fine. I'll be here all afternoon."

Savannah quickly put away the papers she had been working on and walked into the front office. "I may be gone the rest of the day, Betty. If I get any calls, just take messages."

"Will do," she replied.

CHAPTER 101

Savannah pulled up at the Sheriff's office and parked next to one of their patrol cars. It was an old Crown Victoria. The "Vic" had lots of power, but was definitely now showing signs of wear and tear, not only from age, but also from picking up the usual Saturday night inebriated patrons from the local bars.

"Good afternoon, Savannah," said Jean Melancon, Sheriff Breaux's top deputy and his right arm in investigations.

"Hi Jean. Could you please let Charles know that I'm here? He's expecting me."

Jean dialed the extension on the Sheriff's phone and stated, "Senator Devereaux is here to see you." Then after a brief exchange, she turned her head back to Savannah and said with a smile, "You can go in."

"Thanks." When Savannah walked into the office, Charles had already gotten up from behind his desk and started toward the door to meet her.

"How are you doing today, Savannah?" Charles asked. He knew something was bothering her, but wanted to let her bring it up.

"I'm not sure," Savannah responded.

Charles shook her hand and pointed to a chair. As she was going to sit down he went to the door and closed it. Savannah was relieved. She didn't want everybody in the office to hear what she was going to say.

"Charles, I didn't tell you everything I knew about Tracy."

The sheriff looked surprised.

Savannah continued, "When he called me to ask me to meet him at Jim's Place, he told me he had some important information that I needed to be made aware of. He said it concerned Mike. Once I got there he told me so many things, I really didn't know what to believe any more. He told me that Mike's death may not have been an accident, and that our lives may be in danger too."

"You've got to be kidding me!" shouted out Charles in utter astonishment. "Savannah, why didn't you tell me all of this before?"

"I had just met the man. And quite frankly, I wasn't sure how much I trusted him. He was supposed to call me the next day, but of course he never did. When a week went by with no more calls from him, I just thought it must have been some kind of a sick prank. He even implied that Dylan may not be who he says he is. I just couldn't believe him after that. Now that he's dead …" her voice trailed off. After a brief pause, she began again. "Charles, I'm so upset. I don't know what to think or do anymore."

"Savannah, why did he say that Mike may not have had an accident?"

"I want to tell you, but I just can't yet," said Savannah with a terrorized look on her face.

"How can I protect you if I don't know what I'm fighting against? And why was he suspicious of Dylan?" asked Sheriff Breaux.

"I guess I shouldn't have come in. I'm not sure I believe much of what he told me. On top of that, I just can't bear the thought of hurting Dylan with unfounded accusations when we've gotten so close. I can't help but believe he is Mike's son."

"Savannah, you are way too soft-hearted. Dylan could be an axe murderer, or worse, for all you know. If Dylan is not really Mike's son, and Tracy found out, Dylan would have had the perfect motive to kill Tracy.

"Oh, Charles. You don't really think that, do you?"

"I don't know what to think at this point," said Charles. "But I want to make sure you are safe. Maybe you should tell Dylan you think it would be best if he moved out to a place of his own now."

"I just told him he could stay until he got on his feet again. I know he would think it was strange if all of the sudden I tell him he has to move out. He's such a sweet person, and he reminds me so much of Mike," insisted Savannah.

"Well, it's up to you," Charles said with great reservation. "But I want you to program my cell number into your phone. If anything – anything at all – happens that concerns you, if he even looks at you in the wrong way, I want you to call me immediately. Understand?" He wrote down his personal cell phone number and handed it to Savannah.

"Thank you Charles. You're such a good friend. But I really do think we're misjudging Dylan. He just has to be Mike's son. He even looks like him. The way he smiles and his eyes ... he just has to be Mike's son."

"I hope for your sake that you're right, said Charles. But keep my number close at hand until we're sure. And Savannah, please call me if you need me."

Savannah felt relieved she had talked to Charles. Although she had not been able to tell him much, at least now if anything happened, he would know that a thorough investigation would be warranted.

"Oh, one last thing Charles – Tommy said there was a private in-vestigator named Sammy Rodriguez who told him that he had been hired to follow Brian Handy. He also led Tommy to believe that he was working with you on some investigation." Before Savannah could continue Charles broke in.

"Yeah, Tommy told me that too. I don't know where this guy gets off telling people something like that. I never met the guy and sure don't need his help to do my job."

"The reason I brought it up," Savannah continued, "was because I just recently found out that he bought a house in New Roads. Don't you find that strange? Just think about it. This man named Sammy

Rodriguez shows up and says he's been hired as a private detective to follow a man named Brian Handy. Brian Handy gets murdered. Now suddenly, Sammy Rodriguez moves into town and buys a house."

"That sure is peculiar," said Charles. "I'll have to make some calls and find out what our good friend Sammy's up to. Thanks for filling me in."

CHAPTER 102

Another week had come and just about gone. It was already Friday morning and Savannah was looking forward to the weekend. As she drove out of her driveway, she noticed a lone car sitting across the road. *"I guess Charles decided to send an undercover deputy to watch the house for me. I need to call him and tell him that's not necessary. It looks like everything is finally starting to settle down. I'll call him later and thank him anyway."*

When she walked into the office, Betty smiled and said, "Good morning Ms. Savannah. How you doin' today?"

"I'm doing fine, thank you," replied Savannah. "I'm going to get some coffee. Would you like another cup?" she asked Betty after noticing the empty coffee cup on her desk.

"If I have any more, I might float off," she laughed.

Jim and Macy were both there; Jim more animated than usual. "I may have sold two houses yesterday," he boasted when he saw Savannah.

"Great!" exclaimed Savannah. "Which houses?"

"One of the houses is the one I showed last week to Shelly and Donald Juneau. They had looked at it twice, but just couldn't decide. Finally yesterday morning they called me and wanted to see the house once more. After only ten minutes, they signed a purchase agreement.

Before I could get back to the office, I got a call from a woman named Faun Fenderson who had been looking at some condominiums. I met her at the one she was interested in and let her go through it. She loved the place and, bam, I had another signed purchase agreement."

"It doesn't get much better than that," Savannah said, with a big smile on her face.

"Now comes the fun part," he said sarcastically. "Pulling it all together."

"Life's tough, Jim," Savannah teased.

Betty had been giving all the incoming calls to Jim or Macy to take care of so, except for a few personal calls, Savannah's desk looked pretty clear. She took care of the paperwork Mike used to handle and then went for another cup of coffee.

Around ten-thirty Savannah remembered that she had wanted to call Charles to thank him for sending someone out to watch the house for her. She walked into her office and closed the door behind her. When she got Charles on the phone she said, "Charles, I appreciate your concern for me, but you really don't need to have a deputy sitting outside my house during the day. Tony keeps a pretty close tab on things for me."

Charles sounded surprised. "Savannah," he said, "I didn't send anybody out to watch your house. I told the guys that when they were out on patrol, to pass by your house just to make sure everything looked all right, but nobody was assigned to sit in front of your house. What did the car look like?"

"It was a white LTD Crown Victoria. I just assumed it was the one I had seen in your parking lot on Monday."

"Afraid not Savannah. I loved our 'Vics.' They were great cars in their day, but the only "Vic" we had left was on its last leg. Lately it stayed in the shop more than out. It got so old and the upkeep was so expensive, I finally had to let it go. Old "Vic" went into retirement on Wednesday. If the truth be told, I bet they had a difficult time getting it to the scrap yard."

"Charles, if that wasn't a deputy, I'm worried about Tony. He stays at the house all day long working around the yard and doing whatever needs to be done. Could you have someone go over there and check on him for me?"

"I'll go myself," Charles answered. "Give me a chance to check it out and I'll call you back as soon as I find out something. Are you going to be at the office?"

"Yes," she said. "Thanks, Charles. I'll be waiting to hear from you."

After Savannah talked with Charles, she began to think about the car once again. *"Why didn't I pay more attention to what the car looked like and who was inside it?"* It was over an hour before Charles finally called her back.

"Savannah, we had a little trouble, but we finally caught your intruder. When I got to your house I saw his car in your driveway. I called for backup and my men were there in no time. Tony had already seen the car and went out to talk to the man. He told Tony that he had come out to give an estimate on what it would take to put a new roof on your house. He said that you wanted to have the roof changed out."

"What?" said Savannah, appalled by his boldness.

"Don't worry," Charles continued. "Tony said he knew you would never plan something that major without talking to him first. He saw my men drive up, so he tried to play along until they blocked him in. As soon as the man saw my deputies, he took off running across your backyard. He gave them a good run for their money," laughed Charles. He escaped through the woods, so we put out an all points bulletin on him. It wasn't even 15 minutes later when he was seen by another deputy patrolling the area. My men were there in a flash and they picked him up and brought him in.

It appears your stalker has been a very busy man. His name came up as having a number of outstanding warrants against him: some drug and petty theft charges; and more recently, an attempted bank robbery where a teller got shot.

We have enough on him to hold him for a while. Hopefully, during that time we'll be able to find out what his game is. He may have been casing out your house for a possible heist."

"Thank goodness you caught him, Charles. Was Tony upset by all this?"

Charles began to laugh. "You know, Savannah, I think that boy's a born deputy. My men were really impressed by his actions. If you ever decide to let him go, send him my way."

CHAPTER 103

Friday night Savannah, Dylan, and Tony stayed up late discussing the events of the day. Strangely enough, Savannah was finally beginning to relax. The man that had obviously been following her was in jail, Tony had proved himself to be a great protector, and Dylan seemed to be excited about his work at the plant.

By the time Dylan left for work Saturday morning, Tony had come back to check on Savannah.

"Tony," Savannah said, "I can't thank you enough for everything you did, but in the future, if anyone comes snooping around the house, I want you to call the sheriff's office. Don't try to confront them. I don't know what I'd do if anything happened to you."

"Yes ma'am," Tony replied with a silly grin.

Savannah may have been older than Tony, but he still recognized a beautiful woman when he saw one. And, although he knew there would never be anything between them, he still had a special place in his heart for Savannah.

CHAPTER 104

Sunday morning Savannah got ready for church and slipped quietly out of the house, so as not to wake up Dylan. She wished he was going with her, but that was something she would have to work on. It was a beautiful morning and Savannah was in an incredibly upbeat mood.

After the services, Joe Granger approached her on the outside steps of the church where he had been waiting for her. "Senator Devereaux," he began hesitantly, "I'm sorry about the incident at the plant. Dylan was a good worker and I hated to see him go."

"Incident at the plant?" questioned Savannah.

"He didn't tell you?"

"Tell me what?" she insisted.

"I'm sorry, but I thought you knew. Dylan was fired on Wednesday. One of the men reported money missing from his locker. Then, Terri, our secretary, couldn't find the money she left in her desk drawer that was supposed to be deposited Wednesday afternoon. Dylan was the only one left in the office at lunchtime.

When they confronted him, he got mad and started swinging at one of the guys on the crew. That boy of yours has a mean right hook. He broke Ken's nose. As soon as Mr. Mercer heard what happened, he fired Dylan on the spot."

"I don't know what to say, Joe," Savannah mumbled in total disbelief. "I just don't understand. Are they sure Dylan was the one to take the money?"

"Senator, I don't think anyone knows for sure. Frankly, I have my doubts, but he was the only one left in the office during lunch, and starting a fight sure didn't help his cause."

"Thanks for telling me, Joe. I appreciate you giving him the job, and I'm sorry it didn't work out."

Savannah felt like the wind had been taken out of her sails. It was hard to fathom Dylan doing something so detestable. It was even harder to believe that he didn't tell her he was fired.

"Hi," Dylan said cheerily as soon as Savannah walked into the house. The minute he saw the expression on her face, he knew that something was wrong. "What's the matter?"

"Dylan, why didn't you tell me you'd been fired? Where've you been going every day?"

Dylan's whole attitude changed. "I'm sorry Savannah. I thought I could find another job before you found out. After everything you did for me, I couldn't stand the thought of letting you down."

"They say you stole money from the office and from one of the workers. Is that true?"

"No! I swear on a stack of bibles, I never took anything. When they started accusing me of being a thief, I got so mad I hit Ken. That's when Mr. Mercer fired me."

"Dylan, you have to learn to trust me. When something goes wrong I would much rather hear it from you than from someone else. Do you know how embarrassing it was for me to find out about this at church? What have you been doing with yourself since you got fired?"

"I went to the unemployment office first. They told me about a laborer job they had and I went and talked to the people there. Somehow word had already gotten around about me being fired from the plant. Then I went to Baton Rouge to see if I could find something over there. I have my application in at a number of places."

Savannah had put her reputation on the line when she recommended Dylan for a job at the plant. She was a little more hesitant to rush into doing the same thing again. She wanted to believe he didn't take the missing money, but how could she know for sure. Of course, being new, he would be the perfect patsy for a thief at work.

Little more was said until Dylan asked to use the truck again to go fill out more job applications. Savannah agreed, anxious to have some time to herself to sort out what she was going to do next.

Dylan had no sooner left, than Tony's truck turned into the driveway, going to his house in the back. Savannah walked quickly out the back door, and was walking toward the driveway as Tony neared. "Good morning, Ms. Savannah. Nice day, isn't it."

"It sure is, Tony." Her voice faltered, but then she continued. "Have you got a minute to talk?"

"Sure, Ms. Savannah. What can I do for you?"

"Tony, you know how much I value your opinion. I was just wondering what you thought about Dylan."

"What do you mean, Ms. Savannah?" he asked cautiously.

"I want you to be honest with me. I don't really know Dylan that well, and I would like to give him the benefit of the doubt. But this past week he got fired from his job and never told me about it. I didn't find out until this morning after church that he had been let go on Wednesday. I know he's had some hard breaks, but honesty is high on my list of priorities."

"Yes, ma'am. I can understand that," Tony said. Then very hesitantly he began. "I'm not exactly sure what you want me to tell you. I do know that Dylan didn't work on Thursday because he had some friends over. They were out by the pool drinking and got awfully rowdy. I figured it was none of my business so I tried to steer clear of them.

I think you need to be careful when it comes to Dylan. He may be Mr. Mike's son, but I'm just not sure he is the kind of person that you and Mr. Mike have been used to having around you."

Startled, Savannah said "What do you mean, Tony?"

"I'm sorry, Ms. Savannah. Sometimes I talk too much."

"No you don't, Tony. Finish what you were going to say," Savannah insisted. "What happened?"

"No big deal, Ms. Savannah. It's just that Thursday when I was coming back from town, I drove my truck along the driveway like I always do. Dylan was over here with his friends and he started yelling at me, saying that I was stirring up too much dust when I went by. Ms. Savannah, you know me and how I drive. I remember many times passing by your house when you and Mr. Mike were out by the pool, and it never seemed to bother either one of you.

Anyway, Dylan told me that from now on when he was out by the pool with his friends I was not to drive by the house. I tried to tell him that was the only way I had to get back to my place, and that you had never complained before. I guess I shouldn't have said that because he got mad. He told me that since he has now moved in, I was going to have to learn to take orders from him too. I think he was just trying to show off for his friends, so I told him I would try not to bother them again."

Savannah was furious. Tony was like one of the family, and she loved him dearly. "Tony I'm so sorry that he treated you that way. You should have told me immediately. I can tell you now, it won't happen again. I'll talk to Dylan tonight."

"Ms. Savannah, I don't want to cause any trouble between you and Dylan."

"No Tony," Savannah shot back. "If Dylan's going to stay in this house he has to fit in with us, not the other way around. Please promise me that you'll let me know if you have any more problems with Dylan."

"Yes ma'am. Thanks. Oh, and one more thing," Tony said before leaving. "My parents invited me to have dinner and watch a movie with them this evening. I thought I'd spend the night, if you're not going to need me the rest of the day."

"That's fine, Tony. I hope you have a wonderful time. Give my love to your parents."

"Yes ma'am, I will."

Savannah turned around and started walking back toward the house. With each step she took, she became more incensed by Dylan's actions.

CHAPTER 105

Dylan didn't get home until after ten p.m. Savannah wasn't sure, but she thought he had been drinking. He was more talkative than usual and his eyes looked glazed over. "Dylan" she said, "we need to talk."

Dylan walked over to Savannah and put his arm around her. "Don't look so glum little momma," he said. "What'su problem?"

Savannah had never seen Dylan act this way. "Have you been drinking?" she asked point blank.

"I had a few beers with some guys I met today. So?" he asked sarcastically. His mannerisms were completely out of character with the Dylan she had grown accustomed to.

"Where'd you get the money to go drinking?"

"I didn't need any. My friends insisted on treating me. I told them they could come over here and go swimming whenever they wanted. I knew you wouldn't mind."

"What do you mean, you knew I wouldn't mind? I opened up my home to you and you repay me by inviting strangers to my home without even asking me! On top of that, I understand you were rude to Tony on Thursday when your so-called friends came over."

Dylan was starting to slur his words more each time he talked. "Ahh, I was just havin' sum fun. Sheesh, I didn't know you'd get so worked up about everything. Maybe you got a little sumthin' going on with your yard boy, Tony, huh?"

Savannah was livid. She had finally been pushed past her breaking point. "This is not working out Dylan. I think it's time you find a place of your own. I'll give you until Wednesday to make other arrangements."

Dylan's whole demeanor changed. He became belligerent and started yelling at her. "You're not going to get rid of me that easy. I'll go when I'm good and ready, and not before. I'm Mike's son, and if you try to kick me out, I'll tell this whole town what you did, and how Mike turned against me when I needed him the most. What do you think your precious townspeople would think of you and Mike then?"

"I can't believe that you're Mike's son," said Savannah almost in tears. "Mike could never be as mean and vindictive as you are. And as far as Mike's concerned, nobody would believe you if you started telling lies like that about him."

"I wouldn't have to tell lies. You don't know all there is to know about dear old mom and dad."

Savannah froze. Did Dylan know more about Mike and Christine than he had let on? Was it something she should know? She wanted to know what Dylan was talking about, but she was not going to give him the satisfaction of asking.

"I want you out of here by tomorrow morning," Savannah yelled. I want nothing more to do with you. She stormed out of the room and went into her bedroom where she slammed and locked the door behind her. Savannah looked down at her hands and realized she was shaking uncontrollably. Tears were streaming down her face as she tried to muffle her cries. She leaned against the door sobbing.

Suddenly she felt the door start to shake. Dylan was turning the doorknob trying to get in! She ran for her cell phone which was sitting on the nightstand in her bedroom. She pressed the number Charles had told her to program into her phone. Charles answered almost immediately.

"Charles, I'm scared," she whispered. "Dylan has been out drinking and now he's trying to break into my bedroom. He's acting like a mad man."

"Is Tony there?" he asked.

"No. He went to see his parents this afternoon. He told me he may spend the night over there."

"I'm on my way," said Charles. Don't let Dylan into your room. Go into your bathroom and lock the door just in case he gets into the bedroom." Charles didn't even wait for a response. He was on his way out of his house before he had even finished the conversation.

Savannah ran into the bathroom with her cell phone in hand. She did as Charles had said and locked the door. She was trying to keep as quiet as possible so Dylan would not know what she was doing.

After what seemed like an eternity to Savannah, she heard a siren coming down the driveway. "Thank God," she thought. She listened intently to see if she could hear anything going on in the house.

As the doorbell rang, she could hear Dylan start to cuss. Then there was a loud banging on the kitchen door. Finally she heard glass crashing to the floor. Charles had called his deputy, Josh, who drove up to Savannah's house right after Charles had arrived, and together the two men broke into the house by way of one of the back windows. Almost immediately after the security alarm went off, she heard Charles's voice at the bedroom door.

"It's okay, Savannah. It's me, Charles. You can come out now. You're safe."

Savannah threw open the bathroom door and ran to the bedroom door. When she opened it and saw Charles she grabbed his jacket and leaned into it, crying hysterically. The phone was ringing. It was the security company wanting to know if everything was all right. Savannah had to give them the pass code and go turn the alarm off.

"I can't believe how wrong I was about Dylan," Savannah sobbed. "He's going to try to make my life miserable and I don't know what to do about it. Mike and I have always tried to do the right thing, and now he is talking about defaming our names with lies. I just can't stand it."

Josh went through all the rooms, including those upstairs and could find no one. "It looks like he got out by using the upstairs bedroom door to the balcony. He could have easily used that big tree by the balcony to get down to the ground below," Josh told the sheriff.

"Don't worry Savannah," Charles said. "We'll find Dylan, and when we do, he can cool his heels for a while in jail. In the meantime, I want you to call Tony and ask him to come back over here. You've got so many extra bedrooms in this house, maybe he wouldn't mind staying here in the house tonight. I don't want to leave you alone in case Dylan decides to come back."

"Maybe you're right," said Savannah, her eyes still swollen from crying. She called Tony while Charles and Josh searched the outside perimeter. In record time, Tony was back at the house.

Charles pulled Tony aside and said, "Tony, if Ms. Savannah doesn't mind, would you spend the night in the house here until we find Dylan? I don't want him coming back and upsetting her again tonight. If he does make his way back, I want you to call me immediately. Understand?"

"Yes sir," said Tony.

Savannah hardly knew what to say when she walked up to Tony. "Thank you for coming back. I'm sorry I had to call you and mess up your evening with your parents."

"I would've been upset if you hadn't called me, Ms. Savannah. You just try to relax. Nobody's going to bother you again tonight. Not as long as I'm here."

"I'll replace your window tomorrow, Savannah," Charles broke in. "I thought Dylan was still in the house, and I knew if he was, I needed to get to you fast."

"Don't you dare think twice about it," replied Savannah. A window's easy to replace. If you hadn't gotten to me when you did, I might have gone crazy from fear. I can't say thank you enough for being here for me."

If you want, Ms. Savannah, I have a piece of ply board in the shed that I can nail over the window for tonight," said Tony. "Then tomorrow I can get a new piece of glass and replace the window for you."

"Okay Savannah, I can tell I'm leaving you in capable hands," Charles said. "If y'all need me, don't hesitate to call."

After everything settled down, Savannah offered to fix something for Tony to eat, but neither one of them was really hungry. They ended up snacking on Cokes and popcorn. Savannah was glad that Tony wanted to stay up and watch television for a while. She knew she wouldn't be able to get to sleep and was happy to have someone to talk with.

Eventually Savannah did fall asleep on the sofa, and Tony nodded off in the chair beside her.

CHAPTER 106

Savannah woke up and tried to stretch some of the stiffness out of her body after having spent the night on the sofa. Then she looked over affectionately at Tony, still asleep in the recliner. "My good and faithful friend," she whispered as she silently rose from the sofa. "I'll make us some coffee for when you get up." She looked at the glass still scattered on the carpet by the window. She didn't know if she would ever feel safe in her home again.

Once she started the coffee Savannah slipped back down the hall into her bathroom. She took a shower and changed clothes. Then she quietly headed back to the kitchen. When she reached the living room she realized that Tony had already gotten up and gone into the kitchen.

"You hungry?" she asked. "I was going to fix us some breakfast."

"That sounds really good. How are you feeling this morning?"

"Much better, thanks to you. I don't think I could have slept a wink in this big house by myself last night. I have to admit, I don't get scared often, but last night I was petrified."

"If you don't mind me asking," Ms. Savannah, "what happened?"

"Dylan had been drinking when he came home last night. We had words, and it just escalated from there."

"It wasn't because of what I told you about his friends coming over, was it? I don't think I could've forgiven myself if he'd hurt you because of what I said."

"Tony, nothing that happened last night was your fault. Normal people don't act the way Dylan was acting when he came in."

"What are you going to do now?" Tony inquired.

"I'm not really sure," answered Savannah. "I guess I'll call Charles and see if they found Dylan last night. I'm worried about leaving the house in case he comes back. This is so upsetting."

"If you need to go out, I'll watch the house for you. As soon as the glass company opens up, I'll check with you to see if they found Dylan. If they did, I need to run to town to pick up some glass so I can fix your window. If there's anything else you need, just let me know."

"Thank you so much, Tony."

After breakfast Savannah called the Sheriff's office. Charles had not made it in yet, so she spoke with Jean.

"I was worried about you when I heard what happened last night," Jean confided. Charles was out most of the night looking for Dylan. He finally found him this morning around four a.m. in an old cabin on the island side of False River. They booked him into the Detention Center and then Charles went home to get a few hours of sleep. Do you want me to ask him to call you when he gets in?"

"Yes, I'd appreciate it. Thanks Jean." Savannah felt a sudden rush of relief at the thought that Dylan was now under lock and key at the prison. Around eight-thirty she placed a call to the office.

"Good morning. Devereaux Real Estate Company. Betty Cormier speaking."

"Good morning Betty. This is Savannah."

Before Savannah could continue, Betty jumped in and said, "I heard you had problems with Dylan last night."

"Good grief Betty. How'd you hear news like that so fast?"

"Cal's sister works at the prison, and she was there when they brought Dylan in."

"So what's the gossip mill spreading this morning?" asked Savannah.

"They say that when Dylan was brought in he was shouting and cussin' and causing a tremendous ruckus. It took three deputies to get him into his cell. Savannah, he was also saying things about getting even with you. Do you want me to come over and stay with you for a while?"

"No, Betty. I appreciate it, but Tony's here. Besides, now that I know Dylan's in jail, I don't have anything to worry about."

"What happened last night?" Betty asked.

"I really don't want to get into it right now, Betty. Just tell Macy and Jim that I won't be in today. I'll talk to y'all later." Small towns — Savannah should have known there would be no way to hide what went on last night.

"Okay, but let me know if you need anything," Betty said, somewhat disappointed that she was unable to get the lowdown on what happened.

Tony came in just as Savannah had finished her conversation with Betty. "I called the glass company and gave them the measurements for your window. They're having a piece of glass cut to fit it. They said they wouldn't be able to get out here until tomorrow to replace it, so I'm going to pick it up and fix it myself. I don't want you to have to be here without your alarm working. Are you going to be all right until I get back?"

"I know it's terrible to say, but now that it's daytime and I know Dylan's in jail, I feel much better. I'm sure they won't release him before Charles gets back in, so I'm fine for now."

Sheriff Breaux returned Savannah's call by mid morning. "Savannah, I'm sorry about the awkward position you've been put in with Dylan being arrested. I wanted to let you know that you have a lot of friends ready to stand by you if you need them. By the time I got up this morning, there were already four calls on my answering machine asking how you were.

In fact, I just got off the phone with Judge Best. He's really concerned about your safety. I told him that I was going to try to encourage you to press charges against Dylan. If I can keep him locked up long enough, we may be able to find out what's going on. We really need time to check him out."

"Whatever you think is best," responded Savannah sadly.

While Tony went to get the replacement glass for the window pane, Savannah picked up all the the big pieces of broken glass, and got the vacuum cleaner out to get up the smaller pieces. She could have left it all for Mary to do when she came in, but Savannah couldn't stand the thought of being reminded of what had happened the night before every time she looked at all the glass.

Tony was not gone long, and when he returned, he was able to repair the window in a remarkably short time. He was also able to reconnect the alarm system to the window that had been broken. Slowly, Savannah was beginning to regain her confidence, and in the light of day, her home was once again beginning to feel safe.

"Do you want for me to stay overnight in the house again tonight?" Tony asked.

"I think as long as my alarm system is working, I should be all right Tony. But thank you for asking." Secretly she wondered what she would do when Dylan was let out of jail. But that was something she would worry about when the time came. For now, she felt relatively safe.

CHAPTER 107

Savannah woke up to the sound of incessant rain beating against her window pane. Loud claps of thunder seemed to shake the house down to its very foundation. She covered her head with the sheet and bedspread, trying her best to get back to sleep. It was only four o'clock in the morning and she was not prepared to get up yet.

The harder it rained, the more conscious Savannah became of all the problems she was going to have to face. She tried to focus on Mike and how happy they had been, but it was no use. Her thoughts kept drifting back to Dylan and how violent he had become in such a short time.

Something just wasn't right. How could he have been so kind and sweet to her and then turn on her like he did? It just didn't make any sense. Finally, when she could take it no more, she got up from bed, slipped into her robe and slippers, and wandered into the kitchen. *"Why did I fall for Dylan's deceptive ways so easily?"* she thought. *"I guess mom was right. She always said I was too tenderhearted and way too gullible."*

In the kitchen, the long double paned glass windows were covered only by the palest sheer curtains. Bolts of lightning from the powerful and fierce storm shot surges of light through every nook and cranny, illuminating the entire oversized room. Shadows from the trees outside cast ghostly figures on the walls. The stormy weather made Savannah incredibly nervous, but there was no shutting it out.

Savannah pulled out the coffee from the cabinet next to her coffee pot and mechanically placed the loose coffee in the filter. Once it started brewing, she took out a cup and put a single packet of Equal into it.

"I don't know why I'm so worried. I've lived a good life with a man I deeply loved. I've been blessed with good friends and family, lived in a beautiful home … quite honestly, I've had it all. If I died today, I could not have had a better life."

Savannah heard a car coming down the driveway and saw the illumination from its headlights as it turned in under the covered part of the driveway that led to the garage. It was Johnny Robinson, her paper man. She was the last house on this part of his route so, as a favor to her, instead of throwing the paper at the end of the driveway, he drove all the way down the driveway and threw the paper by her back door.

She waited for Johnny to drive off before going out to pick up her paper. She didn't like anyone seeing her still in her robe, regardless of the time. She turned off the security alarm before opening the door, but after retrieving her paper she decided it might not be such a bad idea to turn the alarm back on once she was safely inside again.

The thunder and lightning finally stopped, and the downpour had turned into a steady light rain that was almost relaxing. Savannah thought of trying to go back to bed, but by this time she was already on her second cup of coffee, had her paper spread out over the table, and was wide awake.

She scanned the headlines on the front page and then glanced at the articles. She turned the pages and continued in this manner until suddenly she realized she didn't remember a thing she had read. Her mind was a million miles away. She knew she might as well put the paper aside to read later.

She wasn't really hungry, so she made some toast to eat with her coffee. When she finished she went back into her bedroom, pulled out the clothes she would wear that day, and laid them out on the bed. She filled up the large Jacuzzi tub in the bathroom and added some bath oil beads. Savannah began to relax as she lowered her first leg into the water.

For a very short time she forgot about the rain and all the troubles surrounding her, and concentrated on sinking down further into the comforting and strangely healing water. She became totally serene and probably would have remained that way for some time, if it had not been for the music on her cell phone bringing her back to reality.

"Hello," she answered hesitantly.

"Ms. Savannah, this is Tony. I saw your lights on and since it was so early, I wanted to check to make sure you were all right."

"Oh, Tony. I'm fine. I just couldn't sleep with the all the stormy weather. Thanks for calling though. How are you this morning?" she continued.

"I'm fine. It looks like there may be some loose shingles on my roof, though, because I can see the early stages of a water stain on the ceiling in my bedroom. I'll try to take care of that as soon as the weather clears up a little. I don't think it will be much of a problem."

"Good," Savannah continued. "Be sure to get whatever you need and just go ahead and put it on our account ... '*Our account...*'" Savannah still talked like Mike was there. She didn't correct herself. She knew that Tony understood.

When she finished with her bath, Savannah lazily got out of the Jacuzzi and dressed. It was early, but she decided to go to the office anyway. She needed something to occupy her mind besides Dylan's trouble with the law, Mike's passing away, and Tony's loose shingles.

CHAPTER 108

Dylan, once again considered a "loner," sat in the confines of the Pointe Coupee Parish Detention Center. The initial charges against him – disturbing the peace, drunkenness, and attempted assault – had now been upgraded to include conspiracy to commit murder.

His fingerprints had been run through the system. When they came back with the name Hank Meyers, no one seemed more surprised than Dylan. His insistence that he had never heard the name Hank Meyers did little to convince the authorities. Savannah decided that the time had come for her to confront Dylan about his bizarre behavior.

When she first arrived at the prison, and pressed the button on the side wall next to the front door, she heard a woman's voice come from the small speaker. "You need to take your purse and cell phone back to your car and leave them there. You cannot bring a purse into the detention center."

"Yes ma'am," replied Savannah obediently, unsure with whom she had just communicated. On her second trip back she once again pressed the button. Almost instantly she heard the sound of the unlocking door, and without hesitation, she rushed inside.

Tuesday was visiting day at the prison. Savannah stood in line and followed the example of the other visitors who seemed well versed in the proper procedures to follow. As each visitor approached the desk, the deputy asked, "Who are you here to see?" followed by, "I need to see some identification." After giving the information requested, each visitor found a chair to sit in on either side of the entrance hallway until all the chairs were filled. The overflow of visitors had to find chairs inside the main lobby.

Savannah, dressed in obviously expensive clothes that clearly set her apart from the rest, felt the isolation thrust upon her. It was all so degrading. She had done nothing wrong. Yet she sat segregated from the others as if she were some type of oddity. She didn't belong here. She knew it and they knew it.

When the names of the first five prisoners were called out, the people there to visit them walked back to another room. After fifteen minutes or so, the visitors came out and left the prison. Then the next five names were read out, and the cycle continued.

Dylan's name was finally called along with four others. Savannah followed the other visitors, all women, into a room that was akin to a long hall with spaces partitioned off. Each woman walked into one of the partitioned spaces and began watching through the thick glass window as the prisoners were brought in, one at a time. The room the five prisoners were ushered into mirrored the side that the visitors occupied. Telephone receivers hung on the petitions ready for conversations to begin.

As Dylan was escorted in, Savannah felt strong emotions welling up inside her. She was torn between anger and sorrow. Anger, that Dylan had subjected her to this whole process, and a twinge of sorrow. She had vowed not to be weak, but when she saw the dejected look on Dylan's face as he approached the glass, her heart started to ache.

"I'm so sorry you had to come here Savannah," he said. "I don't know what else to say."

"You can start by telling me what's going on," replied Savannah, trying to sound stronger than she felt. "Sheriff Breaux said that the fingerprints they took from you belong to someone named Hank Myers. Can you explain that?"

"No," said Dylan. "I don't know what's going on. I never heard of Hank Myers. I swear to you, I don't know what's happening. I feel like I'm in the twilight zone."

"I trusted you Dylan. How could you let me down like this?"

His eyes began to look like he was fighting back tears. She was such a soft touch. She knew she couldn't let him get to her like this.

"It seems that no matter what I do, it always turns out wrong. I really tried this time. I just don't know what happened," whispered Dylan as his voice trailed off.

Savannah wondered if this was just another con game, or if Dylan was sincere. It didn't matter. She knew she could never again let her guard down with him. "You can start making amends by explaining to me what was wrong with you when you came home Sunday night. I've never seen you like that."

"I wish I could explain it, Savannah. I know it sounds crazy, but it's like I'm being framed for things I didn't do, and I don't know why."

Savannah wanted to say, "Give me a break, Dylan," but she refrained.

Dylan continued. "I went for a drink at the Daiquiri Diner. Two guys came in and we struck up a conversation. They bought me a couple of drinks, but that was all. The next thing I know I'm waking up in jail. I don't remember anything that happened in between. It's like I had been drugged."

It was the weirdest story Savannah had ever heard. In fact, in was so strange that Savannah began to wonder if maybe it might have an element of truth to it. *"Could it be possible that Dylan was drugged?"* Savannah contemplated. She knew Dylan had looked different when he came in that night. His eyes had a strange wild and sinister look to them. He was like a man possessed. *"Drugs."* Savannah had never thought about that. And drugs would definitely account for his bizarre behavior.

"You need to prove to me that you're sorry about what happened by being honest with Sheriff Breaux. You need to tell him everything: like who were the two men you were with at the bar?"

"I promise you Savannah, I don't know. I had just met them. One called himself Beau, the other was called Sammy."

"Sammy? Sammy Rodriguez?" asked Savannah with a shocked look.

"I don't know what his last name was," replied Dylan. Why, is that important?"

"I'm not sure yet," said Savannah. "I'm afraid this may all be tied in with the murder on False River."

"I promise you, Savannah, I don't know anything about that. I had some drinks with these two guys and the next thing I remember was waking up in jail. I honestly don't remember anything else. I do recall some horrible nightmares I was having before I woke up. You and me had a terrible argument. I went back to town and met up with the same guys again. They told me I could spend the night with them at their cabin on False River.

They were going to visit some friends, but the one named Beau said he would drop me off at the cabin and then meet back up with Sammy. When we got to the campsite, Beau couldn't find his key so we had to climb in through the window. He told me I could stay there as long as I wanted to."

"That wasn't all a dream," reported Savannah. "You came in the house in a wild rage and I had to call the sheriff out. It was very embarrassing."

Savannah, I never cared about anybody in my whole life like I care about you. You have to trust me. I would never do anything intentionally to hurt you. I just honestly don't remember what happened."

Savannah didn't like the way this was going. She had hoped Dylan would be a royal pain, and then she could have easily walked away. Instead, he was starting to get to her again. "Dylan, are you telling me that you don't remember our fighting? That you don't remember our discussion about Tony?"

"We were fighting?" questioned a stunned Dylan. "Did I hurt you?" he asked with a look of horror on his face.

"No," but you scared me," she answered. "No matter what I feel right now," she continued, "you've made some very serious mistakes, and now you're going to have to pay the price. If you're honest from this point on and cooperate with the sheriff, I'll ask him to do what he can to help you. But, even with that, you're still in a lot of trouble."

"I'll tell him everything I know, for whatever it's worth. But," he continued, "you have to believe me when I say, I am not Hank Meyers. I'm Mike's son, whether you like it or not, and somehow I am going to find a way to prove it. I got framed once before because I sat back and let it happen. I don't plan on things going down like that again."

"I don't know what to say," Savannah replied. "I just need some time to think things over." Immediately upon having uttered those flimsy words, she admitted to herself that this was an unrealistic statement. Dylan didn't have time. His trial would be coming up soon, and if he were assigned a public defender, she knew they would have neither the time, nor the resources needed to defend him.

She stared at Dylan one more time before leaving the jail. What was wrong with her? In front of her stood a man who had turned her life upside down, and still she felt sorry for him.

Savannah left the jail feeling totally deflated. She had no idea of what to do.

It didn't take long for the word to reach the press. Soon a feeding frenzy started taking place in the news media.

Headlines read: **LONG LOST SON OF LOCAL REAL ESTATE MOGUL FACING CHARGES OF MURDER ON FALSE RIVER: Initial investigations indicate murder may be part of a cover up involving family members of Senator Savannah Devereaux and possibly even the Senator herself.**

Savannah had been shocked and horrified that such a story could be printed. The local papers had been kinder to her than some of the larger metropolitan papers. Still, it was their duty to report the news and she would have to deal with whatever they felt necessary to print.

CHAPTER 109

Savannah pulled out her cell phone and called the office. "Betty, I have some things I need to take care of this afternoon, so I'm not going to be back in the office for the rest of the day. Is there anything going on over there that I need to know about?"

"Macy said that if you called she wanted to talk with you," answered Betty. "Do you want to wait a minute so I can get her on the line?"

"Sure," said Savannah.

Soon Macy was answering her phone. Her voice was bubbly and full of excitement. "I'm in the process of setting up a closing date with the Robillards and the Bertrands. Since we have a preapproved loan for the Bertrands, it looks like we may be able to close within a week. Oh, and catch this. The Bertrands don't even have to have their house sold in order to buy the Robillard's place. Isn't that great!"

"That is great, Macy. Congratulations. You're a real go-getter."

"I don't think I could have pulled it off without you, Savannah. You're the best."

"Thanks Macy, but I think you give me more credit than I'm due. Tomorrow, I'm taking you out to lunch to celebrate." Macy was so excited Savannah doubted she even heard her.

After their call, Savannah decided she would stop by the Bertrand's house to congratulate them on the purchase of their new home. It was only a matter of a few turns before she was on the side street by the gate blocking entrance to their driveway. She got out and tried to open the latch on the gate. It was locked.

"*Rats,*" she thought. "*I should have known they'd have that gate locked during the day. Now I'll have to walk around to the front, and hope that gate's not locked too.''* Savannah laughed out loud as she said, "You'd think the exercise was going to kill me."

Before she could reach the front gate, she noticed a man coming out of the house across the street. *"That's the house that Sammy Rodriguez just bought,"* she thought. Her heart skipped a beat when she saw the man get into an older model Honda Accord. *"That's him,"* she gasped. *"That's the man that was following Macy and me. What's he doing at Sammy Rodriguez' house?"* Savannah decided the Bertrand's would have to wait. Her curiosity had gotten the best of her. She was going to follow "Mr. Honda Accord" and see what he was up to.

She rushed back around the corner to her car, got in, and scooted down low enough to make sure he wouldn't notice her as he drove by. After he passed the side street she was parked on, Savannah waited a few minutes longer before starting her car. She didn't want him to observe her in his rear view mirror.

The Honda Accord drove on, while Savannah followed in pursuit, remaining far enough behind to avoid being detected. Finally both vehicles arrived on the island side of False River. "Mr. Accord" pulled into the driveway of a small rundown camp. Although there was no 'For Sale' sign on the property, it looked as if it had been abandoned for some time.

Savannah passed the camp and drove a little further, until finally she was able to turn around and come back on the opposite side of the road. Directly across from the camp she had spotted the perfect place to park her car and still not be seen. The lot was overgrown with weeds, large trees and lots of intermingling underbrush and shrubs.

She maneuvered her car to the backside of the otherwise empty lot and parked close to one of the large trees. When she was sure her car was well hidden, she slid out and ran across the highway to the camp. There, she carefully edged her way along the side of the house, trying her best not to make any noise. Once she got in close proximity to the kitchen window, she began to hear voices from inside.

When she got closer and heard the name "Beau," Savannah had to hold her hand over her mouth to keep from screaming. *"It's true,"* she thought. *"Dylan was right. This is the cabin Beau brought him to. I've got to find out from Charles if this is where they found Dylan."*

She ran back to her car, started it up, and ten minutes later was rushing into Sheriff Breaux's office. Jean was working on some paperwork when she arrived. "Jean, I need to see Charles right away. Is he busy?" she blurted out.

"He's not here right now, Savannah," said Jean. "He should be back in about an hour. Is there something I can do for you?"

"No thanks, Jean. I really need to see Charles."

"Let me give him a call, and let him know you need to talk to him," Jean responded.

After a few calls, Jean said, "Savannah, he's not answering his cell, his pager, or his home number. He's probably where he can't call back right now. I've left messages so I'm sure that as soon as he sees I've called, he'll get back in touch with me."

"Thanks, Jean. When you do get hold of him, would you ask him to give me a call on my cell phone? Tell him I need to talk with him as soon as possible."

On the way home, Savannah tried to sort out what all this meant. *"Was Dylan really innocent, or was he involved in Tracy's death, and now trying to shift the blame to Beau and Sammy? Could this be some sort of conspiracy involving the CIA?"* At first, Savannah had refused to believe Tracy's claims that Dylan might not be Mike's son, but after the Sunday night incident when Dylan turned on her, she wasn't sure of anything anymore.

Savannah was sitting at her kitchen table, solemnly looking at the glass of tea in her hand, completely immersed in her thoughts. When the phone rang, the loud noise startled her. Her hand jerked upwards, causing the tea in her glass to come dangerously close to spilling over the brim. To her relief, it was Sheriff Breaux.

"Charles," she began, "I went to visit Dylan today. While I was there, he told me an incredible story that I'm starting to think might be true. There's a possibility that he may have been drugged by two men who befriended him the night I called you out to my house. One was named Beau, and the other Sammy."

"Oh really?" said Charles with a sarcastic tone in his voice. "Well, at least we have to give him credit for being creative."

"I know you're probably right, Charles, but what if — just *if* — he might be telling the truth? Don't you think we should at least check it out? I saw the guy called Beau come out of Sammy Rodriguez's house and drive over to a cabin on the island side of False River about a half an hour ago."

"What were you doing over there?" asked Charles, slightly miffed.

"It's a long story. I can tell you about it on the way to the cabin when we go to check it out."

"Savannah, you're going to be the death of me yet," Sheriff Breaux complained. "All right," he said with some reservation. "I'm on my way over."

When Charles arrived at Savannah's house, she was outside waiting for him. She quickly jumped into the passenger side of Sheriff Breaux's vehicle, and in seconds the two of them were en route to the island side of False River. On the way, Charles called for backup to meet him at the camp, just in case they ran into trouble.

Charles pulled his Ford Explorer onto the dirt driveway at the camp and stopped a few feet before he got to the makeshift sidewalk. "You wait here," he told Savannah as he got out. His backup arrived as soon as he started walking towards the cabin. When Charles saw them, he motioned for them to go to the other side of the house. Charles pulled out his gun, and with it hanging down by his side, he started walking slowly towards the cabin.

Savannah felt the rush of adrenalin pulsating through her entire body. It was a nervous excitement unlike anything she had ever experienced before.

When Charles disappeared from sight it seemed like forever before he reappeared. She was just about to get out and go looking for him when she saw him emerge from the back of the cabin with his two deputies. After they finished their conversation, the deputies went back to their police unit and Charles opened the door to the Explorer.

"Dry run" he said. "Nobody in there. Looks just like we left it after we picked up Dylan."

"So this is the cabin Dylan was talking about. What do we do now?" asked Savannah.

"What do **we** do now?" groaned Charles.

"Okay. What's your next move?" continued Savannah without any hesitation.

CHAPTER 110

Months had passed, and still Dylan sat in jail, no closer to obtaining his freedom. Except for the hordes of news media personnel trying to get the inside scoop on the most exciting story to ever hit the small town of New Roads, his arraignment had been uneventful. Savannah had hired an attorney for Dylan, but that was all she was prepared to do. Doubts as to his innocence still plagued her.

Because of the delay in finding an attorney, the decision on where the trial should take place, the selection of the jury, and even who should be indicted, the trial itself was postponed until March.

Christmas Eve looked like any other day at the Devereaux home. There were no signs of Christmas decorations – not even a tiny artificial Christmas tree. Savannah scrunched down into the recliner in her bedroom. The house seemed extremely quiet, and as the evening hours descended upon her, so did a dark and foreboding sense of despair and loneliness.

"Could I have completely misjudged Dylan?" she wondered. *"He seemed so sincere. Maybe that was because I wanted to believe in him so much. If only Mike had confided in me more about his past. I never pressed him for details, but maybe I should have."* The doorbell rang, pulling her out of her reverie. Savannah rose and hesitantly walked towards the back door.

"Big Brown, it's you," she said with relief as she opened the door. "I didn't hear your UPS van come down the driveway."

"What you doing all by yourself on Christmas Eve, Senator?" he asked.

"I guess I'm enjoying the moment," she laughed half-heartedly.

"What are you doing working late on Christmas Eve?"

"This is my last delivery. Actually, I'd already finished my route, but when I saw your name on this package I told J.B. I'd deliver it for him. I wanted to have a chance to wish you a Merry Christmas."

"That's so sweet of you. Thank you. I hope you and your family have a wonderful Christmas too." Savannah closed the door behind him, and as she walked back to her bedroom she began to examine the package in her hand.

"This is from Saundra," she blurted out excitedly as she spotted Saundra's return address. "It must be the necklace and earrings Mike told her to make for me." She sat back down in her recliner and with trembling hands she began opening the package. Inside were two black velvet boxes – the first one held a pair of earrings unlike anything Savannah had ever seen. As she tried them on, she couldn't help but admire the intricate Fleur De Lis design. The earrings themselves were long enough to gently dangle from her ears, accenting her long slender neck. Delicately shaped diamonds were embedded in the silver and antique metal with a small Vera Cruz Amethyst at the bottom.

The second velvet box contained the matching necklace. In the center of the Fleur de Lis was a larger Vera Cruz Amethyst. The exquisiteness and fine workmanship of both pieces overwhelmed her. *"How ironic it is that when I need you the most, you're still here for me,"* thought Savannah as she clutched the boxes close to her heart. *"I miss you so much, Mike."*

She began crying softly. It wasn't until she brushed away her tears that she noticed there was still something left in the package. It was a small white envelope. "What's this?" she said to herself as she gently pulled the sticky flap apart. To her surprise, there was a small gold key with the word Mosler on it. A number was printed on the opposite side. There was no note or explanation included with it.

"This is strange," thought Savannah, still looking for a note. She

picked up her cell phone and pressed the name with the number she had programmed in for Saundra. Within two rings Saundra answered. "Saundra, this is Savannah Devereaux ..."

Before she could continue Saundra jumped in. "Oh, Ms. Savannah. How do you like your jewelry?"

"I love it!" she exclaimed. "It's incredible. I can't thank you enough, Saundra. It's really beautiful. But there's something I wanted to ask you about."

"Sure," said Saundra, a little apprehensive. "Is there a problem?"

"Absolutely not," stated Savannah emphatically. "I just wanted to ask you about the envelope that was included in the package."

"Oh yes, that," said Saundra a little slower. "That was kind of strange. I wasn't sure what to do about it. About three weeks ago a young boy, probably about 12 or 13, came to my house. He said that some man gave him twenty dollars to bring the envelope to me. It had a typed message attached to it. Wait just a second. I have it on my desk. Let me get it and I can read it to you."

Savannah could clearly hear Saundra moving about, and papers rustling in the background.

"Here it is," said Saundra. "It says: 'I was told that if anything happened to Michael Devereaux before the Christmas gifts for his wife were completed, that I was to send you this envelope and ask that you include it with the gifts for her. As I'm sure you're aware by now, Mike has passed away, so please add this to the package you will be sending. Thanks.'

That's all it says. There's no name or address included on the note. The boy that delivered it was just about worthless when it came to giving me a description of the man."

"So you have no idea what this is all about?" asked Savannah.

"No ma'am. I wish I could help you."

"You've already done plenty," replied Savannah. "Thank you again so much for the gorgeous jewelry. Mike would have been so pleased to see the results of your work."

After they hung up, Savannah stared at the key in her hand wondering what it was for. Eventually, she pulled out her key chain and slipped the key onto it. It was Christmas Eve and it was unlikely that she would be able to pursue this any further until after Christmas.

CHAPTER 111

New Year's Eve fell on a Friday, so Savannah gave her staff off for the holidays, starting on Wednesday. Friday morning found Savannah sitting alone in her house, as she had done throughout most of the Christmas holidays. In the quiet solitude of her home, it dawned on her that she had never checked out the extra key that came with the jewelry from Saundra.

Suddenly it occurred to her that she had seen a similar key in a box of keys that Mike had when they first got married. She ran into their room and pulled out the box. The key was no longer there. *"Now I remember!"* she thought. *"This goes to that safe deposit box Mike has at Chase Bank in Baton Rouge. He took me to sign the signature card, even though I've never been in the safe deposit box."*

A feeling of urgency engulfed her. Savannah looked at her watch and realized she was going to have to rush if she was going to get to the bank before it closed. *"I'm sure they'll shut down early today since it's New Year's Eve,"* she thought.

Savannah arrived downtown shortly before noon, and pulled into a parking spot on the street in front of the bank. Most of the state workers had taken off early, which prompted the closure of a number of other nearby establishments. Downtown Baton Rouge was fast taking on the appearance of a ghost town.

Savannah pushed open the heavy doors leading into the bank and rushed over to the down escalator. She had barely gotten off at the bottom when she turned and saw Lindsey. The attractive young woman had, just moments earlier, found herself mulling over the agonizingly slow day she had been experiencing.

"May I help you?" questioned Lindsey.

"Yes," replied Savannah while trying to coax a feigned smile. "I'd like to get into our safe deposit box. It should be under the name of Mike and Savannah Devereaux."

Before she could continue the woman replied, "Oh yes, Senator. I was so sorry to hear about your husband. I'm Lindsey. I'll be happy to assist you."

"Thank you," said Savannah, her voice becoming softer. Lindsey got Savannah's signature on the bank card, and escorted her into the secured area that housed all the safe deposit boxes. Once inside, she inserted the bank key while Savannah inserted her key into the lock box. The outer box was unlocked and the inside box taken out and placed on a table. Then Lindsey moved away to give Savannah privacy.

Savannah quickly opened the metal box. Crammed inside were two large and bulky envelopes. Hurriedly, Savannah emptied the contents of the safe deposit box into the oversized shoulder bag she brought with her, closed the metal box and slipped it back into the wall space from which it had been taken. When she was finished, Lindsey came over and locked the outside door back. "Happy New Year, Senator!" she recited as they parted company.

Once outside, Savannah walked briskly to her car. She was anxious to open the envelopes, but decided to wait until she was safe in the confines of her home. On the way home, her mind kept replaying all the events of the past months. Without realizing how much time had passed, she was startled to discover she was nearing her house.

"I must be living right," she mused aloud. "I can't believe I made it back so fast and didn't even get a ticket." As she approached her home, she noticed a vehicle pulling out of her driveway. She immediately recognized the car – it was the same Honda Accord that she had seen at Sammy Rodriguez' house, and then later at the camp on False River. As the car pulled out, it sped off.

"Oh, no you don't!" she shouted out loud. "I'm not going to let you get away this time. I'm going to find out who you are, and what you're up to, once and for all." She sped up in hot pursuit of the all-too-familiar car. Savannah was glad she had decided to take Mike's truck instead of her Corvette. She hoped whoever was in the car ahead wouldn't notice her until she could find out where he was going.

After a considerable amount of time, Savannah realized she may have made a big mistake following the car as far as she had. She had driven all the way to Marksville. When the car she had been following turned right beside McDonalds, and again left, she knew he was going into the Paragon Casino Parking Lot.

Savannah pulled into the McDonalds parking lot across the street and drove around to the drive through side. When she was sure she had given the driver of the Honda enough time to park in the Casino lot, she continued on to the parking garage herself. Immediately she spotted the car on the first floor. She passed it and drove up to the second level parking. There, she pulled in between two other trucks.

"What am I doing?" she thought. *"I must be losing my mind."*

CHAPTER 112

New Year's Eve brought a large crowd to the Casino which, Savannah decided, would make it easier to blend in with the other patrons. As she left the safety of her locked truck and ventured inside the Casino, Savannah became conscious of the fact that, other than it appeared to be a man, she had no idea of what the person driving the Honda Accord looked like. She could come face to face with him and not know it.

It didn't matter. She was tired, and hungry, and had to eat before she went into a deep depression. The silence of the parking lot brought tears to her eyes. *"What did I do that was so wrong that God would punish me like this? How could I go from being on top of the world to the depths of despair in such a short time?"*

Self-pity was not like Savannah, but tonight was different. In the darkness surrounding her, everything looked bleak and destitute. She made her way into the crowded casino, studying the faces of everyone she passed. The gambling area held no attraction for her. Savannah ignored the slot machines as she made her way to the buffet. She hated eating alone, but tonight it was her preference.

After paying, she wandered through the various buffet lines in the food court, filled her plate, and found a quiet table where she could sit and eat in peace. She took one bite of food and then pulled out one of the large envelopes in her bag. There were two envelopes inside the larger envelope. The first envelope was addressed to her. She opened it and began to read the enclosed letter:

> *My Darling Savannah,*
> *This letter is difficult to write. There are so many things I*

should have told you. I will try my best to explain all that I can.

My life before meeting you was very complicated. I was drawn into the CIA as an undercover agent. My involvement initially was only intended to prove the innocence of a friend, but once I became a part of their network, I was unable to break the ties that kept me there. Very few people know of this, and for the sake of many people, it is imperative that no one else finds out.

Because of my connection with the CIA, my relationship with my first wife, Christine, became strained. I never seemed to be there for her when she needed me the most. The same was true of my son, Dylan.

I was never able to tell you about Dylan. How could I? I felt like such a failure on so many points. I always loved Dylan, but never knew how to show it.

I was wrong, Savannah, on so many counts. Until my last day on this earth, I will always believe that Christine died because I wasn't there for her, and that Dylan went to jail for a crime he didn't commit because I wasn't there for him.

My identity with the CIA as an undercover agent was somehow leaked to the press. This changed everything. With me still alive, everyone close to me was in danger. Don't you see darling, I could never let anything bad happen to you. That is why, with the help of the CIA, I was forced to fake my death."

Savannah's hands began to shake violently. What does this mean? Is Mike still alive? It took her a minute before she could continue. Her mind could not immediately comprehend the meaning of the words before her.

"I was promised that if I went into the Witness Protection Program you would remain safe and protected for the rest of your life. My dearest Savannah — please believe me when I say that this was the hardest decision I have ever made. I loved you the minute I saw you, and that will never change. Living without you for the

rest of my life will be the worst punishment I could ever endure for the grievous offenses of my past.

Inside the accompanying envelope is a letter I wrote to Dylan asking for his forgiveness. I don't expect it, but maybe if he knows how truly sorry I am, one day he may be able to realize that none of us are perfect. The money I enclosed can never repay the suffering I caused him, but perhaps it will help him make a better life for himself.

My darling, I am so sorry for all the heartaches and dangerous perils I may have subjected you to. My hope is, if Dylan is half the man that I think he is, he will seek you out and watch over you like I should have. Please take care of yourself my love, and whatever you do — never doubt my undying love for you!

Always,

Mike

Savannah took a deep breath and cried out in a soft whisper, "Oh Mike."

CHAPTER 113

When Savannah finished reading the letter from Mike, she took out the second envelope. It was held closed by a large rubber band. Glancing inside she saw a letter addressed to Dylan and a large sum of money. She estimated there must be at least $500,000 in large bills inside.

Replacing the rubber band around the envelope, she placed it back in the larger envelope with her letter. Then she took the second large envelope out and opened it.

Inside she found a stack of envelopes. Some were addressed to Mr. and Mrs. Mike Devereaux, others were addressed just to Mrs. Christine Devereaux. All of them were still sealed, and all of them had the return address of Dylan Devereaux, East Carroll Detention Center. Obviously Mike had never opened the letters, nor given them to Christine. A strange sensation came over Savannah.

"Dylan was telling the truth. I should never have doubted him," she thought. *"I have to let Dylan know, but how? He's in jail and there's no way to get in touch with him, especially not tonight."*

As Savannah sat contemplating what to do next, she heard two men talking in hushed voices at the table opposite from her. There was a partition between them and obviously they had not seen her sit down to eat. She probably would not have paid any attention to them had they not been talking in such whispered tones.

A very deep and raspy voice said, "Well Beau, old buddy. I think we've just about done it – pulled off the perfect caper. Got rid of the two people Senator Lancaster wanted out of the way, and by the end of the night, we'll have discredited Devereaux's wife and blamed the whole thing on his son."They started laughing.

*"My God, what are they saying!"*thought Savannah. *"It sounds like they're talking about me! Blame Dylan? Did he get out of jail? What's going on?!"*

Beau replied, "I'm still nervous about Dylan, though. I know he tried to call her from jail. It's a good thing prisoners can't make collect calls to cell phones from prison. The only calls they can make are collect calls to land lines. She probably wouldn't have taken his calls anyway. We have her convinced the kid is part of some kind of conspiracy against his old man."

The raspy voice started back again. "Yeah, I know. It was a stroke of genius to get those fingerprint reports changed out. Now, no one will believe anything he has to say. They all think he even lied about his name. Are you sure the police won't be able to find out about the switch in the fingerprints sent over?"

"No. That's the beauty of having inside connections. Our fingerprint expert at the lab they sent the prints to has two kids in college. I guess there are very few people that can't be bought," he chuckled. "One other thing though – we can't be sure just how much Dylan knows. He may have found out more than he should have from Butch. Just our luck they shared a cell when Dylan was picked up."

Beau responded, "Not to worry my man. Butch's tragic accident after getting out of jail means there's no one to back up the kid's story."

The man with the raspy voice answered, "Good!" When the waitress came by their table to see if they needed anything else, the hushed voices stopped almost as quickly as they had started.

Savannah felt like she was going to be sick. She rushed out of the restaurant and headed for the ladies room. Once inside, she splashed some cold water onto her face. *"I have to pull myself together. What am I going to do?"*she thought. She grabbed the cell phone from her bag and pressed the number for Sheriff Breaux. His voice mail immediately picked up "... please leave a message at the sound of the beep..."

Undeterred, Savannah continued, "Charles," she whispered. "I found out about the murder on False River. I have to talk to you immediately. Please call me back as soon as you get this message."

She hurriedly dropped her phone into her purse and rushed out through the large hallway of the women's restroom. Without warning, she made a quick turn to the left and ran straight into a tall, heavy set man. The force from the impact caused her to lose her grip on her shoulder bag, and it flew across the floor. The man quickly walked over, picked it up, and brought it back to her. Something drew her to his face. He looked strangely familiar.

"Oh, I'm sorry," she said as she gazed into his eyes.

"No problem, lady," he replied in a deep raspy voice.

Savannah knew she was looking straight into the face of the man who had bragged about all of the destruction he had caused in her life. A chill went through her body. Speechless, she turned and walked briskly down the short hallway. When she got to the end, she quickly turned back to see the man right behind her. "Are you following me?" she demanded.

"No ma'am," he said. "Sorry." With that he turned, dropped his head downward, and started walking in the opposite direction. But it was too late. She had gotten a good look at his face and would be able to identify him. She was certain that he knew she had overheard him, and realized he had to be thinking the same thing.

Savannah headed straight for the elevator leading to the parking garage. Inside the elevator, Savannah wasted no time in pulling the keys to the Silverado out of her bag. Her thumb automatically went into position over the unlock button on her keyless entry remote so there would be no delay in opening the door. As soon as she got close to the Silverado she would press the button, jump in, and just as quickly lock the door.

When she got off the elevator on the second floor of the parking garage she could feel her heart racing out of control. Fear was pumping through every vein in her body. There was no one on the second floor but her. She had to reach her truck quickly before the madman could get there. *"Surely he doesn't know where my truck is!"* she thought. *"Surely he couldn't have gotten there already!"* She knew she had to hurry.

Once on the second floor parking lot she went straight for the truck, got in, and locked the door behind her. She started up the engine and drove to the exit ramp out of the parking garage. As she circled around to the first floor she began to relax ever so slightly. If she could get on the road before he had time to see where she was going, she could calm down a little more and try to call Charles back again.

As she reached the exit to the parking garage on the first floor, there he was! The man was sitting in the Honda Accord with the motor running. He was obviously waiting for her. Stopping to ask for help was out of the question. There was no one in sight, and even if there was, how could you know who to trust? As she passed his car, he pulled out behind her. She revved up her engine as she raced out of the parking garage, trying to get as far away from him as quickly as possible. When she got to the traffic light she reached into her bag for her phone.

"My phone's gone! This is not possible. Where could it be?" she yelled out loud. Then she remembered the man bumping into her at the casino. That had to be it. He must have taken her phone when he collided with her.

"No," she screamed, "It has to be here!" Frantically she continued to search for her phone, until at last she realized she was going to run off the road if she didn't start concentrating more on her driving. The phone search would have to wait until after she got to a stopping point. It was getting dark and there were no cars on the road. Savannah dreaded the long journey home. She was scared.

CHAPTER 114

Savannah had now ventured onto another long stretch of dark, isolated, winding rural highway. The only significant light to illuminate the road came from street lights when passing through small towns. It would be a while before she could anticipate more lights.

For the first time in her life, she hoped a policeman would stop her for speeding, so she would have some protection from the maniac following her. As she sped up, so did the car behind her. Each curve seemed more ominous at the speed she was traveling. With her hands griped tightly on the steering wheel, she took the next curve like a seasoned pro, determined not to cross the center line.

After successfully maneuvering the curve, Savannah watched in horror as a pick-up truck on the opposite side of the road headed straight for her. Panic-stricken she honked her horn frantically, but it kept coming. They were going to have a head on collision. There was no shoulder on the road and nothing else to do but go for the ditch.

Screeching noises filled the air: the sound of glass breaking; the propulsion of her truck flipping over and over into the ditch below; and finally, complete silence. She had slipped into unconsciousness.

Awakening to a terrifying state of semi-consciousness, Savannah felt excruciating pain; too much pain to move or even open her eyes. It was hard to breathe. Her mouth felt wet. But the odd taste was not that of blood. Strange voices came from the distance. As they neared, Savannah recognized the voice of the man from the Casino. He whispered, "Do you think anyone saw you?"

The other voice responded, "Look Sammy, you think I'm stupid or something? No, nobody was around. I wasn't sure she was going to take to the ditch at first. Good thing she did. Otherwise, we'd both be lying in that ditch right now. Her door wouldn't open, but the glass on the window broke out, so I poured Jack Daniels down her throat and left the open bottle in the wreckage. Makes it look like she was drinking and lost control of the truck."

"Good idea," said Sammy. "You wiped the bottle clean, right? I don't want some forensic expert to find your fingerprints on it."

There was a hearty laugh. "Forensic experts in Pointe Coupee? I doubt it. Most likely this will be considered another drunk driving incident."

"You gotta be kidding," replied Sammy. "Remember who we're dealing with here. This was a senator who just bit the dust."

"Like I said, don't worry. Everything was wiped down. It'll look obvious what happened, no matter who investigates the wreck."

"All right then. Go ahead and take off. I'll call in the accident to the police."

Savannah could hear a vehicle driving off, and then Sammy's voice saying, "I'd like to report an accident on LA 1. There's a woman in the truck. I think she's dead. I don't see anyone else around. The accident happened about five miles past Keller, headed towards Simmesport."

Savannah was terrified. She knew what was going on. They were on to her. She had been deliberately run off the road to keep her from talking. What would they do if they discovered she was still alive?

Time passed agonizingly slow for Savannah before she heard the sound of another vehicle drive by. The man from the car came rushing over and asked, "What happened?"

"I saw this truck in the ditch and called it in. The police are on their way."

The other man continued, "It looks like someone's still in there."

"I know. There's a woman inside, but I think she's dead. I tried to get the door open, but it's stuck."

"Come on, let's see if together we can get the door open," urged the other man. When they yanked on the door it flew open.

"Man, look at all the blood," Sammy said. "There's no way she can still be alive. Looks like she was drinking too. See that bottle on the floor?"

The other man reached in, unfastened her seat belt, and then ever so gently lifted her out of the truck, as if she were a feather in his arms. Tenderly he laid her in the grass on the side of the ditch. The man bent down and whispered in her ear comfortingly, "You must be one of God's angels. He was definitely watching out for you tonight."

The sirens blaring in the distance got louder as they approached the accident scene, and the man who had taken her out of the car, quickly disappeared into the night. Muffled voices surrounded Savannah, "What are they saying?" she thought as her head began to throb and the dizziness intensified. "I'm so tired. What's happening to me?"

Someone touched her neck and then her wrist, looking for a pulse. "We've got to get her to the hospital immediately. She's got a pulse, but it's very weak." Savannah was lifted up and put on a stretcher. She felt a sharp prick, a needle going into her arm, and an oxygen mask being placed over her face. That was the last she remembered.

PART VI – 2012

CHAPTER 115

Slowly, Savannah began to awaken to what she thought would be another abject day. To her surprise, she heard someone with a soft and soothing voice in the room talking to her.

"Good morning, Senator Devereaux," the voice said cheerfully.

Savannah recognized the voice. It was Linda Babin, Dr. Trahan's nurse.

"Oh," she was saying, "I see on your chart that today is your birthday. Happy Birthday, Senator Devereaux!"

Savannah felt the patting of her hand and the gently movement to take her pulse. Then suddenly she felt her eyelids grow heavy. Without warning, her eyes opened and a multitude of emotions, pent up for so long, flooded out along with her tears.

"You're awake!" exclaimed Linda.

Savannah's hand slowly and painstakingly moved up to her face, wiping away the tears.

Linda quickly pushed the "call" button on the side of the hospital bed and soon doctors and nurses began rushing into her room to witness the miracle. In the midst of it all, one lone orderly stood quietly in the background looking over adoringly at the frail, but undeterred woman. "*She's so beautiful,*" he thought.

Throughout the ensuing commotion, no one noticed him as he walked over to the television hanging high on the wall opposite Savannah's hospital bed. Holding on to the back of the chair he had just dragged over, he stepped on top of the seat. Reaching up, he found the manual control and turned off the program that was just coming on. It was a FOX news documentary entitled: "*Drug Lords in America.*"

He stepped off the chair carefully, and looked back lovingly at Savannah. For one brief moment, their eyes met. She knew him! It was Mike! A nurse stepped in front of the orderly as Savannah tried desperately to get her to move. The doctor had begun checking her vital signs.

"Wait …" She finally managed to force the one word out from her weakened vocal cords. Savannah tried to yell more forcefully, but again her voice failed her, and her attempted cry produced little more than a feeble utterance, "… please move."

Finally, in one last desperate attempt, she drew from every ounce of strength left in her, and screamed, "**M-o-o-o-v-e!**"

The surprised doctor jumped back to reveal an empty space where the orderly had been.

"Where is he? Where is the orderly that was just in here?" She began to choke on the words she so desperately wanted to get out.

"What orderly?" asked the doctor as his eyes scanned the room.

"I think she might have been dreaming when she came out of the coma," answered Linda.

"No, I wasn't!" Savannah insisted emphatically upon hearing her comment. "He was just in here. He turned off the television."

The doctor turned to Savannah with a questioning look. One of the other nurses whispered back to the doctor, "The television hasn't been turned on in this room since she was admitted."

"It's all right, Senator Devereaux," the doctor said reassuringly. "I want you to try to relax. You've been through a lot, but you're going to be all right now."

Savannah could not understand what was happening to her. As the doctor began examining her again, she answered his questions with a yes or no, seldom elaborating more than that. She wasn't sure if she knew what was real or not anymore.

Throughout the rest of the day, a flurry of excited people rushed in and out of her room. Sheriff Breaux came by as soon as his deputy notified him of Savannah's progress. She told him everything she re-membered about the men who tried to kill her and about what they had done to frame Dylan.

"I guarantee you, Savannah, as soon as we can verify the informa-tion you've given us regarding Dylan, I'll personally see to it that the paperwork is completed for his release," Sheriff Breaux assured her. "Just one more thing I want to ask of you: Please don't discuss any of the details that you've given to me with anyone else. At least, not until we have Sammy Rodriguez and his co-conspirators behind bars.

CHAPTER 116

Early Monday morning, Savannah was awakened by a soft knock on her hospital door. "Come in," she called out, still in a somewhat strained voice. The door opened slowly, a head poking in. Savannah smiled, inviting, "Charles, come in."

Sheriff Breaux's smile turned into a big grin as he walked into the room. "Good news, Savannah! We arrested Sammy and his buddy last night. I guess they got over-confident, with you being in the hospital for so long, and not able to talk to anybody.

I talked to Dylan too, and told him we would be releasing him as soon as all the paperwork is completed. We couldn't do anything over the weekend since he had to be processed through the system first. Hopefully, by tomorrow afternoon, he'll be cleared of all the charges against him and be able to walk out a free man. It looks like your nightmare is about over. I'm sorry you had to go through so much, Savannah."

"Thank you, Charles. You're a good friend," Savannah nodded.

On leaving, Sheriff Breaux added: "Just so you'll know – I'm going to release my deputy from his watch at your door. With Sammy and his friend in jail, I think you're safe now."

Later that morning, Dr. Trahan came in. "How are you feeling today?" he questioned.

"I'm doing better now that I can talk," Savannah answered quietly.

"Good," he replied. "If you keep this up, and eat well today, I'm going to discharge you tomorrow. Do you have someone who can stay with you until you feel strong enough to care for yourself?"

"I can assure you that won't be a problem. My problem will be keeping everyone away," Savannah whispered, as the edges of her mouth turned upwards into a smile.

Dr. Trahan gently touched Savannah's arm, and then with all the affection of a doting father said, "If you need me for anything, anything at all, just let me know."

"I will. Thank you so much for everything, Dr. T."

Suddenly, Savannah realized that she was beginning to feel better. She must be getting better! She was going home tomorrow! The IV and feeding tube had been removed and she was slowly regaining her freedom. News of her impending discharge spread quickly. Soon her hospital room began to resemble Grand Central Station. As if by magic, visitors and flowers appeared from out of nowhere.

"It will be good to go home tomorrow," she thought. *"I can use some rest."*

Nightfall came and Savannah was finally able to doze off into oblivion. An indeterminate amount of time passed when suddenly, either from the results of a restless dream, or a noise in the room, Savannah awoke.

She gasped at the sight of the shadowy figure near the foot of her bed. As her eyes began to focus, the outline became sharper. It was the orderly she had seen earlier. She refused to let her imagination play tricks on her again. As she patiently waited to see what he was going to do, he approached her bedside.

"Mike!" she cried as he leaned over and kissed her. "I knew it was you," she sobbed. "I knew it was you!"

"Yes, darling, it's me. But you can't tell anyone. I'm not supposed to be here ... only ... I just had to see you one more time. If anyone finds out, this visit jeopardizes my cover in the Witness Protection Program. Do you understand?"

"Yes, I understand. But you can't leave me now. Please take me with you."

"No, Savannah. The time's not right — it may never be right. Regardless of what may come about, I want you to always remember how much I love you, and want you to be happy. That means, that if one day you meet someone else, and realize the time has come to get on with your life, I will understand."

"That'll never happen, Mike. I'll always love you. After I get better, no matter what you say or think, one day I'll find you, and we'll be together again."

Mike smiled at Savannah. "Somehow I believe you," he said. "But for now, I've got to leave before anyone sees me." Mike reached over and released the button for the side rail of the hospital bed. Once it dropped down, he bent over, and stroking Savannah's hair ever so gently, he gazed into her eyes and kissed her. After a moment's hesitation, he turned away and began walking towards the door.

The night nurse, coming in to bring Savannah her medicine, paid little attention to Mike as he held the door open for her. Once she was in, he walked out, letting the door slowly pull to behind him.

As the nurse approached Savannah's bed she noticed the bedrail was down, and could see that she had been crying. "Are you all right?" she asked in a worried tone of voice.

"You know what?" Savannah asked rhetorically. For the first time in a very long time, I think I am."

ACKNOWLEDGEMENTS

Without the invaluable help of those listed below, and countless others that I'm sure I unintentionally forgot to mention (mea culpa, mea culpa, mea maxima culpa), I would have been stuck in the murky waters of research/False River taking eons more time than I had to finish this book. Therefore, I humbly thank, and will always remember fondly, the following:

➢ My wonderful family who put up with me through all the hours of self-imposed isolation while I tried to "finish my book,"
➢ "Chris" Paul Manuel, who served as a consultant on several key issues, was the first to read my book in its' entirety, and who continued to give me great constructive criticism throughout "numerous" drafts;
➢ Ty Chaney, Deputy Coroner/Chief Investigator, Board Certified Member of the American Board of Medicolegal Death Investigators, Pointe Coupee Parish, who answered my tons of questions and worked with me through some pretty strange death scenarios;
➢ Yvonne Chenevert, Manager, False River Regional Airport, who supplied me with brochures on airplanes and described operations at the False River Regional Airport;
➢ Marty Teriot, Mortician at Niland's Funeral Home in New Roads who explained the true and beautiful art of preparing a loved one's body for their final viewing, and scenarios for what can happen to a body under different circumstances;
➢ Christee Atwood, who gave me countless tips on getting my book published, and her husband David, who loaned me his EMS ambulance book for reference;
➢ Erica Marie Kennedy, who talked me into joining NANO

WRIMO which actually launched me into writing this book;

➢ The staff of three of my favorite libraries which I frequented when writing: The Pointe Coupee Parish Library in New Roads, Louisiana; The Rapides Parish Westside Regional Library in Alexandria, Louisiana (mom and I will always treasure and think of Study Room B as "our office on the go"); and The Zachary Parish Library in Zachary, Louisiana; and

➢ For all the people who generously let me use their names in my book without suing me … thanks to you all!

CPSIA information can be obtained at www.ICGtesting.com
Printed in the USA
LVOW040303280912

300634LV00002B/1/P